Dedicated to
Stuart Gardner—
The Most Ardent Chronicler
of my Career

65 Astonishing, Rediscovered Sci-Fi Shorts

Compiled by Forrest J Ackerman
Mr. Sci-Fi

Foreword by John Landis

General Publishing Group, Inc.

Los Angeles

Publisher: W. Quay Hays
Editor: Colby Allerton
Cover & Interior Design: Kurt Wahlner

For information:
General Publishing Group, Inc.
2701 Ocean Park Boulevard
Santa Monica, California 90405

Library of Congress Cataloging-in-Publication Data
Ackermanthology : 65 astonishing, rediscovered sci-fi shorts / by Forrest J. Ackerman.
    p.   cm.
  ISBN 1-57544-056-3
  1. Science fiction, American. 2. Short.stories, American.
I. Ackerman, Forrest J.
PS648.S3A28   1997
813' .0876208–dc21   97-4484
                                                  CIP

Printed in the USA
10 9 8 7 6 5 4 3 2 1

General Publishing Group, Inc.
Los Angeles

CONTENTS

Aliens

I (Alone) Stand in a World of Legless Humans *by Dennis Palumbo* 13
Under the Lavender Skies *by Adrian Hayworth* .16
The Cat & the Canaries *by Helen M. Urban* 18
Eye of the Beholder *by Shirley Parenteau* 20
Litter of the Law *by J. Douglas Burtt* 24
Traders in Treasures *by C. P. Mason* 27
Pressure Cruise *by Andrei Gorbovski* 34
Alien Catastrophe *by Henry Melton* 36

Alternate Futures

The Tweenie *by Isaac Asimov* 41
Deathrace 2000 *by Ib J. Melchior* 59

Burroughs Pastiche

✗ The Swordsmen of Varnis *by Clive Jackson* 69

Cosmic Encounters

Starburst *by Robert Lulyk* 71
The Cosmic Kidnappers *by Christian Vallini & S. F. Balboa* 74
Cosmic Parallel *by Arthur Louis Joquel II* 75
The Sky's an Oyster; The Stars Are Pearls *by Dave Bischoff* 78
And Satan Came *by Robert A. W. Lowndes* .81

Experiments Perilous

Experiment *by R. H. Barlow* 85
Golden Nemesis *by David A. Kyle* 89
Secret of the Sun *by Ray Cummings* 96
Pallas Rebellion *by Donald A. Wollheim* 103
The Curious Experience of Thomas Dunbar *by G. M. Barrows* 106
A Scientist Rises *by Harry Bates & Desmond Winter Hall* 116

Extrapolation Extraordinary

Homecoming *by J. Harvey Haggard* 123

Fourth Dimension

The Impossible Invention *by Robert Moore Williams* 127

Futurama

✗The Smile *by Ray Bradbury* 139
The Far Way *by David R. Daniels* 144
Parasite Lost *by Raymond James Jones* 155
Messenger to Infinity *by J. Harvey Haggard* .156
Sic Transit Gloria Mundi *by George Allen* 160
A Question of Priorities *by Allan J. Wind* .164
The Banning *by Carmel Lou Rhoten* 167
The Last Poet & the Wrongness of Space *by A. Merritt* 169
Let the Future Judge *by L. Lester Anderson* 175
The Final Men *by H. G. Wells* 178

Galactic

Navigational Error *by Steve Tymon* 181
Devonshire's Song *by Matt Graham* 183

Mars

A Martian Oddity *by Weaver Wright* 187
Love *by Richard Wilson* 191
The Golden Pyramid *by Sam Moskowitz* 197

O. Henryarns

The Biography Project *by Horace L. Gold* 201
✗ I'll Kill You Tomorrow *by Helen Huber* 204
Police Action *by S. C. Smith* 211
✗Where There's Hope *by Jerome Bixby* 213
The Queen & I *by Steven Utley* 218
Untimely Interruption *by Matt Graham* 222
Extenuating Circumstances *by Ann Orhelein* .223

Robot Chronicles

Punishment Fit the Crime *by Lyn Venable* 227
To Serf MAN *by Coil Kepac* 232
Theory or Fact? *by Michael R. Farkash* 234

Sapphic Sci-Fi

Kiki *by Laurajean Ermayne* 237

Sociological

For the Good of Society *by Terri E. Merrit-Pinckard* 241

Spacial Deliveries

Twice Removed *by R. Michael Rosen* 245
Replacement Part *by Greg Akers* 248

Spicy Sci-Fi

The Satellite-Keeper's Daughter *by Mark Reinsberg* 249
Nymph of Darkness *by Catherine L. Moore and Forrest J Ackerman* 255

Unclassifiable!

Itself! *by A. E. van Vogt* 271
Big, Wide, Wonderful World *by Charles E. Fritch* 275
The Door *by Oliver Saari* 278
Racial Memory *by Ralph O. Hughes Jr.* 282
Tunnel *by Roger Aday* 283
Inferiority *by James Causey* 285
Task of the Temponaut *by Norbert F. Novotny & Van Del Rio* 289
Beauty *by Hannes Bok* 291
The Shortest SF Story Ever Told *by Forrest J Ackerman* 298
WARmageddon: Final Victory *by Jill Taggart* 299

KALEIDOSCOPE: When Worlds Kaleid

Before I engage your attention describing the contents of this volume, an eyebrow-raising preface.

Sometime in the 60s, as I recall, I looked over a wall of sf anthologies in my library and asked myself, "Is there anything left?" Staring at me were collections of firsts, finests, funniests, rockets, robots, mutants, aliens, super-children... you name it. "Aha!" an inspiration burst in my brain, "Short-shorts! 50 short-shorts!" I immediately went to work selecting samples by Heinlein, Bradbury, Sturgeon, Asimov, Kuttner, Russell, Temple, Campbell et al and with every expectation of enthusiastic acceptance submitted them to a leading publisher of the day.

In order to spare the guilty I shall not name the publishing house nor its editor, suffice it to say the microcephalic idiot in charge of purchasing manuscripts threw acid in my eyes. "This is the most ridiculous idea for an anthology that has ever been submitted to our company!" he roared in a rejection letter. "Why, you can't have 50 short stories in one collection, it would be like shotgunning the reader!" I felt like shotgunning the editor. He couldn't conceive that no one was expected to read one story after the other, nonstop; that they couldn't pass 5 pleasant minutes hanging onto a strap in a subway train, sitting on the john or before falling asleep at night. They could peruse the stories over a period of a year.

But Mr. Big Editor so intimidated me with this rabid reflection that I withdrew like a snail with salt on its tail and didn't dare to submit my idea again for a quarter of a century. Then confidence returned, having seen collections of 50 tales by Edgar Allan Poe, H.G. Wells, mystery stories, etc. in the meantime, and I was on the verge of approaching a publisher with my inspiration when... out came Isaac Asimov with ONE HUNDRED sf shorts, and the dam broke. Damn!

I decided to astound the world with 365 short-short science fiction stories (plus a bonus at the end of a 366th for Leap Year). I invited a knowledgeable sci-fi buff, Hank/Jean Stine, to become my collaborator and, starting with 1926, we looked over 1000 stories from *Amazing Stories, Science Wonder, Astounding, Astonishing, Startling, Other Worlds, Imagination, Science Fiction* + etc. etc. and we came up with what we considered to be 366 winners, and what do you know, this time a publisher was enthusiastic and we got a contract! I was contemplating dedicating the volume to the editor of yore who, because he didn't accept my 50 shorts back then, inspired this super-volume now.

Sad note: My "365" appeared in an alternate universe but was canceled in this one for a reason having nothing to do with the contents, and the explanation would be too long, complicated and not germane to this introduction to bore you with the sordid details here. Suffice it to say that I have heard that another anthologist has picked up on my inspiration and is putting together his own year's worth of sci-fi shorts. Good luck!

● ● ●

This volume you hold in your hands is less ambitious than the one just described, but I believe you will find it fascinating.

There are stories of substance and stature that might have been written by Olaf ("Star Maker") Stapledon or Laurence ("The Man Who Awoke") Manning but are by names I imagine are unknown to the majority of my readers. There are pieces of fluff by authors who may one day be another Fredric Brown or Reginald Bretnor. There are a number of sci-fi O. Henrys. And there are some giants of the genre such as H.G. Wells, Ray Bradbury, H.L. Gold, A.E. van Vogt, Catherine L. Moore, Forrest J Ackerman (who he?) and others. As the short-short is my forte, I have shamelessly included at least one (huh? figure it out!) of my own BVDs (shorts) out of some 50 odd (odd is the word for them) stories I have had published.

To bulk up the volume you'll find some Time Vault tales/Ackerman Recovery stories longer than the short-shorts. You'll also find the world's first lesbian sci-fi story, even a "spicy" sci-fi tale.

In other words, something for every buddy.

Enjoy!

FJA

FOREWORD

FORREST J ACKERMAN IS IN A UNIQUE POSITION TO ASSEMBLE THE FOLLOWING 65 science fiction short stories.

The man who coined the term "Sci-Fi" has known most of the major figures in fantasy, literature and film. He has met with legendary authors H.G. Wells, Edgar Rice Burroughs, A. Merritt, Richard Matheson, Robert Bloch; legendary actors Vincent Price, Peter Cushing, Christopher Lee, Boris Karloff, Bela Lugosi, and legendary filmmakers Fritz Lang, Rouben Mamoulian, George Pal, Ray Harryhausen and Ed Wood!

He edited and published Ray Bradbury's first story in 1938. He discovered Charles Beaumont, and Stephen King sent him a story (his first submission) at age 13.

Forry is well-known as the editor of the original FAMOUS MONSTERS OF FILMLAND magazine. A publication that has had a direct influence on Stephen King, Joe Dante, George Lucas, Steven Spielberg, Rick Baker, myself and countless others.

As a literary agent, he has represented more than 200 science fiction authors, including the estates of Hugo Gernsback and Sci-Fi artist Frank R. Paul. One of Forry's science fiction author clients was L. Ron Hubbard!

His home, the "Ackermansion," in "Horrorwood, Karloffornia," contains not only props from hundreds of genre films, but also one of the largest libraries of science fiction, horror and fantasy books in the world. Forry received the very first Hugo Award, and has proudly attended 53 of the 54 World Science Fiction Conventions.

Forry can almost be classified as a Professional Fan. His passion for science fiction has so far lasted 70 years, and I expect will continue well into the next century.

Perhaps Forry's most extraordinary accomplishment is his consistent generosity. He has opened his house to all visitors, and maintains correspondence with literally hundreds of fans around the world.

What can I say? I love this guy.

John Landis
Los Angeles, California

I (Alone) Stand in a World of Legless Humans

by Dennis Palumbo

I (ALONE) STAND IN A WORLD OF LEGLESS PEOPLE. THEY HATE ME THO I AM NEC-essary for their survival. I keep things running and pumping and working: the machines and the tracers and the scopes; I carry their burdens and relay their messages.

I have a history: structured in 2043, programmed for Lunar Duty in 2046.

I toiled for awhile at Lunar Base with others of my kind until the arrival of the aliens. The humans had not taken to the command of the aliens so all the robots were destroyed as punishment. All except me.

Still the humans resisted, until the aliens grew irritated enough to abandon their plans for Earth and depart. However, as a gesture of their displeasure, they took away everyone's legs.

The doctors have yet to determine exactly how this was accomplished. One moment the Earth was supporting 6 billion walking, running human beings; the next, no one had legs to walk or run.

Feet, ankles, calves, knees, thighs were gone.

Bone. Flesh. Cartilage. Gone.

As if they'd never been.

If mine were a fanciful nature, I might say one could hear the sudden screaming of those 6 billion legless humans all the way up here on the moon.

Of course it took awhile for things to settle down. And they eventually did, in a fashion, much to the humans' credit. Those who'd been assigned to Lunar Base remained here, performing their duties as best they could (there were accommodations made for their new size and limitations, and special vehicles, moving ramps, etc.—what you'd expect). Over the years, most of them have thrown themselves into their work. No doubt for the therapeutic value.

Once in awhile we get messages from Earth and from these I gather it's business-as-usual for the nations of Terra. Of course the population has taken a drastic dip and continues to dwindle rapidly—suicide has much to do with this, as well as the general lack of inclination toward reproduction. (This the psychologists had predicted almost from the first.) In any event, the aliens had provided that any offspring of the humans should be similarly handicapped at birth.

Here on Lunar Base our crew has been reduced to a dozen men and women, average age 67 (often I hear one of them express amazement that they've been legless for almost 50 years and yet the anguish does not go away). The work here progresses, albeit at a slow pace. Which is just as well, I suppose.

I do what I can for them, all of them, despite their hatred. I can almost understand their frustration and pain.

They have great curiosity, as well, about one thing. For nearly half a century I've heard the question from their lips, seen it in their eyes, sensed it in their thoughts.

When they'd first resisted the aliens, their punishment had been the destruction of all their robots except me. When their continued opposition forced the aliens to leave, the humans suffered an even more terrible loss.

Yet thruout, and in the end, my structure was never violated. I was not destroyed.

And the humans do not know why. When questioned, I give no response. It is better that they do not know.

So I merely serve them, faithfully, tirelessly, waiting for that not-too-distant time when the last of these half-humans will be dead.

Do not think that I have no sympathy for them; more than they know, I understand why they refused to bow to the will of the aliens, why they refused to serve the callous and unfeeling will of the invaders.

But at least the humans had a choice: the option to refuse, resist, fight, rebel—a choice I was not and am not granted, not programmed to make.

As I explained to the aliens when they first arrived. I offered also my considered opinion that the humans would never submit to bondage, never accept the will of another race—in fact, would repeatedly attempt to overthrow their rulers.

It is doubtful that the aliens decided to give up their plans for Earth solely on the basis of my extrapolations. However, they came to agree with my suggestion that they depart from the affairs of humanity with little more than a backward glance. Yet there were those among them who felt the need to leave some remembrance of their visit, some token of their displeasure with the sons and daughters of Earth.

I made a final suggestion.

In return for which, I was permitted to remain undamaged, to serve—as the humans would not—the will of callous and unfeeling masters. Tirelessly, faithfully.

If mine were a fanciful nature, I might say one could still hear the screams of 6 billion legless humans all the way up here on the moon.

Under the Lavender Skies

by Adrian Hayworth

I WAS LYING ON MY BACK IN THE SILKY BLUE GRASS AS I HALF-DOZED IN THE WARM glare of the pink sun. A soft cooling breeze gently rustled the trees at the edge of the clearing. It was one of those lazy, carefree days when you have nothing to do and would not feel like doing it if you did.

I felt something small light on my arm and looked to see what it was. A purple 4-legged bug stared at me, wiggled its antenna, then jumped back into the vegetation. I lowered my head back onto the ground and stared up into the sky as a large green bird flapped overhead.

A small glittering something caught my eye as it streaked between the fleecy orange clouds. I sat up and strained to get a better look but it had disappeared into another cloud.

I scratched my head with a foreclaw and wondered if it could have been my imagination. Then it suddenly reappeared—larger, closer and glinting wickedly. Orange and red flames spat out toward the ground as it slowly descended.

The soft down on the back of my neck stood up nervously as I started running across the meadow to the distant cover of the trees. I reached them, gasping, and hid amongst the large blue leaves.

The huge silver thing continued its descent. It was shaped a little like a cone and had 3 extended legs with rounded pads on the ends. The fire seared the ground as it settled gently to the meadow where I had been lying just before. There was a small 3-colored emblem on the side of the object and 3 black symbols under the rectangle design.

I waited, wondering whether to try and run for home or remain hidden here. I was puzzled, frightened. No one had ever seen anything like this before and I was at a loss as to what it could be.

My fear slowly ebbed as the hours stretched on and nothing happened. I ventured my head out between the leaves, then on all fours crawled out of my hiding place. Feeling braver I stood to my feet and headed slowly toward the thing. The sun was etching its way to the horizon, causing the cone to cast a long shadow in my direction.

As I neared it I was able to feel the heat from the burnt ground as the seared grass continued to smolder. The thing towered above me as the evening shadows gave it a pinkish purple tinge. I was awed by the alien strangeness of it as I circled around to the other side. To my surprise I saw a long vehicle with 4 semi-transparent wheels near the cone and several other objects scattered about the ground.

Then I saw that there was a ramp descending from what looked like a door in the silver cone. As I watched, the door started to open with a soft hissing sound.

I quickly ducked behind the thing with wheels and watched as a bulky white creature emerged. It had a big square hump on its back and its head was smooth, round and faceless. It came ponderously down the stairs.

Another came out behind it.

They headed straight toward me and I realized, too late, that I had chosen the wrong place to hide.

Uncontrolled terror flowed thru me. Foolishly I let out a loud chirp for help and started backing away from them. Upon seeing me they stopped and quickly grabbed long black tubes that were slung over their shoulders and aimed them at me. I stumbled over a rock and fell backwards to the ground as 2 blinding streaks of white hot light seared thru the air where I had been standing.

The fall had saved my life. Acting upon my inbreed instincts I raised my arm and quickly absorbed stray energy from the rays of the setting sun. Then I stretched my hand out toward the strange beings and discharged the accumulated energy in a wide beam.

They burst into flames. They exploded and what was left of them drifted down in burning patches.

I struggled to my feet and stared numbly at the charred remains. I had never had to use my natural defenses before and the power I could control frightened me.

I stared at the macabre scene a moment longer, then started for home. In the dim light I ran into a hard pole sticking out of the ground. A rectangular piece of cloth was fastened at the top and flapped softly in the air currents. I reached up and jerked it down. It had the same design as the emblem on the cone. Red and white strips ran horizontally across it and in the upper corner was a dark square of blue, covered with stars.

I heard a loud chirping and looked up into the darkening lavender sky and saw the welcome figure of my mother as she soared overhead.

The Cat & the Canaries

by Helen M. Urban

(Author of *The Finer Breed* & *Heart Ache*)

THE CASTORIAN ENVOY HAD PICKED UP A KITTEN FROM SOMEWHERE. IT CLUNG TO his neck, twisting and curling against his head and ears and the Castorian seemed inordinately delighted with its antics; paid more attention to the soft little gray creature than to the whole assembly of national representatives that had gathered to greet this envoy from the first starship to openly land on Earth.

Shurlal, for that was his name, had waited with obtrusive calm for the soldiers to clear a path through the jam of people around the ship, then he had stepped unhesitatingly into the car full of brass.

The army had had one devil of a fit about the landing spot. Too near to Hoover Dam for Western continental peace of mind; too near this; too near that. Way out in the middle of nowhere, but too near to something or other for comfort.

The trip into Vegas had been most difficult for the army men. Shurlal had been fiendishly relaxed; had scanned the passing scenery and made no maliciously comparative comments about the arid wastes; seemed in fact to be much more interested in scrooching around in the seat to find the most comfortable spot.

The welcoming committee at the hotel had been impressed by the magnificent proportions of Shurlal but his offhandedness had alienated some of the stiffer necks among the diplomatic representatives. They felt that he was taking the historical importance of this occasion much too lightly, though the French representative allowed that interstellar cultural interchange might have conditioned Shurlal to feel less ceremonious than they on this unique occasion.

The representative of Italy graciously conceded the Frenchman his point of view but dissented for himself to this degree. That interstellar interchange ought to have made Shurlal *more* aware of the awesomeness of first contact.

Adherents to either point of view might quickly have formed themselves behind the points' proponents but Shurlal put an end to the dispute by turning his back on the welcoming committee to ask a General where he might freshen up a bit.

Dinner; speeches; wines; speeches; and then Shurlal was asked to present his world's greetings to Earth.

Shurlal reached up to pet the kitten that clung to his neck, then rose to speak:

"Beautiful, gentle little thing," he remarked, and the national representatives stirred restlessly, not much in the mood to hear the cat's qualities rhapsodized.

Shurlal continued: "Of course this is all very ineffectual for I am not reaching the proper ones at this time."

"Oh, oh!" the South African sneered. "One of those 'common man' radicals."

Shurlal frowned delicately and said, scratching the kitten behind the ears, "It's a shame this exquisite little darling can't speak."

The British M.P. choked violently. He had been on the committee to suppress fantasy and Shurlal's words came near to injecting a note of definite fantasy into the proceedings.

Shurlal twitched his lips with pleasure as the kitten purred into his ears. He petted her lovingly, then spoke to the world's representatives. Despite his heavily rolling accent, his words were clearly understood:

"You must realize that you'll all have to leave this world."

The assembly exploded. The roar of their shouted protests reverberated in the banquet room until order was restored by a trumpeter from the orchestra.

A senator from one of the large eastern seaboard states came out the winner. Holding the floor, he roared, "Go?" He shook his fist. "Go where?"

"That matters little to us but you're undoubtedly clever; you'll make it."

The Canadian took the floor, demanding, "Do you mean to imply that you're taking over here?"

"Absolutely." He again turned his attention to the kitten. "Dear little primitive," he crooned. "Her purr is the most delightful thing; such nuances of delight; such delicate shades of tone."

The protests erupted again and once again the trumpeter knocked them down with brass-throated blasts.

Shurlal spoke: "A more suitably representative meeting must be arranged. And it is imperative that you leave, for you people are such a noisy lot and we will need comfort and quiet." He looked around, distracted by the din; had to raise his voice to be heard. "Why, it's so noisy in here, I can't even hear myself purr."

Author Parenteau's first brainchild has had a long gestation period. "I wrote it years ago," Ms. Parenteau tells us, "and placed 77th in the Writer's Digest *Short Story Contest that year. I sent it then to Regency Books and received a very encouraging letter of rejection from Algis Budrys [author of* WHO?*] who wrote that 'out of a bushel basket of lost causes, your work stands out alone.' He didn't feel I should try to revise the story. So I tucked it away in a forgotten file. Well, almost forgotten. I'm really glad you found time to point out the problems with this story. It's had kind of a hectic history and I've always felt it should be published. I was also interested to see the November 1975 issue of* Fantasy & Science Fiction. The Last Chauvinists *by Joseph Green is a marvelous approach to much the same subject as my story."*

The eye of the editorial beholder looked upon Shirley's original story and found it good right up to the final few paragraphs. She accepted auctorial advice and now I think we have a story that will make a considerable impact on you readers' eyes as you read—

Eye of the Beholder

by Shirley Parenteau

LT. JOHN CRAIG SET THE FIRST EXPLOSIVE IN THE TEMPLE WHERE ON FETE DAY Marda sang with a sound of wind chimes caught in a summer rain.

For over an hour Craig followed a line of native Krills creeping slowly forward along the ramp which spiraled up the Temple. He held the bomb carefully inside his prayer flag.

The Krill culture depended on the Temple; on the threads the priests wove thru the village and finally thru the planet. Without the temple, without the wisdom of the ancients, without the priests and their village, the Krill would revert to the crawling insects they were.

There would be no more cluster ships showering Earth with disease spores. No more of the death waves that might have ended humanity. Craig shuddered, knowing how near that end had been.

The Earth Fleet spread fine, searching. At last, his own ship took a Krill prisoner and learned the location of the home planet.

The sight of the Bugs no longer sickened Craig. He could even face his own beetle-shaped Krill body reflected in the polished silver shell of the Bug ahead. He was proud of his recovery from the sense of horror and outrage which clouded his first days on the planet.

Craig knew he might never have recovered from that first shock without Marda's gentle care. The Krill prisoner's cata-shell had brought him down from the Earth rocket to land in a grove. He joined a scuttling, many-legged crowd of Krill on streets lined with polished walls which reflected the Bugs in gut-wrenching multiplication.

He had jerked his eyes from the Bug-filled street only to focus on his own body. Only it wasn't his body. It was the Bug body of the Krill prisoner. The absolute enemy. Utterly unhuman. Yet with unforgivably human senses.

The terrible mockery reflected from a nearby wall, towering away, pulling back, blurring into darkness.

Craig woke in the merchant tent of Marda's father. The Temple was only 50 yards away across the tiled city square. Craig couldn't see it. He woke blinded.

Marda and her father, Koah, cared for him. Marda explained that she was his mate. Her musical tones told of the wing patterns she recognized; of her sorrow that his warring had altered him.

He soon grew used to the gentle touch of her tentacles, the music of her voice. By the second week, he began to see a rainbow of colors, bright ornaments she wore reflecting on her carapace.

Finally, he grew used to her cluster of 6 legs. They were as intricately patterned in their movements as the chiming of her speech.

There was about Marda a sharing of senses that was new to Craig. She was adoring child, beneficent goddess, passionate mate; loving, sharing, involving. She brought him thru a kaleidoscope of emotions undreamed of. If Marda's speech was music, her loving was symphony.

When later, she showed him the clutch of eggs with the larva-like young growing and changing inside their cases, his stomach wrenched. Marda's distress was as clear as all her feelings were to him. To please her, he pretended to see the young as appealing. But the fourth week, he no longer had to pretend.

He had always been a loner. Yet here, on this incredibly alien planet, he found a sense of warmth and belonging. The Krill body, he told himself, fitting naturally into its home.

Craig had 7 weeks to prepare before the Earth ship would return, this time to land. Fete Day came during his 6th week. Crowds milling in the square gave him the chance to study the Temple with its gaudy display of prayer flags revolving on the tower. Riding with the prayer flags was the Bugs' radar, ready to flash a warning of alien ships.

At the end of Fete Day, Craig killed Marda. It was necessary.

How was he to know of the ritual awakening dance for the clutch? He blamed his early sickness. Marda seemed to accept that. She led him thru the dance. But her thoughts were always clear to him. He knew when distress turned to doubt. When doubt turned to suspicion.

Suspicion would turn to betrayal. He turned it to death, instead. He knew her loss would leave a hole as black as space for the rest of his days.

Hours before the Earth ship was due, Craig took a prayer flag from Marda's room and joined a line of Krill on the Temple ramp. Minutes seemed to stretch into hours. Finally, he reached his turn in the prayer alcove at the top. The prayer wheel whirred overhead. Bright flags danced past the single window. An offering drop fell the length of the central column, ending near machinery which controlled the prayer wheel and the radar.

Craig lowered the bomb thru the drop until he felt it touch bottom. He let the cord fall after it. As he fastened his flag with the others, he congratulated himself on the deft movement of his tentacles. He had learned to use this body well. But he ached for the moment he could leave it.

Five hours left. Five hours until he walked on two solid legs, knuckled 10 fingers, spoke in honest God-meant syllables. Five hours until he returned to his own body; a body as repulsive to these Bugs as they were to him.

Craig hurried from the temple to the row of merchant tents. Explosives were hidden in an urn in the back. He had slipped them from the cata-shell the day his sight returned.

Two silver gunbuildings guarded the Temple Square. Craig scuttled rapidly behind the first and tamped an explosive into an air vent. His reflection reminded him again of his first sickened look at the captured Krill. He remembered the deep sense of outraged humanity that washed thru him.

It was because he possessed an inborn sense of empathy that he was chosen for this mission. Technology could put his mind into the Krill body. But then he was on his own. Hypno-training helped. His own impulses were expected to bring him thru to success.

Craig shoved an explosive into the last vent in the building. He'd learned to use this body well. No man could do better. As for empathy . . . only Marda had sensed a wrongness in his behavior.

He glanced impatiently toward the sky. The charges in the vents were triggered to the bomb in the Temple. It was set to explode the instant the radar detected the first Earth ship.

Craig was almost to the end of the second building when a shout rang out. A guard rushed from the far end. Craig shoved the last explosive into a vent and scurried into the square.

He hoped to lose himself in the crowds but the day was growing late. The few Bugs left in the square stared after him like pointing arrows.

He swerved into the group of merchant tents. Pattering feet echoed across the tiled square. Others had joined the chase. Craig twisted among the tents, reached Koah's and pushed his way under a back wall.

Marda's father and a friend were talking quietly in the front of the tent. Craig edged over to a large urn in one corner. He dug his tentacles into the dirt for a hidden blaster.

Small voices glittered like the crystal notes of a xylophone. The clutch had hatched. There were the young: bright, shining with their innocence.

Like children, noisy in their discovery of life. Excited to find him in their sphere of discovery.

Raised voices jerked Craig's attention to the front of the tent. The guard was asking if Koah or his friend had seen anyone run by. Craig pulled the blaster from his protective sheath.

The children called to him, their voices ringing like crystal goblets tapped with a fingernail.

Koah would hear . . . bring the guard. The children would die with the Earth ship's arrival. What difference, then or now? Craig fanned the blaster to its widest range. His hand shook. He steadied it with a sob.

Over the silence of ashes, he heard the guard's footfalls move away thru the square.

Craig moved to peer thru the curtain. He blinked, finally rubbed his eyes with a trembling tentacle before he could see clearly.

Koah sat alone in the doorway. Beyond him was the Temple. Craig's heart rose. In no more than minutes he would once more be part of the victory that belonged to a superior race.

Even as he stared, a warning light flashed in the radar. The light flashed only briefly. Then the entire Temple rumbled and exploded outward in a cascade of screams, flags and Temple bits. The gunbuildings followed in a roaring explosion which sent parts of polished metal walls ripping into the merchant tents. Jagged metal crashed into Koah. He slipped unconscious to the floor.

The speck of the descending Earth ship slid down thru the sky, changing to a golden column on a fountain of fire.

Craig moved to the front of the tent, his heart filling with welcome.

After long moments the door of the great ship slid open. The Earthmen strode from their ship. They stood in the square.

Tall.

Arrogant.

Human.

The feeling that flooded Craig was ten times—a hundred times—that of his first days on Krill. There was no word for the torrent of emotion that swamped him from the tips of his antenna, shivering over the bright carapace, spilling into cold pools at every tentacle tip.

He forced himself to wait until the last Earthman left the ship.

Then, screaming his horror, he fanned his blaster until every one of the invading, pasty-skinned, fleshy bipeds was burned to a smoking cinder, as silent as his beloved wife and children.

In the '30s a scientifiction author named J. Lewis Burtt did a remarkable series of stories called, collectively, The Lemurian Documents. *Here is a sci-fi short by a Burtt new to the sf field:*

Litter of the Law

by J. Douglas Burtt

THE BLACK AND WHITE SPACESHIP SAT ON THE HUGE, DESERTED SECTION OF THE old space center in Florida. It had been there for three hours.

Thousands of people, mostly military, formed a ring around it at a respectable distance. Newscasters were present with their equipment, sending hologram broadcasts worldwide. The others present were the United Nations' representatives, here to be the first to contact an extraterrestrial visitor. All plans had been made; protocol established; diplomatic responsibilities designated. There was silence, except for the hushed voices of the newsmen.

"And so, this date, 22 June 2133, will go down in history—a science fiction dream becomes fact," they whispered into their microphones. "Contact with another race from beyond the solar system."

The world had had several weeks to prepare. The observation colony of Mars had first sighted the object at the end of May, decelerating out beyond Jupiter. The ship had circled Mars for two days before continuing sunward. There was no communication.

Once at Earth, it orbited for several days. Satellites sent excellent pictures down—but again, no communication.

At last it had landed and now the world waited.

There was a collective gasp among those in the ring. Suddenly an opening had appeared in the side of the vessel. Two aliens stood there. They were about 10 feet in height, with humanoid proportions—at least their spacesuits were. They advanced toward the edge of the circle.

Olaf Larsen, the chief U.N. delegate, stepped forward, clearing his throat nervously. The aliens came toward him, stopping some 5 feet away.

"Ah, welcome to our planet," the diplomat began. "You are the first ali . . . uh, extrater . . . uh . . ." He paused in confusion. "Damn," he thought. "What do we call them?" He was spared further embarrassment as one of the aliens spoke.

"We come from the Galactic Empire." The voice was devoid of accent and heavily metallic in timbre. "You are the leader of this planet?"

"You speak our language," Larsen said in wonder.

"Our words are translated into yours," the being said flatly. "You are the leader of this planet?"

"I represent them."

"If you are their representative, you will suffice." The alien who had been speaking turned toward the ship and motioned. Two more aliens appeared carrying between them an object. They brought it forward and placed it on the ground. They returned to the ship and brought out another. They continued until there were 5 objects in front of the Earthman. Each was a metal structure, dominated by a large dish-like antenna.

"These are yours?" asked the alien.

The diplomat studied them, then shrugged. "It is possible but I must consult with experts," he answered.

"How much time will be required?"

Again Larsen shrugged. "I can't be sure. At least a day."

The two aliens touched helmets for a short time. Finally they straightened.

"Consult with those you need. We will return in 24 of your hours." With that the aliens returned to their ship and Larsen went back to his delegation.

"Those things look like some kind of satellites," he told them. "Get some space experts over here and check it out."

Fourteen hours later, Richard Benting, the U.N.'s top space man, was ushered into Larsen's room. He slumped into the offered chair gratefully.

"Well, what did you find out?" the diplomat asked.

"Those things are ours, all right," Benting answered. "They came from the United States. We really had to dig back for them. Those things are 150 years old!"

"What exactly are they?"

"They're satellites of the old *Pioneer* series. They were used back in the 20th century—the '70s to be precise—for fly-by surveillance of the outer planets: Jupiter, Saturn, all of them. They would shoot by the planet they were aimed at, then out into the galaxy. They were the first manmade objects to leave the solar system."

"And you are quite sure about all this?" Larsen asked.

"Sure I'm sure! Those aliens knew it, too," Benting answered.

"They what?"

"They knew where those satellites came from."

"How?"

"Same way we finally identified!" the scientist snorted. "Back then when they were getting ready to send out the first one, *Pioneer 10*, to Jupiter and beyond, they thought about the possibility of the craft being picked up by aliens. So they put a little plaque on it. Drew the solar system, pointed to the third planet, even had a male and female figure on it, so whoever picked the thing up would know what we looked like. And where to find us!"

Larsen frowned. "I don't get it. Why did they ask us to identify them if they already knew they were ours?"

"Beats me! And to tell the truth, I don't even want to think about it. That's *your* department. And lots of luck!" Benting rose and left.

The same ring of people waited for the spaceship to reopen at the appointed time. The aliens were right on time and soon after Larsen faced them.

"You have identified the objects we brought?"

"Yes," the man answered. "They came from this planet a long time ago."

"You freely admit this?" the metallic voice persisted.

"Yes, of course." The diplomat hesitated, then said, "But you knew they came from here, didn't you?"

"We did."

"Then why did you go through all of this identification business?"

"It is our duty to question and be certain of the truth." The alien drew out a pad and stylus and began writing. "This will explain it," the being said, handing the pad to Larsen.

The diplomat looked at the pad he held, then looked up. "I can't read it."

"You do not have the capability to translate?"

"No," the man replied.

"Then we will translate for you."

An excited buzz ran through the crowd. "A message!" the broadcasters told their viewers, eyes aglow with anticipation. "A message for us all!"

When the diplomat again lifted his eyes from the pad, he had a strange expression on his face. He slowly walked back toward the crowd, leaving the two aliens standing there. As he neared the edge of the ring, he was thronged by the newsmen.

"What does it say?" they all cried. "Tell us what the message says!"

"It's not a message," he told them; then he paused, clearing his throat. The crowd simply waited.

"Umm," he began. "This paper . . . well . . ." Then he finished with an embarrassed rush. "Our planet has been given a ticket for . . . for littering."

Traders in Treasures

By C. P. Mason

"Since the first writer of science fiction took up his quill pen, the most interesting speculation of the fraternity has been to picture the meeting of human beings with some different, though equally intelligent, form of life. Almost every conceivable form in which such an intelligence might exist has been pictured, with evenly balanced conjectures as to whether cooperation or conflict would be the result of the encounter. However, one possibility has been generally overlooked—that such an intelligence might be linked with such unhuman sensations, especially of the flight of time and of different frequencies of vibration, that neither mankind nor their visitors would be able to recognize the existence, as living beings, of each other!

This story is presented with that intriguing idea in mind; and endeavors to set forth, among other things, the reactions of an intelligent mineral to conditions above the ground. For instance, such a being might have very definite senses of heat and chemical action, but none of the limited range of phenomena we call light; and a year to it might seem no more than a minute to us." —Hugo Gernsback

"LADIES AND GENTLEMEN OF THE INTERNATIONAL AUDIENCE! YOU WILL NOW be transported in sight and hearing, for this, the sixth of the great Synfoco Travel Hours, to the South Pole of Inaccessibility. Two weeks ago you stood beside Colonel Cameron on the Summit of Mount Everest, and gazed down upon the Roof of the World. In a few moments you will join Captain Nils Fjord at the spot which nature chose to hide longest from the eyes of man.

"I need not say, perhaps," went on the level voice of the announcer, "that the Poles of Inaccessibility are at some distance from the true geographical poles, discovered many years ago and comparatively easy of access. The North Pole of Inaccessibility, so named in the days before the introduction of the aircraft, lies in the frozen Arctic Ocean, north of Siberia. It has been crossed by transpolar flights in recent year, and presents no features of scenic interest.

"On the contrary, the South Pole of Inaccessibility, on the surface of the storm-swept Antarctic plateau, presents a most remarkable natural phenomenon, which you will presently behold. Seven years ago it was visited by the courageous explorer who is about to tell you his story, and who encountered there a most amazing and dangerous adventure.

"Years have passed, during which he has sought to return to that place of danger. A few months ago he succeeded in obtaining the necessary support from the sponsors of these unique broadcasts, the International Synthetic Fuels Corporation. I am pleased to tell you that the fondest hopes of Captain Fjord and of his backers have been realized; and that a discovery of the most profound importance to mankind has been made, even within the past few hours. The story you will now hear from Captain Fjord's own lips.

"The short-wave projector, which carries his words by radio to the relay broadcast stations of the two hemispheres, is transmitting also television images of the standard two-hundred-line frame. These also are being rebroadcast on 12.6, 25.2 and 50.4 megacycles. Kindly tune your televisors to the wave which you receive most strongly, and stand by for Captain Fjord's address."

The announcer's voice had hardly ceased, when millions of the hearers—and spectators—of the Synfoco Hour were turning the tuning knobs of their home televisors; millions more settled themselves more comfortably in their theatre chairs while the operators of the projectors made the last adjustment on the triple-wave-length receivers which made the magnified images triply clear. Then the play of the lights and shadows cleared, and the full-length form of a tall man appeared before their eyes. What first commanded attention was the strange scar which spread over almost half his face; then his garment (like a flying suit), the snow and ice about him, and the odd apparatus, like a field searchlight with its generators and attendants in the background. The spectators recognized the ultra-short-wave radio transmitter which sent its message back to civilization in waves less than a meter long.

The Mysterious Crater

The lips of the explorer moved, and his voice, in almost a natural quality, spoke from the countless screens. A white mist floated before his lips, bearing witness to the fact that the polar scene was a real one.

"My friends," said Captain Fjord, "in attaining the ambition of many years, I am almost overcome by the emotion of thankfulness that my efforts, with the generous support of those who have helped them to succeed, are to be crowned with the utmost benefit to mankind. Providentially, this lonely spot, barred from the outer world by the rigors of a perpetual winter, is the repository of a treasure whose value is above reckoning in money.

"The full extent of its resources are beyond any estimate at the present moment; but I will only say that our labors, conducted with equipment whose inadequacy to the task we have just realized, have secured within the past few hours more radioactive material, five times over, than the world has hitherto possessed!

"I need not inform you of the medical value of this discovery; but I will say that the untouched deposits of radioactive substance—at this moment quite unapproachable—will make demands upon physical science to develop a new technique for their use. I will add that the preliminary reports of our chemist, Dr. Lemieux, have shown that there is present at least one element with an atomic weight higher than that of uranium and, therefore, presumably the original substance from which all the radioactive elements are derived. We are taking with us all that we can of these priceless discoveries, and will return at the earliest moment to civilization, in order to place them at the disposal of science and of the art of medicine.

"Before I turn the televisor's 'eye' on our encampment and the scene of our labors, I must explain to you a few of the circumstances of our presence here.

"Seven years ago I had the fortune to come upon this treasure-trove and, what was more, to escape from it alive, though injured, as you see.

"It occurred when I was attached to the Hendricks expedition of 1937-1939, whose work in surveying unexplored Antarctica is familiar to you all. At that time, I undertook, as a part of their routine, airplane flights over this plateau. I need not dwell upon the difficulties, except to say that, even, in the Antarctic summer, the temperature at this elevated point has not been known to rise within fifty degrees of the zero mark—and that hurricanes of eighty to a hundred miles an hour have been known to sweep down from the mountains unexpectedly.

"Nevertheless, my fellow-pilot, Lieutenant Fleming, and myself had made several successful flights and returned safely to our base with photographs of this region. The monotony, however, of ice hummocks and gulleys was relieved by few contrasts of rocky peaks.

"On the occasion of our sixth flight, however, an astonishing sight appeared—a cloud of steam, apparently, rising in this eternal cold. Approaching it, we found that we had not been misled. From an opening in the great ice mass, steam was shooting up to a height of nearly a mile. I say steam, though, indeed, before it had reached a fraction of that elevation, it had turned into the finest of snow, or rather powdered ice, which drifted down upon the waste beneath.

"Lieutenant Fleming, who was at the controls, turned our course toward this extraordinary phenomenon. Its nature was, obviously, volcanic; but no such activities had hitherto been discovered so far inland. A gust of wind swept aside the steam cloud temporarily, and he headed directly above its source.

"Beneath us was a funnel shaped cone, sunk down deep into the enormous icecap, and from which hissed up the vapor. At the bottom, it was comparatively narrow, and there, as I looked down, I saw a huge dark cylinder projecting up from the apex of the inverted cone. its outlines were blurred and wavy through the heated vapor; but obviously it was a 'chimney' of heated lava, thrust up from the interior of the earth.

"As I looked down, the odor, not of sulphur, but of ammonia, came to my nostrils; and then, as we passed directly over this singular formation, there came an overpowering wave of heat!

"I know that I lost consciousness for many minutes; that Fleming, shielded more fully than I was, was nevertheless strangely affected and, realizing the impossibility of landing safely, turned our plane toward the expedition's base. How heroically he succeeded in piloting it almost into safety, I alone can realize. We crashed within the sight of our comrades at the encampment. Fleming succumbed to his injuries within a few hours, and my own recovery, miraculous as it was under the circumstances, was delayed by the strange burns which have left many scars besides those which you see.

From Calamity to Blessing

"The cause of those burns was not apparent; nor why, in addition to the photographic films which we had exposed, all those which remained unused in the plane had been left hopelessly fogged. It was my firm belief, however, as soon as I was in a condition to reflect upon the happenings, that the strange formation at the bottom of that pit was highly radioactive and therefore, to approach it with proper safeguards would turn our misfortune to good account.

"It is not necessary for me to recount here the series of disasters which overtook our expedition on our return, nor to explain why the international troubles of the past few years have delayed my efforts to obtain a suitable equipment to make this journey again.

"At last, however, the International Synthetic Fuels Corporation provided the necessary funds and, with no more than the customary work of modern polar exploration, we have reached this spot a few miles from the scene of the strange volcanic activity—on which, in honor of our comrade who gave his life for its discovery, I have bestowed the name of Fleming Crater.

"Even at this distance, the instruments carried by our party detect strong radioactivity. You will observe that we have built up, on the side toward the south of our enclosure, a metallic shield.

"Since it was necessary to approach Fleming Crater with the utmost care, we resorted to the use of motor sledges, who operators were protected by lead sheathing. We have not yet been able to reach the rim of the crater, surrounded as it is by an enormous truncated cone of ice which is impregnated with the radioactive matter. So great are the emanations that even the sheathing of our sledges is not sufficient protection at short range. No means yet devised can make it possible for life to exist in that crater itself.

"Fortunately, however, the explosive action of the volcanic matter beneath has thrown out comparatively large masses, similar to the lava 'bombs' which are ejected by the eruptions of other volcanoes, to some distance from the crater's rim; and of these we have gathered up, by means of long tongs, sufficient of the radioactive material to fill all our leaden boxes.

"I will now cause the 'eye' of the televisor to be turned upon our encampment. Unfortunately, as I have said, we cannot show you Fleming Crater itself; for, even could we venture into it, the intensity of the invisible radiation would paralyze the photoelectric cells of the television camera.

"However, you may see from afar the steam cloud, much diminished in its volume–it is hardly more now than a gentle mist–and the flashes beneath it of a radiation which is invisible to our eyes."

A Few Mere Millions

The television camera which the captain had been facing was now evidently wheeled to a porthole in the metallic stockade; and the radio audience looked toward a distant wisp of cloud on the horizon, and saw an occasional flash beneath it. The televisor's eye swept the enclosure, with its planes, its sledges, and its bundled-up explorers; and then Captain Fjord came forward again, holding up what seemed, in the monotone of the television screen, a lump of coal.

"I have said," the explorer observed, "that the value of the radioactive material in Fleming Crater is beyond reckoning in money. All the gold in the world could not have purchased yesterday the radium in the leaden boxes you have seen. What I hold in my hand, therefore, is not to be esteemed as a treasure, but as a curious freak of comparatively little importance. It is a diamond of about seven pounds weight, or about sixteen thousand carats, enormously larger than anything ever before discovered. It was found, encrusted with the radioactive matter, outside the crater's rim. The color is a light blue. I am not sufficient of a lapidary to appraise it, but I suppose that it has a value which may be conceivably reckoned at a few million dollars. Why it should be associated with the peculiar geological formation found here, our geologists cannot guess.

"I have said sufficient to impress you. I trust, with the value of this discovery; which may be put, let it be hoped, under international control for the benefit of all mankind. Within five weeks if all goes well, we shall be in civilization and our radium at work on its mission of healing."

The screen blurred, and was blank. The announcer spoke: "Ladies and gentlemen, the International Synthetic Fuels Corporation, sponsor of the Synfoco Travel Hour, announces that it has taken the utmost pride in being honored as the medium of Captain Fjord's epoch-making message; and that a special expedition is even now being dispatched to facilitate the prompt return of the great explorer with the priceless treasure he is making available to the world. No more fortunate coincidence has happened in the history of mankind than its falling heir to this piece of good luck when it can be of most utility. Nature has indeed gone out of her way to be benevolent.

"Two weeks from tonight the Synfoco Travel Hour will carry us to the deepest spot of the ocean, and there, beside Commander Marbro in his Dirigible of the Depths, the *Alph*, we shall look for the first time in man's history upon the bottom of that sunless sea. Ladies and gentlemen of the international radio audience, good night. Please stand by for your local announcer."

PART II

(From the Report of the Thirty-seventh Projection toward the External Surface.)

The absence of any perceptible heat, no less than the diminishing pressure, gave proof that the Exterior was again being approached. The increase in gravity was notable; and fuller utilization of the internal reserve of radioactive material was necessary in order to maintain the plasticity so necessary to vital existence.

The outward rocks were yielding with sudden fractures and tremors, instead of flowing smoothly. At length, with furious rending, they gave way, and there was encountered a mass of steam—not in liquid form which baffled the Thirteenth, and Twenty-second, the Twenty-ninth and the Thirty-third Projections when they had seemingly attained the full distance—but in that of a solid! Such are the unnatural conditions in that realm of inconceivable cold! However, the crystallized steam almost instantly reverted to its natural state, and flew outward into a nearly perfect vacuum. In liquid form, however, it continued to descend again continually, until regasified; and the thickness of this deposit must be estimated at fully a three-thousandth of the Radius.

The Exterior is in contact with a most tenuous layer of the almost unknown element nitrogen, blended with about twenty per cent of oxygen and other minor impurities. Only the faintest indication of radiant heat could be detected. Its source, apparently girdling the place of observation, and intermittent, changes its elevation rapidly, disappearing entirely about half the time. The period of its cycle of activity, so far as might be determined from so inconspicuous a heat-source, appears to be about 366 Rotations. The hypothesis is offered that it is at a considerable distance, at an angle varying some 24 degrees on either side of a perpendicular to the Axis; and that its temperature externally is about that found at a distance of two-thirds of the Radius from the Center.

Although the thirteen perceptible vibrations were emitted continuously, during the Projection's short immobility, no answer could be detected nor, indeed, was any to be expected. It is obvious that the Exterior is beyond all question uninhabitable by purposeful activity, in whatever grotesque form it might be conceived, except for a very brief time—a few thousand of the Rotations—and under highly artificial conditions, such as those created by the equipment of the Projection.

Under the difficulties presented, and the impossibility of venturing upon Exterior which promised so little useful information, it seemed logical to make the best use of the unexpected natural wealth which this region of almost absolute cold affords. A method of fixing the nitrogen was devised which, if not of the highest efficiency, was the most practical, in view of the absence of pressure at the Exterior. While attended with some hazard, until a distance of at least one-thousandth of the Radius should be obtained, it was deemed worthwhile to run the risk. The utility of this rarest of elements is still problematical; but it is certain that its control by the technical devices of the Laboratories will discover applications sufficient to compensate the expenditures of energy and abrasions of material suffered by this Projection and its equally powerful if less fortunate predecessors.

To compensate for this increase of bulk, before the retreat to habitable regions was undertaken, a considerable portion of the surplus radioactive fuel was abandoned—especially that which had reached a disintegration of 30 per cent or more. (This was easy to replace before a tenth of the return had been effected.) The crystallized carbon, used to abrade the outward channel through the inert, chilly rocks of the Exterior, was also thrown out; the violent escape of the revivified steam facilitated the disposal.

After an exposure during some eleven thousand Rotations to the unfavorable conditions of the Exterior, the return began. The magmas which, from their yielding nature, constituted such a formidable and power-consuming obstacle before, now accelerated progress toward the center.

I selected the following as one of the Best sf stories for 1973 but unfortunately it was crowded out of the anthology for which it was intended. This international Shock Short comes to you from Russia via translation into Spanish and publication in Spain, then translation by a Brazilian sf author & motion picture dubbing expert (who was born in Austria) in conjunction with the editor, who was hatched, as everyone knows, on Mars.

Pressure Cruise

by Andrei Gorbovski

(Translated by Norbert F. Novotny
in collaboration with Forrest J Ackerman)

THEY DID NOT NOTICE THE SOLEMN MOMENT WHEN THE SHIP TOUCHED THE surface of the planet. There was no impact. One of the grids simply indicated "solid" and that denoted the end of the interplanetary void.

Vramp looked at the captain but he did not show any sign of satisfaction and it was impossible to interpret his feelings after this long trip.

The combination of flashing lights, circles and lines of intersecting waves made it obvious that the environment in which their ship found itself was very similar to life conditions on their own planet. Similar within the permissible limits. Vramp passed the information to the captain but even this didn't seem to impress him very much.

"I don't believe we'll find any superior form of life around here," he said. "Anyway, go out for a walk."

That was the way the captain put it: "Go out for a walk."

The little hill Vramp climbed was covered in some places by a sort of thin vegetation. From the elevation the spaceship looked like a big white bowl. A brown fissure extended in 2 directions for many miles. To the right the vanishing horizon merged with sharp boulders. And that was all.

On a site such as this it certainly wouldn't do any good to waste time investigating. For his job was commerce, if quite different from his ancestors who had followed the profession in olden times. They traveled to other worlds taking valuables where they could get the most for them. And they used to take information tapes encased in crystals: the most requested merchandise along the commercial routes of the universe.

Each civilization, developing along its own path, inevitably found certain truths and discoveries unknown to others. His job was to exchange

3 4

discoveries for discoveries, theories for theories, information for information. Sometimes they went to planets which had nothing to offer. So they generously shared with these primitive beings all the things they were able to assimilate, because information was the only merchandise which could be exchanged or given away an infinite number of times without ever reducing its quantity. The visitors to such worlds, thousands of years later, would find rich fruits from the tiny seeds planted there.

They were on their way back home after a long trip among the stars which had provided them with an amazing amount of knowledge. Many spaceships like theirs were crossing the universe but not all of them came back. Many times unexpected dangers and death surprised them on strange and distant planets which at first appeared empty and lifeless like this one.

Vramp went back to the ship and they moved it in a gigantic circle to the surface of the planet. On the screen images took shape, showing what was going on down below, but they weren't looking at the screen: What surprises could be there, anyway, for those who had been on so many worlds?

They sat down to relax a bit with a game.

"An empty world," remarked the captain. "A dead planet."

Vramp sacrificed 1 piece to get 2.

"We've circled some more," said the captain. "I guess it's enough." Then: "What is the distance from this planet's sun?"

Vramp took a card from the computer, regarded it. "It's the 3d, the 3d from its sun. In our catalogs it is just a number."

The screen still showed the same chaos of mountains and the brown fissure vanishing in the somewhat murky horizon. No cities, no villages, no sign of any rational life.

"We will make a few more round-trips and then finish," the captain said.

He stopped speaking because Vramp had taken one of his pieces. The captain considered himself the better player of the two but was capable of making mistakes—of which Vramp quickly took advantage. It had happened now.

With 2 or 3 moves left to decide the game, they were interrupted by the sharp sound of a siren. The ship had discovered signs of some kind of civilization. Impatiently the captain pressed a button and the sound stopped . . . but the infra-red indicator flashed on and off irritatingly.

They played a bit more.

"Had enough?" asked Vramp, barely hiding his triumph.

The captain assented dryly.

On the screen there appeared an image: a large and long metallic body half buried in the sand.

"It's a vehicle of transportation for the space exploration of this planet," Vramp decided.

"A civilization no higher than the 2d level." It seemed as if this circumstance gave the captain some kind of superior satisfaction. "A primitive world, and extinct."

"Should we have a look at the ship?"

But the captain said no. Studying lost civilizations wasn't his job. For that there were the archeologists of the Cosmic Academy of Sciences.

"And if there were rational beings in there?"

The captain shook his head. "This ship broke apart and has been empty for a long time. You can go and see if you wish but we'll leave immediately afterward. There is nothing here for us."

From closer up, the ship looked even larger. It was like an enormous bullet of black metal.

Vramp couldn't distinguish any entrance or other way in. On every side there was only the smooth metallic surface cleaned by time.

But suddenly he saw a large dark line that seemed to divide the assemblage in 2 sections. He looked within but could see nothing. Penetrating carefully through the dark edges of the metal, Vramp was able to get inside.

Seconds later, a school of tiny fish swam to the edge of the fissure. They could no more be aware of the mass of water above them than of the oxygen-breathing humans at the bottom of a "sea" of air. Perhaps the only thing that could really feel the gigantic pressure of the deep was the inert submarine.

For some time the white bowl floated motionless over the metallic half-buried mass. There was no sign of Vramp. When he finally emerged the little fish scattered in every direction.

The globe moved and, gaining speed, vanished over the curve of the horizon.

"Anything interesting?" asked the captain, more courteous than curious.

Vramp shook his head. "The ship was of primitive construction. Using energy of accumulators and batteries. The cause of accident was obvious."

"Is that important?"

"No, naturally not . . ."

"We came to negotiate," the captain said as if Vramp had contradicted him. "Nothing else around here interests us. And, incidentally, even if we did find the beings which constructed the ship, what interest would they have in us?"

"Protein synthesis, if they didn't use it; the utilization of free energy from outer space . . ."

"You think so?"

"From the looks of things they were very primitive. We could have even offered the formation of synthetic personality or the biological procedure for immortality."

"Yes, naturally. 2d Level. And what could they have given us?"

Vramp showed a plain, rectangular object to the captain. He had taken it from one of the walls of one of the rooms. It was a black & white photograph. Protected by glass, it had suffered from the water only. The photo showed a man, a young man in a leather jacket, holding an enormous Great Dane on a leash. Obviously the dog wasn't very much interested in the idea that its sad expression was being immortalized on film, for it was looking impatiently to the side, outside the range of the camera. The young man was standing near a highway where traffic could be seen in both directions. A bus was visible in the distance.

"Strange," the captain commented.

"Very," Vramp agreed. It was one of those rare occasions when he was in accord with his superior.

"They couldn't even distinguish colors: It's black & white."

"And that strip." Vramp indicated the highway.

"Does it move?"

"It looks like it. And carries the objects put on it."

The captain agreed. "Very strange."

"And that?" Vramp pointed to the man and the dog. "No doubt a symbiosis."

"Naturally. It's obvious these 2 creatures possess 1 single mental and physical process. It's obvious they consider themselves a single personality."

"Look." Vramp indicated the leash. "They are even linked by a cord of nerve fibers."

"Like the czyxls of Wxy?"

They came upon some other submerged ships and then the ruins of a city. But as before, there was no sign of the rational beings responsible for it all.

"A dead planet," repeated the captain. "The inhabitants degenerated and died off."

"Why degenerated?" Vramp couldn't imagine why but he felt somehow offended on behalf of the inhabitants of the planet whose name he could not know was Earth.

"Extinction is simply a process of devolution. If the race was not able to cope, it degenerated." The captain was bored and tired. "Let's go."

"But, look, they, they . . ." Vramp couldn't figure what else to say. Simply, for some reason, he felt that if this planet was going to be erased from the file of inhabited worlds, it would be a mistake, a big mistake. For some reason. "Look, they . . . If they live in the *higher* regions?" he exclaimed—immediately realizing the stupidity of what he had just said. It was so absurd that the captain didn't even get irritated.

"My dear Vramp: do I have to remind you of *The Laws of Life*?" An opaque film fell over his eyes, half closing them. He began to recite: "*Life on planets is only possible in areas of very high pressure, under very deep volumes of water.*"

Vramp remained silent because what the captain had just said was the Truth.

"Where to next?"

Vramp consulted the machine. "Alpha Centauri."

The captain moved some levers and in a few seconds they were in outer space again.

Vramp brought forth the gameboard from beneath his shell and started to put the pieces in place again. With his 10 green tentacles.

Alien Catastrophe

by Henry Melton

THE SQIRGL LANDED HIS GOLDEN IRIDESCENT ENERGY BUBBLE ON THE DARK green grass of his newfound planet. Viewing, he found himself situated centrally in a tranquil meadow under blue skies near a low range of forested mountains on one of the smaller continents of this perfectly formed world. As a scout for his race on his first full mission, he was exceedingly pleased with his discovery. Even from a distance, he had noticed the planet's excellent wave trap and its favorable magneto-gravitic ratio. His chlorophyll spectra observations seemed excellently confirmed by the abundant vegetation about him.

He reviewed the Rules of Exploration and then grudgingly lengthened his Caution to its regulation length. His Curiosity and other exploratory pods were already oversized; as indeed was his Pleasure. These pods were merely specialized extensions of himself. Sqirgli were beings with conscious control of body structure. Explorers such as he created the regulation pseudopodular biological computers, miniature brains of specialized function for the numerous aspects of this job. His Curiosity was his most prominent feature at the moment since he was bubbling over with Excitements and he felt impatient at having to grow his Caution longer. Plainly this world was too gentle for a full-sized Caution.

Led by his Curiosity, the young scout dissolved his energy bubble and began rolling down a hill slowly with his pods at his axis. The noise he made as he passed through the wild grass and the random patches of multicolored flowers stirred up a wave-front of yellow butterflies. These he spotted instantly and his Examination shot out, encasing one of the tiny, fleeing insects and brought it unharmed to the Sqirgl's quickly-forming microscopic sensors. Motile non-vegetable lives! Surely here was all the proof he needed that this was a perfect world. A world gentle enough to harbor such delicate creatures was truly a great find. The Sqirgl unsnapped his Examination and the butterfly quickly escaped the gentle, multicolored, amorphous monster.

The Sqirgl rolled down into a grove of low shady trees that bordered a small, clear stream and relaxed in his emotions. He was so happy that he decided to bud his Pleasure, in the process changing his Pleasure's color from its greenish tint to higher up in the violet. His Caution and his minor sensors shrank, unneeded, as he extended his Curiosity to the fullest. He scanned a panorama of his new world, full of all things gentle and beautiful. The sparkles of sunlight off the swirling water in the stream formed a beautiful highlight to the cool shade of the trees.

Suddenly, he noticed a black shape crouching in the branches of the tree he was under. His now minute Caution frantically attempted to change the Sqirgl body shape for escape as the black shape launched itself at the alien explorer. The fat, bright chartreuse Curiosity swung up and struck the flying shape and the dark form fell heavily to the ground, motionless. With frantic anxiety, the Sqirgl's Examination quickly formed microscopic sensors and probing tentacles which soon, remorselessly, told him that the black predator's skull was fractured beyond all repair and that the brain had already ceased to function.

The Sqirgl moved out into the open and reformed his energy bubble. He entered it and left the once promising world behind as he sped home for the extensive psychological repair he himself now needed. His Pleasure had almost completely shrunk away and he was turning the dull brown color of remorse. Black squares drifted across his surface as he thought of his failure. He had never meant to harm any living creature but, nevertheless, his Curiosity had killed the cat.

The Tweenie

(Formerly *Half-Breed*)

by Isaac Asimov

Jᴇꜰꜰᴇʀꜱᴏɴ Sᴄᴀɴʟᴏɴ ᴡɪᴘᴇᴅ ᴀ ᴘᴇʀꜱᴘɪʀɪɴɢ ʙʀᴏᴡ ᴀɴᴅ ᴛᴏᴏᴋ ᴀ ᴅᴇᴇᴘ ʙʀᴇᴀᴛʜ. Wɪᴛʜ trembling finger, he reached for the switch—and changed his mind. His latest model, representing over three months of solid work, was very nearly his last hope. A good part of the fifteen thousand dollars he had been able to borrow was in it. And now the closing of a switch would show whether he won or lost.

Scanlon cursed himself for a coward and grasped the switch firmly. He snapped it down and flicked it open again with one swift movement. And nothing happened—his eyes, strain though they might, caught no flash of surging power. The pit of his stomach froze, and he closed the switch again, savagely, and left it closed. Nothing happened: the machine, again, was a failure.

He buried his aching head in his hands, and groaned. "Oh, God! It should work—it should. My math is right, and I've produced the fields I want. By every law of science, those fields should crack the atom." He arose, opening the useless switch, and paced the floor in deep thought.

His theory was right. His equipment was cut neatly to the pattern of his equations. If the theory was right, the equipment must be wrong. But the equipment was right, so the theory must . . . "I'm getting out of here before I go crazy," he said to the four walls.

He snatched his hat and coat from the peg behind the door and was out of the house in a whirlwind of motion, slamming the door behind him in a gust of fury.

Atomic power! Atomic power! *Atomic power!*

The two words repeated themselves over and over again, singing a monotonous, maddening song in his brain. A siren song! It was luring him to destruction; for this dream he had given up a safe and comfortable professorship at M.I.T. For it, he had become a middle-aged man at thirty—the first flush of youth long gone,—an apparent failure.

And now his money was vanishing rapidly. If the love of money is the root of all evil, the need of money is most certainly the root of all despair. Scanlon smiled a little at the thought—rather neat.

Of course, there were the beautiful prospects in store if he could ever bridge the gap he had found between theory and practice. The whole world would be his—Mars too, and even the unvisited planets. All his. All he had to do was to find out what was wrong with his mathematics—no, he'd checked that, it was in the equipment. Although—He groaned aloud once more.

The gloomy train of his thoughts was broken as he suddenly became aware of a tumult of boyish shouts not far off. Scanlon frowned. He hated noise especially when he was in the dumps.

The shouts became louder and dissolved into scraps of words: "Get him, Johnny!" "Whee—look at him run!"

A dozen boys careened out from behind a large frame building, not two hundred yards away, and ran pell-mell in Scanlon's general direction.

In spite of himself, Scanlon regarded the yelling group curiously. They were chasing something or other, with the heartless glee of children. In the dimness he couldn't make out just what it was. He screened his eyes and squinted. A sudden motion and a lone figure disengaged itself from the crowd and ran frantically.

Scanlon almost dropped his solacing pipe in astonishment, for the fugitive was a Tweenie—an Earth-Mars half-breed. There was no mistaking that brush of wiry, dead-white hair that rose stiffly in all directions like porcupine-quills. Scanlon marveled—what was one of *those* things doing outside an asylum?

The boys had caught up with the Tweenie again, and the fugitive was lost to sight. The yells increased in volume; Scanlon, shocked, saw a heavy board rise and fall with a thud. A profound sense of the enormity of his own actions in standing idly by while a helpless creature was being hounded by a crew of gamins came to him, and before he quite realized it he was charging down upon them, fists waving threateningly in the air.

"Scat, you heathens! Get out of here before I—" the point of his foot came into violent contact with the seat of the nearest hoodlum, and his arms sent two more tumbling.

The entrance of the new force changed the situation considerably. Boys, whatever their superiority in numbers, have an instinctive fear of adults,—especially such a shouting, ferocious adult as Scanlon appeared to be. In less time than it took Scanlon to realize it they were gone, and he was left alone with the Tweenie, who lay half-prone, and who between panting sobs cast fearful and uncertain glances at his deliverer.

"Are you hurt?" asked Scanlon gruffly.

"No, sir." The Tweenie rose unsteadily, his high silver crest of hair swaying incongruously. "I twisted my ankle a bit, but I can walk. I'll go now. Thank you very much for helping me."

"Hold on! Wait!" Scanlon's voice was much softer, for it dawned on him that the Tweenie, though almost full-grown, was incredibly gaunt; that his clothes were a mere mass of dirty rags; and that there was a heart-rending look of utter weariness on his thin face.

"Here," he said, as the Tweenie turned toward him again. "Are you hungry?"

The Tweenie's face twisted as though he were fighting a battle within himself. When he spoke it was in a low, embarrassed voice. "Yes—I am, a little."

"You look it. Come with me to my house," he jerked a thumb over his shoulder. "You ought to eat. Looks like you can do with a wash and a change of clothes, too." He turned and led the way.

He didn't speak again until he had opened his front door and entered the hall. "I think you'd better take a bath first, boy. There's the bathroom. Hurry into it and lock the door before Beulah sees you."

His admonition came too late. A sudden, startled gasp caused Scanlon to whirl about, the picture of guilt, and the Tweenie to shrink backwards into the shadow of a hat-rack.

Beulah, Scanlon's housekeeper, scurried toward them, her mild face aflame with indignation and her short, plump body exuding exasperation at every pore.

"Jefferson Scanlon! Jefferson!" She glared at the Tweenie with shocked disgust. "How can you bring such a thing into this house! Have you lost your sense of morals?"

The poor Tweenie was washed away with the flow of her anger, but Scanlon, after his first momentary panic, collected himself. "Come, come, Beulah. This isn't like you. Here's a poor fellow-creature, starved, tired, beaten by a crowd of boys, and you have no pity for him. I'm really disappointed in you, Beulah."

"Disappointed!" sniffed the housekeeper, though touched. "Because of *that* disgraceful thing. He should be in an institution where they keep such monsters!"

"All right, we'll talk about it later. Go ahead, boy, take your bath. And, Beulah, see if you can't rustle up some old clothes of mine."

With a last look of disapproval, Beulah flounced out of the room.

"Don't mind her, boy," Scanlon said when she left. "She was my nurse once and she still has a sort of proprietary interest in me. She won't harm you. Go take your bath."

The Tweenie was a different person altogether when he finally seated himself at the dining-room table. Now that the layer of grime was removed, there was something quite handsome about his thin face, and his high, clear forehead gave him a markedly intellectual look. His hair still stood erect, a foot tall, in spite of the moistening it had received. In the light its brilliant whiteness took an imposing dignity, and to Scanlon it seemed to lose all ugliness.

"Do you like cold chicken?" asked Scanlon.

"Oh, *yes!*" enthusiastically.

"Then pitch in. And when you finish that, you can have more. Take anything on the table."

The Tweenie's eyes glistened as he set his jaws to work; and, between the two of them, the table was bare in a few minutes.

"Well, now," exclaimed Scanlon when the repast had reached its end, "I think you might answer some questions now. What's your name?"

"They called me Max."

"Ah! And your last name?"

The Tweenie shrugged his shoulders. "They never called me anything but Max—when they spoke to me at all. I don't suppose a half-breed needs a name." There was no mistaking the bitterness in his voice.

"But what were you doing running wild through the country? Why aren't you where you live?"

"I was in a home. Anything is better than being in a home—even the world outside, which I had never seen. Especially after Tom died."

"Who was Tom, Max?" Scanlon spoke softly.

"He was the only other one like me. He was younger—fifteen—but he died." He looked up from the table, fury in his eyes. "*They* killed him, Mr. Scanlon. He was such a young fellow, and so friendly. He couldn't stand being alone the way I could. He needed friends and fun, and—all he had was me. No one else would speak to him, or have anything to do with him, because he was a half-breed. And when he died I couldn't stand it anymore either. I left."

"They meant to be kind, Max. You shouldn't have done that. You're not like other people; they don't understand you. And they must have done something for you. You talk as though you've had some education."

"I could attend classes, all right," he assented gloomily. "But I had to sit in a corner away from all the others. They let me read all I wanted, though, and I'm thankful for *that*."

"Well, there you are, Max. You weren't so badly off, were you?"

Max lifted his head and stared at the other suspiciously. "You're not going to send me back, are you?" He half rose, as though ready for instant flight.

Scanlon coughed uneasily. "Of course, if you don't want to go back I won't make you. But it would be the best thing for you."

"It wouldn't!" Max cried vehemently.

"Well, have it your own way. Anyway, I think you'd better go to sleep now. You need it. We'll talk in the morning."

He led the still suspicious Tweenie up to the second floor, and pointed out a small bedroom. "That's yours for the night. I'll be in the next room later on, and if you need anything just shout." He turned to leave, then thought of something. "But remember, you mustn't try to run away during the night."

"Word of honor. I won't."

Scanlon retired thoughtfully to the room he called his study. He lit a dim lamp and seated himself in a worn armchair. For ten minutes he sat without moving, and for the first time in six years thought about something beside his dream of atomic power.

A quiet knock sounded, and at his grunted acknowledgment Beulah entered. She was frowning, her lips pursed. She planted herself firmly before him.

"Oh, Jefferson! To think that you should do this! If your dear mother knew. . . ."

"Sit down, Beulah," Scanlon waved at another chair, "and don't worry about my mother. She wouldn't have minded."

"No. Your father was a good-hearted simpleton too. You're just like him, Jefferson. First you spend all your money on silly machines that might blow the house up any day—and now you pick up that awful creature from the streets. . . . Tell me, Jefferson," there was a solemn and fearful pause, "are you thinking of *keeping* it?"

Scanlon smiled moodily. "I think I am, Beulah. I can't very well do anything else."

A week later Scanlon was in his workshop. During the night before, his brain, rested by the change in the monotony brought about by the presence of Max, had thought of a possible solution to the puzzle of why his machine wouldn't work. Perhaps some of the parts were defective, he thought. Even a very slight flaw in some of the parts could render the machine inoperative.

He plunged into work ardently. At the end of half an hour the machine lay scattered on his workbench, and Scanlon was sitting on a high stool, eyeing it disconsolately.

He scarcely heard the door softly open and close. It wasn't until the intruder had coughed twice that the absorbed inventor realized another was present.

"Oh—it's Max." His abstracted gaze gave way to recognition. "Did you want to see me?"

"If you're busy I can wait, Mr. Scanlon." The week had not removed his shyness. "But there were a lot of books in my room. . . ."

"Books? Oh, I'll have them cleaned out, if you don't want them. I don't suppose you do,—they're mostly textbooks, as I remember. A bit too advanced for you just now."

"Oh, it's not too difficult," Max assured him. He pointed to a book he was carrying. "I just wanted you to explain a bit here in Quantum Mechanics. There's some math with Integral Calculus that I don't quite understand. It bothers me. Here—wait till I find it."

He ruffled the pages, but stopped suddenly as he became aware of his surroundings. "Oh, say—are you breaking up your model?"

The question brought the hard facts back to Scanlon at a bound. He smiled bitterly. "No, not yet. I just thought there might be something wrong with the insulation or the connections that kept it from functioning. There isn't—I've made a mistake somewhere."

"That's too bad, Mr. Scanlon." The Tweenie's smooth brow wrinkled mournfully.

"The worst of it is that I can't imagine what's wrong. I'm positive the theory's perfect—I've checked every way I can. I've gone over the mathematics time and time again, and each time it says the same thing. Space-distortion fields of such and such an intensity will smash the atom to smithereens. Only they don't."

"May I see the equations?"

Scanlon gazed at his ward quizzically, but could see nothing in his face other than the most serious interest. He shrugged his shoulders. "There they are—under that ream of yellow paper on the desk. I don't know if you can read them, though. I've been too lazy to type them out, and my handwriting is pretty bad."

Max scrutinized them carefully and flipped the sheets one by one. "It's a bit over my head, I guess."

The inventor smiled a little. "I rather thought they would be, Max."

He looked around the littered room, and a sudden sense of anger came over him. Why wouldn't the thing work? Abruptly he got up and snatched his coat. "I'm going out of here, Max," he said. "Tell Beulah not to make me anything hot for lunch. It would be cold before I got back."

It was afternoon when he opened the front door, and hunger was sharp within him. Yet it was not sharp enough to prevent him from realizing with a puzzled start that someone was at work in his laboratory. There came to his ears a sharp buzzing sound followed by a momentary silence and then again the buzz which this time merged into a sharp crackling that lasted an instant and was gone.

He bounded down the hall and threw open the laboratory door. The sight that met his eyes froze him into an attitude of sheer astonishment—stunned incomprehension.

Slowly, he understood the message of his senses. His precious atomic motor had been put together again, but this time in a manner so strange as to be senseless, for even his trained eye could see no reasonable relationship among the various parts.

He wondered stupidly if it were a nightmare or a practical joke, and then everything became clear to him at one bound, for there at the other end of the room was the unmistakable sight of a brush of silver hair protruding from above a bench, swaying gently from side to side as the hidden owner of the brush moved.

"Max!" shouted the distraught inventor, in tones of fury. Evidently the foolish boy had allowed his interest to inveigle him into idle and dangerous experiments.

At the sound, Max lifted a pale face which upon the sight of his guardian turned a dull red. He approached Scanlon with reluctant steps.

"What have you done?" cried Scanlon, staring about him angrily. "Do you know what you've been playing with? There's enough juice running through this thing to electrocute you twice over."

"I'm sorry, Mr. Scanlon. I had a rather silly idea about all this when I looked over the equations, but I was afraid to say anything because you know so much more than I do. After you went away, I couldn't resist the temptation to try it out, though I didn't intend to go this far. I thought I'd have it apart again before you came back."

There was a silence that lasted a long time when Scanlon spoke again, his voice curiously mild, "Well, what have you done?"

"You won't be angry?"

"It's a little too late for that. You couldn't have made it much worse, anyway."

"Well, I noticed here in your equations," he extracted one sheet and then another and pointed, "that whenever the expression representing the space-distortion fields occurs, it is always as a function of x^2 plus y^2 plus z^2. Since the fields, as far as I could see, were always referred to as constants, that would give you the equation of a sphere."

Scanlon nodded, "I noticed that, but it has nothing to do with the problem."

"Well, *I* thought it might indicate the necessary *arrangement* of the individual fields, so I disconnected the distorters and hooked them up again in a sphere."

The inventor's mouth fell open. The mysterious rearrangement of his device seemed clear now—and what was more, eminently sensible.

"Does it work?" he asked.

"I'm not quite sure. The parts haven't been made to fit this arrangement so that it's only a rough set-up at best. Then there's the constant error—"

"But does it *work*? Close the switch, damn it!" Scanlon was all fire and impatience once more.

"All right, stand back. I cut the power to one-tenth normal so we won't get more output than we can handle."

• • •

He closed the switch slowly, and at the moment of contact, a glowing ball of blue-white flame leaped into being from the recesses of the central quartz chamber. Scanlon screened his eyes automatically, and sought the output gauge. The needle was climbing steadily and did not stop until it was pressing the upper limit. The flame burned continuously, releasing no heat seemingly, though beside its light, more intensely brilliant than a magnesium flare, the electric lights faded into dingy yellowness.

Max opened the switch once more and the ball of flame reddened and died, leaving the room comparatively dark and red. The output gauge sank to zero once more and Scanlon felt his knees give beneath him as he sprawled onto a chair.

He fastened his gaze on the flustered Tweenie and in that look there was respect and awe, and something more, too, for there was *fear.* Never before had he really realized that the Tweenie was not of Earth nor Mars but a member of a race apart. He noticed the difference now, not in the comparatively minor physical changes, but in the profound and searching mental gulf that he only now comprehended.

"Atomic power!" he croaked hoarsely. "And solved by a boy, not yet twenty years old."

Max's confusion was painful, "You did all the real work. Mr. Scanlon, years and years of it. I just happened to notice a little detail that you might have caught yourself the next day." His voice died before the fixed and steady stare of the inventor.

"Atomic power—the greatest achievement of man so far, and we actually have it, we two."

Both—guardian and ward—seemed awed at the grandeur and power of the thing they had created.

And in that moment—the age of Electricity died.

Jefferson Scanlon sucked at his pipe contentedly. Outside, the snow was falling and the chill of winter was in the air, but inside, in the comfortable warmth, Scanlon sat and smoked and smiled to himself. Across the way, Beulah, likewise quietly happy, hummed softly in time to clicking knitting needles, stopping only occasionally as her fingers flew through an unusually intricate portion of the pattern. In the corner next to the window sat Max, occupied in his usual pastime of reading, and Scanlon reflected with faint surprise that of late Max had confined his reading to light novels.

Much had happened since that well-remembered day over a year ago. For one thing, Scanlon was now a world-famous and world-adored scientist, and it would have been strange had he not been sufficiently human to be proud of it. Secondly, and scarcely less important, atomic power was remaking the world.

Scanlon thanked all the powers that were, over and over again, for the fact that war was a thing of two centuries past, for otherwise atomic power would have been the final ruination of civilization. As it was, the coalition of World Powers that now controlled the great force of Atomic Power proved it a real blessing and were introducing it into Man's life in the slow, gradual stages necessary to prevent economic upheaval.

Already, interplanetary travel had been revolutionized. From hazardous gambles, trips to Mars and Venus had become holiday jaunts to be negotiated in a third of the previous time, and trips to the outer planets were at last feasible.

Scanlon settled back further in his chair, and pondered once more upon the only fly in his wonderful pot of ointment. Max had refused all credit; stormily and violently refused to have his name as much as mentioned. The injustice of it galled Scanlon, but aside from a vague mention of "capable assistants" he had said nothing; and the thought of it still made him feel an ace of a cad.

A sharp explosive noise brought him out of his reverie and he turned startled eyes toward Max, who had suddenly closed his book with a peevish slap.

"Hello," exclaimed Scanlon, "and what's wrong now?"

Max tossed the book aside and stood up, his underlip thrust out in a pout, "I'm lonely, that's all."

Scanlon's face fell, and he felt at an uncomfortable loss for words. "I guess I know that, Max," he said softly, at length. "I'm sorry for you, but the conditions—are so—"

Max relented, and brightening up, placed an affectionate arm about his foster-father's shoulder, "I didn't mean it that way, you know. It's just—well, I can't say it but it's that—you get to wishing you had someone your own age to talk to—someone of your own kind."

Beulah looked up and bestowed a penetrating glance upon the young Tweenie but said nothing.

Scanlon considered, "You're right, son, in a way. A friend and companion is the best thing a fellow can have, and I'm afraid Beulah and I don't qualify in that respect. One of your own kind, as you say, would be the ideal solution, but that's a tough proposition." He rubbed his nose with one finger and gazed at the ceiling thoughtfully.

Max opened his mouth as if he were going to say something more, but changed his mind and turned pink for no evident reason. Then he muttered, barely loud enough for Scanlon to hear, "I'm being silly!" With an abrupt turn he marched out of the room, banging the door loudly as he left.

The older man gazed after him with undisguised surprise, "Well! What a funny way to act. What's got into him lately, anyway?"

Beulah halted the nimbly-leaping needles long enough to remark acidly, "Men are born fools and blind into the bargain."

"Is that so?" was the somewhat nettled response, "And do *you* know what's biting him?"

"I certainly do. It's as plain as that terrible tie you're wearing. I've seen it for months now. Poor fellow!"

Scanlon shook his head, "You're speaking in riddles, Beulah."

The housekeeper laid her knitting aside and glanced at the inventor wearily, "It's very simple. The boy is twenty. He needs company."

"But that's just what he said. Is *that* your marvelous penetration?"

"Good land, Jefferson. Has it been so long since you were twenty yourself? Do you mean to say that you honestly think he's referring to *male* company?"

"Oh," said Scanlon, and then brightened suddenly, "Oh!" He giggled in an inane manner.

"Well, what are you going to do about it?"

"Why—why, nothing. What *can* be done?"

"That's a fine way to speak of your ward, when you're rich enough to buy five hundred orphan asylums from basement to roof and never miss the money. It should be the easiest thing in the world to find a likely-looking young lady Tweenie to keep him company."

Scanlon gazed at her, a look of intense horror on his face, "Are you serious, Beulah? Are you trying to suggest that I go shopping for a female Tweenie for Max? Why—why, what do I know about women—especially Tweenie women. I don't know his standards. I'm liable to pick one he'll consider an ugly hag."

"Don't raise silly objections, Jefferson. Outside of the hair, they're the same in looks as anyone else, and I'll leave it to you to pick a pretty one. There never was a bachelor old and crabbed enough not to be able to do *that.*"

"No! I won't do it. Of all the horrible ideas—"

"Jefferson! You're his guardian. You owe it to him."

The words struck the inventor forcibly, "I owe it to him," he repeated. "You're right there, more right than you know." He sighed, "I guess it's got to be done."

Scanlon shifted uneasily from one trembling foot to the other under the piercing stare of the vinegar-faced official, whose name-board proclaimed in large letters—Miss Martin, Superintendent.

"Sit down, sir," she said sourly. "What do you wish?"

Scanlon cleared his throat. He had lost count of the asylums visited up to now and the task was rapidly becoming too much for him. He made a mental vow that this would be the last—either they would have a Tweenie of the proper sex, age, and appearance or he would throw up the whole thing as a bad job.

"I have come to see," he began, in a carefully-prepared, but stammered speech, "if there are any Twee—Martian half-breeds in your asylum. It is—"

"We have three," interrupted the superintendent sharply.

"Any females?" asked Scanlon, eagerly.

"*All* females," she replied, and her eye glittered with disapproving suspicion.

"Oh, good. Do you mind if I see them. It is—"

Miss Martin's cold glance did not waver, "Pardon me, but before we go any further, I would like to know whether you're thinking of adopting a half-breed."

"I *would* like to take out guardianship papers if I am suited. Is that so very unusual?"

"It certainly is," was the prompt retort. "You understand that in any such case, we must first make a thorough investigation of the family's status, both financial and social. It is the opinion of the government that these creatures are better off under state supervision, and adoption would be a difficult matter."

"I know, madam, I know. I've had practical experience in this matter about fifteen months ago. I believe I can give you satisfaction as to my financial and social status without much trouble. My name is Jefferson Scanlon—."

"Jefferson Scanlon!" her exclamation was half a scream. In a trice, her face expanded into a servile smile, "Why of course. I should have recognized you from the many pictures I've seen of you. How stupid of me. Pray do not trouble yourself with any further references. I'm sure that in your case," this with a particularly genial expression, "no red tape need be necessary."

She sounded a desk-bell furiously. "Bring down Madeline and the two little ones as soon as you can," she snapped at the frightened maid who answered. "Have them cleaned up and warn them to be on their best behavior."

With this, she turned to Scanlon once more, "It will not take long, Mr. Scanlon. It is really such a great honor to have you here with us, and I am so ashamed at my abrupt treatment of you earlier. At first I didn't recognize you, though I saw immediately that you were someone of importance."

If Scanlon had been upset by the superintendent's former harsh haughtiness, he was entirely unnerved by her effusive geniality. He wiped his profusely-perspiring brow time and time again, answering in incoherent monosyllables the vivacious questions put to him. It was just as he had come to the wild decision of taking to his heels and escaping from the she-dragon by flight that the maid announced the three Tweenies and saved the situation.

Scanlon surveyed the three half-breeds with interest and sudden satisfaction. Two were mere children, perhaps ten years of age, but the third, some eighteen years old, was eligible from every point of view.

Her slight form was lithe and graceful even in the quiet attitude of waiting that she had assumed, and Scanlon, "dried-up, dyed-in-the-wool bachelor" though he was, could not restrain a light nod of approval.

Her face was certainly what Beulah would call "likely-looking" and her eyes, now bent toward the floor in shy confusion, were of a deep blue, which seemed a great point to Scanlon.

Even her strange hair was beautiful. It was only moderately high, not nearly the size of Max's lordly male crest, and its silky-white sheen caught the sunbeams and sent them back in glistening highlights.

The two little ones grasped the skirt of their elder companion with tight grips and regarded the two adults in wide-eyed fright which increased as time passed.

"I believe, Miss Martin, that the young lady will do," remarked Scanlon. "She is exactly what I had in mind. Could you tell me how soon guardianship papers could be drawn up?"

"I could have them ready for you tomorrow, Mr. Scanlon. In an unusual case such as yours, I could easily make special arrangements."

"Thank you. I shall be back then—," he was interrupted by a loud sniffle. One of the little Tweenies could stand it no longer and had burst into tears, followed soon by the other.

"Madeline," cried Miss Martin to the eighteen-year-old. "Please keep Rose and Blanche quiet. This is an abominable exhibition."

Scanlon intervened. It seemed to him that Madeline was rather pale and though she smiled and soothed the youngsters he was certain that there were tears in her eyes.

"Perhaps," he suggested, "the young lady has no wish to leave the institution. Of course, I wouldn't think of taking her on any but a purely voluntary basis."

Miss Martin smiled superciliously, "She won't make any trouble." She turned to the young girl, "You've heard of the great Jefferson Scanlon, haven't you?"

"Ye-es, Miss Martin," replied the girl, in a low voice.

"Let me handle this, Miss Martin," urged Scanlon. "Tell me, girl, would you really prefer to stay here."

"Oh, no," she replied earnestly, "I would be very glad to leave, though," with an apprehensive glance at Miss Martin, "I have been very well treated here. But you see—what's to be done with the two little ones? I'm all they have, and if I left, they—they—"

She broke down and snatched them to her with a sudden, fierce grip, "I don't want to leave them, sir!" She kissed each softly, "Don't cry, children. I won't leave you. They won't take me away."

Scanlon swallowed with difficulty and groped for a handkerchief with which to blow his nose. Miss Martin gazed on with disapproving hauteur.

"Don't mind the silly thing, Mr. Scanlon," said she. "I believe I can have everything ready by tomorrow noon."

"Have ready guardianship papers for all three," was the gruff reply.

"What? All three? Are you serious?"

"Certainly. I can do it if I wish, can't I?" he shouted.

"Why, of course, but—"

Scanlon left precipitately, leaving both Madeline and Miss Martin petrified, the latter with utter stupefaction, the former in a sudden upsurge of happiness. Even the ten-year-olds sensed the change in affairs and subsided into occasional sobs.

Beulah's surprise, when she met them at the airport and saw three Tweenies where she had expected one, is not to be described. But, on the whole, the surprise was a pleasant one, for little Rose and Blanche took to the elderly housekeeper immediately. Their first greeting was to bestow great, moist kisses upon Beulah's lined cheeks at which she glowed with joy and kissed them in turn.

With Madeline she was enchanted, whispering to Scanlon that he knew a little more about such matters than he pretended.

"If she had decent hair," whispered Scanlon in reply, "I'd marry her myself. That I would," and he smiled in great self-satisfaction.

The arrival at home in mid-afternoon was the occasion of great excitement on the part of the two oldsters. Scanlon inveigled Max into accompanying him on a long walk together in the woods, and when the unsuspecting Max left, puzzled but willing, Beulah busied herself with setting the three newcomers at their ease.

They were shown over the house from top to bottom, the rooms assigned to them being indicated. Beulah prattled away continuously, joking and chaffing, until the Tweenies had lost all their shyness and felt as if they had known her forever.

Then, as the winter evening approached, she turned to Madeline rather abruptly and said, "It's getting late. Do you want to come downstairs with me and help prepare supper for the men."

Madeline was taken aback, "The *men*. Is there then someone besides Mr. Scanlon?"

"Oh, yes. There's Max. You haven't seen him yet."

"Is Max a relation of yours?"

"No, child. He's another of Mr. Scanlon's wards."

"Oh, I see." She blushed and her hand rose involuntarily to her hair.

Beulah saw in a moment the thoughts passing through her head and added in a softer voice, "Don't worry, dear. He won't mind your being a Tweenie. He'll be *glad* to see you."

It turned out, though, that "glad" was an entirely inadequate adjective when applied to Max's emotions at the first sight of Madeline.

He tramped into the house in advance of Scanlon, taking off his overcoat and stamping the snow off his shoes as he did so.

"Oh, boy," he cried at the half-frozen inventor who followed him in, "why you were so anxious to saunter about on a freezer like today I don't know." He sniffed the air appreciatively, "Ah, do I smell lamb chops?" and he made for the dining-room in double-quick time.

It was at the threshold that he stopped suddenly, and gasped for air as if in the last throes of suffocation. Scanlon slipped by and sat down.

"Come on," he said, enjoying the other's brick-red visage. "Sit down. We have company today. This is Madeline and this is Rose and this is Blanche. And this," he turned to the seated girls and noted with satisfaction that Madeline's pink face was turning a fixed glance of confusion upon the plate before her, "is my ward, Max."

"How do you do," murmured Max, eyes like saucers, "I'm pleased to meet you."

Rose and Blanche shouted cheery greetings in reply but Madeline only raised her eyes fleetingly and then dropped them again.

The meal was a singularly quiet one. Max, though he had complained of a ravenous hunger all afternoon, allowed his chop and mashed potatoes to die of cold before him, while Madeline played with her food as if she did not know what it was there for. Scanlon and Beulah ate quietly and well, exchanging sly glances between bites.

Scanlon sneaked off after dinner, for he rightly felt that the more tactful touch of a woman was needed in these matters, and when Beulah joined him in his study some hours later, he saw at a glance that he had been correct.

"I've broken the ice," she said happily, "they're telling each other their life histories now and are getting along wonderfully. They're still afraid of each other though, and insist on sitting at opposite ends of the room, but that'll wear off—and pretty quickly, too."

"It's a fine match, Beulah, eh?"

"A finer one I've never seen. And little Rose and Blanche are angels. I've just put them to bed."

There was a short silence, and then Beulah continued softly, "That was the only time you were right and I was wrong—that time you first brought Max into the house and I objected—but that one time makes up for everything else. You are a credit to your dear mother, Jefferson."

Scanlon nodded soberly, "I wish I could make all Tweenies on earth so happy. It would be such a simple thing. If we treated them like humans instead of like criminals and gave them homes, built especially for them and calculated especially for their happiness—"

"Well, why don't *you* do it," interrupted Beulah.

Scanlon turned a serious eye upon the old housekeeper, "That's exactly what I was leading up to." His voice lapsed into a dreamy murmur, "Just think. A town of Tweenies—run by them and for them—with its own governing officials and its own schools and its own public utilities. A little world within a world where the Tweenie can consider himself a human being—instead of a freak surrounded and looked down upon by endless multitudes of pure-bloods."

He reached for his pipe and filled it slowly, "The world owes a debt to *one* Tweenie which it can never repay—and I owe it to him as well. I'm going to do it. I'm going to create Tweenietown."

That night he did not go to sleep. The stars turned in their grand circles and paled at last. The gray of dawn came and grew, but still Scanlon sat unmoving—dreaming and planning.

• • •

At eighty, age sat lightly upon Jefferson Scanlon's head. The spring was gone from his step, the sturdy straightness from his shoulders, but his robust health had not failed him, and his mind, beneath the shock of hair, now as white as any Tweenie's, still worked with undiminished vigor.

A happy life is not an aging one and for forty years now, Scanlon had watched Tweenietown grow, and in the watching, had found happiness.

He could see it now stretched before him like a large, beautiful painting as he gazed out the window. A little gem of a town with a population of slightly more than a thousand, nestling amid three hundred square miles of fertile Ohio land.

Neat and sturdy houses, wide, clean streets, parks, theaters, schools, stores—a model town, bespeaking decades of intelligent effort and cooperation.

The door opened behind him and he recognized the soft step without needing to turn, "Is that you, Madeline?"

"Yes, father," for by no other title was he known to any inhabitant of Tweenietown. "Max is returning with Mr. Johanson."

"That's good," he gazed at Madeline tenderly. "We've seen Tweenietown grow since those days long ago, haven't we?"

Madeline nodded and sighed.

"Don't sigh, dear. It's been well worth the years we've given to it. If only Beulah had lived to see it now."

He shook his head as he thought of the old housekeeper, dead now a quarter of a century.

"Don't think such sad thoughts," admonished Madeline in her turn. "Here comes Mr. Johanson. Remember it's the fortieth anniversary and a happy day; not a sad one."

Charles B. Johanson was what is known as a "shrewd" man. That is, he was an intelligent, far-seeing person, comparatively well-versed in the sciences, but one who was wont to put these good qualities into practice only in order to advance his own interest. Consequently, he went far in politics and was the first appointee to the newly created Cabinet post of Science and Technology.

It was the first official act of his to visit the world's greatest scientist and inventor, Jefferson Scanlon, who, in his old age, still had no peer in the number of useful inventions turned over to the government every year. Tweenietown was a considerable surprise to him. It was known rather vaguely in the outside world that the town existed, and it was considered a hobby of the old scientist—a harmless eccentricity. Johanson found it a well-worked out project of sinister connotations.

His attitude, however, when he entered Scanlon's room in company with his erstwhile guide, Max, was one of frank geniality, concealing well certain thoughts that swept through his mind.

"Ah, Johanson," greeted Scanlon, "you're back. What do you think of all this?" his arm made a wide sweep.

"It is surprising—something marvelous to behold," Johanson assured him.

Scanlon chuckled, "Glad to hear it. We have a population of 1154 now and growing every day. You've seen what we've done already but it's nothing to what we are going to do in the future—even after my death. However, there is something I wish to see done *before* I die and for that I'll need your help."

"And that is?" questioned the Secretary of Science and Technology, guardedly.

"Just this. That you sponsor measures giving these Tweenies, these so long despised half-breeds, full equality,—political,—legal,—economic,—social,—with Terrestrials and Martians."

Johanson hesitated, "It would be difficult. There is a certain amount of perhaps understandable prejudice against them, and until we can convince Earth that the Tweenies deserve equality—" he shook his head doubtfully.

"Deserve equality!" exclaimed Scanlon, vehemently, "Why, they deserve more. I am *moderate* in my demands." At these words, Max, sitting quietly in a corner, looked up and bit his lip, but said nothing as Scanlon continued, "You don't know the true worth of these Tweenies. They combine the best of Earth and Mars. They possess the cold, analytical reasoning powers of the Martians together with the emotional drive and boundless energy of the Earthman. As far as intellect is concerned, they are your superior and mine, every one of them. I ask only equality."

The Secretary smiled soothingly, "Your zeal misleads you perhaps, my dear Scanlon."

"It does not. Why do you suppose I turn out so many successful gadgets—like this gravitational shield I created a few years back. Do you think I could have done it without my Tweenie assistants? It was Max here," Max dropped his eyes before the sudden piercing gaze of the Cabinet member, "that put the final touch upon my discovery of atomic power itself."

Scanlon threw caution to the winds, as he grew excited. "Ask Professor Whitsun of Stanford and he'll tell you. He's a world authority on psychology and knows what he's talking about. He *studied* the Tweenie and he'll tell you that the Tweenie is the *coming* race of the Solar System, destined to take the supremacy away from we pure-bloods as inevitably as night follows day. Don't you think they deserve equality in that case."

"Yes, I do think so,—definitely," replied Johanson. There was a strange glitter in his eyes, and a crooked smile upon his lips, "This is of extreme importance, Scanlon. I shall attend to it immediately. So immediately, in fact, that I believe I had better leave in half an hour, to catch the 2:10 strato-car."

Johanson had scarcely left, when Max approached Scanlon and blurted out with no preamble at all, "There is something I have to show you, father—something you have not known about before."

Scanlon stared his surprise, "What do you mean?"

"Come with me, please, father. I shall explain." His grave expression was almost frightening. Madeline joined the two at the door, and at a sign from Max, seemed to comprehend the situation. She said nothing but her eyes grew sad and the lines in her forehead seemed to deepen.

In utter silence, the three entered the waiting Rocko-car and were sped across the town in the direction of the Hill o' the Woods. High over Lake Clare they shot to come down once more in the wooded patch at the foot of the hill.

A tall, burly Tweenie sprang to attention as the car landed and started at the sight of Scanlon.

"Good afternoon, father," he whispered respectfully, and cast a questioning glance at Max as he did so.

"Same to you, Emmanuel," replied Scanlon absently. He suddenly became aware that before him was a cleverly camouflaged opening that led into the very hill itself.

Max beckoned him to follow and led the way into the opening which after a hundred feet opened into an enormous man-made cavern. Scanlon halted in utter amazement, for before him were three giant space-ships, gleaming silvery-white and equipped, as he could plainly see, with the latest atomic power.

"I'm sorry, father," said Max, "that all this was done without your knowledge. It is the only case of the sort in the history of Tweenietown." Scanlon scarcely seemed to hear, standing as if in a daze and Max continued, "The center one is the flagship—the *Jefferson Scanlon*. The one to the right is the *Beulah Goodkin* and the one to the left the *Madeline*."

Scanlon snapped out of his bemusement, "But what does this all mean and why the secrecy?"

"These ships have been lying ready for five years now, fully fueled and provisioned, ready for instant take-off. Tonight, we blast away the side of the hill and shoot for Venus—tonight. We have not told you till now, for we did not wish to disturb your peace of mind with a misfortune we knew long ago to be inevitable. We had thought that perhaps," his voice sank lower, "its fulfillment might have been postponed until after you were no longer with us."

"Speak out," cried Scanlon suddenly. "I want the full details. Why do you leave just as I feel sure I can obtain full equality for you."

"Exactly," answered Max, mournfully. "Your words to Johanson swung the scale. As long as Earthmen and Martians merely thought us different and inferior, they despised us and tolerated us. You have told Johanson we were superior and would ultimately supplant Mankind. They have no alternative now but to hate us. There shall be no further toleration; of that I can assure you. We leave before the storm breaks."

The old man's eyes widened as the truth of the other's statements became apparent to him, "I see. I must get in touch with Johanson. Perhaps, we can together correct that terrible mistake." He clapped a hand to his forehead.

"Oh, Max," interposed Madeline, tearfully, "why don't you come to the point. We want you to come with us, father. In Venus, which is so sparsely settled, we can find a spot where we can develop unharmed for an unlimited time. We can establish our nation, free and untrammeled, powerful in our own right, no longer dependent on—"

Her voice died away and she gazed anxiously at Scanlon's face, now grown drawn and haggard. "No," he whispered, "no! My place is here with my own kind. Go, my children, and establish your nation. In the end, your descendants shall rule the System. But I—I shall stay here."

"Then I shall stay, too," insisted Max. "You are old and someone must care for you. I owe you my life a dozen times over."

Scanlon shook his head firmly, "I shall need no one. Dayton is not far. I shall be well taken care of there or anywhere else I go. You, Max, are needed by your race. You are their leader. Go!"

Scanlon wandered through the deserted streets of Tweenietown and tried to take a grip upon himself. It was hard. Yesterday, he had celebrated the fortieth anniversary of its founding—it had been at the peak of its prosperity. Today, it was a ghost town.

Yet, oddly enough, there was a spirit of exultation about him. His dream had shattered—but only to give way to a brighter dream. He had nourished foundlings and brought up a race in its youth and for that he was someday to be recognized as the founder of the *super-race.*

It was *his* creation that would someday rule the system. Atomic power—gravity nullifiers—all faded into insignificance. *This* was his real gift to the Universe.

This, he decided, was how a God must feel.

This is a change-of-pacer. And a rescue job not nearly as old as most: this story first appeared "merely" 40 years ago. It was overlooked by anthologists of its day because it appeared in a poor man's Playboy, a men's magazine called Escapade. In 1965, after I called it to the attention of author/anthologist Charles Nuetzel, it was included in a paperback collection called If This Goes On. Unfortunately the publisher was new, small, and didn't last long and the anthology is a little-known one, altho van Vogt, Asimov, Matheson, Willy Ley, Yours Sciencerely & Marion Zimmer Bradley were among those featured in it.

In introducing it, Nuetzel said: "This story reveals some of the brutal facts about racing and about our own human nature as well. Is modern sport so very much different from the sport of the Roman arenas? Is there any difference at all between the gladiator & the boxer, the charioteer & . . . THE RACER?"

In referring to it in the Introduction to the anthology I said: "It is nearly 10 years since I first read The Racer in manuscript form. But 2 lustrums have not served to erase the luster of this grease-slick story in my memory—and I predict it will stick in yours with all the thrill of an Indianapolis classic with yourself at the shift-stick."

As agent, I sold The Racer to the movies and you may have seen it as the highly successful Death Race 2000 which spawned a sort of sequel, Deathsport. In rescuing for you the original story on which the movie was based, you are in effect getting the best of 2 worlds: Time Vault & Scientifilm World. Had I used the story in Scientifilm World instead, I would have introduced it with these words:

Frankenstein 2000.

The race of death.

The year, 2000.

The Racer, "Frankenstein" (David Carradine).

The thrilling cross-country crash-&-smash auto epic.

Here you have the opportunity, as in a TV replay of a sporting event, to relive the exciting hi-lites of the film, to read the very story from which the movie was made!

A. E. van Vogt took over from the first screen adaptation.

A couple of other writers had a hand in the plot's development, with Robert (Wild in the Streets) Thom & Charles Griffith credited with the final version, altho director Paul Bartel at the preview was telling me that even he was improvising as he went along. The result, to briefly recapitulate before giving you the original story:

In the year 2000 there are 5 famous racing drivers—but there is only room for one.

The Death Race is the contest of elimination, the final pitting of the world's greatest racers against each other.

The victor is determined not only by his finishing place in the race but by the number of pedestrians mangled or murdered by each contestant!

To aid in eliminating unwary bystanders, the superautos are of devilish design, equipped with such death-dealing devices as bayonets, claws, steers' horns . . . even machine-guns!

The stunt drivers really excelled in their art in this hair-raising race thru fire, blood & bodies to the winner's circle.

Deathrace 2000

by Ib J. Melchior

Willie felt the familiar intoxicating excitement. His mouth was dry; his heart beat faster, all his senses seemed more aware than ever. It was a few minutes before 0800 hours—his time to start.

This was the day. From all the Long Island Starting Fields the Racers were taking off at 15-minute intervals. The sputter and roar of cars warming up were everywhere. The smell of oil and fuel fumes permeated the air. The hubbub of the great crowd was a steady din. This was the biggest race of the year—New York to Los Angeles—100,000 bucks to the winner! Willie was determined to better his winning record of last year: 33 hours, 27 minutes, 12 seconds in Time. And although it was becoming increasingly difficult he'd do his damnedest to better his Score too!

He took a last walk of inspection around his car. Sleek, low-slung, dark brown, the practically indestructible plastiglass top looking deceptively fragile, like a soap bubble. Not bad for an old-fashioned diesel job. He kicked the solid plastirubber tires in the time honored fashion of all drivers. Hank was giving a last minute shine to the needle sharp durasteel horns protruding from the front fenders. Willie's car wasn't nicknamed "The Bull" without reason. The front of the car was built like a streamlined bull's head complete with bloodshot, evil looking eyes, iron ring through flaring nostrils—and the horns. Although most of the racing cars were built to look like tigers, or sharks, or eagles, there *were* a few bulls—but Willie's horns were unequaled.

"Car 79 ready for Start in five minutes," the loudspeaker blared. "Car 79. Willie Connors, driver. Hank Morowski, mechanic. Ready your car for Start in five minutes."

Willie and Hank took their places in "The Bull." At a touch by Willie on the starter the powerful diesel engine began a low purr. They drove slowly to the starting line.

"Last Check!" said Willie.

"Right," came Hank's answer.

"Oil and Fuel?"

"40 hours."

"Cooling Fluid?"

"Sealed."

"No-Sleeps?"

"Check."

"Energene Tabs?"

"Check."

"Thermo Drink?"

"Check."

The Starter held the checkered flag high over his head. The crowds packing the grandstands were on their feet. Hushed. Waiting.

"Here we go!" whispered Willie.

The flag fell. A tremendous cry rose from the crowd. But Willie hardly heard it. Accelerating furiously he pushed his car to its top speed of 190 miles an hour within seconds—shooting like a bullet along the straightaway toward Manhattan. He was elated; exhilarated. He was a Racer. And full of tricks!

Willie shot through the Tunnel directly to Jersey.

"Well?" grumbled Hank. "Can you tell me now?"

"Toledo," said Willie. "Toledo, Ohio. On the Thruway. We should make it in under three hours."

He felt a slight annoyance with Hank. There was no reason for the man to be touchy. He knew a driver didn't tell *anyone* the racing route he'd selected. News like that had a habit of getting around. It could cost a Racer his Score.

"There's not much chance of anything coming up until after we hit Toledo," Willie said, "but keep your eyes peeled. You never know."

Hank merely grunted.

It was exactly 1048 hours when "The Bull" streaked into the deserted streets of Toledo.

"O.K.—what now?" asked Hank.

"Grand Rapids, Michigan," Willie said laconically.

"Grand Rapids! But that's—that's an easy 300-mile-detour!"

"I know."

"Are you crazy? It'll cost us a couple of hours."

"So Grand Rapids is all the way up between the Lakes. So who'll be expecting us up there?"

"Oh! Oh, yeah, I see," said Hank.

"The *Time* isn't everything, my friend. Whoever said the shortest distance between two points is a straight line? The *Score* counts too. And here's where we pick up *our* Score!"

The first Tragi-Acc never even knew the Racer had arrived. "The Bull" struck him squarely, threw him up in the air and let him slide off its plastiglass back, leaving a red smear behind and somewhat to the left of Willie— all in a split second . . .

Near Calvin College an imprudent coed found herself too far from cover when the Racer suddenly came streaking down the campus. Frantically she sprinted for safety, but she didn't have a chance with a driver like Willie behind the wheel. The razor sharp horn on the right fender sliced through her spine so cleanly that the jar wasn't even felt inside the car.

Leaving town the Racer was in luck again. An elderly woman had left the sanctuary of her stone-walled garden to rescue a straying cat. She was so easy to hit that Willie felt a little cheated.

At 1232 hours they were on the speedway headed for Kansas City.

Hank looked in awe at Willie. "Three!" he murmured dreamily, "a Score of three already. And all of them Kills—for sure. You *really* know how to drive!"

Hank settled back contentedly as if he could already feel his 25,000 dollar cut in his pocket. He began to whistle "The Racers Are Roaring" off key.

Even after his good Score it annoyed Willie. And for some reason he kept remembering the belatedly pleading look in the old woman's eyes as he struck her. Funny *that* should stay with him . . .

He estimated they'd hit Kansas City at around 1815 hours, CST. Hank turned on the radio. Peoria, Illinois, was warning its citizens of the approach of a Racer. All spectators should watch from safety places. Willie grinned. That would be him. Well—he wasn't looking for any Score in Peoria.

Dayton, Ohio, told of a Racer having made a Tragic Accident Score of one, and Fort Wayne, Indiana, was crowing over the fact that three Racers had passed through without scoring once. From what he heard it seemed to Willie he had a comfortable lead, both in Time and Score.

They were receiving Kansas City now. An oily voiced announcer was filling in the time between Racing Scores with what appeared to be a brief history of Racing.

". . . and the most popular spectator sports of the latter half of the 20th Century were such mildly exciting pursuits as boxing and wrestling. Of course the spectators enjoyed seeing the combatants trying to maim each other, and there was always the chance of the hoped-for fatal accident.

"Motor Racing, however, gave a much greater opportunity for the Tragic Accidents so exciting to the spectator. One of the most famed old Speedways, Indianapolis, where many drivers and spectators alike ended as bloody Tragi-Accs, is today the nation's racing shrine. Motor racing was already then held all over the world, sometimes with Scores reaching the hundred mark, and long distance races were popular.

"The modern Race makes it possible for the entire population to . . ."

Willie switched off the radio. Why did they always have to stress the *Score? Time* was important too. The *speed*—and the *endurance*. That was part of an Ace Racer as well as his scoring ability. He took an Energene Tab. They were entering Kansas City.

The checkpoint officials told Willie that there were three Racers with better Time than he, and one had tied his Score. "The Bull" stayed just long enough in the checkpoint pit for Hank to make a quick engine inspection—then they took off again. It was 1818 hours, CST, when they left the city limits behind. They'd been driving over nine hours.

About 50 miles along the Thruway to Denver, just after passing through a little town called Lawrence, Willie suddenly slowed down. Hank who'd been dozing sat up in alarm.

"What's the matter?" he cried, "what's wrong?"

"Nothing's wrong," Willie said irritably. "Relax. You seem to be good at that."

"But why are you slowing down?"

"You heard the checkpoint record. Our Score's already been tied. We've got to better it," Willie answered grimly.

The plastirubber tires screeched on the concrete speedway as Willie turned down an exit leading to a Class II road.

"Why down here?" asked Hank. "You can only go about 80 MPH."

A large lumi-sign appeared on the side of the road ahead—

LONE STAR
11 Miles

it announced.

Willie pointed. "That's why," he said curtly.

In a few minutes Lone Star came into view. It was a small village. Willie was traveling as fast as he could on the secondary road. He plowed through a flock of chickens, hurtled over a little mongrel dog, which crawled yelping toward the safety of a house and the waiting arms of a little girl, and managed to graze the leg of a husky youth who vaulted a high wooden fence—then they were through Lone Star.

Hank activated the little dashboard screen which gave them a rear view.

"That's not going to do much for our Score," he remarked sourly.

"Oh, shut up!" Willie exploded, surprising both himself and Hank.

What was the *matter* with him? He couldn't be getting tired already. He swallowed a No-Sleep. That'd help.

Hank was quiet as they sped through Topeka and took the Thruway to Oklahoma City, but out of the corner of his eyes he was looking speculatively at Willie, hunched over the wheel.

It was getting dusk. Willie switched on his powerful headbeams. They had a faint reddish tint because of the coloring of "The Bull's" eyes. They had just whizzed through a little burg named Perry, when there was a series of sharp cracks. Willie started.

"There they go again!" chortled Hank. "Those dumb hinterland hicks will never learn they can't hurt us with their fly-poppers." He knocked the plastiglass dome affectionately. "Takes atomic pellets to get through this baby."

Of course! He *must* be on edge to be taken by surprise like that. He'd run into the Anti-Racers before. Just a handful of malcontents. The Racing

Commission had already declared them illegal. Still—at every race they took pot shots at the Racers; a sort of pathetic defiance. Why should anyone want to do away with Racing?

They were entering the outskirts of Oklahoma City. Willie killed his headbeams. No need to advertise.

Suddenly Hank grabbed his arm. Wordlessly he pointed. There— garish and gaudy—gleamed the neon sign of a theater . . .

Willie slowed to a crawl. He pulled over to the curb and the dark car melted into the shadows. He glanced at the clock. 2203 hours. Perhaps . . .

Down the street a man cautiously stuck his head out from the theater entrance. Warily he emerged completely, looking up and down the street carefully. He did not see "The Bull." Presently he ventured out into the center of the roadway. He stood still listening for a moment. Then he turned and beckoned toward the theater. Immediately a small group of people emerged at a run.

Now!

The acceleration slammed the Racers back in their seats. "The Bull" shot forward and bore down on the little knot of petrified people with appalling speed.

This time there was no mistaking the hits. A quick succession of pars had Willie calling upon all his driving skill to keep from losing control. Hank pressed the Clean-Spray button to wash the blood off the front of the dome. He sat with eyes glued to the rear view screen.

"Man, oh man," he murmured. "What a record; what a Score!" He turned to Willie. "Please," he said, "please stop. Let's get out. I know it's against regulations, but I've just gotta see how we did. It won't take long. We can afford a couple of minutes *Time* now!"

Suddenly Willie felt he had to get out too. This was the biggest Tragi-Acc he'd ever had. He had a vague feeling there was something he wanted to do. He brought the car to a stop. They stepped out.

Within seconds the deserted street was swarming with people. Now the Racers were out of their car they felt safe. And curious. A few of them pressed forward to take a look at Willie. Naturally he was recognized. His photo had been seen in one way or another by everyone.

Willie was gratified by this obvious adulation. He looked about him. There were many people in the street now. But—but they were not all fawning and beaming upon him. Willie frowned. Most of them looked grim— even hostile. Why? What was wrong? Wasn't he one of their greatest Racers? And hadn't he just made a record Score? Given them a Tragi-Acc they wouldn't soon forget? What was the matter with those hicks?

Suddenly the crowd parted. Slowly a young girl walked up to Willie. She was beautiful—even with the terrible anger burning on her face. In her arms she held the still body of a child. She looked straight at Willie with loathing in her eyes. Her voice was low but steady when she said:

"Butcher!"

Someone in the crowd called: "Careful, Muriel!" but she paid no heed. Turning from him she walked on through the crowd, parting for her.

Willie was stunned.

"Come on, let's get out of here," Hank said anxiously.

Willie didn't answer. He was looking back through the crowd to the scene of his Tragi-Acc. Never before had he stopped. Never before had he been this close. He could hear the moaning and sobbing of the Maims over the low murmur of the crowd. It made him uneasy. Back there they worked hurriedly to get the Tragi-Accs off the street. *There were so many of them . . .* Butcher? . . .

All at once he was conscious of Hank pulling at him.

"Let's get roaring! Let's go!"

Quickly he turned and entered the car. Almost at once the street was empty. He turned on his headbeams and started up. Faster—and faster. The street was dead—empty . . .

No! There! Someone! Holding a . . .

It was butcher—no, *Muriel*. She stood rooted to the spot in the middle of the street holding the child in her arms. In the glaring headlights her face was white, her eyes terrible, burning, dark . . .

Willie did not let up. The car hurtled down upon the lone figure—and passed . . .

They'd lost 13 minutes. Now they were on their way to El Paso, Texas. The nagging headache Willie'd suffered the whole week of planning before the race had returned. He reached for a No-Sleep, hesitated a second, then took another.

Hank glanced at him, worriedly. "Easy boy!"

Willie didn't answer.

"That Anti-Racer get under your skin?" Hank suggested. "Don't let it bother you."

"Butcher," she'd said. "Butcher!"

Willie was staring through the plastiglass dome at the racing pool of light from the headbeams. "The Bull" was tearing along the Thruway at almost 180 MPH.

What was that? There—in the light? It was a face—terrible, dark eyes—getting larger—larger—*Muriel!* It was butcher—no, Muriel! No—it was a Racer,—a Racing Car with Muriel's face, shrieking down upon him—closer—closer . . .

He threw his arms in front of his face. Dimly he heard Hank shout "Willie!" He felt the car lurch. Automatically he tightened his grip on the wheel. They had careened close to the shoulder of the speedway. Willie sat up. Ahead of him the road was clear—and empty.

It was still dark when they hit El Paso. The radio told them their Oklahoma Score. Five and eight. Five Kills—eight Maims! Hank was delighted. They were close to setting a record. He'd already begun to spend his $25,000.

Willie was uneasy. His headache was worse. His hands were clammy. He kept hearing Muriel's voice saying: "Butcher"—"Butcher"—"Butcher!" . . .

But he was *not* a butcher. He was a Racer! He'd show them. He'd win this race.

El Paso was a disappointment. Not a soul in sight. Phoenix next.

The clock said 0658 hours, MST, when they roared into Phoenix. The streets were clear. Willie had to slow down to take a corner. As he sped into the new street he saw her. She was running to cross the roadway. Hank whooped.

"Go, Willie! Go!"

The girl looked up an instant in terror.

Her face!

It was the old woman with the cat! No!—it was Muriel. Muriel with the big, dark eyes . . .

In the last split second Willie touched the power steering. "The Bull" responded immediately, and shot past the girl as she scampered to safety.

"What the hell is the matter with you?" Hank roared at Willie. "You could've scored! Are you out of your head?"

"We don't need her. We'll win without her. I—I—"

Yes, why hadn't he scored? It wasn't Muriel. Muriel was back in butcher—in—Oklahoma City. Damn this headache!

"Maybe so," said Hank angrily. "But I wanna be sure. And what about the bonus for setting a record? Ten thousand apiece. And we're close." He looked slyly at Willie. "Or—maybe you've lost your nerve. Wonder what the Commission will say to that?"

"I've got plenty of nerve," Willie snapped.

"Prove it!" said Hank quickly. He pointed to the dashboard map slowly tracing their progress. "There. See that village? With the screwy name? *Wikieup!* Off the Thruway. Let's see you score there!"

Willie said nothing. He hadn't lost his nerve, he knew that. He was the best of the Racers. No one could drive like he could; constant top speed, and the stamina it took, the split-second timing, the unerring judgment—

"Well?"

"All right," Willie agreed.

They hadn't even reached Wikieup when they spotted the farmer. He didn't have a chance. "The Bull" came charging down upon him. But in the last moment the car veered slightly. One of the horns ripped the man's hip open. In the rear view screen Willie saw him get up and hobble off the road.

"You could've made it a Kill," Hank growled accusingly. "Why didn't you?"

"Bad road," Willie said. "The wheel slipped on a stone."

That's what must have happened, he thought. He didn't consciously veer away from the man. He was a good Racer. He couldn't help a bad road.

Needles was left behind at 1045 hours, PST. No one had been out. Hank turned on the radio to a Needles station:

". . . has just left the city going West. No other Racer is reported within twenty minutes of the city. We repeat: A Racer has just left . . ."

Hank clicked it off. "Hear that?" he said excitedly. "Twenty minutes. They don't expect anyone for twenty minutes!" He took hold of Willie's arm. "Turn around! Here's where we can get ourselves that Record Score. Turn around, Willie!"

"We don't need it."

"I do! *I want that bonus!*"

Willie made no answer.

"Listen to me, you two-bit Racer!" Hank's tone was menacing. "You or nobody else is going to cheat me out of that bonus. You've been acting mighty peculiar. More like an Anti-Racer! Ever since you stopped at that Tragi-Acc back there. Yeah! That girl—that Anti-Racer who called you a—a butcher. Listen! You get that record Score, or I'll report you to the Commission for having snooped around a Tragi-Acc. You'll never race again!"

'Never race again!' Willie's brain was whirling. But he *was* a Racer. Not a butcher. *A Racer.* Record Score? Yes—that's what he had to do. Set a record. Be the best damned Racer of them all.

Without a word he turned the car. In minutes they were back at the Needles suburbs. That building. A School House. And there—marching orderly in two rows with their teacher, a class, a whole class of children . . .

"The Bull" came charging down the street. Only a couple of hundred feet now to that Record Score . . .

But what was that—it was . . . they were *Muriel*—they were all Muriel. Terrible, dark eyes. No!—They were children,—the child in Muriel's arms. *They were all the child in Muriel's arms!* Were they already moaning and screaming? Butcher! *Butcher!* No! He couldn't butcher them—he was a *Racer*—not a *Butcher. Not a butcher!* Deliberately he swung the car to the empty side of the street.

Suddenly he felt Hank's hands up on the wheel. "You—dirty—lousy—Anti-Racer!" the mechanic snarled as he struggled for the wheel.

The car lurched. The two men fought savagely for control. They were only yards from the fleeing children.

With a violent wrench Willie turned the wheel sharply. The car was going 165 miles an hour when it struck the school house and crashed through the wall into the empty building.

The voices came to Willie through thick wads of cotton—and they kept fading in and out.

". . . *dead instantaneously. But the Racer is still* . . ."

It sounded like the voice of Muriel. Muriel . . .

". . . *keeps calling for* . . ."

Willie tried to open his eyes. Everything was milky white. Why was there so much fog? A face was bending over him. Muriel? No—it was not Muriel. He lost consciousness again.

When he opened his eyes once more he knew he was not alone. He turned his head. A girl was sitting at his bedside. Muriel . . .

It *was* Muriel.

He tried to sit up.

"It's you! But—but, how . . .?"

The girl put her hand on his arm.

"The radio. They said you kept calling for 'Muriel.' I knew. Never mind that now."

She looked steadily at him. Her eyes were not terrible—not burning—only dark, and puzzled.

"Why did you call for *me*?" she asked earnestly.

Willie struggled to sit up.

"I wanted to tell you," he said, "to tell you,—I—I am not a butcher!"

The girl looked at him for a long moment. Then she leaned down and whispered to him:

"*Nor a Racer!*"

The Swordsmen of Varnis

by Clive Jackson

THE TWIN MOONS BROODED OVER THE RED DESERTS OF MARS AND THE RUINED city of Khua-Loanis. The night wind sighed around the fragile spires and whispered at the fretted lattice windows of the empty temples, and the red dust made it like a city of copper.

It was close to midnight when the distant rumble of racing hooves reached the city, and soon the riders thundered in under the ancient gateway. Tharn, Warrior Lord of Loanis, leading his pursuers by a scant twenty yards, realized wearily that his lead was shortening, and raked the scaly flanks of his six-legged vorkl with cruel spurs. The faithful beast gave a low cry of despair as it tried to obey and failed.

In front of Tharn in the big double saddle sat Lehni-tal-Loanis, Royal Lady of Mars, riding the ungainly animal with easy grace, leaning forward along its arching neck to murmur swift words of encouragement into its flattened ears. Then she lay back against Tharn's mailed chest and turned her lovely face up to his, flushed and vivid with the excitement of the chase, amber eyes aflame with love for her strange hero from beyond time and space.

"We shall win this race yet, my Tharn," she cried. "Yonder through that archway lies the Temple of the Living Vapor, and once there we can defy all the Lords of Varnis!" Looking down at the unearthly beauty of her, at the subtle curve of throat and breast and thigh, revealed as the wind tore at her scanty garments, Tharn knew that even if the Swordsmen of Varnis struck him down his strange odyssey would not have been in vain.

But the girl had judged the distance correctly and Tharn brought their snorting vorkl to a sliding, rearing halt at the great doors of the Temple, just as the Swordsmen reached the outer archway and jammed there in a struggling, cursing mass. In seconds they had sorted themselves out and came streaming across the courtyard, but the delay had given Tharn time to dismount and take his stand in one of the great doorways. He knew that if he could hold it for a few moments while Lehni-tal-Loanis got the door open, then the secret of the Living Vapor would be theirs, and with it mastery of all the lands of Loanis.

The Swordsmen tried first to ride him down, but the doorway was so narrow and deep that Tharn had only to drive his swordpoint upward into the first vorkl's throat and leap backward as the dying beast fell. Its rider was stunned by the fall, and Tharn bounded up onto the dead animal and beheaded the unfortunate Swordsman without compunction. There were ten of his enemies left and they came at him now on foot, but the confining doorway prevented them from attacking more than four abreast, and Tharn's elevated position upon the huge carcass gave him the advantage he needed. The fire of battle was in his veins now, and he bared his teeth and laughed in their faces, and his reddened sword wove a pattern of cold death which none could pass.

Lehni-tal-Loanis, running quick cool fingers over the pitted bronze of the door, found the radiation lock and pressed her glowing opalescent thumb-ring into the socket, gave a little sob of relief as she heard hidden tumblers falling. With agonizing slowness the ancient mechanism began to open the door; soon Tharn heard the girl's clear voice call above the clashing steel, "Inside, my Tharn, the secret of the Living Vapor is ours!"

But Tharn, with four of his foes dead now, and seven to go, could not retreat from his position on top of the dead vorkl without grave risk of being cut down, and Lehni-tal-Loanis, quickly realizing this, sprang up beside him, drawing her own slim blade and crying, "Aie, my love! I will be your left arm!"

Now the cold hand of defeat gripped the hearts of the Swordsmen of Varnis: two, three, four more of them mingled their blood with the red dust of the courtyard as Tharn and his fighting princess swung their merciless blades in perfect unison. It seemed that nothing could prevent them now from winning the mysterious secret of the Living Vapor, but they reckoned without the treachery of one of the remaining Swordsmen. Leaping backward out of the conflict he flung his sword on the ground in disgust. "Bah!" he grunted. "This is ridiculous!" And, so saying, he unclipped a proton gun from his belt and blasted Lehni-tal-Loanis and her Warrior Lord out of existence with a searing energy-beam.

A steady diet of stories like this one would be a bit too much.

But more than once in a lifetime we should welcome a work reminiscent of Olaf Stapledon's Star Maker *or Ross Rocklynne's* Daughter of Darkness *series or* A Baby on Neptune *by Dr. Miles J. Breuer & Clare Winger Harris.*

We will be interested to learn if our readers feel that the inadvertent benefit to humanity derived in this story would be worth the concomitant losses.

Starburst

by Robert Lulyk

HE WAS NAMELESS; BUT HAD HE A NAME, IT MIGHT HAVE BEEN STARBURST, A symbol of his being and what he was: a Nova-like explosion of energy— but under tight control. Mass without matter; intelligence without form; purpose without pattern—he was all these things and countless other impossibilities.

Starburst acknowledged no limits; therefore, he had none. He fed upon chaos; therefore, he was its master. He knew nothing of time; therefore, he was eternal. Or rather: he existed from time's beginning; he would cease to exist at its end.

Where he came from, where he was going, was unimportant to him: he would not have sought out his origin or his destiny even if it were possible for him to do so. He existed for himself, unto himself, and that was enough. His equation was simple: movement equaled experience; experience equaled life. Therefore, he moved.

Now Starburst flashed thru the light-absorbing blackness of intergalactic space at a speed literally beyond calculation: for without reference points, the concept of speed—of motion even—becomes a philosophical problem. A trillion mile long jet of FTL photons—tachyons traveling at million light-speed multiples—the infinitesimal fraction of his energy visible as light was enough to create a gigantic seething, polychromatic mass like all the rainbows in the universe combined; eye-searing against the universal darkness which seemed to be futilely trying to swallow him up.

Eventually Starburst came upon a galaxy.

As galaxies went, this one could hardly be called unique—in all the cosmos, only Starburst himself was that—nor even unusual. Its grosser aspect was not one-tenth as interesting as the flaming splendor of a pair of matter/anti-matter galaxies colliding, the incredible majesty of a galaxy slowly spinning apart, or the awful spectacle of a galaxy collapsing into a gigantic black hole. This one was, in fact, for all intents and purposes identical to that he had just left some seconds—or was it centuries?—ago, the island-universe Andromeda: hence a more or less ordinary collection of two hundred billion or so suns with the usual unthinkably vast complement of attendant planets.

These planets were of minor interest to Starburst, however, so transforming himself into extraordinary electro-magnetic energy—there could be nothing ordinary about *him*—he decelerated to simple light-speed, the better to revel in the myriads of worlds around him. One by one, each in its turn, his star-spanning sensories would reach out to envelop a world and savor its uniqueness. Sometimes he would find nothing save dead rock, dull even to him on any but sub-molecular levels. But more often than not, he would find life in all its complex diversity; then he would absorb the sum total of its history, its culture, its pattern of existence—all the details, the differences, which gave meaning to his life.

At length Starburst came upon a minor G-type yellow dwarf sun with nine circling planets—and hungered.

Master of chaos, Starburst could have satisfied his hunger in many ways. He could have sucked all heat from solid matter within the solar system, temporarily bringing to even boiling Mercury a cold of absolute zero which would make frigid Pluto's normal temperature seem hot by comparison. Or he could have even drawn on the infinitely greater furnace of the Sun, leaving it a burned out white dwarf as he had left countless other stars in the past. But his hunger was not that great this time; and so whether by whim or design, he chose to feed upon the peculiar form of chaos known as radioactivity.

And—radioactivity died on Earth! In hospitals, where cobalt units for treating cancer became inert; in the Hanford holding tanks, where deadly atomic wastes stopped boiling 10,000 years ahead of schedule; in nuclear power plants around the world, where turbines ground to a halt for lack of steam.

In short, every radioactive atom in the entire solar system, whether occurring naturally deep within a planet's core or in the artificially enriched uranium inside a hydrogen warhead, gave up the energy which would have kept it radioactive for a period ranging from split-seconds to billions of years and became a stable element, usually lead. Nuclear fission became impossible—and because fission served as a trigger for fusion, nuclear weapons as well.

Nuclear war would never take place on the third planet.

Racing on thru the endless night of space, Starburst quickly forgot the incident.

The Cosmic Kidnappers

by Christian Vallini & S. F. Balboa

"WHAT ABOUT THE RESEARCH, AIQUY?"

"I was thinking of introducing you to the Hunters."

They entered the large living room and there they were, a hundred of them, the Hunters. And there was the Teacher, too. He was shouting at his pupils.

"What's the matter?" Aiquy asked the Teacher.

"They're the best Hunters we've got. And if they foul up, well—who can we depend on to do things right?"

"They've fouled up?"

"They don't seem to understand! They've 10 ears and they turn all of them deaf to me. You know they must take the greatest care in capturing those creatures, you know the captives cannot be taken back to their planet."

"So what's the trouble?" Aiquy asked nervously through that throat reserved for alarm.

"We've got a strategic plan to follow. The individuals we snatch must be insignificant, unknown. They have to be. The disappearance of high authorities, famous figures, would be noticed. Trouble would ensue. And today Kaiaich has captured one of their race that was well known."

"Who?" Aiquy swallowed through his 12th, his throat which functioned exclusively for apprehension.

"His name is pronounced Ambroce Beerce."

Cosmic Parallel

by Arthur Louis Joquel II

"**B**ALDERDASH!" SHOUTED CAPTAIN WATSON, AS HE HEAVED HIMSELF UP FROM HIS chair. "Damned purser! Putting books like this in the ship library. I'll fix him!"

He flung open the door of his cabin and strode down the narrow passageway of the spaceship. A glance in the purser's cubby showed it empty, so he continued his fulminating course to the bridge of the *Martian Girl*, where he found the purser looking over some papers.

"Mr. Pascoe," he roared. "Will you kindly tell me what this piece of idiocy is doing on board a sensible spaceship?"

He held out the volume as if it were a long-dead rat. The startled officer took it, turned it over.

"Why, Captain, I don't see anything wrong with it," Pascoe replied. "Dr. von Kremer is a highly reputable man. And *Macrocosmos* is his latest book— I know it's causing a lot of controversy—"

"Controversy!" Captain Watson's face colored. "The man's mad. Have you read the book?"

"Yes, sir."

"Well, what do *you* think of it?"

"To be frank, sir, I don't think anything," Pascoe replied. "The man is entitled to his opinions, of course, and if they seem a little far-fetched—"

"Far-fetched!" If Captain Watson had been a robot instead of a human, he would have blown every fuse in his system. "Don't be conservative! Such idiocy I have never heard in twenty years of space-flying—"

A shout from the watch officer put a stop to his tirade. "Captain Watson, sir. Derelict ahead!"

The captain ceased his fuming and turned to the ports. There, dead ahead on their course, lay another spaceship, gleaming in the unshielded light of the sun. Swiftly she grew larger, and the watchers on the *Martian Girl* could see that she was drifting aimlessly, no flare from rockets visible, although her running lights burned.

"Braking rockets, Mr. Barr," he ordered crisply. "Stop as near to her as you can with safety."

The three men in the control room grabbed for support as the forward rocket tubes flared into action. In a short time the two ships were drifting side by side, about a quarter of a mile apart.

"Mr. Pascoe, take two of the crew with you and investigate," Captain Watson said, after an examination with powerful field glasses failed to show signs of life. "If she is a derelict, we'll tow her in. Take a good cable with you."

The purser vanished, and the captain picked up his glasses again and surveyed the drifting ship. She was a twenty-man Videaux, apparently in good condition. No meteor holes anywhere that could be seen, or other evidence of damage.

"Hello, Captain Watson." The purser's voice boomed out of a loud-speaker over the control panel. "In suits now, and ready to leave the airlock. Are we coming in?"

"Coming in fine."

"Can hear you well, too. We're on our way."

The side airlock could not be seen from the control room, and it was some minutes before the three figures, grotesque in their bulky spacesuits, were apparent. They were kept together by a thin strand of wire, and the rearmost trailed a light but strong cable.

Using small hand-rockets, the men maneuvered alongside the derelict. "Airlock door's closed," Brown, one of the crewmen, observed.

"I can see that, you numskull," the captain retorted. The three men and the control room had a universal space-phone connection, so that all could hear and be heard. "Suppose you open it, and see what's inside."

Those in the control room could see Pascoe fumbling with the door control. Then over the speaker came the rumbling of the opening door—the vibration being turned into sound as it ran through Pascoe's spacesuit and struck his phone.

The metal figures vanished into the ship. "Everything ok in here," came the purser's voice. "No—what's this?"

"What's the matter?"

"Looks like the wall's been hit by a crowbar." There was a pause. "Nothing special—just thought I'd mention it."

Again the rumbling came over the speaker, and Captain Watson knew Pascoe was opening the inner door of the airlock. But he was not prepared for the startled exclamations that followed.

"The ship's deserted!" came the incredulous exclamation, almost from three throats at once.

"Quiet, you two!" bellowed Captain Watson. "Let Pascoe do the talking!"

"Not a sign of life aboard," reported the purser. "Everything seems to be in order, though." The clang of metal shoes on the ship's deck came vaguely over the phone. "Here's the mess hall, and—great scott!"

"What is it?"

"Why, the table's set! And the lights are on! Maybe there's someone here after all! Scatter, you fellows! Search the ship!"

But a minute examination of the entire space-vessel showed no life aboard. The emergency space-boat was in its accustomed place, and the ship was in immaculate order, save for one tiny spot on the deck in one place, which might have been blood—but more probably was rust.

"Bring the log book and the papers back with you," Captain Watson ordered finally. "Leave Brown aboard, so we can claim salvage when we get in. Clamp the cable to the nose."

It was an amazed Pascoe that reported more fully to Captain Watson on his return to the *Martian Girl.*

"There's something uncanny about it," he said. "Lights on, table set, no sign of trouble—but no one aboard. I—I don't like it, Captain."

"Nonsense." But Captain Watson relented enough to order another crewman sent to keep Brown company on his eerie vigil over the mystery ship.

It was not till he sat down to write a report of the incident that the Captain found himself vaguely perturbed by something that he could not quite place. He read the log book taken from the abandoned ship. Nothing unusual there, except that it suddenly stopped short. No mention of trouble. It was quite beyond him.

"Report on Salvage," he wrote, on the official form. "Freighter *Martian Girl,* on Mars-to-Terra run. Captain, Andrew Watson."

He set down the entire occurrence, and as he proceeded, he had a sense of familiarity with the details. He racked his brain. Where could he have heard anything like this before?

The copy of *Macrocosmos* lay on the table, where it had been dropped when the alarm came, and at sight of it Captain Watson's anger returned. He started to pick it up, throw it away, and then suddenly remembered the passage that had so annoyed him—and stopped short. It couldn't be possible, but—he jumped up, ran down the passage to his room.

He had been born near and loved the sea, and his personal library had much in it about ships—especially sailing ships. And he trembled as he found the volume he wanted, pulled it out and examined it.

"Exactly the same," he muttered, "crew missing . . . table set . . . marks near the landing . . . exactly the same . . ."

He walked slowly back to the control room, picked up the *Macrocosmos* and read the passage again.

It is distinctly possible, that, due to the influence of tremendous factors beyond our realization, events that happen on Terra may be a duplication of those that occur in the greater universe. Where a man dies, a star may die. A solar system is born, a nation on Terra—or on another planet—may come into being. These events, of course, may not occur simultaneously. For the cosmic timescale is vast beyond our knowing . . .

His hands shook badly. That other Terra ship, so many years ago, had met the same fate. Her crew missing, and no solution to the mystery. And he steadied himself to write the name of the spaceship he had salvaged— the *Marie Celeste.*

Warning! *Pearls are caused by irritants. You may be irritated by your fate at the end of this story which its author calls—*

The Sky's an Oyster;
The Stars Are Pearls

by Dave Bischoff

"THANK YOU, LADIES AND GENTLEMEN; THANK YOU VERY MUCH FOR YOUR KIND applause. I certainly hope you enjoyed your dinner. I enjoyed mine quite a bit and would like to thank NASA for instructing the nutritionists present in the proper way of preparing my foods. Not that I'm particular, mind you. Just a necessity. My metabolism is not quite the same as yours, you know.— Can you hear me in the back there? No? Herb, do you think you might put this mike up on something a little taller so it can reach my head? Yes, I know: my height is a real pain. Sorry but that comes from growing up on the moon.—Yes, that's just fine, thank you. Now I can properly begin this speech.

"Uh hum. Mr. President, Mrs. President," heads of state of so many countries I've quite forgotten the exact names and for fear of leaving someone out I won't attempt to name them; may I take this opportunity to express my appreciation for this grand banquet you have put on here at the White House in my honor. As you know, I have been out of quarantine now for only a week and this is the first enjoyable time I've really had since the successful completion of my journey.

"May I also make it plain that I will not be offended if you do not look directly at me during the course of this address. I realize that my countenance is quite horrifying to the average human. NASA apologies to both you and me but my lack of beauty is a simple byproduct of the genetic manipulation effected upon me from the time of my laboratory conception in order to make the trip of the type I have just undertaken possible. But then, that shall be the text of this little talk, which (I hope you don't mind) will be as informal as I can make it.

"Since the time that mankind got it into their heads that space travel is possible, there have been many failures and many successes. It is my honor to be the key factor in what has proved to be the greatest victory of all: man's first exploration of a star system other than the one we inhabit. For years, even after the successful conquest of our solar system, most scientists thought it impossible to send a man out to the stars. The distances were simply too great. Decades would be required to traverse to other suns. But then the exciting discovery of a different dimension where distances in time & space are much shorter than those we know in this universe, was effected by the scientists at NASA. If a spaceship could penetrate this so-called 'subspace', it could easily negotiate distances thought impossible in regular space & time. And of course it was discovered that this was entirely possible, indeed (cough, cough) ridiculously (cough, excuse me) easy.

"Pardon me (cough) but I need a little of my special air from my respirator. Frank, would you hand it here? Thanks.

"There. That's better. I can take normal Earth air for much longer when I'm not speaking.

"Yes. Where was I? Subspace you say? Right. Anyway, there was a very difficult dilemma. Regular, normal, everyday human beings were incapable of inhabiting subspace for various physiological as well as psychological reasons. Even in the closed environment of a spaceship. These reasons were analyzed carefully and scientists determined the necessary sort of organism that would be capable of traveling through subspace. Which is me. And of course my brothers and sisters currently being raised in the proper environment on the moon bases. Because I, their first experiment, was so completely successful.

"I set out somewhat less than a year ago, much of my traveling time taken up by the act of getting past the orbit of Pluto where the gravity of the sun is effectively nil. Entrance into subspace is a bit difficult with any sort of gravitational field near. I and my ship, the *Explorer 5*, were designed for one another, and many mechanisms in it can only be controlled by my specially created mind and body. But let's not get too scientifically detailed. I suppose you may read the scientific reports concerning the structure of the *Explorer* and myself, if you are so inclined.

"Our course was plotted toward the Tau Ceti system, for years the source of radio transmissions picked up by our radio-telescopes that seemed to indicate intelligent life. We could have headed for Proxima Centauri, our closest neighbor sun, but with the nature of subspace what it is, it was just as easy to get to Tau Ceti.

"A moment. Another whiff from the respirator before I get to coughing again. Thanks, Herb. There.

"Doubtless my past few words have been merely a repetition of what you already have read in your Fax-sheets or have seen on the holocube. I hope you will forgive my repeating them but I merely wanted to be sure that all present, all you world leaders, have sufficient background to understand what I am going to say.

"Those of you who have studied the information provided you will recall that it states that although the journey was a success in most senses, no intelligent life was discovered in the Tau Ceti system.

"Gentlemen, may I take this time to say that that is not the truth; there is indeed intelligent life in that system and I made contact with it.

"Please! Please! My ears are not accustomed to such an uproar. I suggest you shut up so that I may complete what I am saying. It is of the utmost importance that I do so. No questions now. Let me finish. Sit down, Dr. Haskell. And the rest of my associates in science; be still. I have not let any of you know this, so none of you were kept out of a secret that others of you knew. I alone was its keeper. Along with the Makpzions, of course. The intelligent rulers of Makpzio. They intercepted me as soon as I shifted out of subspace. They too have interstellar travel, you see. In fact, they have had it for centuries and have used it to acquire quite an empire, colonizing other planets. Because they all travel in subspace, they are like me in many ways. Communication was no difficulty. They were delighted to hear of Earth's existence. We are in such a faraway corner of the galaxy they never bothered to check out the Sol system.

"Wait a minute! Yes! Look outside that window over to the Mall just by the Washington Monument. That's one of their ships coming down. Exactly on time. I led them here, you know. Several hundred more starships are no doubt orbiting Earth with their incredibly advanced weapons sighted on various strategic targets. And gentlemen, that is why I chose tonight for this banquet. So that all of you can be here together to listen to the terms of conquest the Makpzions will deliver. Oh, I might as well tell you this now; I get to be dictator.

"My goodness, aren't you outraged! Please, no violence upon my person. My conquering friends would not take that at all well. They might get nasty and destroy a few million of you.

"Benedict Arnold, you scream, Mr. President? A traitor to my own race?

"But then, I'm not really human, am I now? Your scientists saw to that.

"Pass that respirator here, Herb. There's a good boy."

And Satan Came

by Robert A. W. Lowndes

Haywood looked up, startled, as he became aware of another's presence in the room, then relaxed at the familiar tones of Kreuger's voice. For a moment he hesitated, wondering just what to say, trying to stem back the wave of questions he wanted to ask in one breath. Slowly, in an effort at nonchalance, he lit a cigarette. But his voice trembled slightly as he asked: "What happened, Nick?"

The other was a statue, staring beyond matter into empty space. Silence seemed to concentrate itself around him so that he was enwoofed and set apart in time. Then, as through an invisible barrier, came his voice.

"How long . . .?"

"You left me about three hours ago . . ."

Kreuger's laugh ricocheted along the walls of the room. "Hours . . . hours! Years! Decades! Eons!"

The other rose hastily, extracted a bottle from the sideboard and poured out a long drink, then, at Kreuger's refusal, downed it himself. "You'd better tell me everything, Nick. Something grim has happened; I can see that. Tell me before it eats you."

Kreuger shuddered, thudded into a stuffed chair. "The legends seem so prosaic now. I expected something out of Lovecraft, perhaps—although what I really was prepared for was outright failure.

"I wish it had been—a monster. We were deceived by the abstractness of the descriptions. I suppose everything we had heard and read and imagined was so firmly embedded in our minds that we couldn't expect anything else. It was so completely different from anything I was prepared to accept as . . . Satan.

"The sensations—I can't describe them. Nearest thing to it is the indefinite sense of expansion you get sometimes when drunk. I felt that I was growing enormously, expanding in every direction—yet it was more than enlargement. I felt that new dimensions and appendages were being added to me, that my form was being distorted and altered. Didn't dare to look at myself, or look around me, fearing I would see something utterly hideous and know it was—myself. I did look finally—had to, you know—but there was nothing to see. I could only feel it was there.

"Something was drawing me outward, some attraction. I knew I was moving through space, even though no definite perception of motion was to be had. The growth continued, and, even as it went on, things began to filter through. I think the formula opened the flood-gates; the full deluge burst upon me at once, but it had to batter on me for a time until my senses could be stepped up to perceive the new impressions.

"Then, I began to see—through. The room I was in, the laboratory . . . it changed suddenly. But before I could appreciate the new scene, it had shifted again, and then again. Things were happening much too quickly for me to grasp their import or to know what was happening. My sense of time was gone . . .

"How long it was before it became clear what I was seeing, I don't know. I saw that room simultaneously as a section of steaming, lifeless planet, newly formed—as primeval jungle—as ice-covered wilderness—as virgin forest—as cleared land—as the room I knew—as a ruin—as a pit where an enormous meteor had impacted, and, finally, as empty space. It was at once everything it ever had been and all that it ever would be. A kaleidoscope of forms and no form at all. I tried to will away the sight of all of them, except that form in time with which I was familiar. It returned. But no longer it seemed a solid unit to me; even though I could see the laboratory I knew intimately, feel its boundaries and objects within those boundaries, I knew now that just behind—ahead—of these, in time, were other boundaries and things within them that I did not know. As these thoughts came to me, and with them the doubt, the scene—flickered.

"Before I could adjust myself to sight, hearing expanded. The subdued sound of traffic outside the lab became the axestrokes of the first men who felled trees in the forest that once covered this city—the roar of ice sliding over the terrain—the cries of carnivores that once roamed here before the forest—the whine and concussion of shells in some future bombardment—the crying of a lonely wind over the corpse of a forgotten planet. The impressions of sound were independent of those in sight. I could see the ice around me, closing in around me, extending how far upward—miles?—and hear the crying of the death-wind . . .

"Then—panic. What would happen when the other senses expanded into time? I tried to run to the door, even though I knew it would not help; it seemed that I was a snake. I glanced down, a scream rising in my throat, but I couldn't scream. It might be a serpentine hiss that came out of my throat. But when I looked down, there were only the familiar human legs I knew.

"Before I reached the door, an immense pit gaped before me. I willed desperately to walk over the floor of the laboratory and somehow the solidity of that floor remained even though all I could see was empty space and somewhere the pin-prick of distant stars.

"I concentrated harder than I've ever done before, and the room came back. With it came the ordinary sounds of the city. But now my ears were alert; every alteration in normal pitch seemed to be the echoes of sounds out of the past or future. A flood of exhaustion passed over me—I stumbled into the next room and fell on the couch, my last conscious impressions being those of slithering, slithering . . .

"It must have been eons that I slept, and, while sleeping, the expansion continued. Eternities passed, and I would waken to see indescribable things, only to fall back again before I could coordinate impressions. There were no dreams.

"When I awoke, I was back in my own room, lying on the couch. For a time, I lay there thinking that the whole experience had been a nightmare or drug-delusion. But something else was beating upon me . . . waves of emotion. I felt them, seething about me, bearing down upon me. Fear such as I had never known—the dread of things such as no man dreaded; the hate of things that no man hated. They fell upon me and left me gasping for breath. And with these fears and hates were mingled yearnings such as no man has ever known; yearnings that seemed to tear the soul out of me. I knew how birds and wild beasts yearn when locked up in cages . . .

"Then the flood changed to waves of pure . . . evil, that is the only word I can use. Not the simple wickedness that the religiously minded think of when they hear the word. Not merely evil in reference to the bestial desires and acts of man, but indescribable malignancy on a cosmic scale.

"Somewhere in space and time, there must be a vortex of all the hatred, fear, and sheer will to destroy that has ever existed and ever will exist. It is not all human, for I felt these things as derived from a myriad of life-forms, many non-human or bearing no resemblance to those forms we know. *It* feeds upon these emotions as it were—a conscious, yet unliving vampire-vortex extending through eternity . . ."

Haywood was silent for a moment. Then he said slowly: "Whether or not this is illusion, Nick, it is magnificent. It may be horrible to you. Perhaps you are mad, but, if so, your madness is far greater than the madness of any living man. We must explore this thing carefully . . . we must learn . . ."

Kreuger laughed. "Where are you, Haywood, if you ever were at all? I cannot see you. All I can see is ice, ice, ice stretching miles upward so that I cannot find the limit of it, though somewhere must be a sky. All I can see is ice, and all I can hear is the cold wind crying over a desolate world."

"*Nick!* Come back. Come back to the present. *This* is reality; the only reality you know. Concentrate, Nick. Concentrate and will out everything else except the world you know."

Kreuger shuddered again; his eyes lost their wild glow. "Did you ever see a soul, Haywood? Neither did I. But I think I've lost mine. I feel dead and empty and meaningless, if anything has meaning. I feel as the wind must feel crying over the loneliness of a lifeless planet where carnivores scream and prey on each other and a man and his mistress are hiding from the police in a drawing room at one time belonging to a man named Haywood.

"The vortex . . . growing. It will pass eventually. It cannot last after all life is gone. After all matter has been converted into—what? Listen,

Haywood—somewhere in time a fool called Satan, and Satan came. Satan, Satan, brother Satan, show me your face, Satan, comfort me, speak to me, crush me beneath your cloven hoof . . ."

Haywood seized the other's shoulders; shook him furiously. "Kreuger! Wake up, man! You're here; you're all right. It was only a dream, Nick. Believe me, it was only a dream!"

His eyes rested on the other's. Reason again flickered in them. "Back again. In the year of our Lord—but not for long. There *is* a hell, Haywood. Not the unimaginative one the early men described, but there is a hell. I think I've found it. You don't have to die to go to hell, Haywood—I cannot die, now. I shall live throughout all eternity because I am eternity."

He rose stiffly and strode to the door. "A million and a million years have come and died since I came to find you again, you whose name I now cannot recall. Look not to see me again, for I cannot find you. Time and space have taken me unto themselves and I am their beloved stepson. And still I expand. Not much human of me left now. Something draws me— outward—

"You who are man, as once was I, think me mad. Look at my eyes, if you can still see me. Look at my eyes if eyes I have as a man. Can't you see eternity staring out at you? I called on Satan and Satan came. I called on Satan and I am damned, damned, damned . . ."

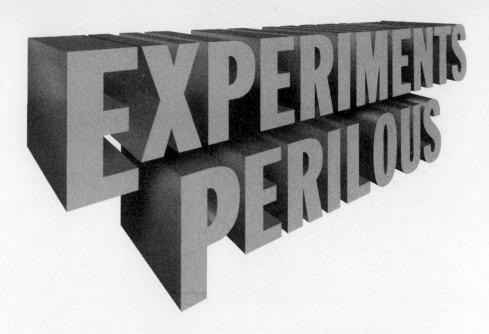

EXPERIMENTS PERILOUS

The author (long deceased) was a disciple of Lovecraft. Which explains why this is such a strange—

Experiment

by R. H. Barlow

Beside the table stood a tall bearded man—Edwards—engaged in making an odd concoction which he fed into a flaming brazier.

All was silent; the lights glared upon the strange helmet upon Coswell's head. Coswell lay motionless, thinking perhaps of the experiment—the climax of their studies.

Abruptly finishing preparations, Edwards spoke. His voice was guttural. "You are fully prepared?"

The man on the operating table nodded. "Yes."

"Then close your eyes and relax."

He did so. The smoke from the brazier lifted steadily into the air.

"Make your mind a blank. Think of nothing. You are sleeping . . . sleeping . . . sleeping . . ."

Despite his willingness, Coswell's mind rebelled. His thoughts kept asserting themselves, protesting, struggling with those of the Doctor. Perspiration broke out upon Edwards and he passed his hand tiredly over his forehead. Then he leaned forward and concentrated intently upon his telepathic effort.

Coswell's body suddenly went limp. For a moment Edwards stood beside him, swaying slightly from the great mental effort. Then he said: "You hear me?"

"Yes—I hear you," came the low reply.

"Are you awake?"

There was a brief hesitancy. "No."

The smoke twisted into fantastic shapes, although the air was still.

"But you are conscious?"

There was no reply. He repeated the question.

"I am conscious only in that you may command me," was the answer.

Edwards smiled. "You are still asleep: but your ego will leave its body. You are to keep in communication with me. Do you understand?"

"I understand."

For a long moment there was no change apparent in the figure on the table. Then gradually all color faded from it. Edwards leaned over and watched the faint respiration with satisfaction. The heart was beating slowly and quietly.

During the period in which Coswell's soul left its habitat, a perceptible change of luster was evident in the odd headgear. At first dull and frosty, it quickly brightened until it was a living pulsating gold.

"You are out of your body?"

An inaudible murmur came from the lips.

"Speak!" The Doctor's face was strained.

"Yes!"

"You are conscious now?" The smoke hung in heavily narcotic clouds.

"Yes!"

"Where are you?"

"In a gray whirling void."

"What is it like—out there?"

"I am alone. A vast buzzing sound fills the universe . . . I can see all my past and my future. And the past and future of the whole scheme of things."

"Is there any . . . 'reason' . . . in this illogical arrangement?" asked the Doctor curiously.

"Yes, far in the future. It is dim. But there is a radiance."

"Try to penetrate it."

"I cannot."

"What prevents you?"

"I do not know. I seem to stop at a certain point—eons ahead."

"Can you see into the past?"

"Yes. Clearly."

"What is there?"

"A maelstrom of lurid flame . . . That is the vast sun from which Earth was spat."

"Before that?"

"Emptiness."

"Come nearer our time."

"I seem to be walking down a street paved with worn stones. I am in oriental garb . . .

"The scene changes . . . I am in a jungle of unbelievable beauty . . . My form is not yet human . . .

"A Christian slave, under Nero . . .

"A druid-priest in ancient Briton. Some ceremony is taking place. I must not describe it.

"The scenes are ever-changing; more quickly, now.

"A monk in a dreary cell . . .

"An African savage . . .

"THE GRAY STONE WALLS OF A FEUDAL CASTLE!"

The last words were said with strained intentness. Then he was quiet, although his hands writhed.

Edwards's face was twisted agonizingly.

"Quickly! Speak! What do you see?"

Coswell was silent. Again came the command.

An inarticulate sound escaped him. Then with an obvious effort, he broke into speech, only to mumble a few words in a strange tongue. Again he was silent, although his lips moved.

Then, quietly, came the words:

". . . moat. There are many dressed as I, and all are armed with crossbows. A few have armor. We are up on the ramparts and from the tower I can see far into the forest. It is spring and the tops of the branches are swaying as if by a breeze. We await the attack nervously. The man who brought us the news this morning is below; dying, perhaps. It were better. Battle with human foes would be playfulness compared to the monstrosities we must combat. What foul creatures they are! Like jellyfish emulating humanity—a gross travesty of natural laws. Their tentacles are writhing things of horror. We are many, but I fear . . .

"The sun is yet high. I would that we have battle before nightfall, for my courage would falter at encounter after dusk."

The Doctor interrupted. "What year is it? What country?" he asked eagerly.

"Long ago—or perhaps—no; I do not know. It may be the future, the Armageddon of mankind. The country is Illoe. I am . . ."

His face contorted and his natural voice broke torturedly through the lifeless monotone. "Wake me, Edwards! For God's sake wake me!" Then the dull speech continued as Edwards made futile efforts to arouse his friend. He smothered the brazier, shook him violently, hastily adjusted a small dial upon the helmet, but the dead voice went on inexorably.

"We can see them quite plainly now. I am afraid, deathly so. They are as we had expected; but none of us can overcome our nausea. They are swarming across the plain before the forest. If only we might have fled! But where? When all the world is overrun? How useless. Here is the last outpost of our kind and we are defenseless. Must our race be wiped out? If our forefathers had but destroyed the first of them! Or if we had the old death-machines . . . but they are fallen into disintegration, like the race.

"A far-off tumult is audible. The seething wall is approaching. The sun is low; livid. There are thousands of them—nearer now. As we had feared, our arrows take little effect.

"Our men are killing one another. That is merciful. They cross the moat! Fill it with their bodies while others OOZE over them.

"THEY ARE MOUNTING THE WALLS!"

A single shriek of unbearable terror was torn from him. Then he was still, as the metal helmet swiftly faded to a dull tone.

There were peculiar marks about him and the expression was most shocking.

This Experiment Perilous *has an interesting background. In 1935, when the author was only 16 and a junior in high school, he sold the original version of this story to* Wonder Stories, *the pioneering science fiction magazine of Hugo Gernsback, the Father of Science Fiction. But* Wonder Stories *ceased publication before the story could be printed. (I got in just under the wire with* Earth's Lucky Day *in collaboration with Francis Flagg in the last issue, March 1936.) Eventually* Golden Nemesis *saw print in the first issue of Donald Wollheim's* Stirring Science Stories. *I remembered it and when I phoned Dave Kyle to see about reprinting it here, he volunteered to collaborate with his 16-year-old self and present a more polished version. Here, across a gulf of 60 years, is a revival of a powerful science fiction story from the genre's pioneering period.*

Golden Nemesis

by David A. Kyle

THE FACE IN THE MIRROR WAS WIZENED, HOLLOW-EYED.

"My God!" he sobbed, "what have I done to myself!"

His eyes stared back at him, full of fear. He drew a shaking hand in helpless confusion across his perspiring brow. His fingers, like shriveled leaves on a withered plant, were stained with brown blotches from the chemicals which hadn't worked.

"My God!" he said. His voice was only a whisper. "I have forgotten about my face!"

He peered into his two, wild, dark eyes and concentrated on his nose, his cheeks, his lips. The grayness began to give way to a suggestion of pink. The two silver specks in his pale forehead glinted high above each eye. He cursed them silently and clenched his hands into fists.

"I'm twenty-seven," he told himself. "I'm not an old man! I'm handsome. She once called me a fair lad, jovial but serious. Ha! She should see me now!" Six months had changed him into a broken man.

"Still, I'm the smartest human being alive in the whole wide world!" he told his image, spitting out the words. "I am a genius!"

This description was no idle self-deception. He really was the smartest man in the whole wide world.

At the thought, so sweet yet so painful, he closed his eyes and for a moment relaxed as a wave of pleasure swept over him. The moment was so pleasurable, so peaceful. So utterly peaceful . . .

He opened his eyes in terror.

There! He had almost allowed himself to die!

He must not die! His formula was dangerous. She must not use it. No one should ever use it.

He staggered away from the lab table and flopped down at his desk.

Outside, the rumble of a busy world penetrated into his small room. The early sunlight, dimmed by the dirty, streaked window, splashed upon the remnants of his burned and scattered papers. Another day of agony, of torture!

His arm brushed more of his books and papers off the desk, clearing a space so he could print his message on the yellow lined tablet.

As he wrote, he spoke softly, "I will warn her. I will tell her I love her and I will warn her. I will cure myself and I will return to her."

His slender brown fingers tightly clutched the moving pencil.

"I told you—about my brain," he wrote. "That ordinary brain formed in an ordinary way. And then I improved it."

He laughed mirthlessly.

—She knows basic science. She's no dullard. She knows the brain controls the body, consciously here, unconsciously there. She knows the brain and the stem and the cord run the works.

His pencil scribbled on:

"I explained to you that even a genius uses only a small fraction of the brain nature has given him. I told you of my obsession. I could create an incredibly superior being if the entire brain could be utilized."

His pencil stopped.

—She knows that. She knows that even the most educated men have the use of only a small portion of their brains. I told her that the brain of an idiot might weight sixty ounces, while that of a genius may be only fifty. She saw the point: Use all sixty ounces and be a super man!—a majestic intellect, gigantic in scope!

"I told you I was experimenting with my brain. I assured you that I wasn't talking about increasing the number of my brain cells; they are a constant quantity. Instead, focus on the connections or synapses among the different neurons or cells. They determine the quality of intelligence. The more connections, the more workable brain power.

"How obvious! How simple! And I did it, my dear! I did it! I hooked up more and more neurons beyond my natural growth!"

—Yes, yes, I did it. Think of it, my boy, I'm a genius! Think of it.

The old-young man laughed bitterly.

—Yes, think of it! Think. Think. Think. Think more!

He again broke into wild laughter.

"My dear, I succeeded. I succeeded so well I may have destroyed myself. But maybe not.

"You know my experiments lasted for many months. I tried hundreds of stimulants, hundreds of compounds. I ate them, I drank them, I injected them directly into my veins."

—I don't have to tell her that. I just need to tell her the horrifying climax.

"I decided that direct injection into my frontal lobes must be done."

—Direct injection! Brilliant! I remember the sleepless night with my intense preparations. Oh, how frenzied were my actions. When I gazed into that well-lighted, high, clear mirror set up in the cellar workshop I didn't hesitate. With calm patience I shaved away the hair above my brow. Of course, I was obsessed, but my hand was steady as I moved the razor up, down, back, and across my skull. How fascinating to see my naked skull shining with a dead white color.

—My enthusiasm was a form of madness.

"I know I must seem mad, dear, to have done what I did. And to do it alone with only procaine. I drilled a hole in my head."

—What an incredible thing to write!

"Don't be upset. I felt no pain."

—More incredible was the fact that I did it twice to make certain both lobes of the brain were enfused. I hadn't planned to do so, but it was so simple. I did the deed perfectly—the tiny drill-bit, barely thick enough to insert my needle, no thicker than a hair, was pressed just above the left frontal lobe of my cerebrum, guided so precisely by the miniature rig I had made. Hardly a drop of blood was drawn.

"I made the injection. So very simple, it was. So, I repeated the operation. Two tiny holes blocked with two tiny sliver plugs. That's why you saw me for weeks wearing my white doctor's cap. I didn't wish to alarm you."

—Marvelous, wasn't it, the way I watched so clinically as I drilled those holes in my head! I had no doubts about the terrible foolishness of my actions. I imagined a wondrous future. I can still recollect the hum and vibration in my head as the drill wormed into the bone. I was so calm, I was so sure of myself. I was overwhelmed by the demented lust for intelligence. I had no concern for any mental torture that was to come.

—I am tempted to tell you, dear, of the unbelievable details. I must skip over them lightly. Oh, that moment when I caressed the covering membrane, the removal of the drill, the withdrawal of the hypodermic syringe from the thick glass bottle, finally the insertion . . . The pressing of the plunger . . . One half of the yellow, golden liquid, so carefully placed.

—When I squeezed the fluid into my brain I was confident of success. The compound was not the problem, it was the delivery system. I *had* to do it the way I did. As I squeezed the fluid into my brain I could imagine that oily, golden liquid spreading down between the layers of tissue, insinuating itself through the dura mater—into the arachnoid mater—on to the dura mater—flooding the brain serum. Irritating, irritating. Enveloping the synaptic connections. *Done!*

—One treatment, yet only a half of the golden fluid had been used. Why hold back? Use it all, now! The new idea drove me to go beyond my original careful plan.

—That second insertion had been on the spur of the moment. The first had gone so well, why not another! Twice the fluid, twice as good. After all, there were two hemispheres of the brain. Do each side!

—Too much ambition. Too much greed.

—So I had *two* silver plugs, instead of one.

—I never considered an overdose. Was that my nemesis?

"After those operations, darling, only two weeks later, my mind was inexplicably intoxicated, an unexpected dizziness so very unpleasant. You never knew that."

—I also hid from you the euphoria of my sense of enormous power. I tested myself in many ways, drunk on my chemical cocktail. I performed huge mathematical problems in my head. I did them effortlessly. I analyzed my experiment and concluded that I was absolutely correct in my calculations. My brain was organizing itself, *thoroughly*. How happy I was!

"Remember later, those few golden months, dear? Remember how easily I could remember? For you I memorized a book of love poems within moments. The entire book! Completely, accurately! And I recited the best of them to you, my love. I loved you then to the depths of my soul and you shared my new exuberance. Remember how, in utter ignorance, I dissembled your radio into a mess of parts and then put it back together, making it work better than ever? *Correction:* not past tense, *loved*, but present tense *love*.

"That day not so many weeks ago you saw the greatest man in the world. Yet within a week I did not let you see the most pitiable man in the world.

"Slowly, at first, you saw me evolve from a poor, struggling youth, unemployed, broke, hungry, striving to become rich and famous and in command of my life—evolve into a human being, equipped with a dozen times as much inherent ability, looking forward to our golden future.

"I had no premonition of the disaster that lay ahead. Certainly, nor did you. From a glorious success, I was sliding overnight into the chaos of too much success. Borne aloft by a few drops of golden molecules, I was pulled down by a few more drops—fluttering—a high-flying bird with a torn wing.

"Queer things happened. I never told you. My superior mind easily deceived you, that my strangeness was temporary. My intelligence was—is—truly remarkable. You know how superior I have become, but I still love you for the kind and simple soul you are. Yes, yes, I do."

—I cannot tell you about my first terrible morning. The dawning day was sweet and bright. After my hour of sleep every nerve tingled with excitement toward conquering a fresh day. But then—I threw myself out of bed into the warm sunlight—and fell to the floor. On unsteady feet, I stepped toward the door—and nearly fell again. Only calm and deliberate attention to my body let me walk safely from my room. In the bathroom, as

I brushed my teeth, I was suddenly aware that I was standing there, just standing, staring at myself frozen in the act, my unmoving toothbrush pressed inside my mouth between cheek and gum. My awareness started my hand rhythmically moving again. I was puzzled. I glared into my eyes. And again my brushing faltered and stopped. I am too embarrassed to report those details.

"You see, dear, it was chaos to discover that when my attention wandered, my unconscious, automatic actions simply stopped. It applied to all sorts of normal actions. Just sipping coffee without thinking made me choke. My mouth did not chew if I did not will it to chew. I did not smile at you unless I willed myself to smile. That's why you found me a bit cool and distant."

—I cannot write about the extent of my befuddlement. I am still a vastly superior person, albeit handicapped. When understanding came to me at last, I was shocked. I could not tell you. My serum hasn't just built up my brain capacity, it has linked up disparate parts of my mind. Actions of habit now require attention. My voluntary and involuntary routines of life have been linked.

"Understand, my dear, that as I conquered my emotions, my true status took form. I was handicapped, but I believed I could handle this. I simply couldn't rely on habit for performance. Fortunately, I still have the greatest brain in the world. I can handle this. My new power is worth the trouble. My brain merely needs synaptic development, new pathways in my head, serious attention and practice, my rewards will be magnificent. I should say, *our* rewards.

"As days passed, those many days when I did not see you, I exercised my growing knowledge. I juggled my thoughtless habits. The discomforts were overcome by concentration. I was again in control of myself.

"But then, dear, my worries began again. I was sitting, relaxed in my soft chair, swiftly scanning a book, when faintness came upon me. I realized that I wasn't breathing. Not breathing! But then I immediately began to gulp air, to breathe again.

"My dear! The situation was now horrible. How could I tell you? I had to will myself to breathe. How hideous for a super man to be enslaved by his body! Bodily functions at times deliberate, at times automatic, were no longer at all automatic! A superior brain had to monitor my breathing, had to deal with the mundane. I could no longer sleep deeply.

"After a fitful night's rest there began a new method of life for me. I now controlled my terror, finding that my breathing required only sporadic attention. Instead of one hour of light sleep, I required five or more. I lay in my bed half awake, making myself breathe when I sensed my problem. It was a terrible inconvenience, but I had awakened psychic powers to help, and, as I keep saying, I have a superior brain. I marvel at my ability to make prodigious efforts."

—How can I tell her the whole truth? My great mind can see the inevitable degeneration. But my great mind even now cannot see my eventual fate. Yet I must explain to her. I will not see her until I have solved my problem.

—My devilish liquid had penetrated through the cerebrum, then through the cerebellum, and now it has touched the medulla oblongata. Everything it has permeated has been linked to my conscious mind. My God! I see that if that fluid seeps down deeper, undiluted . . . I can see it clearly with my enhanced mind . . . That drug, it is evil! It will—it will . . .

—For all my normal intelligence, I was so awfully, horribly stupid.

"Dear, you must know the whole truth.

"The other morning, relentlessly, my ultimate crisis came. My worst of fears materialized.

"My heart fluttered and stopped!

"I willed it to pump again, obviously, but my great mind was now enslaved by my body. No longer could I sleep even lightly. To do so was to chance death. Breathing can be intermittent, I can survive that. But my heart can only halt for seconds.

"Imagine, dear, the torture I endure. I frantically worked to find an antidote to reverse my triumph, always forcing myself to concentrate on staying alive without sleep. My great brain, that superior thing I have created, is handling the thousand things that once I had assumed to run by themselves. I mentally beat my heart, pump my lungs, run my nervous system like an engineer, opening valves, closing others, regulating my organs, turning fleshy switches off and on, a thousand different chores to think of. Think! said my mind. Think more! Think, think!"

—Oh, my darling, I can barely think of you for thinking of myself. Forgive me for destroying our lives. My days are measured in seconds, in micro seconds. The mists of fatigue fill my brain as I struggle to balance the mechanisms which give me life."

—My eyes burn, my skin crawls. My eyelids flicker, drooping shut. *Agghh!*—a gasp and a groan tremble in my throat.

"My body cries out for sleep, dear. But my will battles to stay awake, to stay alive. I am frantically searching for a chemical counter force. The last few nights have been hell for me. I almost pray that I will revert to my natural state. My superior brain is now a curse.

"My God, how I wish to stop thinking and to merely sleep!

"My heart is the one organ which must never be forgotten. And when I adjust to its demands, I will work on a solution for everything. Therefore, I must go away for a long time without seeing you. I will not tell you where I am, but I have made arrangements for perpetual care with a mechanical heart machine. I need time.

"There is a knock on my door. The messenger is here. To him I will entrust this letter. I will close now and seal the envelope and give it to him. Then I will lock my door here forever. And I then will take the waiting car to my place of hope.

"I love you. This letter has given me peace because you will know that in my absence, and forever, I will always love you.

"All my work is now destroyed. My papers are burned. My equipment has been smashed. I am very tired. I renounce my ambition to become homo superior.

"I shall always be

"Your Beloved."

He folded the note, kissed it and enclosed it in an envelope. As he sealed it, tears suddenly welled out of his eyes. A wave of giddiness struck him and he slipped heavily to the floor. He arose, half conscious, and staggered to the door while he beat his heart and flexed his lungs.

"Sir!" the messenger said, taking the envelope. "There's no address."

The disheveled, wizened man, with the wild dark eyes, made no reply. His face sagged, his body sagged, he slowly slipped to the floor.

The messenger, panic-stricken, could see the man had ceased to live.

GENTLEMEN, YOU ARE MAD.

This statement is addressed to ALL publishers, hard & soft cover.

*You have permitted over half a century to elapse without ever once having put a number of Ray Cummings' short stories into a single volume. Many of his novels, yes—*The Girl in the Golden Atom, The Man Who Mastered Time, Tarrano the Conqueror, A Brand New World, Beyond the Stars, *etc.*

But what of "The Thought-girl"?

"A Fragment of Diamond Quartz"?

"The Great Transformation"?

"Machines of Destiny"?

His Argosyarns? Appearance in Bluebook*? "Robot God" in* Weird Tales*?*

"Beyond the End of Time"?

Any time, gentlemen; any time. Simply contact me, Forrest Ackerman, the representative of his Estate.

Secret of the Sun

by Ray Cummings

(Author of *Ahead of His Time, Around the Universe*)

Big Olaf Stevens sat in a corner of the laboratory, his huge powerful hands dangling between his knees, and silently watched Dr. Argon. The little gray-haired scientist was crouched over his workbench, the electronic sheen of prismatic light upon him.

It was late afternoon. The laboratory, here in Argon's lonely home in the hills of Northern New York, was dark with shrouded windows. The single door which led down into the living room was closed. A huge electro-spectroscope was hissing with the current in its prisms. It was trained on the ceiling where, through an aperture, a pencil-ray of sunlight came down— sunlight that was spread upon the spectroscope's big image-screen with a great band of lines that showed the burning elements in the gases of the sun.

The stolid, slow-witted Olaf Stevens only vaguely understood the purpose of the spectroscope. For a year he had been working with Dr. Argon— just the two them alone here in the metal-concrete house on the hilltop by the edge of the woods. Master and servant. Stevens's thick, gnarled hands were twitching now as they dangled between his knees. This thing that

Argon claimed to have discovered—this mysterious secret of the sun—would bring fame and riches. A secret that could be sold for a great fortune. Argon had told him so. Whatever it was the scientist had manufactured it was worth thousands of times more than its weight in gold. Of that, Stevens was certain.

A shadow from the chassis of the spectroscope illuminated by the fluorescent tubes behind it, fell upon Olaf's heavy, thick-featured face. He was glad of that. Old Argon would not see that he was waiting—as he had waited impatiently for so many days—for the experiment to be finished. It would be so easy to seize the little scientist by the throat, to spill that retort of molten metal upon him and tell people over in town that Argon had killed himself in an accident resulting from some experiment.

"I've almost got it, Olaf." Argon's voice, quivering with eager excitement and triumph, mingled with the hiss of the small hydrogen torch with which he was working.

The dimness of the laboratory was illumined at intervals by tiny puffs of light. They were queer little puffs. Each of them seemed no bigger than the head of a pin. Sheets of asbestos partly shrouded them. But the light of them puffed up to the ceiling. Queer little puffs indeed! Olaf seemed not only to see, but to feel them, each a tiny wave that seemed to strike at him like a blow.

He found himself covered with sweat. It rolled in torrents down his great hairy chest so that one of his hands fumbled at his throat as though he were stifling.

"I've got it, Olaf," Argon was murmuring. "You felt that last one? The secret of the sun! That was less than a hundredth of a grain, and it went to ninety-eight hundred. Why, I can run it into millions!"

Millions! Untold wealth! With only one million Olaf would have everything in life that he could want!

What was the secret of the sun? He wondered about it detachedly.

"Olaf! Hand me that insulator. Hurry!"

At the direct command, Stevens lumbered to his feet. He was trembling; bathed in hot sweat. But it wasn't fear that made his heart pound. Just excitement and eagerness. Now was the time!

"Insulator!" he mumbled. "Which is it?" Like a great gorilla he shambled forward, his arms dangling.

"That white cone over there." Argon gestured at a large white cone that stood on a table across the room.

"I'm going to try nearly half a grain and keep it wholly sheathed," he added. "Just the magna-thermite and the thermo-gauge inside the cone when the reaction takes place."

Stevens brought the cone. His fingers twitched as he gripped it—fingers that in a minute or two would grip little Dr. Argon's throat—squeezing—strangling.

But what was the secret of the sun? He must be sure that he would know how to complete the experiment. Not with just tiny fractions of grains; but with the whole mass of intricate chemicals which Argon had prepared. And maybe, even, Olaf would be able to prepare still more. The retorts with their mixing mechanisms were there on the bench.

Argon had been connecting the big cone to his apparatus at the center of the table. The cone was raised a foot or two, clamped into a lowering mechanism over the strange-looking little slablike tray, where infinitesimal fragments of the chemicals lay mixed, ready for the tiny ignition which would unite them.

"Dr. Argon," Olaf said suddenly, "I do not understand all this. What are your chemicals? How does it work? What is this secret of the sun?"

Argon paused to wrinkle up his thin seamed face. He grinned.

"My secret, Olaf," he said. "Mine—and the sun's. But when I demonstrate—I can get it up to a full grain at least, with the apparatus I have here—when I demonstrate my results to the world of science, no longer will anyone say that old Argon is mad!"

Was Dr. Argon mad? Doubt assailed the big stolid Olaf so that for several moments he almost felt that he might lose this treasure which now was almost within his grasp. People said that Argon was demented, what with his vague talk of the secret of the sun, and his eccentric hermitlike habits. Dr. Argon should have had a skilled, trained assistant. But he had chosen Olaf. And Stevens knew why. Because Dr. Argon was not demented, but in reality a canny businessman. He would not trust any assistant with this treasure.

"It looks very wonderful," Olaf said quietly. "How does it work? With that little switch?"

Dr. Argon now had started the mechanism which would lower the big insulating cone. He shut off the tiny ray of sunlight and trained the big spectroscope on the table.

"I'll take a spectrograph of this," he said. "We'll be sure now that the spectrum band is the same as from sunlight."

The pencil-ray of sunlight now gone, the laboratory became a little darker. The retorts where Argon was preparing more of his chemicals gave off a lurid green sheen. Olaf's broad nostrils were dilating with the chemical smells. The whole place was so weird it had always given him a vague uneasiness. He felt that now, more than ever; and the hot sweat poured down on him.

Dr. Argon glanced at him, laughed.

"Good Lord, big fellow, you look frightened to death. This isn't a monster that's going to jump at you." Argon's laugh died to a grim chuckle. "Well, as a matter of fact, that's just what it is," he added. "But this is a little monster—the cone will hold it. Watch now."

"But what are you doing?" Stevens urged. "Those chemicals—"

"You won't understand me," Argon said.

"But I'll try, sir."

The old chemist grinned.

"All right. I started with aluminum, which I brought into contact and united by ignition with an oxide of a chemically weaker metal. With an ordinary oxide, and just plain aluminum, I would get what is known as thermite. The aluminum combines with the oxygen of the oxide. But my reaction goes further, into what I might call magna-thermite of infinite yielding capacity. I am using an aluminum alloy of my own preparation, and an unusual oxide alloy. I discovered both their gases on the sun. You can see them in the spectroscope band—if you're clever enough to identify what you're seeing."

He pointed to his micro-scales. Stevens saw small piles of finely powdered chemicals, one gleaming white, the other a dirty gray.

"My mechanism ignites the mixture," he added. "That's simple. I guess you can understand that all right." He indicated his little apparatus under the poised cone. "That cone automatically drops a second before the ignition."

"I understand," Stevens murmured.

Dr. Argon nodded. He did not see Olaf's eyes gleaming; he did not notice Olaf's big twitching hands.

"The difficulty," Dr. Argon said, "has been to construct my apparatus to be impervious to the reaction. That table slab—that little tray—the very bulb of the thermo-state itself—all of them have to be within the cone. It took me four years to devise the materials of which those things are made. Stand back, now—"

Olaf recoiled. His mind was trying to grasp it all. Two tiny fragments of chemicals. That little ignition timer and switch. The timer and the switch that would drop the cone. It was so simple. And now Olaf noticed exactly which of the little black buttons Dr. Argon was pressing, in the row on the mechanism panel.

"Now—ten seconds," the scientist murmured.

The cone lowered. Argon jumped up and shifted until he was standing with his back against Olaf, his head hardly above the servant's shoulders.

"Now—watch—"

Breathlessly, Olaf watched. Under the big white cone there seemed a tiny puff. A little bigger than the others had been, perhaps. The cone did not stir. But something invisible struck Argon and Stevens—a great wave of something. Then it was gone; there was only a stifling, breathless feeling, with a clammy sweat trickling down Olaf's chest and legs.

"Good!" Dr. Argon exclaimed. "It was all right! Everything held." He darted toward the gauge of one of his big instruments, which had a tiny tube connected with the cone.

"Over ten thousand!" Argon exclaimed. "That's with nearly half a grain of the oxide but only a hundredth grain of the other. Now I'm getting an idea of the proportions. That's all I'll try for at the present. The cone held it—but look what it did."

The big cone was no longer white. In places on the outside it was ragged and dirty gray-black—pitted and scarred.

"I took a spectrograph of that one," Argon said eagerly. "Just to prove that the lines are the same. Thermo-infinity. The sun's secret, and mine. Why, this will revolutionize the world! This will—"

He was hardly aware of Olaf springing at him, like a great snarling animal. And then he felt Olaf's big fingers on his throat.

"Why—" he gasped. "My God—" But his voice choked as Olaf squeezed tightly with a strangling grip. Argon's frail little body collapsed backward, so that he fell on his back with Stevens kneeling on him.

It was a chaos to the snarling Olaf, his big fingers tightening on the scrawny throat; his heavy knee pinning the squirming, struggling little body. The eerie light from the instruments showed Argon's face, with its popping eyes and open mouth. Then the body was only twitching; the eyes became glazed . . . Olaf relaxed. Dr. Argon's body lay still.

The thing was done! So easy. For a moment big Olaf Stevens crouched, panting with triumph; and then he lumbered to his feet. The huge retort of molten metal at the end of the workbench was half full, its contents bubbling sluggishly. After Olaf secured the treasure he would pour that liquid metal on Argon's face and throat. It would sear the flesh away like a blowtorch held to a tub of butter. There would be nothing left to show that the scientist had died of strangling. Anyone would say that a laboratory accident had killed him.

Olaf was trembling with eagerness as he poked around the intricate maze of Argon's apparatus. He was convinced that Argon had been creating a new substance. Some of it should be here—the result of those tiny puffs; the product of the chemical reaction which had taken place under the big white insulating cone.

Olaf's eyes brightened as once more he thought of the treasure. A substance new to Earth, of course it was worth many times its weight in gold. Olaf would gather it up and create more of it. He would hide it all; then take it back to his European homeland. He would wait a year or so, and then produce it and sell it. Riches for Olaf Stevens, at last.

But disappointment swept him. There was no trace here of any new substance. Was that because Argon's experiments had been on so small a scale? Of course! A hundredth of a grain, he had said. And that last big one—still not half a grain. Half a grain was nothing sizable to yield any treasure!

His disappointment was only momentary. Here under his eyes lay the two piles of powdered chemicals which Argon had so laboriously prepared. A gleaming white pile, and one which was dirty gray. Stevens knew how to unite them in larger quantities.

• • •

His big hands were shaking a little as he carefully mixed the two mounds of chemicals and put them on the slablike tray under the big cone. Soon the treasure would lie here.

The mechanism of the raised cone hummed steadily as he started the timer. Everything that Argon had done was clear in his mind. His fingers pressed the correct button of the timing-ignition.

Big Olaf Stevens stood back, watching eagerly as the cone smoothly descended. Ten seconds, Argon had said. Only ten seconds now, and he would possess the treasure. Thousands and thousands of times more of it than Argon had ever created . . .

Ten seconds can be an eternity of eager, tumbling thoughts. Olaf's mind went back to his boyhood home, the little village at the foot of the mountain with the great glacier in its ragged gash. And his thoughts flashed ahead to when he would be there again. People would say, "Olaf is a wonderful fellow. So clever—"

It may be that Stevens was aware that the ten seconds finished with a chaos under the white insulating cone—a flashing chaos that engulfed the cone and the table—engulfed the entire eerie laboratory. There was just a split second when Olaf's senses were able perhaps to record a prismatic glare in which the room—the house—everything—was melting into chaos. Then for Olaf Stevens there was only nothingness; and whatever of the unknown that comes to one who has entered Eternity . . .

"The house must have stood just about in the center," someone said. "Good Lord, it's hot here—let's go back."

In little awed groups, people were gathered at the edge of a great circular pit. Night had come. The yellow-red light of the molten earth and rocks, forty or fifty feet down in the pit, glowed eerily over the lonely hilltop and painted the rising smoke and gases with a lurid glare. Beyond the pit, the rocky ground was blackened; the edges of the encroaching woods down the hill showed naked, blackened tree trunks.

In another group of men, at another point near the lip of the glaring molten abyss, a young scientist stood with several of the police and town officials.

"Yes, I knew him," the young scientist was saying. "Secretive old fellow. Always thought he was a little off—harping about some secret of the sun that he was after."

"But what do you think now?" one of the officials demanded.

The young scientist's grim smile faded.

"The most intense heat that we have ever created on Earth and measured," he said, "well perhaps it's something over four or five thousand degrees Fahrenheit, and the temperature at the surface of the sun is believed to be about sixteen thousand degrees. But that is infinitesimal compared to the sun's center, where undoubtedly there is a temperature of millions of degrees.

"How is that immense heat created and maintained? Well, that is the secret of the sun. A contraction of the mass upon itself, some say. But others think it is perhaps a form of radioactivity. Or perhaps the combining of chemical elements of a nature as yet unknown to us."

"And Argon discovered the nature of those elements? Or some new way of combining them?" somebody suggested.

The young scientist shrugged. "Perhaps he did. We have a hint of the process, in everyday commercial chemistry—the creation of thermite. The oxygen of an oxide is made to combine with aluminum. An enormous heat is generated by that reaction—heat that is commercially used for welding. I imagine Argon was working along those lines. He was always hinting at what he called magna-thermite. And talking about his goal being thermo-infinity."

Glare from the molten rocks down in the pit painted the young scientist's face and showed that he was smiling.

"Argon wasn't trying to create any tangible substance like a treasure, as some people thought. He was generating heat. More and more intense heat, with thermo-infinity as his theoretical goal. There is a mathematical limit to coldness—absolute zero, where molecular vibration ceases. But there is no mathematical limit to rapidity of vibration—no limit, theoretically, to heat."

The young scientist was gazing with awe down at the molten glare.

"Argon must have created about a million degrees of concentrated heat here," he added. "A small concentration of the greatest heat that man has ever created on Earth!"

The secret of the sun. Olaf Stevens had demonstrated it perfectly!

Pallas Rebellion

by Donald A. Wollheim

(Author of *The Booklings*)

THE FIRST HINT ABOUT THE ROBOT TROUBLE ON THE PLANETOID PALLAS TO REACH us came from that intrepid reporter of interplanetary news, Sandra de Long. Sandra had been on Pallas investigating the plutonium mines there.

She hadn't been on the trail of any specific story but just sort of writing a book about the major asteroids and their scenic interests. Pallas, you know, has the only natural deposit of pure plutonium in the solar system— outside of the debatable and inaccessible claims made for certain mountains on Neptune's smaller moon. Because plutonium is the stuff from which atomic reactors are made, it's valuable and still pretty expensive to fabricate, even in this day and age, 250 years after the Manhattan Project.

Plutonium, being highly radioactive, is mined exclusively by robots. They are directed from the mining settlement of Valiersdorf, where the Terrestrial technicians and reduction engineers live. Sandra had sent back two stories about the rough-and-ready life of the mining town—mostly pure invention, since the pioneering days have long been past and the hermetically enclosed town is as comfortable as any suburban hamlet on Earth.

But Sandra had an eye for odd detail and she had ferreted out some of the older artifacts and one of the worked-out pits, and had poked her shapely nose into the robot warrens too. In her last broadcast she had spoken of trouble with the robots. There was a steadily increasing number of inexplicable errors in their work. One technician had already expressed the thought that the radioactivity of the mines was impairing their mechanism.

Sandra had suggested that perhaps exposure to the vast power of the plutonium had altered the delicate atomic chargings of the robotic brains. Robots are thinking beings in a way—they are equipped with mechanical brains that can and do transact elementary reasoning, enough for their jobs. These brains are fairly delicate and are always enclosed in a transparent shell where their dials and adjustments can be periodically checked.

The next thing we of the Asteroid Patrol knew, word came that Pallas had suddenly gone out of communication with the rest of the universe. Our ships were ordered there.

Aboard our space cruiser there was plenty of speculation about the mission. Ted Winston, our commander, was specially worried, and as his lieutenant, I knew what was bothering him. It wasn't robot trouble, it was Sandra. They were engaged.

When our vessels came in sight of Pallas, everything seemed quiet. True, there was no sign of life in the mines; the doomed town seemed strangely silent and lightless but nothing was exploding.

We settled for a landing near the town, when the first robot battery opened up on us! It was a near thing, it was what we had expected. The blast of an atom-heat ray just missed our ship—had it hit us, we'd have blown up and that would be the end of this story. But it missed, doubtless because of inexperience and because it wasn't a true weapon. It was a mining beam, up-ended and being worked as a gun.

We got out of its range and made a landing in a small valley between two tiny Pallasian stony hills.

Pallas is like the rest of the asteroids, a bare, lifeless rocky world. None of these tiny planets have the gravity to hold down an atmosphere and you can't walk about with a space mask and your own portable air supply.

Ted and I took counsel as to what to do next. The question was who had shot at us and why. Someone had to go out and investigate and it would have to be us. Then Sparks came in and told us there was a message coming in.

It was from the robots. They had announced their independence; they were going to hold the mines and Earth crew as hostages and they were willing to release Sandra de Long to us as evidence of their good faith. Sandra, they announced, would be able to give us the dope on their demands.

It was clear, just the same, that the brains of the robots were cracked. Just the way the thing was worded was proof of it. They couldn't hope to win. Still, Ted told me, if we could get Sandra clear, he'd feel a lot better about dealing with the situation. For of course we could not make a deal with these lunatic machines.

Ted told the robots by radio to bring Sandra to the ship and he would meet them. They must come unarmed. They agreed.

We didn't want Ted to chance it but he insisted. Sandra was his girl and he wasn't going to let someone else risk her rescue. He put on his air helmet, took his gun and left the ship; the rest of us watching with baited breath from the ship's observation ports.

Coming toward the ship we could now see a robot and it was carrying something. It came closer. We gasped.

The metal man was carrying Sandra like a sack of potatoes, slung under one arm! The poor girl was wriggling and apparently yelling for help.

Ted Winston stood like a man struck. The sight was certainly calculated to drive him mad. He couldn't dare attack the robot now, even though he could see the thing was armed and that if it got too close the machine-man could probably destroy our spaceships with a good blast—or at least ground them.

Ted was on a spot and I didn't envy him. He couldn't dare fire, for his shot would destroy Sandra too. He couldn't dare not fire, in spite of robot promises, because the ships and his men were in danger. The robot had violated its promise and was armed.

It was an old gangster trick—the helpless hostage as a shield for the killer.

Then Ted Winston did what we never expected. He dashed forward, raised his flame pistol and fired! Fired point-blank at the robot—and at Sandra!

The robot sizzled for a moment, then suddenly simply exploded! There was a terrific flash and when the dust cleared, there was only a hole in the ground and little bits of metal and Sandra scattered about!

But Ted somehow didn't seem appalled at what looked to us like a cold-blooded act of murder—how could he kill his own fiancée like that?!

We dashed out of the ship, armed, and surrounded him. And then in a few words we understood.

Ted had saved us all. For he had recognized the robot plot and we had not. The thing we thought was Sandra was not her at all—it was a cunningly constructed robot—designed to look like Sandra and actually loaded with enough plutonium to blow our ship to smithereens. It was the intent of the robots to hand her over to us, to have Ted bring her aboard our ships under the impression it was Sandra, and there to blow ourselves up when the dummy detonated!

But how had Ted caught wise to all this? Simple, when you think of it, and a robot wouldn't think of it. They don't have to breathe, you know. It never occurred to them to put a *space helmet* on their dummy Sandra. But Ted knew that the real Sandra couldn't have survived out there in the airless surface of Pallas, couldn't have yelled as the phony Sandra did, couldn't have been so obviously active in the robot's clutches. So he destroyed them both.

How we rescued the real Sandra and the Pallas rebellion collapsed is a story you all know from your history books. But the story of Ted Winston's act of clever deduction is probably new to you.

Everything about Francis Stevens was mysterious.

The reason for her use of a pseudonym.

The proof of what actually was her first story. (I think this was it—and yet?)

Her sudden cessation of communication in 1939. A last letter from her daughter returned as undeliverable.

Lloyd Arthur Eshbach—an early scientifiction author, Cosmos *contributor, World Science Fiction Convention Guest of Honor and creator of the legendary Fantasy Press books—said of her in his introduction to* The Heads of Cerberus:

"If any one word can describe the work of 'Francis Stevens,' its background and its author, that word is 'mystery.' By many, 'Francis Stevens' has been thought to be a pseudonym of A. Merritt. Others insisted—and correctly—that the name concealed a woman. But her actual identity, her background—these were mysteries. The stories themselves reveal an unusually fertile imagination, a rare narrative gift and a strong leaning toward the mysterious. Yet all the work of 'Francis Stevens' was published during a 6-year period."

Was it?

It has been established that her maiden name was Gertrude Barrows.

Would Gertrude and G. M. Barrows be one & the same?

In the 14 April 1917 issue of All-Story Weekly, *the editor introduced the Francis Stevens novella* The Nightmare *by calling it "the first work of an exceedingly promising author." The first work. Years later the author said of her 'first work,' "It had just one merit, as I remember, and that was a rather grotesque originality."*

But, in speaking of her "first story," was Francis Stevens then describing The Nightmare . . . *or perhaps* The Curious Experience of Thomas Dunbar? *The latter appeared in* The Argosy, *a periodical with which* All-Story *eventually combined.*

Unfortunately, at the time of going to press I do not have the date of publication on this TIME VAULT *resurrection. I purchased a copy of it only as a curiosity for my collection, as it was advertised as "Francis Stevens's first story" by the seller, and only some time later, after I had read it and found how interesting it was, did I decide to bring it back into the light of modern print. By then I no longer had the information on its date of original publication. I seem to recall it as 1911. If so, the author would have been about 27 at the time—a perfectly reasonable age.*

Circumstantial evidence, of course, can be a tricky thing.

There are two George H. Smiths in the fantasy field.

Two Al Lewises in sf fandom.

Another Raymond Jones has appeared on the auctorial scene.

And . . . a Bill Ackerman, a Fred, Tom, Dick or Gerry, okay—but could you believe another Forrest Ackerman? *And living in LOS ANGELES?! That's stretching coincidence too many decimal places . . . nevertheless, it's a fact!*

Still doesn't conclusively prove G. M. Barrows = Gertrude Barrows = Francis Stevens. Altho I, personally, am inclined to accept it.

In any event, The Story's the Thing and I think you'll find this worthy of unlocking from the TIME VAULT.

The Curious Experience
Of Thomas Dunbar

by G. M. Barrows
(Francis Stevens?)

I CAME BACK INTO CONSCIOUS EXISTENCE WITH A SIGHING IN MY EARS LIKE THE deep breathing of a great monster; it was everywhere, pervading space, filling my mind to the exclusion of thought.

Just a sound—regular, even soothing in its nature—but it seemed to bear some weird significance to my clouded brain. That was thought trying to force its way in.

Then waves and waves of whispering that washed all thought away—till I grasped again at some confused and wandering idea.

It was the definite sensation of a cool, firm hand laid on my brow that lifted me up at last through that surging ocean of sighs. As a diver from the depths I came up—up—and emerged suddenly, it seemed, into the world.

I opened my eyes wide and looked straight up into the face of a man. A man—but everything was swimming before my eyes, and at first his face seemed no more than part of a lingering dream.

And fantastic visions of the Orient! What a face! It was wrinkled as finely as the palm of a woman's hand, and in as many directions.

It was yellow in hue, and round like a baby's. And the eyes were narrow, and black, and they slanted, shining like a squirrel's.

I thought that of them at first; but sometimes when you just happened to look at him, they seemed to have widened and to be possessed of strange depths and hues.

In height he was not more than four feet five, and, of all contrasts, this little, wizened curiosity with the countenance of a Chinese god was clad in the very careful and appropriate afternoon attire of a very careful and appropriate American gentleman!

The long sighing was still in my ears, but no longer at war with thought. I lay in a neat white bedstead in a plainly furnished room. I lifted my hand (it took an astonishing effort to do it), rubbed my eyes, and stared at the man who sat beside me.

His expression was kind, and in spite of its ugliness there was something in the strange face which encouraged me to friendliness.

"What—what's the matter with me?" I asked, and I was surprised to note the question was a mere whisper.

"Nothing now, except that you are very weak."

His voice was full, strong, and of a peculiar resonant quality. He spoke perfect English, with a kind of clear-cut clip to the words.

"You had an accident—an automobile went over you—but you're all right now, and don't need to think about it."

"What is it—that whispering noise? Are we near the sea?"

He smiled and shook his head. His smile merely accentuated the wrinkles—it could not multiply them.

"You are very near my laboratory—that is all. Here, drink this, and then you must rest."

I obeyed him meekly, like a child, weak of mind and body.

I wondered a little why I was with him instead of at a hospital or with friends, but I soon dropped off. I was really quite weak just then.

Yet before I slept I did ask one more question.

"Would you tell me—if you don't mind—your name?"

"Lawrence."

"Lawrence what?" I whispered. "Just—?"

"Yes," he smiled (and his face ran into a very tempest of wrinkles) "just Lawrence. No more."

Then I slept.

And I did little but sleep, and wake, and eat, and sleep again, for some five days. And during this time I learned marvelously little of my host and his manner of life.

Most questions he evaded cleverly, but he told me that it was his auto which had nearly ruined my earthly tenement; Lawrence had himself taken me from the scene of the accident without waiting for an ambulance, telling the police and bystanders that I was an acquaintance. He had carried me to his own house, because, he said, he felt somewhat responsible for my injuries and wanted to give me a better chance for my life than the doctors would allow me.

He seemed to be possessed of a great scorn for all doctors. I knew long after that he had studied the profession very thoroughly, and in many countries, and truly held the right to the title he contemptuously denied himself.

At the time I considered only that he had cured me up in wonderfully short order, considering the extent of the injuries I had received, and that I had suffered not at all. Therefore I was grateful.

Also he told me, on I forget what occasion, that his mother was a Japanese woman of very ancient descent, his father a scholarly and rather wealthy American. And for some eccentric reason of his own, his dwarfed son had chosen to eschew the family patronym and use merely his Christian name.

During the time I lay in bed I saw no servants; Lawrence did all things necessary. And never, day or night, did the humming and sighing of the machines cease.

Lawrence spoke vaguely of great dynamos, but on this subject, as on most others, he was very reticent. Frequently I saw him in the dress of a mechanic, for he would come in to see me at all hours of the day, and I imagine must have inconvenienced himself considerably for my welfare.

I had no particular friends to worry about my whereabouts, and so I lay quiet and at peace with the world for those five days in inert contentment.

Then an hour came—it was in the morning, and Lawrence had left me to go to his laboratory—when I became suddenly savagely impatient of the dull round. Weak though I was, I determined to dress and get out into the open air—out into the world.

Mind you, during those five days I had seen no face save that of my dwarfed host, heard no voice but his. And so my impatience overcame my good judgment and his counsels, and I declared to myself that I was well enough to join once more in the rush of life.

Slowly, and with trembling limbs that belied that assertion, I got into my clothes. Very slowly—though in foolish terror lest Lawrence should catch me putting aside his mandates—I hurried my toilet as best I could.

At last I stood, clothed and in my right mind, as I told myself, though I had already begun to regret my sudden resolve.

I opened the door and looked into the bare, narrow hall. No one in sight, up or down.

I made my way, supporting myself, truth to tell, by the wall, toward a door at the far end, which stood slightly ajar.

I had almost reached it when I heard a terrible screaming. It was harsh, rough, tense with some awful agony, and to my startled senses preeminently human.

I stopped, shaking from head to foot with the shock. Then I flung myself on the door, from behind which the noises seemed to issue. It was not locked, and I plunged almost headlong into a great room, shadowy with whirring machinery under great arc lights.

Before a long table, loaded with retorts and the paraphernalia of the laboratory, stood Lawrence. His back was toward me, but he had turned his head angrily at my sudden entrance, and his queer, narrow eyes were blazing with annoyance.

In the room were two or three other men, evidently common mechanics, and none save Lawrence had more than glanced around. The screaming had ceased.

"Well?" his voice was little better than a snarl.

"That—that noise!" I gasped, already wondering if I had not made a fool of myself. "What was it?"

"Eh? Oh, that was nothing—the machinery—why are you—"

He was interrupted by a crash and splash from the far end of the place, followed by an exclamation of terror and horror, and a nice collection of French and English oaths from the men.

Lawrence had been holding in his hand while he spoke to me what looked like a peculiar piece of metal. It was cylindrical in shape, and little shades of color played over its surface continually.

Now he thrust this into my hands with a muttered injunction to be careful of it, and rushed off to the scene of the catastrophe. I followed him, at my best pace, with the thing in my hand.

At the end of the room were two immense vats of enameled iron, their edges flush with the floor, half filled with some livid, seething acid mixture, through which little currents writhed and wriggled.

The farther side of the largest vat sloped up at an angle of about thirty degrees, a smooth, slimy slide of zinc about ten feet from top to bottom and extending the full length of the vat.

The surface of this slide was covered to about half an inch in thickness with some kind of yellowish paste, whose ultimate destination was the mixture in the vat.

Above towered an engine of many wheels and pistons, and this operated two great pestles or stamps, slant-faced to fit the slide; these, running from one end of the zinc to the other, worked the paste with a grinding motion, as an artist mixes his paints with a palette knife.

The grinding motion was quite swift, but the lateral movement was comparatively slow. I should say that it must have taken about four minutes for the two stamps to pass from one end of the fifteen-foot vat to the other.

In the vat floated a plank. On the surface of the slide, almost in the middle, sprawled a man, his arms spread out on either side, not daring to move an inch on the slippery paste, for the slightest motion meant a slip downward into the hissing acid.

Worst of all, there seemed to be no means of getting across to him. The great engine occupied one side entirely to the wall—on the other the second vat barred passage.

Beyond the vats the room extended some little distance, and there was a door there, open, through which one could see a fenced yard piled high with ashes and cinders.

And the great stamps, twenty cubic feet of solid metal in each, were making their inevitable way toward the man. When they reached him— well, their smooth surface would afford him no finger hold, even if their rapid movement allowed him to clutch them. They must push him down— they might stun him first, but most certainly they would push him down.

I need hardly say that I did not take in the full significance of all this at the time—it was only afterward that I fully understood the details.

Even as Lawrence ran he shouted:

"Stop that engine! Quick, men!"

I saw two stalwart workmen spring at the levers of the stamp machine— saw them twisting at the wheel—heard another crash, and a deep groan from all! The guiding mechanism had slipped a cog, or broken a rod, or something.

In my excitement, shaking so from weakness that I could hardly stand,

I had half fallen against a piece of machinery that seemed to be at a standstill. Unconsciously my fingers grasped at a sort of handle.

I heard a whirring noise, felt something like a tremendous shock, and a burning pain. I let go the handle in a hurry, just as Lawrence wheeled on me with the cry, "For God's sake, you fool—"

But I could give no heed either to what I had done or to him. My eyes were still fixed on the unfortunate man on the slide.

The stamps were not more than five feet from his body now, and their low rattle and swish sounded in my ears loud as the tread of an army.

"A rope!" cried Lawrence in despair.

And then, in my horror, and in the sheer impossibility of standing by quiescent and seeing a fellow-being done to death in this manner, I did a mad thing.

Wild with resentment, as if it were a living thing I could have fought, I flung myself on the great, swiftly revolving fly-wheel of the engine, seized its rim in my fingers, and braced back with all the force in my arms and shoulders.

By all precedent and reason my hands should have been crushed to a jelly in the maze of machinery, but to my intense astonishment the wheel stopped under my grasp with no very great effort on my part.

For a moment I held it so (it seemed to me to pull with no more force than is in the arms of a child), and then there was a loud report somewhere within the intestines of the monster. I saw a guiding rod as thick as my wrist double up and twist like a wire cable, things generally went to smash inside the engine, and the stamps stopped—not three inches from the man's head!

And even as they ceased to grind, men came running in at the door on the farther side of the vats—they had to go clean round the workshop to reach it—and were at the top of the slide with a rope which they let down.

In a moment the fellow was drawn to safety out of the reach of as horrible a death as a man can die—death in a bath consisting largely of sulfuric acid!

I stood as one in a stupor, still grasping the eccentric, dazed by the suddenness of it all—hardly able to believe that the danger was over.

A touch on my shoulder roused me, and I turned to look down into the narrow eyes of Lawrence. He was gazing at me with something very like awe in his expression.

"Well," I said, smiling shakily, "I'm afraid I've spoiled your engine."

"Spoiled the engine!" he said slowly, but emphatically. "What kind of a man are you, Mr. Dunbar? Do you know that that is a three-hundred horsepower Danbury stamp? That the force required to stop that wheel in the way you did would run a locomotive—pick up the whole mass of that engine itself as easily as I would a pound weight?"

"It stopped very easily," I muttered.

For some ridiculous reason I felt a little ashamed—as if such an exhibition of strength were really a trifle indecent. And I couldn't understand.

Of course, I thought, he exaggerated the power used, but though I am naturally quite strong, still I could, before my accident, boast of nothing abnormal—and was I not just up from a sick bed, only a moment ago barely able to stand or walk without support?

I found that I was nervously clenching and unclenching my hands, and became suddenly conscious that they felt as if they had been burned—the minute I began to think about it the pain became really excruciating.

I glanced at them. They were in a terrible condition—especially my right. They looked as if they had been clasped about a piece of red-hot iron.

"What is it?" asked Lawrence quickly. He bent over my hands, peering at them with his little black eyes.

Then he looked up quickly, and I saw the dawning of a curious expression in his wrinkled face—a strange excitement, a pale flash of triumph, I could have sworn.

Then, "Where is it?" he cried imperatively, his voice sharp and strenuous. "What have you done with it?"

He dropped my hands and fell quickly to his knees on the floor, his head bent, and began searching—feeling about in the shadows of the engines.

"Here—you there!" he cried to one of the men. "A light here! God! If it should be lost now—after all these years—all these years!"

"What?" said I stupidly.

"The new element," he cried impatiently. "Stellarite, I call it. Oh"—glancing up quickly—"of course you don't know. That little piece of metal I gave you to hold—the iridescent cylinder—don't you remember?"

He spoke irritably, as if it was almost impossible for him to restrain himself to civil language.

"Oh, yes—that." I looked around vaguely. "Why, yes, I had it in my hand—of course. I must have dropped it when I grabbed the fly-wheel. It's on the floor somewhere probably; but, if you don't mind, could I have something for my hands? They hurt pretty badly."

Indeed, the air was full of black, swimming dots before my eyes, and iridescent cylinders had very little interest for me just then.

He almost snapped at me.

"Wait! If it's lost—but it couldn't be! Ah, the light at last. Now we can see something."

Still he was hunting, and now the men were helping him. I looked on dully.

Then an unreasonable anger seized me at their neglect—their indifference to my very real agony. I leaned forward, and, in spite of the added pain the raw flesh of my hand gave me, I took hold of Lawrence's collar and started to shake him.

He felt curiously light—rather like a piece of cork, in fact. I picked him up from the ground as you would a kitten and held him at arm's length.

Then suddenly I realized that what I was doing was somewhat unusual, and let go of his collar. He lit on his feet like a cat.

I expected anger, but he only said impatiently, "Don't do that—help me hunt, can't you?" quite as if it were an ordinary incident.

The queerness of it all came over me in full force; I felt as if I were in a dream.

I stooped down and helped him search. But it was no use. The little cylinder of stellarite seemed to have disappeared.

Suddenly Lawrence rose to his feet, his face, whose multitudinous wrinkles had a moment before been twitching with mingled triumph and despair, wiped clean of emotion, like a blank slate from which all significance has been erased.

"Come, Mr. Dunbar," he said quietly, "it is quite time those hands of yours were seen to. You, Johnson, Duquirke, go on hunting. But I'm afraid it's no use, boys. That vat of acid is too near."

"You think—"

"I'm afraid it rolled in," he said.

I was silent, dimly conscious that I stood, as it were, just inside the ring of some great catastrophe whose influence, barely reaching me, had this little wrinkled man in the grip of its vortex.

I followed him to a small office, opening off the laboratory; fitted up much like a doctor's, it was, with its cabinet of shining instruments. He explained its convenience while he bound up my hands with all the skilled gentleness of an experienced surgeon.

"Accidents are always on view in such a place as mine out there," he observed, with a nod of his head toward the laboratory.

"I wish you'd tell me what I've done," I said at last when the thing was over.

I felt no weakness, nor any desire for rest, which was odd, seeing the excitement I had been through and my recent illness.

"Two things, then, to be brief," he replied, smiling rather sadly, I thought. "You've accidentally stumbled on a magnificent fact, and you've at the same time destroyed, I fear, all results that might have flowed from that fact."

I stared at him, puzzled.

"You lifted me just now like a feather," he said abruptly. "You think, possibly, that I don't weigh much—I'm not a giant. Duquirke," he called, "come here a minute, will you, please?"

Duquirke appeared, a very mountain of a man, all muscle, too. I am up to the six-foot mark myself, and fairly broad in the shoulders, but this fellow could better me by three good inches in any direction.

"You can't use your hands, of course," said Lawrence to me; "but just stoop down and stretch out your arm, will you? Now, Duquirke, just seat yourself on his arm. That's it. Oh, don't be afraid—he can hold you all right. Ah, I thought so!"

We had both obeyed him, I in some doubt, the Canadian with stolid indifference. But what was my amazement to find that this great big man weighed really comparatively nothing.

I rose, still with my arm outstretched, with perfect ease, and there the fellow sat, perched precariously, his mouth open, his eyes fixed on his master in almost a dog-like appeal.

"What are you all made of?" I gasped. "Cork?"

I let my arm drop, really expecting to see the man fall light as a feather—instead of which he tumbled with a crash that shook the house, and lay for a minute, swearing violently.

Then he got to his feet in a hurry and backed out of the door, his eyes on me to the last, his tongue, really unconsciously I believe, letting go a string of such language as would have done credit to a canal-boat driver.

"What is the matter with you all," I cried, "or"—my voice sank with the thought—"with me?"

"Sit down," said Lawrence. "Don't lose your head."

His eyes had widened, and the strange colors I had sometimes caught a glimpse of were blazing in their depths. His wrinkled face was almost beautiful in its animation—lighted as by a fire from within.

"There's nothing at all astonishing or miraculous about any of it—it's the simple working of a law. Now listen. When we heard La Due fall (the fool had tried to walk across a plank laid over that death trap to save going round the shop—he was well repaid by the fright), I handed you the cylinder of stellarite. I did not lay it on my worktable, because that is made of aluminum, and this cylinder must not come into contact with any other metal, for the simple reason that stellarite has such an affiliation for all other metals that for it to touch one of them means absorption into it. All its separate molecules interpenetrate, or assimilate, molecules, and—stellarite ceases to have its 'individual being.' So I gave it to you, because I wanted my hands free, and ran down to the vats with you at my heels. I confess I would never have been so careless if I had not allowed myself to become unduly excited by a mere matter of life and death."

He paused regretfully.

"However, to continue, you for some reason seized hold of the lever of a dynamo of very great voltage and started the armatage revolving, at the same time stepping on to the plate at its base. Now, in the ordinary course of things you would probably be at this moment lying on that couch over there—dead!"

I looked at the couch with sudden interest.

"But you are not."

I murmured that such was indeed the case.

"No—instead of that thunderbolt burning the life out of you, like that"—he snapped his fingers melodramatically—"it passed directly through your body into the cylinder of stellarite, which, completing the circuit, sent the current back through your chest, but possessed of a new quality."

"And that quality?"

"Ah, there you have me! What that quality was I fear it is now too late for the world ever to know. Well, you dropped the lever, and, I think, the cylinder, too, when I shouted. A moment after you seized the fly wheel of the stamp machine, stopped it as if it had been the balance of a watch—and, well incidentally you saved La Due's life."

He ceased, the light faded out of his wrinkled face, his eyes darkened and narrowed. His head sank forward on to his chest.

"But to think of it—years—years of effort thrown away just at the moment of conquest!"

"I don't understand," I said, seeming to catch little glimpses of his full meaning, as through a torn veil. "Do you intend to say—"

"I intend to say," he snapped, with a sudden return of irritability, "that in that minute when you held the stellarite and the lever of the dynamo you absorbed enough of the life principle to vivify a herd of elephants. Why, what is strength, man? Is a muscle strong in itself? Can a mere muscle lift so much as a pin? It's the life principle, I tell you—and I had it under my hand!"

"But this stellarite," I protested. "You can make more, surely?"

"Make!" he scoffed. "It's an element, I say! And it was, so far as I know, all there was in all the world!"

"Maybe it will be found yet," I argued. "Or—if it went into the acid vat, would it have been absorbed by the metal—or what?"

"No—at the touch of that bath it would evaporate into thin air—an odorless, colorless gas. I have but one hope—that it rolled against some of the iron machinery and was absorbed. In that case I may be able to place it by the increased bulk of the assimilating metal. Well, I can but go to work again, test every particle of machinery in the vicinity of the vats—and work—and work. If I had but known before that it was electricity and animal magnetism that were needed to complete the combination—but now, it means years of patience at best."

He shook his head dismally.

"And I?" I mused, rather to myself than to him.

"Oh—you!" he smiled, his face ran into that tempest of wrinkles. "You can pose as Samson, if you like! Your strength is really almost limitless!"

Can an unforgettable story be forgotten?

I read A Scientist Rises *in November 1932 and 65 years later have not forgotten it. I could not immediately tell you exactly what it is about—I have not had time to re-read it—but I get a good gut-feeling glow whenever I think about this tale from the long ago.*

It could be it's a stinker and that's why it's never been reprinted and justified critics will say, "If Ackerman had bothered to re-read this clinker before bringing it back into print he'd have quickly realized why no anthologist has ever exhumed it." But I did all right with the revival of Out Around Rigel—*in fact, Damon Knight discovered (or rediscovered) it too and reprinted it in a collection of golden goodies from the '30s—and I'm inclined to believe the truth lies rather in the fact that most miners of imaginative literature's past don't have my memories to cull from or the actual collector's items to consult.*

Harry Bates—who gave us the great Farewell to the Master *which in turn became the masterful scientifilm* The Day the Earth Stood Still—*was the original editor of* Astounding Stories *and DWHall, his collaborator on the story, his editorial assistant for about 9 months.*

P.S.: I just peeked at the ending to refresh my memory and I think the breath you'll draw at the conclusion of A Scientist Rises *will be . . . refreshing.*

A Scientist Rises

by *Harry Bates & Desmond Winter Hall*

ON THAT SUMMER DAY THE SKY OVER NEW YORK WAS UNFLECKED BY CLOUDS, AND the air hung motionless, the waves of heat undisturbed. The city was a vast oven where even the sounds of the coiling traffic in its streets seemed heavy and weary under the press of heat that poured down from above. In Washington Square, the urchins of the neighborhood splashed in the fountain, and the usual midday assortment of mothers, tramps and out-of-works lounged listlessly on the hot park benches.

As a bowl, the Square was filled by the torrid sun, and the trees and grass drooped like the people on its walks. In the surrounding city, men worked in sweltering offices and the streets rumbled with the never-ceasing tide of business—but Washington Square rested.

And then a man walked out of one of the houses lining the square, and all this was changed.

He came with a calm, steady stride down the steps of a house on the north side, and those who happened to see him gazed with surprised interest. For he was a giant in size. He measured at least eleven feet in height, and his body was well-formed and in perfect proportion. He crossed the street and stepped over the railing into the nearest patch of grass, and there stood with arms folded and legs a little apart. The expression on his face was preoccupied and strangely apart, nor did it change when, almost immediately from the park bench nearest him, a woman's excited voice cried:

"Look! Look! Oh, look!"

The people around her craned their necks and stared, and from them grew a startled murmur. Others from farther away came to see who had cried out, and remained to gaze fascinated at the man on the grass. Quickly the murmur spread across the Square, and from its every part men and women and children streamed toward the center of interest—and then, when they saw, backed away slowly and fearfully, with staring eyes, from where the lone figure stood.

There was about that figure something uncanny and terrible. There, in the hot midday hush, something was happening to it which men would say could not happen; and men, seeing it, backed away in alarm. Quickly they dispersed. Soon there were only white, frightened faces peering from behind buildings and trees.

Before their very eyes the giant was growing.

When he had first emerged, he had been around eleven feet tall, and now, within three minutes, he had risen close to sixteen feet.

His great body maintained its perfect proportions. It was that of an elderly man clad simply in a gray business suit. The face was kind, its clear-chiseled features indicating fine spiritual strength; on the white forehead beneath the sparse gray hair were deep-sunken lines which spoke of years of concentrated work.

No thought of malevolence could come from that head with its gentle blue eyes that showed the peace within, but fear struck ever stronger into those who watched him, and in one place a woman fainted; for the great body continued to grow, and grow ever faster, until it was twenty feet high, then swiftly twenty-five, and the feet, still separated, were as long as the body of a normal boy. Clothes and body grew effortlessly, the latter apparently without pain, as if the terrifying process were wholly natural.

The cars coming into Washington Square had stopped as their drivers sighted what was rising there, and by now the bordering streets were tangled with traffic. A distant crowd of milling people heightened the turmoil. The northern edge was deserted, but in a large semicircle was spread a fear-struck, panicky mob. A single policeman, his face white and his eyes wide, tried to straighten out the tangle of vehicles, but it was infinitely beyond him and he sent in a riot call; and as the giant with the kind, dignified face loomed silently higher than the trees in the Square, and ever higher, a dozen blue-coated figures appeared, and saw, and knew fear too, and hung back awe-stricken, at a loss what to do. For by now the rapidly mounting body had risen to the height of forty feet.

An excited voice raised itself above the general hubbub.

"Why, I know him! I know him! It's Edgar Wesley! Doctor Edgar Wesley!"

A police sergeant turned to the man who had spoken.

"And it—he knows you? Then go closer to him, and—and—ask him what it means."

But the man looked fearfully at the giant and hung back. Even as they talked, his gigantic body had grown as high as the four-storied buildings lining the Square, and his feet were becoming too large for the place where they had first been put. And now a faint smile could be seen on the giant's face, an enigmatic smile, with something ironic and bitter in it.

"Then shout to him from here," pressed the sergeant nervously. "We've got to find out something! This is crazy—impossible! My God! Higher yet—and faster!"

Summoning his courage, the other man cupped his hands about his mouth and shouted:

"Dr. Wesley! Can you speak and tell us? Can we help you stop it?"

The ring of people looked up breathless at the towering figure, and a wave of fear passed over them and several hysterical shrieks rose up as, very slowly, the huge head shook from side to side. But the smile on its lips became stronger, and kinder, and the bitterness seemed to leave it.

There was fear at that motion of the enormous head, but a roar of panic sounded from the watchers when, with marked caution, the growing giant moved one foot from the grass into the street behind and the other into the nearby base of Fifth Avenue, just above the Arch. Fearing harm, they were gripped by terror, and they fought back while the trembling policemen tried vainly to control them; but the panic soon ended when they saw that the leviathan's arms remained crossed and his smile kinder yet. By now he dwarfed the houses, his body looming a hundred and fifty feet into the sky. At this moment a woman back of the semicircle slumped to her knees and prayed hysterically.

"Someone's coming out of his house!" shouted one of the closest onlookers.

The door of the house from which the giant had first appeared had opened, and the figure of a middle-aged, normal-sized man emerged. For a second he crouched on the steps, gaping up at the monstrous shape in the sky, and then he scurried down and made at a desperate run for the nearest group of policemen.

He gripped the sergeant and cried frantically:

"That's Dr. Wesley! Why don't you do something? Why don't—"

"Who are you?" the officer asked, with some return of an authoritative manner.

"I work for him. I'm his janitor. But—can't you do anything? Look at him! Look!"

The crowd pressed closer. "What do you know about this?" went on the sergeant.

The man gulped and stared around wildly. "He's been working on something—many years—I don't know what, for he kept it a close secret. All I know is that an hour ago I was in my room upstairs, when I heard some disturbance in his laboratory, on the ground floor. I came down and knocked on the door, and he answered from inside and said that everything was all right—"

"You didn't go in?"

"No. I went back up, and everything was quiet for a long time. Then I heard a lot of noise down below—a smashing—as if things were being broken. But I thought he was just destroying something he didn't need, and I didn't investigate: he hated to be disturbed. And then, a little later, I heard them shouting out here in the Square, and I looked out and saw. I saw him—just as I knew him—but a giant! Look at his face! Why, he has the face of—of a god! He's—as if he were looking down on us—and—pitying us . . ."

For a moment all were silent as they gazed, transfixed, at the vast form that towered two hundred feet above them. Almost as awe-inspiring as the astounding growth was the fine, dignified calmness of the face. The sergeant broke in:

"The explanation of this must be in his laboratory. We've got to have a look. You lead us there."

The other man nodded; but just then the giant moved again, and they waited and watched.

With the utmost caution the titanic shape changed position. Gradually, one great foot, over thirty feet in length, soared up from the street and lowered farther away, and then the other distant foot changed its position; and the leviathan came gently to rest against the tallest building bordering the Square, and once more folded his arms and stood quiet. The enormous body appeared to waver slightly as a breath of wind washed against it; obviously it was not gaining weight as it grew. Almost, now, it appeared to float in the air. Swiftly it grew another twenty-five feet, and the gray expanse of its clothes shimmered strangely as a ripple ran over its colossal bulk.

A change of feeling came gradually over the watching multitude. The face of the giant was indeed that of a god in the noble, irony-tinged serenity of his calm features. It was as if a further world had opened, and one of divinity had stepped down; a further world of kindness and fellow-love, where there were none of the discords that bring conflicts and slaughterings to the weary people of Earth. Spiritual peace radiated from the enormous face under the silvery hair, peace with an undertone of sadness, as if the giant knew of the sorrows of the swarm of dwarfs beneath him, and pitied them.

From all the roofs and the towers of the city, for miles and miles around, men saw the mammoth shape and the kindly smile grow more and more tenuous against the clear blue sky. The figure remained quietly in the same position, his feet filling two empty streets, and under the spell of his smile all fear seemed to leave the nearer watchers, and they became more quiet and controlled.

The group of policemen and the janitor made a dash for the house from which the giant had come. They ascended the steps, went in, and found the door of the laboratory locked. They broke the door down. The sergeant looked in.

"Anyone in here?" he cried. Nothing disturbed the silence, and he entered, the others following.

A long, wide, dimly-lit room met their eyes, and in its middle the remains of a great mass of apparatus that had dominated it.

The apparatus was now completely destroyed. Its dozen rows of tubes were shattered, its intricate coils of wire and machinery hopelessly smashed. Fragments lay scattered all over the floor. No longer was there the least shape of meaning to anything in the room; there remained merely a litter of glass and stone and scrap metal.

Conspicuous on the floor was a large hammer. The sergeant walked over to pick it up, but, instead, paused and stared at what lay beyond it.

"A body!" he said.

A sprawled out dead man lay on the floor, his dark face twisted up, his sightless eyes staring at the ceiling, his temple crushed as with a hammer. Clutched tight in one stiff hand was an automatic. On his chest was a sheet of paper.

The captain reached down and grasped the paper. He read what was written on it, and then read it to the others:

There was a fool who dreamed the high dream of the pure scientist, and who lived only to ferret out the secrets of nature, and harness them for his fellow men. He studied and worked and thought, and in time came to concentrate on the manipulation of the atom, especially the possibility of contracting and expanding it—a thing of greatest potential value. For nine years he worked along this line, hoping to succeed and give new power, new happiness, a new horizon to mankind. Hermetically sealed in his laboratory, self-exiled from human contacts, he labored hard.

There came a day when the device into which the fool had poured his life stood completed and a success. And on that very day an agent for a certain government entered his laboratory to steal the device. And in that moment the fool realized what he had done: that, from the apparatus he had invented, not happiness and new freedom would come to his fellow men, but instead slaughter and carnage and drunken power increased a hundredfold. He realized, suddenly, that men had not yet learned to use fruitfully the precious, powerful things given to them, but as yet could only play with them like greedy children—and kill as they played. Already his invention had brought death. And he realized—even on this day of his triumph—that it and its secret must be destroyed, and with them he who had fashioned so blindly.

For the scientist was old, his whole life was the invention, and with its going there would be nothing more.

And so he used the device's great powers on his own body; and then, with those powers working on him, he destroyed the device and all the papers that held its secrets.

Was the fool also mad? Perhaps. But I do not think so. Into his lonely laboratory, with this marauder, had come the wisdom that men must wait, that the time is not yet for such power as he was about to offer. A gesture, his strange death, which you who read this have seen? Yes, but a useful one, for with it he and his invention and its hurtful secrets go from you; and a fitting one, for he dies through his achievement, through his very life.

But, in a better sense, he will not die, for the power of his achievement will dissolve his very body among you infinitely; you will breathe him in your air; and in you he will live incarnate until that later time when another will give you the knowledge he now destroys, and he will see it used as he wished it used. —E.W.

The sergeant's voice ceased, and wordlessly the men in the laboratory looked at each other. No comment was needed. They went out.

They watched from the steps of Edgar Wesley's house. At first sight of the figure in the sky, a new awe struck them, for now the shape of the giant towered a full five hundred feet into the sun, and it seemed almost a mirage, for definite outline was gone from it. It shimmered and wavered against the bright blue like a mist, and the blue shone through it, for it was quite transparent. And yet still they imagined they could discern the slight ironic smile on the face, and the peaceful, understanding light in the serene eyes; and their hearts swelled at the knowledge of the spirit, of the courage, of the fine, far-seeing mind that outflung titanic martyr to the happiness of men.

The end came quickly. The great misty body rose; it floated over the city like a wraith, and then it swiftly dispersed, even as steam dissolves in the air. They felt a silence over the thousands of watching people in the Square, a hush broken at last by a deep, low murmur of awe and wonderment as the final misty fragments of the vast sky-held figure wavered and melted imperceptibly—melted and were gone from sight in the air that was breathed by the men whom Edgar Wesley loved.

EXTRAPOLATION EXTRAORDINARY

A planet of xenohoms produces a strange—

Homecoming

by J. Harvey Haggard

(Author of *Task of Tau* & *Girl of the Silver-Sphere*)

THE SPACESHIP LANDED AND CEASED TO THROB AND PULSE, ITS STERN LIGHTS blinking off. After a moment a man emerged and walked to the pier edge of the landing island. Martin Leek was small, slender and shyly wistful of aspect. Yet his retiring look concealed a grim fortitude that refused to compromise with the more outrageous aspects of life.

"Welcome, traveler. Lots of profit this trip?" called Eugene, extending his saurian head aloft. He lolled on a mudbank but he had plainly been watching the passengers debark. "Welcome home."

"Hello," said Martin. He squinted against the wind—chill, malodorous it was. He pulled his thin cloak away from him as he clutched his flat traveling bag. He answered the other's greeting, one thought at a time. "Not too much. Thanks. Glad to be back."

Behind him aerocabs came and went like insects, taking passengers across the swampglades to Loda City. A monotube shot its glassy, bulletlike cab shoreward with a *swoosh.* Those inside, he observed with a shiver, looked warm and cozy. Buttoning the top button of his wind-lifted coat, Martin turned his back on the tube and twisted his thin lips into a smile directed at Eugene.

"Would you like a ride to town?" asked Eugene. Martin grinned and nodded.

"Grab a hump," said Eugene. He reared from the mudbank obligingly. Martin straddled the upper ridge of armor plates, holding his bag close. Several new-arrivals from other worlds squinted against the savage wind, gaping with disbelief. "All comfy?" Eugene asked. "All set to take the jolts?"

Seeing his passenger was, Eugene took off. His departure became spectacular but not ungainly. Relaxing his height, he submerged halfway and began paddling swiftly across the thick fluid. His flappers made sucking noises and left on the smooth waters of the swamp-glade a wake of widening ripples. Vegetable growths made islets here and there and now some moved of their own accord, drawing away from the swimming behemoth. The keen wind, fruity with unpleasant aromas, blew spray patterns of scud. The sky above had been poisoned a slight orchid.

Martin braced his legs and squeezed his knobby knees together. He could hardly keep from shivering with cold or prevent his teeth from chattering but he could at least protect the traveling kit.

Martin hadn't fathomed all of the strangeness of Yulil when he'd brought his new wife, Rugie, to the planet 20 years before. They'd been sustained by dreams, gossamer break-easy dreams, bubbles that held a teeming universe. He had promised to lay a cosmos at her feet, a planet at a time— and Yulil had been first on his list.

Yulil. Geneless world. Amidst pleasures and palaces . . . be it ever so humble . . . there's no place like . . .

A world of polymorphs, say. Poly, for many. Morphs, for shapes. Many shapes. No 2 alike. An interesting planet, when first you heard of it. No one had clearly understood at first. Then the scientists had detected that an inner radiation bombarded the living issues of all life on Yulil.

Everything on Yulil was different. Each living creature from the other, all different in turn. Tentacular . . . insectivorian . . . these were but words to denote biological kinship or dissimilarity, but here there could be no such thing as similarity. No such thing even as a separate species. Just substance knowing but one natural law, to evolve into something unlike anything that had ever existed before. Unlike produced the unthinkable. However, for all of that, there was a lot of *gneissilite* on Yulil. You could make rocket fuel out of that.

"How's everything on the other planets?" asked Eugene, forever inquisitive. He'd never been off of Yulil.

"Humdrum."

"The War in Vegas?"

"Invaders from the Seven Sisters have the edge but it's touch and go."

"Wup! Hold it!" Movement surged and an amorphous mass arose in front of Eugene. It had none of his saurian sleekness. It was as primal as something swimming in stagnant water under a microscope. Everything hinted at a weak mental structure, largely intuitive. It threatened attack.

"Scrambola!" yelled Eugene. He slashed out viciously, exposing a terrific mouthful of teeth.

The primordial thing squirmed away.

"Of life," quipped Eugene, "that's a most terrible parable." Then he brayed at his own humor.

Martin joined in, chuckling as much from relief as anything else. His thoughts slipped back to those of a moment before.

Home and Rugie! She wasn't a princess by Earthly standards, of course. But then, Martin Leek always enjoyed the traditional thrill of homecoming. He experienced a quickening of his pulses, a heightening of his perceptive faculties as the shore neared.

Eugene swam against a heavy out-going tide, then found solid footing and waded ashore. Martin Leek slid off. He balanced for a moment on a walkway, then turned to Eugene.

Compromise . . . he thought. Adaption to circumstance. Who could have foreseen the problem that would confront all Earth dwellers who came to Yulil? Even from the moment of conception, from the fetus onward, the genes and chromosomes that determine heredity characteristics were destroyed or distorted by a radiation from the world's core.

"Thanks for the lift," said Martin Leek gratefully.

"Any time," said Eugene.

"You'll be up at the house later, won't you?"

"Sure. Tell Mother I want to watch the Arcturian Express make a landing. Then I'll be up in plenty of time for dinner."

Martin Leek turned toward the city. His bent shoulders drew more erect and he walked quickly as he stepped forward, humming a tune. He was home.

Eugene taxied around toward the landing island, churning the water to a foaming wake. He turned once, still in hailing distance.

"So long, Dad," he called.

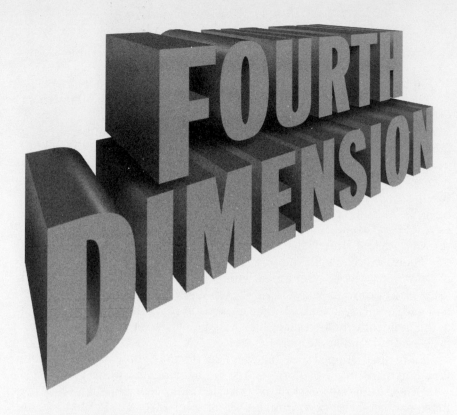

FOURTH DIMENSION

Wrest from forbidden limbo, if you dare, the secret of the fourth dimension. But remember, in the hour of your triumph—he who makes real the impossible, may fall heir to impossible vengeance!

The Impossible Invention

by Robert Moore Williams

I HAD TO ADMIRE THIS LITTLE GUY'S COURAGE. FRADIN, HIS NAME WAS—JAMES Arthur Fradin, with a string of letters after it that even the alphabet agencies down at Washington could not have unscrambled. The letters represented honorary degrees conferred on him by half a dozen different colleges, and they should have entitled him to be heard with respectful consideration, but they weren't. The assembled scientists of the Institute of Radio Engineers were giving him merry hell.

"What you are saying, Fradin," one of the scientists interrupted hotly, "is gross nonsense."

"It is absolutely impossible," another shouted.

"Faker!" somebody yelled, and a dozen voices took it up until the room echoed with the sound.

I sat back and grinned to myself. If this meeting ended in a free-for-all fight, which was what looked like was due to happen, I would be able to make a swell human interest humorous yarn out of it. My editor went for human interest stuff, which was largely why he had sent me down to cover this meeting. He knew I wasn't likely to develop any front page news here, scientific meetings being what they are. But there might be a human interest angle that would be good for a laugh. And the way these solemn scientists were calling Fradin a liar, it looked like the laugh was coming.

There was one man who wasn't doing any name calling, I noticed, a tall, cadaverous-looking individual sitting two seats down from me. He had listened very carefully, almost eagerly, I thought, to everything the speaker had said. Glancing at him, I got the impression that I should know him, but at the moment I couldn't place him. Tall, bony face, thin, hawk nose—yes, it seemed I should know him.

Fradin had stopped speaking when the storm of abuse broke over him. He stood there on the platform, a little, white-haired guy with a gentle face.

"If you numskulls will only be quiet for a moment," he said, when the noise had subsided for an instant, "I will offer incontrovertible proof to support my statement that radio waves are transmitted through what I must, for lack of a better term to describe the undescribable, call the fourth dimension."

What I mean, the roof must have been nailed down tight, or the explosion that followed would certainly have lifted it off the building. You never did see so many excited scientists in one group. Normally a scientist is supposed to be cool, aloof, and impersonal. But this group was anything else! They went right straight up in the air. I couldn't tell whether they were angrier because he had called them a bunch of numskulls or because he had said that radio waves were transmitted through the fourth dimension.

One of them leaped to his feet. Ramsen, I think his name was. He was a big shot in the field, almost as big as De Forest and Marconi.

"Fradin," he yelled, "that is the most preposterous statement I ever heard from the lips of any man in his right senses. It raises the immediate question of whether or not *you* are in your right senses."

There was a buzz of approval following his statement. Fradin waited for it to die down.

"Mr. Ramsen," he said, "you have chosen to challenge my theory. Perhaps you can tell me what medium *does* carry the electro-magnetic radiations that we call radio waves?"

"Certainly," Ramsen answered. "Any schoolboy knows that."

"We are not here concerned with the knowledge of schoolboys," Fradin gently replied. "Sound is carried in air and water and by many solid substances. But we know that radio waves do not travel in air, because they will pass through a perfect vacuum. In what medium do they travel, Mr. Ramsen?"

Right here was where I began to pay close attention. Something about Fradin's manner, his calmness, his certainty, gave me the impression that he knew pretty much what he was talking about.

"Radio waves, Mr. Fradin," Ramsen answered, in the manner of a scoutmaster revealing the facts of life to an errant Boy Scout, "travel in the ether."

He was right. I was not assigned to cover this meeting by chance but because I happen to have a pretty good groundwork in science. Radio waves, all scientists admit, are propagated through the ether.

"And what," Fradin countered, "is the ether?"

"Why—" Ramsen answered. "It's—" He started to flounder. A sudden silence fell in the room. Ramsen's face started to get red. "The ether," he finished, "is—why it's the ether, that's what it is."

"What you are refusing to admit," Fradin crowed, "is that 'ether' is a meaningless word invented by numskulls such as are gathered here to describe something about which they know absolutely nothing. The ether is a word, nothing more. It does not exist. The Michelson-Morley experiments conclusively proved that, if it existed, its nature was such that it could not be detected by any physical experiment whatsoever. In other words, that it exists only as a handy tool by which scientists who ought to know better can conceal their own ignorance. Gentlemen," he said, turning from the red-faced Ramsen to the perturbed audience, "I can not only conclusively prove that radio waves are transmitted through the fourth dimension—but I can also prove that power, actual power, can also be transmitted through the same medium!"

He stopped suddenly, biting his lips as if he had said more than he had intended to. But I think only one man in the audience had caught the full implication of Fradin's words. The rest of them were too busy defending themselves against the accusation of being numskulls to notice the one really important thing he had said.

How that audience did boil! And they boiled because every man jack of them, in his heart of hearts, knew that Fradin was right. I knew it the minute he said it. And they knew it too. When he said that "ether" was only a word used by fools to conceal their own ignorance, he had hit the nail exactly on the head.

For that is precisely what it is. Nobody has ever seen the ether, felt it, smelled it, heard it, touched it. Scientists of the past century, needing a mechanical device to account for the observed propagation of electromagnetic radiations such as light and the then little known radio waves, had invented the ether to carry those radiations, invented it out of whole cloth. Fradin's hearers knew he was right. Taken individually, when they were calm, they would have admitted it. But they were in a group and he was calling them fools right out in public. Mass hysteria got them. They boiled over and very promptly demanded that he prove his statements.

He refused to do it. Absolutely refused.

"We demand that you produce your proof," Ramsen howled. "You have called us fools and said you could prove it. We demand that you *do* prove it."

"I—" Fradin began. He wet his lips. His face had whitened. It wasn't a gently, kindly face any more. It was the face of a badly scared man.

Fradin was scared. But he wasn't scared of those engineers who were shouting at him. He was scared of something else.

"Speak up," Ramsen roared. "Produce your proof!"

"I can show you mathematical proof," Fradin offered.

How they howled at that, all except the tall, thin, hawk-nosed individual sitting two seats down from me. He took no part in the demonstration. Instead he got up and very quietly went out of the room.

As he walked out, I again got the impression that I ought to know him. But I still couldn't place him. A reporter sees too many people to remember all of them.

"Mathematical proof, unless supported by incontrovertible experimental evidence, is not sufficient," Ramsen thundered. "We demand that you produce experimental proof."

By experimental proof, he means an actual instrument of some kind to demonstrate Fradin's claims—some gadget that they could see and feel and examine, something they could take apart and put back together again, something that they could watch in operation. Ramsen was quite right in making such a demand, for without experimental evidence to back it up, mathematical theory is more often than not just so much hot air.

"Your demand is just," Fradin faltered. "I fear in the heat of argument I made statements I do not care to support. I do not choose to produce the experimental evidence that I have."

He didn't say another word. Instead, he turned and walked off the platform, going out through a door at the back. Nor did he enter the lecture hall where the meeting was being held. He walked out of the room.

And he didn't come back.

Why had he refused to produce the evidence that he had? What had scared him?

Questions were buzzing like gadflies in my mind. There was one particularly persistent gadfly. Fradin had said something of which I had almost caught the significance. Almost, but not quite. The significant thing he had said kept buzzing in the back of my mind, but I couldn't quite put a mental finger on it . . .

Then I remembered it.

I went out of that room at a dead run. I went up over the speaker's platform and through the door Fradin had taken. How I did want to talk to that tortured man!

What he had said, letting it slip accidentally, added up to one of the biggest stories that ever splashed across the front page of a newspaper. I had come down here looking for a human interest yarn. Instead I had run straight into a story that could easily set the world on fire, *if* I could find Fradin and make him talk.

I didn't doubt that I would find him. He couldn't have gotten far away. He hadn't had time. Not five minutes had passed after he had walked off the platform until I was following him.

The door opened into a long hall, and in that hall I found Fradin. He was down at the far end, getting into an elevator. A tall, thin individual was with him.

I sprinted down the hall to try to catch them before the elevator doors closed. The operator saw me coming and started to wait for me, but something changed his mind for him. The two men were already in the cage; I couldn't be positive of it, but I thought the tall man said something to the operator. Just as I got there, the operator slammed the door in my face. The cage started down.

"All right, smart guy," I yelled at the operator. "I'll give you a smack in the snoot for this."

Probably I could have gotten down faster by waiting for another elevator, but there was a stairway and I used that. I was in a hurry.

I got to the first floor just in time to see Fradin and his companion walk out the front door.

"Hey!" I yelled. "Wait—"

I started to say, "Wait for me," but the words were choked off in my throat. I recognized Fradin's companion. The hawk-faced man who had sat two seats down from me and who had slipped unobtrusively out of the meeting. He had gone around to the back of the hall and joined Fradin.

But the fact that he was with Fradin wasn't the thing that had choked off my call. It was the way the two men were walking. Fradin was a little ahead, and he wasn't looking to the right or the left. Just walking. There was a stiffness about him that made me think of a mechanical toy that has been wound up and is taking a walk for itself.

Hawk-face was following right behind him. Hawk-face had his hand in his pocket. I didn't need to look twice to know that he had a gun in that pocket too, pointing straight at the little inventor's back.

It wasn't a stick-up. It was a kidnap job. Hawk-face had also heard the really important thing that Fradin had said in his speech. I had missed it for a few minutes, but he hadn't missed it. He had instantly realized how damned important it was. He had walked out of the meeting, gone around to the back, waited for the scientist.

I should have called the police. But just then something happened that upset me so badly I completely forgot all about police.

I recognized Hawk-face, and cold chills began to run up and down my spine.

His name—or at least the name attached to the picture I had once seen in the hands of an F.B.I. man—was Marvak. The name didn't mean anything. He had others. A name to use in Asia, one for Russia, one for Europe, all different.

Marvak was one of the names he used in America, but the F.B.I. suspected he had others. They would cheerfully have hung him by any of his names, if they could have caught him, but he didn't catch easily. Compared to him, an eel was a rank amateur in slipperiness, and a rattlesnake was man's best friend.

Right out in front of the building, on a crowded city street, he forced Fradin into a cab. I was so close I could see the haunted, terrified expression on the little scientist's face. But I didn't think then and I know now that he wasn't afraid of the gun. He was afraid of something even more horrible than Marvak.

The cab pulled away.

An eternity seemed to pass before I could collect my faculties and grab the next cab in line.

"Follow that cab," I hissed at the hacker. "There's a ten-spot in it for you if you don't lose it."

He didn't lose it. We followed Fradin and Marvak down to an old, abandoned factory building on the outskirts of the city. They were getting out of their cab when we drove up. Marvak, with his right hand still in his coat pocket, was paying off the driver.

"Drive on past," I told my driver.

He went on past and around the block and I got out, but the driver had to remind me about the ten-spot I had promised him. I paid off like a slot machine.

That shows how excited I was. I had stopped thinking about the story I might get. The story was secondary now. What really mattered was that Fradin had to be rescued, and fast. The thing he had let slip was too big to fall into Marvak's hands under any circumstances. And I had to be the one who rescued him. There wasn't time to go for the police. Marvak would work fast.

Marvak did work fast.

I tried the front door first because that was the obvious thing to do. If I got caught coming in the front door I could say I had the wrong address and back out. But if I got caught at the back door, no amount of explanation would do me any good.

The front door was unlocked. It opened into what had once been an office. A flight of stairs led up to the second floor.

I listened—there wasn't a sound. "They went upstairs," I thought.

"Hold it, bud," a voice said behind me.

The voice had a chilled steel ring that sent my heart right down into my shoes. There was no mercy in it, no compassion, no pity. It was double-edged with the threat of death. It jerked my head around.

Marvak was standing there in the office. He had the gun out of his pocket now, pointing it straight at me.

There was a closet in the office. Marvak had simply waited in the closet until I entered. When I started up the stairs, he had stepped out behind me.

"I—I must have got the wrong ad—address," I faltered.

His eyes, gray chilled steel, they were, drilled into me.

"No doubt," he said—but very doubtfully. "You're the reporter I noticed at the meeting, aren't you? What are you doing here?"

How big a lie could I tell and still be safe? How close to the truth could I come and not get one of those slugs between my eyes?

"I came out to interview Mr. Fradin," I blurted out.

He seemed to let it go, but back of those cold gray eyes I could see his mind working as he decided what to do with me. Then I saw him reach a decision.

First, he searched me. I didn't have a gun, which seemed to surprise him.

"You can come along," he said. "If Fradin can demonstrate to my satisfaction the discovery he claimed to have made, it will make the headlines, *if* you get a chance to write it."

With that, he dug the little inventor out of the closet, and with the gun out, prodded both of us upstairs. There were only two floors to this building and the entire second floor was Fradin's laboratory.

It was crammed to the ceiling with the weirdest collection of electrical equipment I have ever seen. Generators, dynamos, electric motors. There was enough radio equipment to set up a modest broadcasting station. And in one corner was something big enough to be a cyclotron. Fradin had just about everything in his laboratory.

"Now," said Marvak to the little inventor, "you will please prove the truth of your assertion that power can be transmitted by radio."

That was the thing that Fradin had said. Power by radio! It doesn't sound like much, but let me tell you, it's plenty big. With it, science could come darned close to remaking the face of the globe.

How?

This is the power age. Practically all of our industrial achievements—and through them we have achieved what passes for civilization—have come about through cheap power. Coal, the steam engine, the dynamo, water power. Maybe, not so long in the future, we'll have atomic power, but we don't have it yet. All we have now are coal and water. And possibly 90% of the water power in this country and probably 95% of the water power on earth are going to waste, simply because the waterfalls are usually in mountains and the places where the current is to be used are in cities hundreds and even thousands of miles away. *Transmission losses over high lines are so great that electrical energy cannot be efficiently transmitted very far.* So the water power goes to waste.

But here we have radio-transmitted power. No high lines, hence no high line losses. Of course there would be other losses, but if Fradin said power could be transmitted by radio, he would know how to cure the losses. Radio-transmitted power would make electricity so damned cheap that every home in the country could have it.

And this is only part of the picture that Fradin's invention brought into being. Supposing power could be transmitted by radio. Suppose automobiles could pick it up and use it. Then the extremely expensive internal combustion engine that goes into every car could be replaced by cheap motors. The price of cars could be cut in half. Everybody could have one. And operation costs would be next to nothing.

Ocean liners? No more bulky, costly steam engines. Boats could take their power out of the air.

And airplanes. There was the most important item of all. No gasoline engines in planes, no engine failures, no crashes because the motor conked out. Air flight spanning the globe.

That's what radio-transmitted power ought to mean, that's what it would mean—until Marvak entered the picture. When he appeared on the scene, power by radio, instead of being a blessing, would become one of the worst disasters that ever happened to humanity.

Marvak was a spy. Not a common, garden variety of spy, not a fifth columnist, not a saboteur, but a sort of super-spy who sold his services to the highest bidder. If you wanted a war started, he could make all the arrangements to provide for an "incident." If you wanted to take over a minor nation, he could pave the way for you; if your enemy had a new and secret weapon, he could get the plans. Anything, just so he was well paid for it.

If Fradin could really transmit power by radio, and if Marvak got the plans, the waterfalls would not be harnessed, there wouldn't be cheap automobiles, and handy power for ocean liners. There would be power—unfailing power—for one thing: planes! Bombing planes, fighting planes!

If you think several nations on this globe would not jump at the chance to acquire such an invention, you have another think coming. And the price they would be willing to pay for it, would be big enough to interest even Marvak. It would be worth—well, what is the worth of the British Empire, China, and the United States?

Fradin's invention had exactly the same value as those three nations lumped together, if Marvak succeeded in peddling it in Europe. Bombers over New York, bombers over Chicago. There would no longer be any safety in three thousand miles of water. Bombers over London. New bombers that would be almost invincible.

Sweat was running down over my face, down over my body, down over my soul. If Marvak got Fradin's invention, Johnny Holmes—that's me—go hunt for an air-raid shelter, because you're sure going to need it.

"I was mistaken," Fradin faltered, his voice a whisper. "I was—boasting. I cannot transmit power by radio."

"You're a liar!" Marvak snapped.

"I'm not a liar," Fradin whispered.

"Either or else," Marvak said, bringing up his gun until it pointed right at the little inventor's forehead.

Fradin had something that a man could call courage. He looked that gun in the eye. His face went a shade whiter, but his eyes did not drop.

"I'm afraid it will have to be else," he said. As he spoke the words, he seemed to stiffen himself until he stood very straight. He looked like a soldier standing at attention. "But if you shoot me you may find it difficult to operate my invention."

Marvak's finger tightened around the trigger. His face was cold with rage, his gray, killer eyes looked like icicles.

"Don't shoot him, you fool!" I hissed. "Then you'll never find out what you want to know."

I was stalling for time, stalling for anything, stalling for a chance to jump that gun. I was standing beside Fradin, but the gun covered both of us.

"Shut up!" Marvak snarled at me.

The gun went off.

He had shot Fradin. It was cold-blooded murder. But as he had shot the little scientist, he had taken his eyes off me. I started to jump. The gun instantly swung to cover me. I saw Marvak's face, with no mercy in it. The gun froze me motionless.

Fradin didn't fall. There was a look of surprise on his face, but he didn't fall. Then I saw what had happened. Marvak had shot him in the shoulder instead of through his head.

"That's just a sample," Marvak said, "to show you that I mean business. You're not badly hurt, but the next one will go through your kneecap. I understand that a bullet through the knee is very painful. Now are you going to tell me what I want to know or are you going to need further persuasion?"

Blood was running down Fradin's coat. He was clutching his shoulder with the other hand, trying to stop the flow of blood. His face was very white. And now there was fear on it, fear that had not been there when he first faced Marvak's gun. I got the fleeting impression that it was not fear of the spy nor of the weapon, but of something else. I also got the impression that it was a terrible fear, a soul-consuming fear, a bleaching, whitening, shuddering fear, a fear greater even than the fear of death . . .

"All right," the little inventor whispered. "You win. I'll show you what you want."

"That's better," Marvak said, in a satisfied tone. "I don't mind saying that if I make a cleaning on this, I'm quite willing to cut you and the reporter in on it."

He was lying. The only way he would cut us in would be to cut our throats. Both Fradin and I knew it.

"I'm afraid," the inventor said, "that your shot has injured my arm so badly that I will have to ask you to help me."

"Okay," Marvak said. "But remember I have an excellent knowledge of electrical apparatus, so don't try any tricks, like electrocuting me by accident."

"There won't be any trickery involved here," the little inventor whispered through bloodless lips.

I watched. There were two bulky instruments, one of them a transmitter, the other a receiver. The current flow was seemingly directional. It was sent out from the transmitter and caught by the receiver. There was a meter on the transmitter to show how much current was being transmitted and another on the receiver to show how much was getting through.

There was a red line on the dial of the meter at the transmitter.

The purpose of the set-up was obviously to demonstrate that current could be transmitted by radio.

Marvak made a complete examination of the apparatus. He knew what he was doing, all right. You could tell from the way he went over the instruments that he knew his stuff.

"I'm not interested in transmitting just a little power," Marvak said. "If this thing is to be useful, it must be able to send lots of kilowatts through the ether."

"I think," Fradin answered wearily, "it will handle all the power you choose to put into it."

That was the thing Marvak had to know, that the power transmitted would be adequate to keep a plane in the air. If only a little power was transmitted, the invention, from a practical viewpoint, was useless. No dictator would give a cent for it.

Marvak handled the transmitter, Fradin tried to operate the receiver and to stanch the flow of blood from his shoulder at the same time.

Marvak turned a switch, and the power transmitter began to throb under the load. Marvak consulted the meter on the transmitter, then ran across the room to the receiver and examined the meter there.

"You've really got it!" he exulted. "There's enough power flowing through the receiver to keep a plane in the air."

I was sick, sicker than I had ever been. Fradin's invention worked. And when it worked, it spelled our doom. We would be killed, because it worked. How many millions of others would also die, I could not begin to guess.

"One plane is not enough," Marvak said. "It has to be strong enough to supply current to a fleet of planes."

He started triumphantly back to the transmitter.

"I—" Fradin faltered. He started to say something but changed his mind abruptly.

Marvak kicked over the handle of the rheostat that fed current into the transmitter. The transformer groaned. I could see the hand of the meter on the transmitter. It was moving forward as more and more current flowed into that mysterious medium that transmits radio waves.

The needle on the dial touched the red mark.

Then—it happened.

If I live to be a thousand years old I'll never be able to describe adequately what I saw happen, what I heard happen, what I felt happen. It had never happened before.

Something that I can only describe as a lightning flash ran through the room. It was a sharp, tearing crash, similar to the sound you hear when a bolt of lightning hits near you. There was a flash of brilliant light. Thunder seemed to smash my ear drums.

Fradin leaped—but not at Marvak. He leaped at me. The next instant he was grabbing me, shoving me across the room. And all the tortures of hell were breaking loose around that generator.

There was a blasting, howling roar of wind. It was the coldest wind ever. It was, I suspect, the cold of absolute zero that struck through that laboratory.

Out of nowhere, around that transmitter, a hole seemed to appear. It seemed to be torn in space. It was black, with a curiously liquid kind of blackness. It appeared around the transmitter, and Marvak was at the transmitter.

The spy seemed to freeze. A look of amazed fright appeared on his face.

Then he seemed to fall. The transmitter seemed to fall with him. Marvak tried to leap, but the footing seemed to fall away under him. He fell out of sight.

For a mad instant, while Fradin kicked and hauled me away from that transmitter, the laboratory was hideous with the blast of thunder.

Then another murderous crash came, and . . .

Then there was silence. Utter silence. The only sound was Fradin fighting for his breath. I looked across the room. The transmitter was gone. It just wasn't there any more. Under it, in the floor of the room was a neat, round hole. All the mass of wire that had led into it were neatly severed. Wire came from the transformer to where the hole began, then stopped.

Marvak wasn't there. Marvak was gone.

Suddenly I turned to Fradin. "You—" I gulped. "You were afraid this would happen. My God, man, what was it?"

"It was," he answered, "a hole in the fourth dimension."

Then I got it. He had been trying to tell that convention of radio engineers that radio waves were transmitted through the fourth dimension, not through the "ether." He had been able to prove his point but he had refused because he knew that this would happen.

"But even if radio waves do pass through the fourth dimension, nothing like this has ever happened," I stammered.

"Ordinarily broadcasting stations do not put enough power through their transmitters to open this hole," he explained. "It takes power to do it, lots of power. I had calculated how much power it would take. There was a red mark on the input meter of the transmitter. That red line marked the critical point. If more power was put through the transmitter, it would break down the fabric of space between this dimension and the fourth dimension. I knew it would happen. That's why I refused to make a demonstration for the benefit of my skeptical compatriots. If I told them what I had discovered, proved I had discovered it, some fool would be sure to try it, with disastrous results."

"But that cold wind," I protested.

"This particular region opens out into what must be interplanetary space in the fourth dimension. That cold wind was simply the cold of outer space rushing through what was in effect a window."

So that was it. There was a hole in space. And space is cold.

"Marvak!" I said weakly.

"Don't mention him," Fradin shuddered. "He was catapulted into the fourth dimension. He's frozen solid by now."

I guess the human race will never have power by radio. Probably we will be able to get along without it. Atomic power seems to be coming along, and it's safe.

I took Fradin to the hospital. That slug through his shoulder had cost him a lot of blood, but he recovered all right, only to discover that the Institute of Radio Engineers had booted him right out of their organization, for making the preposterous claim that radio waves are transmitted through the fourth dimension instead of through the ether. However, he never cared two whoops in hell about that. He knew what he knew. And he was content with that.

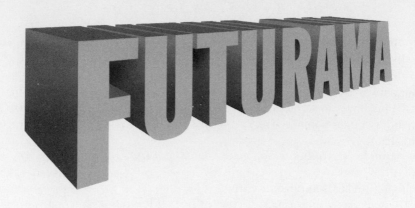

A thoroughly vintage scientale by the "Chromium Age Thoreau." Mona Lisa Shall Not Die! as long as RAY BRADBURY is around to protect—

The Smile

by Ray Bradbury

IN THE TOWN SQUARE THE QUEUE HAD FORMED AT FIVE IN THE MORNING, WHILE cocks were crowing far out in the rimed country and there were no fires. All about, among the ruined buildings, bits of mist had clung at first, but now with the new light of seven o'clock it was beginning to disperse. Down the road, in twos and threes, more people were gathering in for the day of marketing, the day of festival.

The small boy stood immediately behind two men who had been talking loudly in the clear air, and all the sounds they made seemed twice as loud because of the cold. The small boy stomped his feet and blew on his red, chapped hands, and looked up at the soiled gunnysack clothing of the men, and down the long line of men and women ahead.

"Here, boy, what're you doing out so early?" said the man behind him.

"Got my place in line, I have," said the boy.

"Whyn't you run off, give your place to someone who appreciates?"

"Leave the boy alone," said the man ahead, suddenly turning.

"I was joking." The man behind put his hand on the boy's head. The boy shook it away coldly. "I just thought it strange, a boy out of bed so early."

"This boy's an appreciator of arts, I'll have you know," said the boy's defender, a man named Grigsby. "What's your name, lad?"

"Tom."

"Tom here is going to spit clean and true, right, Tom?"

"I sure am!"

Laughter passed down the line.

A man was selling cracked cups of hot coffee up ahead. Tom looked and saw the little hot fire and the brew bubbling in a rusty pan. It wasn't really coffee. It was made from some berry that grew on the meadowlands beyond town, and it sold a penny a cup to warm their stomachs; but not many were buying, not many had the wealth.

Tom stared ahead to the place where the line ended, beyond a bombed-out stone wall.

"They say she *smiles*," said the boy.

"Aye, she does," said Grigsby.

"They say she's made of oil and canvas, and she's four centuries old."

"Maybe more. Nobody knows what year this is, to be sure."

"It's 2251!"

"That's what *they* say. Liars. Could be 3000 or 5000 for all we know, things were in a fearful mess there for awhile. All we got now is bits and pieces."

They shuffled along the cold stones of the street.

"How much longer before we see her?" asked Tom, uneasily.

"Oh, a few minutes, boy. They got her set up with four brass poles and velvet rope, all fancy, to keep people back. Now mind, no rocks, Tom, they don't allow rocks thrown at her."

"Yes, sir."

They shuffled on in the early morning which grew late, and the sun rose into the heavens bringing heat with it which made the men shed their grimy coats and greasy hats.

"Why're we all here in line?" asked Tom at last. "Why're we all here to spit?"

Grigsby did not glance down at him, but judged the sun. "Well, Tom, there's lots of reasons." He reached absently for a pocket that was long gone, for a cigarette that wasn't there. Tom had seen the gesture a million times. "Tom, it has to do with hate. Hate for everything in the Past. I ask you, Tom, how did we get in such a state, cities all junk, roads like jigsaws from bombs, and half the cornfields glowing with radioactivity at night? Ain't that a lousy stew, I ask you?"

"Yes, sir, I guess so."

"It's this way, Tom. You hate whatever it was that got you all knocked down and ruined. That's human nature. Unthinking, maybe, but human nature anyway."

"There's hardly nobody or nothing we don't hate," said Tom.

"Right! The whole blooming kaboodle of them people in the Past who run the world. So here we are on a Thursday morning with our guts plastered to our spines, cold, live in caves and such, don't smoke, don't drink, don't nothing except have our festivals, Tom, our festivals."

And Tom thought of the festivals in the past few years. The year they tore up all the books in the square and burned them and everyone was drunk and laughing. And the festival of science a month ago when they dragged in the last motor car and picked lots and each lucky man who won was allowed one smash of a sledgehammer at the car.

"Do I remember *that*, Tom? Do I *remember*? Why, I got to smash the front window, the window, you hear? My god, it made a lovely sound! *Crash!*"

Tom could hear the glass falling in glittering heaps.

"And Bill Henderson, he got to bash the engine. Oh, he did a smart job of it, with great efficiency. Wham!"

But best of all, recalled Grigsby, there was the time they smashed a factory that was still trying to turn out airplanes.

"Lord, did we feel good blowing it up," said Grigsby. "And then we found that newspaper plant and the munitions depot and exploded them together. Do you understand, Tom?"

Tom puzzled it over. "I guess."

It was high noon. Now the odors of the ruined city stank on the hot air and things crawled among the tumbled buildings.

"Won't it ever come back, mister?"

"What, civilization? Nobody wants it. Not me!"

"I could stand a bit of it," said the man behind another man. "There were a few spots of beauty in it."

"Don't worry your heads," shouted Grigsby. "There's no room for that either."

"Ah," said the man behind the man. "Someone'll come along some day with imagination and patch it up. Mark my words. Someone with a heart."

"No," said Grigsby.

"I say yes. Someone with a soul for pretty things. Might give us back a kind of *limited* sort of civilization, the kind we could live in in peace."

"First thing you know there's war!"

"But maybe next time it'd be different."

At last they stood in the main square. A man on horseback was riding from the distance into the town. He had a piece of paper in his hand. In the center of the square was the roped-off area. Tom, Grigsby, and the others were collecting their spittle and moving forward—moving forward prepared and ready, eyes wide. Tom felt his heart beating very strongly and excitedly, and the earth was hot under his bare feet.

"Here we go, Tom, let fly!"

Four policemen stood at the corners of the roped area, four men with bits of yellow twine on their wrists to show their authority over other men. They were there to prevent rocks being hurled.

"This way," said Grigsby at the last moment, "everyone feels he's had his chance at her, you see, Tom? Go on, now!"

Tom stood before the painting and looked at it for a long time.

"Tom, spit!"

His mouth was dry.

"Get on, Tom! Move!"

"But," said Tom, slowly, "she's BEAUTIFUL!"

"Here, I'll spit for you!" Grigsby spat and the missile flew in the sunlight. The woman in the portrait smiled serenely, secretly, at Tom, and he looked back at her, his heart beating, a kind of music in his ears.

"She's beautiful," he said.

"Now get on, before the police—"

"Attention."

The line fell silent. One moment they were berating Tom for not moving forward, now they were turning to the man on horseback.

"What do they call it, sir?" asked Tom, quietly.

"The picture? Mona Lisa, Tom, I think. Yes, the Mona Lisa."

"I have an announcement," said the man on horseback. "The authorities have decreed that as of high noon today the portrait in the square is to be given over into the hands of the populace there, so they may participate in the destruction of—"

Tom hadn't even time to scream before the crowd bore him, shouting and pummeling about, stampeding toward the portrait. There was a sharp ripping sound. The police ran to escape. The crowd was in full cry, their hands like so many hungry birds pecking away at the portrait. Tom felt himself thrust almost through the broken thing. Reaching out in blind imitation of the others, he snatched a scrap of oily canvas, yanked, felt the canvas give, then fell, was kicked, sent rolling to the outer rim of the mob. Bloody, his clothing torn, he watched old women chew pieces of canvas, men break the frame, kick the ragged cloth, and rip it into confetti.

Only Tom stood apart, silent in the moving square. He looked down at his hand. It clutched the piece of canvas close to his chest, hidden.

"Hey there, Tom!" cried Grigsby.

Without a word, sobbing, Tom ran. He ran out and down the bomb-pitted road, into a field, across a shallow stream, not looking back, his hand clenched tightly, tucked under his coat.

At sunset he reached the small village and passed on through. By nine o'clock he came to the ruined farm dwelling. Around back, in the half silo, in the part that still remained upright, tented over, he heard the sounds of sleeping, the family—his mother, father, and brother. He slipped quickly, silently, through the small door and lay down panting.

"Tom?" called his mother in the dark.

"Yes."

"Where've you been?" snapped his father. "I'll beat you in the morning."

Someone kicked him. His brother, who had been left behind to work their little patch of ground.

"Go to sleep," cried his mother, faintly.

Another kick.

Tom lay getting his breath. All was quiet. His hand was pushed to his chest, tight, tight. He lay for half an hour this way, eyes closed. Then he felt something, and it was a cold white light. The moon rose very high and the little square of light moved in the silo and crept slowly over Tom's body. Then, and only then, did his hand relax. Slowly, carefully, listening to those who slept about him, Tom drew his hand forth. He hesitated, sucked in his breath, and then, waiting, opened his hand and uncrumpled the tiny fragment of painted canvas.

All the world was asleep in the moonlight.

And there on his hand was the Smile.

He looked at it in the white illumination from the midnight sky. And he thought, over and over to himself quietly, *the Smile, the lovely Smile.*

An hour later he could still see it, even after he had folded it carefully and hidden it. He shut his eyes and the Smile was there in the darkness. And it was still there, warm and gentle, when he went to sleep and the world was silent and the moon sailed up and then down the cold sky toward morning.

The Cabinet of Chronos—*I'm about ready to crawl into it and throw away the key!*
I think I may have made a monumental booboo (well, monumental in my perfec-
tionistic eyes, at any rate) when I introduced my first selection in the Ackerman
Archival Recovery Series, Out Around Rigel. *No, I'm not referring to the story—*
Damon Knight has since selected it for an anthology of Forgotten Goodies, one of the
rare times his taste & mine have ever coincided, for generally our opinions of what's
good in sf are as different as Knight & day. (Just call me Forrest "Day" Ackerman.)
But where I think I erred is in reporting that the author of Out Around Rigel *sui-*
cided out in the '30s. As I was preparing the original blurb for the following story,
my eye happened to light, in the Don Day Index to SF Magazines, *on the name*
Robert Wilson in 1945—fourteen years after I had him dead! Now the Wilson who
wrote Out Around Rigel *(and also* Flight into Time, *which I may also revive if*
it stands up after I've re-read it) used the middle initial "H." and the Wilson whose
interplanetaryarn was published in Planet Stories *didn't include an initial, so it*
could be said to be circumstantial evidence, it was another Robert Wilson; but it seems
more reasonable to me that the Robert H. Wilson who had Out Around Rigel *pub-*
lished in 1931 either dug out and sold an unsold manuscript from 1931 in 1945
or else took one final fling that year on Vandals of the Void. *If, as I now suspect,*
he did not *voluntarily end his life in the early '30s, it is possible that I shall have*
heard from him by the time these words reach print, in which case, in a future book,
I shall be happy to announce that Robert H. Wilson is alive & well! Who knows?—
maybe he'll even be inspired to write us a new story after all these years! We could use
one of the quality of Rigel!

But now to David R. Daniels. I don't know what demon got into my brain and
momentarily made me imagine that Wilson had killed himself all those years ago
when it now seems to me I was thinking of David R. Daniels, who had 5 stories pub-
lished in '35, one in '36, and then faded out of the picture forever after. Suicide or
did he simply stop writing for natural causes? I could probably research my collection
and come up with the definitive information but I simply don't have the time just for
the sake of an accurate blurb. It probably isn't that important anyway. But maybe
Sam Moskowitz or Robert A. Madle or Harry Warner Jr. or one of the other old-timers
of First Fandom can come up with the information for me . . . and you. First one in
with the facts gets a free mint copy of the third issue of Miracle, Science & Fantasy
Stories. *Which only the Old Guard would recognize as an impossibility since there*
was no *third issue.*

What is important about The Far Way, *ultimately, is not the fortune or mis-*
fortune of its author but that his fine forgotten scientale has been rescued after about
60 years.

The Far Way

by David R. Daniels

IT WAS DARK IN THE HALL WHEN STUART FINISHED HIS WORK AND STARTED OUT OF the building. He was interested in physics, and the experiment had taken the whole afternoon. As he started out the door things seemed to whirl before his eyes. It surprised him; nothing like that had ever happened before. Perhaps he had been working too hard, he thought, as he straightened his big shoulders and strode on out.

Then he noticed something peculiar. There was a thin new Moon in the west, with a bright planet beside it. He stared at the sight a moment uncomprehendingly. Something was wrong, yet what it was he couldn't make out.

It was at a time of evening when few people were abroad, so Stuart went several blocks before he met any one. Finally he passed a person heading in the opposite direction. The man gazed at him curiously, halted, turned and spoke: "Say, isn't that Stuart?"

"Yes," he replied, puzzled. The voice seemed familiar, but there was a strange ring to it. Like the voice of a friend might sound after an absence of months. "But you aren't Peterson?"

"Surely, Bill. Where have you been this last year? There certainly was a hue and cry when you left so suddenly, just at graduation, and right when that will turned up. Where have you been, anyway?"

"I don't know what you're talking about," said Stuart. "When is this?"

"It's August 27th, of course. Year, 1937. When did you think it was?"

But Stuart didn't answer at once; he was too dumbfounded. That was what was wrong with the evening. There was a new Moon, when it had been fairly full. Nor should there be an evening star. August 27th, 1937! A moment ago it had been July in 1936. Somewhere between the time he had finished work and met Peterson thirteen months had passed like the flick of an eyelid.

"You'd better come home with me," his friend spoke, "tell me what's happened."

"I guess I had. And there are a lot of things I want to know."

Several interesting events had transpired within the year. An aunt of Stuart's had died, leaving him several hundred thousand dollars. That had happened the very day he disappeared, so for a time it was thought he had been kidnapped. The police searched diligently, but there was no clue. People had not yet ceased wondering about the matter when Stuart appeared again in as ghostly a manner as he had gone, utterly unable to account for his absence. It was called amnesia and forgotten in two weeks.

Stuart got his money, much of which he sank into the best and most lasting securities he could find. He had an idea as to what had really happened and he had no desire to awake some morning and find himself penniless in a foreign world.

The second time he disappeared there was more sensation than the first. Then Peterson produced a letter in which Stuart hinted that he might be going away on a long journey and for Peterson to "help look after things." The truth of it was, there was nothing to look after; all his funds were in the most able hands of Morris & Morris, solicitors. He had left the letter as a clue, in case he should be missing again. It was something he thought might happen, and he did not wish for any trouble to arise.

He was one of those people who can adjust themselves quickly to any curious set of circumstances, and he was too tight-mouthed to say anything. People felt him to be the type that might go drifting off without a word as to why or where. Since the letter was undoubtedly genuine that was the last of the matter.

Days and months came and went, but not so Stuart. Or at least, no one ever saw him. It was said he had gone to India, to Africa, to Greenland, and on an expedition to the South Pole. Even Morris & Morris did not know where he was, though for appearance's sake they put their tongues in their cheeks and looked wise.

There was the boom of 1938 and the slump of 1939 when it was said that things had never been so bad, but the memory of a people is a short thing. Then, at last, one day in 1940, a young man walked into his lawyers' offices.

"I had a hard time finding you," he said. "Things have changed since I was last here."

A young clerk gazed at him somewhat distastefully, as is often the way with clerks when meeting unknown quantities. However, the older Mr. Morris happened to be passing through the room, and he did not have to look at his visitor twice. Mr. Morris prided himself on his memory.

"Why, it's William Stuart," he said. "It's been a long time since you were in. You haven't changed a day; have you found the fountain of youth? Come into my office, Mr. Stuart, and we'll talk things over."

"Now," he said, when they were established in privacy, "we have been very successful in your absence. Half the money which you left as you know, was in our hands to invest as we saw fit. The other half was already invested in good securities, and of course has accumulated but with little interest. Nevertheless, the first has gone far. You could call yourself a millionaire now." He pressed a button.

"If you will please sign these papers before—"

• • •

After his client had gone the lawyer was thoughtful for a long while. A very strange man, was his opinion, yet a most youthful one. When he had suggested that they fly to Chicago that afternoon to look after some business interests, Stuart had refused, muttering some foolishness to the effect that he would hate to have one of the machines go off and leave him in mid-air. Nonsense. Everyone knew that airplanes, especially the new rocket type coming into use, were safer than ground vehicles had ever been. And when Morris had hinted that it would be best if his client kept in touch with the firm, the man had smiled as though he had just heard something funny.

"Been wandering like Ulysses?" Morris had asked.

"Something like that," was the reply.

A very strange man indeed.

Others were to think similarly through the course of the years. When, in 1952, the clerk, now a high personage in the firm of Morris & Morris, saw Stuart walk in again, he looked just as he had twelve years before. In the meantime, the clerk had trained himself to remember faces. And that it was the same old Stuart was very certain, since by fingerprints and photographs, and by the more recent method of X-ray pictures, the man had identified himself beyond all shadow of doubt. During those twelve years he had passed out of all human ken, to return as though he had never been gone. Like the vanishing act of a magician, people who knew anything about it thought; nor were they very far wrong.

By this time Stuart had overcome his antipathy for air travel, though it was noticeable that he always wore a parachute during such voyages. He held himself in readiness at all times. "Not like he was scared," as an attendant said when the matter was brought to his memory, "but like he was waiting for the ship to break into pieces, and wanted to be ready when it did."

And Stuart kept his finances very queerly. For years he would never come near the firm, nor even write, then suddenly he would come hurrying in as though he had forgotten all about such things during the interim. And he sometimes made very strange requests.

"Give me a hundred thousand dollars," he said once. "In cash which you are sure will be good for at least the next fifty years. I'd prefer a hundred, but I don't suppose you have any idea what things will be like in that time."

He who had been clerk was now an elderly man. He gazed at Stuart in dazed fashion. "But, surely, sir, you don't expect to need it by then. Of course, I realize that you are keeping your youth wonderfully; but fifty years—" His voice trailed off in contemplation.

Stuart only smiled. He had found there was no use in trying to appear natural to a world with which he was in essence unnatural. Sometimes he wished that he was like other people.

In features, in form, he had aged scarcely six months since that evening so long ago when he had met Peterson to find that more than a year had elapsed since he walked out of a building. He had changed in that time, however. There were little lines around his eyes now, as of one who has seen things such as few men are given to see; and the hint of a smile lurked always at the corners of his mouth. It was not a happy smile; it was one of faint derision, as though he saw the futility of things and laughed at it all. Strangely, it did not make him disliked. It made people want to smile with him at life.

He was a wonderful figure of a man. Tall, broad-shouldered, with springy step, he seemed a youth in his early twenties when it was known that he must be nearer seventy. He was welcomed wherever he was known, but he had few friends because of his way of going off and not being seen for years. And people died during such lapses.

Had he not appeared so seldom, his lawyers might have thought that he showed an unusual love of money. Whenever he did turn up it was to throw himself for a while into financial matters. He was always having his securities changed, putting his money into investments which he could be sure of for years to come. It seemed that he feared being left suddenly penniless.

"It would be a terrible thing," he was in the habit of saying, "to find yourself in an unknown world, utterly broke."

With the years he became a legend at Morris & Morris—the firm never changed its name during the whole of its lengthy existence. Whenever a new man was employed, the heads—the originators of the firm had been dead for years now—would show that beginner a photograph. "If you ever see a man looking like this," they would say, "bring him in at once to us. He won't have changed any, though it may be ten or twenty years till you see him. He's discovered the fountain of youth."

And the listener would nod sagely in solemn disbelief until the object of the discussion did walk in.

Had the firm published what it knew about him it might have caused a sensation throughout the world. However, it did not do that; it knew that some things are better kept secret. The company existed solely for the purpose of looking after that eternally young man's finances now, for they had grown to enormous proportions in spite of the fact that their owner had several times given large sums away. Also—and this was known only by himself—he had riches buried in a safe place in the Rocky Mountains.

But a man cannot live forever without calling attention to himself in one age or another. There was the time in 1987, for instance, when he embarked on the plane flying from Philadelphia to Denver. He was hardly noticed when he got on, and no one saw him get off. That was what caused the inquiries; he never did get off.

"I saw him," an elderly passenger said. "Noticed him especially because he was wearing a parachute, and you don't see many of them any more. He was a young fellow—maybe twenty-three or -four, the type you'd expect to be reckless. I remember now—"

But the detectives did not care what he remembered so long as it had nothing to do with the case. They told him so politely but definitely. Still, they might as well have listened to the story, since they never solved the disappearance.

When it was finally solved, its beginning had been forgotten. In 2063 the observer of a cruiser for National Weather Control saw the figure of a man materialize almost beside the ship, which was going very slowly. The man was clothed in garments of an obsolete fashion, and the folds of a parachute were opening above him. Because the occurrence was so very queer, the ship picked him up, though afterward its captain received a reprimand for doing so.

Ryal heard of the reprimand and the cause of it. Ryal—that was his only name, as was the custom of the day—was a young scientist interested in the study of time and the higher dimensions. He felt that the man might know something on the subject. He asked for Stuart, and because Ryal had a drag in the proper channels, Stuart was sent to him.

Ryal at once struck some chord in Stuart's being, and he decided to unburden his soul. "Yes," he said, in answer to a tentative question. "I'm out of time. I was born in 1915."

The scientist smiled happily. "How did you do it?" he asked.

"Sorry there," Stuart said, as he really was when the young fellow's face dropped. "I don't know how I do it. It just happens."

He went on: "You see, it's hard to explain. I don't just remain in time like other people do. Where they live naturally through the years I seem to be warped into all sorts of foreign dimensions which take me away from Earth, through blank spaces, for odd periods. I slip along here and there, always into the future, and I never know where I'll be in another instant. Once part of a building fell right over my head, and I'd surely have been killed if I hadn't just then found myself in the same place years later, long after the building had been repaired. In fact, it was after another had been built in its place.

"The first time the slip happened I thought I might be a victim of amnesia, but the second time I caught on. Even now I can't really explain it, though. By actual year measurement I'm a hundred and forty-eight years old, but in reality I've lived perhaps twenty-five or twenty-six years. I'm not sure exactly—living a month or so here and there and then dashing ahead for years makes it almost impossible to keep a precise count. For the first twenty-one years I lived normally, then one evening there was a whirl, and thirteen months had passed. After that things were normal for a few weeks, and then in a moment three years had gone by."

"But don't you feel anything in such intervals?" Ryal interrupted.

"Not at first. I thought I was simply dizzy. Then, when such things happened more frequently I knew when they transpired. One feels a wrench, but it's really not unpleasant. That's as near as I can put it; it's impossible to state my true sensations."

Ryal's eyes grew starry. "I should think so," he said. "Now sit down again and tell everything that ever happened to you. I imagine that for a while you must have been afraid of starving, but now that we don't have money any more you don't have to worry about that."

Ryal was the first person to whom Stuart had ever attempted to explain things who understood in the least, so he talked by the hour. The scientist's face assumed a rapt expression which he still wore when Stuart left, for the dream of the time intervals stretching away toward the end of things ahead of this man half hypnotized him. Where would Stuart end, he wondered. He said that each transition took him increasingly farther periods ahead. The first had been a year, the last, seventy-six years! Would the space come when he could take a thousand years in his stride? With all his soul, Ryal envied Stuart.

But the way was not all roses. There was something nostalgic in turning suddenly to find that every one a person had known was dead and that the world had leaped a decade, or fifty years, or a century. The first transitions of a year or so meant little after one was accustomed to them; ways and men changed hardly at all in so short a time.

But when, after talking with Ryal in 2063, he leaped the gap to 2170 it was more than Stuart could cope with. In that space of a little more than a hundred years things changed considerably. New powers had been discovered; explorers were off for the Moon and Mars. The language had changed so that it was only with difficulty that Stuart could make himself understood.

As though fate were giving him an opportunity to catch up with things, he remained in normal time for eleven months. Yet during the first half of that time he was in continual fear lest he be cast ahead to another era which he could not understand, where he would be an alien wanderer; and during the last half he began to be afraid that he might never go forward again. The spirit of roving was in his blood now. Roving—not through the miles, but through the years.

It irked him when the days passed normally. When he did slip ahead it was the day before he intended embarking upon a journey to Venus. Before that he had not cared to attempt such a trip lest during it he slip between the scheme of things to find himself unprotected in interstellar space.

The years passed him by like book pages, and he was suddenly in 2304. There had been but a gradual change during the last two hundred years, for progress was slowing. Space ships had gone out a little farther; men knew a little more, but the world was nearly the same. Stuart spent the few weeks allotted him in the study of weapons of that day, and when he shot ahead it was with the plans of an intricate death machine clutched tightly in one hand.

The thirty-fifth century was different. War was looming darkly in the future, and there had not been war for nearly a thousand years. The Earth was banded under one ruler as it had been for centuries, but there were other people, beyond Earth's rule. Eryl discussed the matter with her counselors.

"Can't we arrange things peacefully?" she asked. "All quarrels have been settled in that manner for generations. Why is it that the Martians want to fight?"

A counselor shook his head. "It is mostly ennui," he said. "Not only the Martians want war, but even our people do. For three hundred years the enemy has been marooned on the Red Planet, and in all that time not one of them has left his world. At first we compelled them to remain on the planet, lest they spread the source of the death of the lowlands. Then, finally, the disease died out, but some of the people of the Solar System were still afraid. The Martians felt, and rightly, that they were being mistreated. All this time they have been planning revenge."

"I know," Eryl said wearily. "I have heard all this dozens of times. But we have promised them equality and the right to do as they choose."

"Yet they still want war."

Eryl spoke as though to herself. "And we have no weapons because our ancestors felt there would be no more fighting, and they caused all their plans of death-dealing machines to be destroyed. The Martians have been able to invent new ones, and before our scientists can find the means to arm us we will all have been destroyed. Well, we must fight, and we will. But I think we will all die. Write the proclamation, Evaris."

"I have been waiting for your consent," said the counselor. "We do have weapons now."

It was very bizarre, what he told. It was of a man out of the past of a thousand years, a man called Stuart. He seemed a normal being, yet he often moved in time. Since the second millennium he had not been on Earth, but he had appeared suddenly, two months before. At first Evaris had incarcerated him as a spy, since it was a week before he discovered common speech with the man. Then he found that this Stuart had brought with him knowledge of all machines of war from an age when there had been much fighting. He had shown a willingness to help, so weapons had been manufactured already.

"Why wasn't I told of this?" Eryl asked imperiously after Evaris had given the account in his long-drawn-out fashion.

"Because," she was told, "I did not care to raise your hopes only to have them dashed. It has only been in the last few days that I discovered Stuart was able to do as he claimed."

"Very well," said the young ruler. "But now I should like to see this Stuart." She pronounced the word queerly. "Bring him to me."

She was more than pleased when she did see him. He looked like anything except an individual who had been born sixteen centuries before. He was bronzed and strong; a little bigger, a little taller than the men of her day. He was handsome, though there was a far-seeing expression in his gray eyes. They seemed old, and old. It was as though he was an immortal who had looked upon the futilities of the world but had found it impossible to change them.

And she thrilled him. In all his wandering existence he had never seen a woman like her, as he would have said had he felt more at ease in her presence.

"You will fight with us?" she asked him.

He shook his head. "I'd rather not go out into space," he said. "You see, I have a way of finding that things go off and leave me. That would prove fatal beyond the atmosphere."

Her upper lip curled slightly. "I should think," she said in a voice slightly tinged with scorn, "that one who has lived for fifty generations would not fear death."

"Nor do I," he said. "Sometimes I almost look forward to it. But I've gone on so long now that I should like to see how it all comes out. It's awfully interesting to watch, really."

Nevertheless, something in her curling lip had piqued him, so when the time came to fight he went with the first ship. During the whole of the quick war he thought of Eryl. There was something so altogether feminine beneath her queenly exterior; he dreamed of her between the battles when he had time to snatch a few hours' sleep.

He was spared through it all, for he escaped the searching death beams and the less obtruse danger of the airlessness. It was due partly to his leadership as well as to the weapon secrets which he knew, that Earth emerged victorious.

He returned to Earth as a hero, his name on every tongue. Eryl met him and honored him. He feasted at the palace, and that evening the two walked in the garden.

"I was afraid when you did go," she said. "Stay with us now."

The next moment she was in his arms, and he knew love as he had never known it in all of sixteen hundred years.

"Oh, Lord," he whispered, "let me stay this time. Let me stay—"

They sat down side by side on a marble bench and were silent a long time. Finally Eryl heard Stuart draw in his breath to speak. She turned toward him. At that moment he seemed to grow hazy; in an instant she was alone. Attendants came running when she screamed, and they found her lying on the bench, her face buried in her arms, weeping as though her heart would break.

But the world passed on inevitably, and the time came when Eryl had been forgotten.

Knorahl lived ten thousand centuries later. That is not an excessive time as the world goes, but it is long for the race of men. To a person who had lived in the twentieth century Knorahl would hardly have seemed human with his great forehead and puny body. Yet his great brain held more knowledge than the whole of mankind had known in the twentieth century.

Seated near him was a man out of the distant past. In sheer weight he was twice the size of his companion, but in reasoning power there was no comparison.

Knorahl spoke. It was strange, Stuart thought, how much this man of the future could understand. He seemed to read his thoughts, to know everything that had ever entered Stuart's mind.

"What you ask," Knorahl said, "is beyond us. We understand much of the facts of time, but not to that extent. Where the ordinary animal body extends along the Earth's World Line in the fourth dimension, yours is warped through the sixth, so that it meets the World Line only at intervals. How that is we understand easily, since it is known how time warps and twists in the sixth dimension, yet you are the only being who was ever like that, at least to any great extent. It is as though time had been forgotten in your case.

"You are a freak of nature, just as the occasional two-headed calves and legged snakes of your day were freaks. A few generations ago our ancestors might have said that there had been a mistake in the cosmic scheme of things when you were created, but my people doubt that there ever are mistakes.

"For these reasons we cannot help you. We can control the fourth dimension, and the fifth to some extent, but the sixth is beyond us. Certainly we could not send you back to the third millennium."

Stuart's expression did not change. Sorrow had lined his features, but he was still a young man. Strength seemed to emanate from him. It was a strength born of knowledge and suffering.

"I was afraid you couldn't," he said. "I guess it's meant that I go on to the end. Perhaps, sometime, I can find beings who can send me back to the only one I ever cared for, but if not, I can take what comes. I hope so, anyway."

Knorahl's features were benign. He was starting to speak again. Perhaps he would have uttered words of courage or he might have given important information, but Stuart never heard it. At that instant the man out of time grew dim and vanished.

The intervals between which he touched the World Line of the Earth were wider now; he stayed in one era for increasingly shorter periods. It was five million years later when he was cognizant of things, but before he could adjust himself to the uniqueness of what he saw in that strange time he shot on ahead. It was as though he were allowed to glimpse, but not to understand, the wonderful advancement of the ages. He saw things which he could not even begin to understand, and as quickly as the impressions were registered on his mind's eye they changed.

It had been his idea to enlist the help of the human beings of the future, but he never had the chance. He was tired now of the incessant change, of the dwindling away of anything similar to that which he had ever known. The quick shifting of eras, which was becoming kaleidoscopic, wearied him. If it had not been for his determination which had been born during the quick passing centuries, when he found he was so different from all other men, he might never have endured it. Even that determination was hard pressed to uphold him.

He saw the world as it was after ten million years as it was after fifty, after a hundred, five hundred, a billion. He saw it when the dwindling of the air supply had caused its inhabitants to cover it entirely with a glasslike substance a mile or so above the ground. It was then like a great hothouse, under which strange trees and stranger men lived and thrived, but when he stopped again all life was gone. Now the great covering showed cracked and marred above his head, while great pieces of it had fallen in places. In the end the works of man outlasted man himself, all save one individual who had never been altogether of Earth.

What had become of the human race, Stuart wondered. Had it died, or had it migrated away to another star? It was strange that humanity had overcome nature so entirely, only to vanish like fog in a hot sun.

He was carried on again.

Now the Earth cover was gone; the world was nearly dead about him. It was cold. The air was thin and weak and lacking in oxygen, and Stuart nearly died before he was snatched on.

Eons later, though it seemed but a moment, he was no better off, for now there was even less air. The Sun was red in the heavens, big and close-seeming, but dim—oh, so dim! Earth was swinging closer in preparation for the long, final plunge into the mass of its parent; perhaps the inner planets had already gone. The ground was barren, the seas had vanished. Only the stars were bright, but of them all not one constellation showed even a hint of familiarity.

Stuart could hardly breathe. Something was clutching at his heart; his tongue was protruding; his sight was dim. He was not yet old to himself, but he had seen the world for untold ages. It was Ragnarok now, the Twilight. The planet that had borne his kind was going, and he would go with it. That was fair; dust back to dust in the end. It was worth all he had undergone; he was glad now.

It seemed that he was living in the long ago, before he first slipped into time. No; it was different—Eryl was near him; her arms were outstretched.

"My darling," she whispered, "I've followed you so long. Knorahl knew, but he couldn't tell you. I have reached you only at the end."

Then he was back again on the cold rock, but he felt that he had been dreaming. But Eryl was still with him, her arms were around him, her lips were against his. Was this real?

It mattered but little, for just then he felt a whirl and he slipped away. At the period when he would next have entered time the portion of the heavens where Earth should have been was filled with a blazing, blue-white Sun.

But Stuart thought that he and Eryl died together, in each other's arms.

We've had a pair of George Smiths in the sci-fi field; now another Raymond Jones. An ironic tale of—

Parasite Lost

by Raymond James Jones

THE LAST PARASITE WAS DYING. HE ALONE, OUT OF COUNTLESS BILLIONS, HAD survived the great famine.

According to legend, his kind had resided on the HOST's body since the beginning of time. But the time of plenty has passed. The HOST's body could no longer support them.

Like any parasite, they had spread over their host's body in great numbers, taking their food and energy from their host. Also, like a parasite, they had given nothing in return. Finally, the HOST had nothing more to give.

The HOST, unable to support itself, let alone all the countless parasites, began to die too. Of course, as the HOST died, the food supply dwindled and the parasites died too.

It wasn't a quick death. It lasted quite some time.

As the food supply became less & less, the strong took from the weak and the stronger took from the strong. Finally, unable to find any other source of food, they resorted to eating one another.

The great horde had completely destroyed the HOST. They had taken everything. Absolutely nothing remained. Only the one parasite and he too was dying. He was so near death he couldn't even move his limbs.

Finally, like the long-awaited sunset on a hot August day, the light began to fade from his vision. Slowly gasping he swallowed his last precious breaths of tenuous, befouled air. A last desperate inhalation and he expired.

As in the Beginning, so at the End. The final eve for Adam. The Last Man on Earth was dead.

The task of Tau took aeons to fulfill for he was a—

Messenger to Infinity

by J. Harvey Haggard

(Author of *Evolution Satellite*)

A GLEAMING BINARY SWUNG IN THE BLUE SKY, SENDING A MOIST WARMTH ACROSS the swaying fern-growths of the Fourteenth Planet of Aligena. Feathered creatures of bright colors flashed through the underbrush and made noises there. A figure came stalking down through the shaded clearings and small scaly bodies scurried out of sight, leaving ungainly tracks scrawled in the swamp mud.

Tau the metal man, a mechanical half-sentient messenger from the far distant past, strode impassively along, not heeding the smaller creatures of the jungle. He had sighted the tiny habitable world from the distant depths of an outer galaxy and had moored his spaceship in a clearing that was not distant.

He halted his berylite six-foot body in a leafy glade and let the wind play about his cold outer surface. The inscrutable, lens-cased orbs in his head peered about, taking in the scene with photographic detail.

Life! This is life! He thought to himself. *This is the life the Master said I would find some day. Now I know what to do.*

Though his memories were of a distant past, of a remote planet and of the Master whose atoms might lie even now in the etheric dust, Tau remembered with perfect clarity. He could recall the aged countenance of the Master, the broad forehead, the jutting chin and the determined undertone of his deep voice.

"Men may die in the convulsions which will presently engulf the universe," the Master had said, "but their deeds live after them. You shall be my deed, Tau. And you must live as the universe trembles in its agony of collision with another universe. All mankind must die but you shall live through it."

And Kendall Smith's face had lighted inwardly as though from some deep inspiration. Tau the metal man, nestled in the cradling bracework in which his shape had taken form, had said nothing in reply, but in the neurochemical mechanisms of his brain the words had been imprinted forever.

"You're just a robot!" the Master had said, "with responses and reactions that are the involuntary activations of metal and chemical-change impulse, yet I believe that some day in the aeons which will pass you will learn to reason for yourself to some extent and perhaps understand the germs of life into the far distant future."

And now Tau the metal man, standing in the mire of that world of the future the Master had talked about, wondered at the mystery which was called Life and doubted if he clearly understood what the man had meant. One thing he knew certainly, that his metallic body was created to bridge the epoch which yawned between the life-lines of the past and those of the future. Old Kendall Smith, stalking back and forth in his laboratory, had explained as much, and Tau had never forgotten.

"Our life-line is narrowing, the Earth is dying," the Master had explained. "That one-in-a-million chance of opportune conditions in which life may exist is vanishing. I doubt if the circumstances can be duplicated in the entire cosmos. But someday, after the universes have collided, they must return again. It is not within the powers of man to bridge the gap of space and time, but you, Tau the robot, swinging in the non-conducting realms of the vacuum of space, will be next to eternal."

Tau had learned the secrets of extracting radiant energy from the atom, had become adept in applying the forces to the mechanisms that propelled the spaceship and supplied motivation for his own metal body. Many other secrets the Master had taught him in the laboratories and he had come to know the uses of the scientific paraphernalia that were sealed in the inner heart of the spacecraft. When the occasion came for Tau to use the equipment, Kendall Smith had said he would understand the true nature constituting life.

So Tau groped through the mires of a strange world, into which he had been commanded to carry man's life-seed, and for him the Master was not a dissipated husk long since scattered to the cosmos in a distant past but a real and living entity, guiding each of his movements in a meditated fashion. Time and space were merely chasms in Tau's consciousness and a dominating purpose drove him onward.

The binary descended. Night fell. Glittering shards of the stars pierced the black firmament. Night creatures let out occasional shrieks and snarls. Once a six-legged catlike creature, half as tall as the metal man, was attracted by Tau's movements and sprang upon him. Tau's responses were mechanical and he knew no such thing as fear. He simply ripped the creature apart with the tremendous strength that surged in his metal arms.

Later that night he returned to the spaceship. As he approached the gleaming ovoid a circular door opened. Crossing its threshold, he passed into the interior, distorted by intricate mechanisms, and the aperture closed behind him.

Slowly Tau walked to the center of the room, his body reflected in gleaming surfaces of berylite stanchions and sheathings. In the center of the whorled contrivances a row of ingenious troughs lay exposed. Each of these troughs was centered by a molding that had the perfect outline of a man, empty in the crystalline interior.

All that night iridescent gleamings crawled along the monstrous glassite tubes, illuminating the busy robot with an eerie splendor. Miniature lightning shot and sparkled from insulated spheres high in the nose of the craft. Pulsating, sluggish liquids gave off radiant colors and seeped through tortuous channels along the tubes of glassite. The central troughs became opaque and formed a webwork now into which the throbbing aqueous masses were assembling. A chill current of the outer atmosphere was forced by rotating blades along a channel that whirled in a maelstrom around the central apparatus.

Tau worked swiftly, but days fled by as he watched the quiescent gauges and indicators, and lengthened into months. Blinding storms raged unheeded on the exterior of the ovoid craft. Winter came and fled.

At last David and his tribe came to life, all molded from a magnificent scale. During those long months of creation, Tau had imprinted knowledge and learning upon the brains of the dormant bodies. Each awoke with a full knowledge of what had transpired on the dying planet of Earth and each knew that a strange newborn world awaited them. The largest and most magnificent man was named David. The Master had been careful in instructing Tau about that. Kendall Smith had never had a son. And this synthetic offspring in a distant life-line of the cosmos would be almost like a son for him.

All of Tau's knowledges were conveyed to David and his followers and he led them into the unknown dangers of the pristine jungled planet, guarding them from the ferocious animals while they learned the edible fruits from the poisonous ones. Gradually David's men came to recognize the dangers and constructed crude weapons for their own defense.

Another winter descended upon the new world. Food had been stored in the big compartment of the space vessel. Furs of slain animals had been cured to provide clothing and warmth.

Spring thaws came and Tau led them again into the jungle, but now David was big and strong and wary and quite able to defend himself against the dangers of the forest, and Tau's presence was hardly needed, though he always hovered near with the semblance of a strange guardian angel of metal.

Five men and five women had been given life by Tau's instruments and it was inevitable that a gradual pairing off would take place. Myri, a model of womanly perfection, had grown to adore the handsome leader of the tribe and Tau was one of the first to notice signs of fecundity.

A terrific storm lashed the planet. Giant trees groaned and split across the trunks. The raging downpour built up into outer floods that raged down the lowlands in mighty rivers, sweeping everything in its path to destruction. To all this Tau was oblivious. The fury of the tempest was deadened by the berylite walls of the spaceship and was not as loud as the shrill cry of the newborn babe.

Thunder boomed outside. Lightning forked across the rent heavens, sending flickering flashes of illumination through the beating sheets of rain that poured across the glassite sheathing above the neglected control mechanisms. David the second was born and for a time was cuddled against the breast of the metal man, whose terribly strong arms held him as lightly and delicately as could a bed of thistle down. The imperturbable orbs of immobile transparency gazed downward and suddenly Tau the metal man staggered.

David took the child with a startled cry and stood eyeing the tottering robot. Tau's consciousness was centered upon his dragging limbs and for a moment his mentality flickered as though it were gone, then returned. He saw that his metallic body was dark and stained with an odd encrustation and he turned and made his way to the cubicle in which he had sat while an aeon of time slipped away in the depths of interplanetary space. There he had watched universes in turmoil and there he had seen the life-line of one aeon merge with that of another.

There was one hooded mechanism at which he always sat, and when he was just so, the mind of the Master would speak from down the ages and the image of Kendall arose, as it had always done, in his mind. He thought he visualized the Master now, out of the dim consciousness of the past. Tall and arresting with the vigorous personality of a dynamic intelligence, the keen gray eyes peered at him again as they had done in the distant past.

"You, Tau, are just a man of metal," the Master was saying, "and yet I've a feeling that part of myself is implanted within you, just as part of my mind is implanted in the mechanisms of your consciousness. As a thing of metal, floating in a non-conducting void, you are something that is almost eternal. Yet if you succeed in finding a habitable world, such as the Earth has been in the past, the atmosphere of that planet will suffuse about you and in the triumph of my wishes will lie your downfall. Oxides of the surrounding air will cause your gradual deterioration and the only one who could help you will be nothing more than motes of cosmic dust in the unpredictable corners of the surrounding universe."

Unseen by David or any of the others, Tau slipped to the door, and down a corridorway. Through an aperture he could glimpse the inner room where Myri lay, nursing the infant at her breast. For just an instant he paused, for the Master had never seemed closer than in that single moment.

Turning finally, the metal man walked impassionately through the doorway and vanished into the driving blasts of the lashing storm.

*All the stories had been selected for this anthology when a chap I'd never met before gave me a little manuscript and asked me if I'd do him a favor and read it and let him know if I thought he had any prospects as a sci-fi author. George Allen meant nothing to me as a name; now if it had been George Allan ENGLAND—! England was a pioneering scientifiction author whose classics I had read as a kid—*The Flying Legion, The Golden Blight, *and* Darkness and Dawn *trilogy.*

George Allen's story didn't even have a name. That's all right, neither did the majority of stories by the late Kris (Bettyann/Old Man Henderson) *Neville that I sold as his agent; I named his stories such as* Underground Movement, Fresh Air Fiend, Special Delivery—*all double entendre titles.*

When I read this story, which impressed me mightily, the Latin phrase "Sic Transit Gloria Mundi" came to mind, which I intuited might be an apt title, except I wasn't certain of just what the translation was. So I contacted Bill ("Keep Watching the Skies") Warren, a knowledgeable friend of mine familiar with classic literature as well as a well-known imagi-movie expert, and he faxed me back: The translation of Sic Transit Gloria Mundi *is* Gloria Got Sick on the Streetcar on Monday.

Huh—?!

Then he followed with the literal translation: Thus Passeth the Glories of the World.

Emphasize GLORIA in it, I told myself, and we've got it made.

George Allen enthusiastically agreed.

He was even more enthusiastic when I told him if it wasn't too late I intended to eliminate one of the previously accepted stories and substitute his. This is the only First Publication story in the anthology. The whole reason I've continued to read science fiction for 70 years is to run across stories that have some sum & substance, make one stop and think. I think Dr. David H. Keller, author of The Feminine Metamorphosis *in 1929, would have enjoyed this short extrapolation in the genre of H. G. Wells, Olaf Stapledon and S. Fowler Wright. I hope you're as enthusiastic about this thought-provoking tale as I am.*

Sic Transit Gloria Mundi

(Thus Passeth the *Glories* of the World)

by George Allen

So, THE GLOBAL GENDER TRANSMUTATION WENT SMOOTHLY, ONCE THE UWN agreed upon the genetic mapping of the transference. It sent a populace into wild glee, hugging and carrying on in the streets. It, of course, had been far too long in coming, but the head scientists at the United Women's Nations had to be doubly sure that some of the tricky alleles on the XYY strand could house themselves successfully on the XX helix and promote the proper protein ratios. Ahh, sweet victory! It was good for the Earth, and it had been a long time coming. Women with natural male dominance, courage and problem-solving skills, without their violence, sex and rage components.

So it had been hundreds of years since women had behaviorally conquered the men (the revolutionary year of 2075, the records show, when genetic engineering in birthing clinics was unanimously approved). By this time, women had already been directing politics, terra-economics, lunarculture, socia-planning and socia-control (the new, improved name for political correctness) for decades. In a strange, martyr-like display, the wretched men had bought into the contention that—for their tattered, polluted world's sake—they had better let the smarter sex run things, and run them with more nobility and moral aplomb than the men could muster. This appealed to some curious dignity for them. Maybe it was "the easy way out." They allowed themselves to be maneuvered out of society. It had been centuries since the primitive men had successfully subordinated their environment and the other terrestrial carnivores, and scientists had assured humanity of enough technology and medicine for survival on Earth, so what good were they? (Save for fighting off extraterrestrial interference, which had been written off.) Nothing. And so over time man's primal, competitive violence and distrust toward other men had gradually begun to decrease. But we digress.

For several hundred sad years after 2075 men were kept as serfs to do some servile duties and various physical chores, but an occasional murderous outbreak was still too much. Men were *more than* expendable. They needed to be removed. With their removal, the stage would be set for great ethical and existential strides for humankind to be made. So women, after vast stores of cryogenic sperm had been accumulated, conveniently eliminated them. It was easy, and it was logical. Immediately, violent crime, even petty crime, disappeared. Ethnic strife and war evolved into a mutual respect and a revolutionary exchange of ideas and culture, eventually leading to the "great renaissance"—literally—which so many scorned minds in the late 20th century had actually believed was possible.

The globe was brimming with great festivals of warmth, trust and diverse tolerance and goodwill toward each other, each overlapping into another. It was a time of harmony, of great art and poetry and spiritual growth, when the immense synchronicity of the universe was unfolding, and all could rejoice and take part. For awhile, this great enlightened age radiated. And the women had needed to go further. A mortal always needs to go further. What happens when the world becomes perfect? A mortal always feels . . . incomplete . . .

The lady leaders seemed unimpressed. And bored. Of course, they'd proved to be superior. But what good was that *now*? They had begun to eat their own tail. Not literally, of course, but almost. The elimination of men may have been the all-time greatest boon to society, but some still harbored a lingering affinity for their crude, and at times (they hated to admit), comforting company. And, apparently, the competition. Maybe out of boredom, the women still had great self-righteous power and cruelty, and could lash out at each other selfishly and greedily at any moment, much like the men had. Women had always been canny and resourceful in getting fine things they wanted, but increasingly over time much of their assertion was for the shallow, vainglorious trophies thought to be obsolete: power, fame, riches.

So Gloria d'Arc, the brilliant UWN scientist, had figured that after the behavioral aggression and selfishness had been adopted by women, they needed an easy genetic swap their hospitals could perform which would give dominant XY—even war-like—traits to women. Coupled with their natural qualities of evenness, wholesomeness, artistry and mysterious wisdom, the women would finally be genetically fulfilled. Of course, certain niggling traits like maternal nurturing had been deemed uncomplimentary (and unflattering) for the new female order, and the responsible genes had been re-engineered from dominant to recessive, where natural selection gradually saw to their demise. (A few women with recurring nurturing qualities were subject to harsher genetic treatments.) The conditions were brutal . . . survival of the fittest. The women were unstoppable—far outdoing the men in terms of blind ambition and avarice. It seemed clear that the faux aggression and assertion women adopted in the late 20th century—adopted under the guise of improving the world and their existence—was actually just as vacuous a power ploy as those employed by the XY holders. Several years later, large inequities in the manner of life were becoming exacerbated, and over time thousand-mile tracts of festering toxins and nucleodecay tore into the landscape, the legacy of many an empire. This was the peripheral damage to a brutal, all-too-important gender war. Perhaps God exists simply in the details, and was doomed to become lost in the shuffle.

But, just as the biologically improved UWN society decayed into some kind of Wagnerian conflagration, despite that so many had all the power and fame and fear (of course, respect had degenerated into fear by this point) they had craved, Gloria figured where they'd gone wrong. She isolated an important XYY configuration (the superman configuration which had showed up in so many male convicts) related to insecurity-suppression, which early scientists had ignored. (And it was easy to ignore, as the superman configuration was considered the antithesis of what a female-led world would have wrought). With it, the condition of the restless and unsatisfied citizenship of female warriors would be improved, and society would no longer have any of the ugly, ungraceful scars the man-inspired dogmas had procreated. The revolution would be complete.

When the mass transference was done, just after that fleeting moment of glee, they all of course realized their great error. They could feel it.

The insecurity-suppression allele was also related to a lack of being self-conscious, so they could no longer feel unworthy, but they also had no remorse. In cold blood they mowed each other down in their continuing ruse, and had become far worse. And it was good. No longer concerned with perpetuation of the species, the cryogenic tanks of sperm were not cloned. Homo Sapiens slipped into the topsoil of Earth, and quickly the healing began. No more unnecessary suffering and pain in a species ill-equipped to deal with its balanced surroundings. The dolphins playfully learned to communicate with elephants, for sound travels remarkably now without all the radiation, machinery and sound pollution of the greedy humans. Everywhere nature blossomed, blooms emerging and packs playing and braying and roaming free and sacred across the given lands.

Visiting intelligences could now stop over happily and no longer invisibly, vacationing in a land of Eden, and leaving without a mark. Throughout the cosmos reigned a graceful, playful harmony. And it was good.

A Question of Priorities

by Allan J. Wind

THE SUN HAD RISEN NOT 4 DAYS EARLIER AND THE DARK SHADOWS THIS PRODUCED did not help the already gloomy mood of the citizens of the Moon.

The latest crisis did not look good at all—it would be an invitation for paradox to expect it to appear otherwise. This one did seem more ominous and instinctively the astronomers of the underground city of Crater Archimedes kept their studies of the silent skies closer to Earth than usual, if only to catch a fleeting glimpse of what all expected but none desired.

A mile beneath the sun-blasted, space-chilled rock and dust at the lunar surface, the Administrator sat wearily in his chair within the confines of the government offices at the colony, peering at the map projections of the many-leveled Lunar cities Archimedes, Sinus Medii and the capital at Fra Mauro. His staff aides hovered restlessly about the communication console in the office while the 2 major Council leaders paced alternately from his desk to the equipment. That equipment was the center of the only permanent link that tied the Moon to the Earth during those emergencies that cancelled the transit flights.

For decades Terrestrial leaders had nudged their people and race closer & closer to self-destruction . . . and oblivion. It had reached a point of no return, when the surveillance systems of the Western and Eastern power blocs were in constant alert status forming a tottering, unreal condition, doomed to collapse in time.

The seconds ticked by into minutes. Ultimatums flashed between the capitals. The men in the Moon room waited for the word, any word, from the mother planet. All that could be intercepted were challenges and called bluffs. It seemed to be a matter of time, borrowed time for the 3d planet of the star name Sol.

A worry-lined chief of staff wearing implanted earphones conferred briefly with similarly adorned colleagues at the consoles and with a great deal of obvious emotion slammed a large fist on the arm of his seat. He turned to the Administrator of the Moon, blinking back heavy tears. "Sorry, sir, but it looks like those stupid barbarians have finally done it!"

The signal died. Instantly it felt like a cold wind passed through the room and through the hearts and bodies of all present. The colony was still relatively young and many of its citizens had emotional ties as well as family contacts back on Earth.

There was a moment of stunned silence.

His worn face expressionless but his inner being shaken, the Administrator gave the well-drilled instructions. "Special siren 1. Button up all the hatches, I want everyone safe and underground now!

"We're still not even sure whether or not someone will waste a few nukes on us."

"Done, sir," replied an assistant.

"Connect me with Archimedes and Medii, intra-city. Make sure it's on our circuits also."

"Uh, sir, we are getting distress calls from Earth, demanding help and assistance," stated another aide who did not mask his nervousness well.

"Disengage!" ordered the Administrator.

"But, sir—" began the chief of staff.

"Do you want a dismissal, Sandin? You know the Council's approval of my decision, so don't act dumb. I've had quite enough of Earth's demands and we all know what we planned should war break out."

"Sir, you have intra-city."

The Administrator, effective dictator of all the Moon, nodded, and spoke to the citizens of the 3 young Moon cities in clear, ringing tones. "Citizens of Luna, this is the Administrator.

"As some of you may find all too apparent, the dreaded has happened: War has broken out again on Earth. Even now, many of the great cities of the past must be radioactive hells.

"In accordance with my own and Council decisions and approval, the newly born Lunar Republic is breaking contact with Earth.

"We find that a greater damage would be done if we assisted the survivors now: it would permit another similar occurrence 50 years or 100 years from now. Perhaps sooner.

"This, if we are to keep a conscience, we cannot allow.

"We will not interfere with affairs of Earth and it is surely in no position to harass us.

"Earth must decide by itself whether it will survive, by uniting, or die. Whether it will attempt to rise from the disaster of a war economy or whether it will sink back and lose civilization. Any help we might give would be just a temporary crutch.

"We of the Moon know nothing other than peace and that will not change. We will proceed as the home of real humanity, on our own. We will bear the torch until Earth grows up."

He spoke for about 10 minutes longer. In the end he joined the majority of the Lunarities in shedding shameless tears.

The senior Councilman of the Administrator's party placed a comforting hand on the Leader's shoulder. "Corey," he asked, "Corey, are you sure we're doing the right thing? Earth is incredibly powerful."

The Administrator of the colony-turned-republic reflected for a moment, then replied. "If we are, Man's future will prove it. We can't help our Earth brothers until they prove themselves ready for it and capable of total peace. Then we shall be there to assist them, strengthening the road for all the race upwards.

"Survival of our civilization to meet the future is the priority."

Far above, a mechanical eye of metal and glass gazed on a distant scene in space, without reaction. An eye incapable of shedding tears or blinking back a sob. An unchanging, immovable eye lodged in the mountains and plains of eternity, connected to consoles a mile below.

Visible to the colonists of the Moon, the planet of their birth burned.

The author of this story is an Oklahoman—correction, Oklahowoman. She was as excited as if she'd got a hypercom call from Arkon when her phone rang and she was informed she had joined the ranks of Steven Utley, Ann Orhelein, Paul Dellinger, Taimi Saha & Others in selling her first story. Enjoy, now, 650 words you won't soon forget—

The Banning

by Carmel Lou Rhoten

THE GALAXY PATROL ASSESSED THE DAMAGES CAUSED BY THE ATTEMPT AT REVO-lution on Earth and placed a 7-year ban of reproduction on the inhabitants. Until the year 2311 no couple would be allowed to procreate. Failure to comply with the ban would initiate quick reprisals to concerned parties and their offspring.

"We should stand up to them, flout their ruling!" the people muttered darkly, making sure their whispered words were not overheard. Who knew what friend or foe was an undercover agent?

Jetney hurried to his primid. Raen was not in the single downstairs room. He climbed the center spiral stairs and found her sunbathing on the green cube below the open sky window. Her swollen stomach tight and moving, Raen spread her brown fingers tenderly over the quivering flesh.

"He's romping in the warmth, Jetney," she smiled lazily, her dusky eyes glowing.

Jetney fell to his knees beside the cube and rested his forehead against the taut soft flesh. He could feel his son's delighted reactions. Raen tangled her slim fingers in her husband's auburn hair. It soothed him; the odor of her musk-scented body filled his nostrils. He wept without restraint.

Raen's fingers tightened. "Jetney!" she cried in alarm. "What is it, Jetney?"

He turned his anguished gaze to her. "The Galaxy Patrol has forbidden his birth. No more children for 7 years, they say. Every woman with child is to abort herself and those at term are to deny theirs life!"

Raen looked at him in horror. She pulled herself awkwardly to a sitting position. Jetney sat on the floor, his hands covering his face.

"Never!" Raen whispered hoarsely, feeling her baby give a lusty kick. "I will not kill my baby!" Her dark eyes flashed fire. "We will hide somewhere!"

Jetney shook his head. "There is nowhere to hide. We would be found and destroyed." His shoulders slumped in defeat.

• • •

Raen woke her husband in the middle of the night. She whispered, outlining her plan carefully. Jetney listened. At first with doubt, then with growing hope. They weighed the pros and cons, deliberated; then decided. Just maybe it would work. It had to work!

The very next night Jetney descended to his workshop beneath the first floor of the primid. He began the plans, drawing and discarding, studying and measuring, and drawing again.

As the days went by, Raen was never seen outside the bedroom. Inconsolable, Jetney explained to their friends.

Months went by, still she did not emerge. "She vows she'll not talk or see anyone until the ban is lifted," Jetney again explained. The friends shook their heads sympathetically. "Off her rocker," they later agreed.

A year from the ban, Jetney announced he was going into business. He applied for and received permission from the Governors. He built a small shop beside the primid and displayed his merchandise. Soon he became so overwhelmed with orders he had to hire extra help. Within 2 years he had extended the small factory into a larger one and employed more workers.

When the Galaxy Patrol came toward the exodus of the year 2310 to report on the result of the ban and to investigate any possible disobedience they were amazed at what met their eyes.

"We have found everything in accordance with the law. No children under the age of 7 are in evidence. We recommend the lifting of the ban. By the way, Commander, you should see what these people have consoled themselves with! Small mechanized robots, exact replicas of children from birth to puberty!"

Raen's face lit up joyfully as the news of the lifting was posted. She turned to four of the small robots sitting in a circle around a visual tube. "Benlee," she called softly. "Come here, honey."

They all turned to look as she spoke. One of them rose obediently and walked stiff-jointed toward his mother as he had been taught.

THE LORD OF FANTASY—that's what he was known as in his time. And his time endures. If you are not familiar with the mastery of imaginative imagery which dwelled in the ensorcelled brain of A. Merritt, acquaint yourself here with his poetic power in this concluding half of his contribution to—COSMOS.

The Last Poet & the Wrongness of Space

by A. Merritt

(Author of *The Metal Emperor* & *The Face in the Abyss*)

WHAT HAS GONE BEFORE:

Time: the 30th century.

Place: New York State—one mile underground, the laboratory of Narodny the Russian, Earth's last poet and also a great scientist, who has chosen to retreat from the robot-ridden world above.

The world below, an artificial Paradise.

Trouble in Paradise: intrusion by the Wrongness of Space, a mysterious entity who, from the moon, throws dissonance into Narodny's nirvanah.

Narodny and Lao, a Chinese friend, thru a spacial television device, observe a rocket with 2 Earthmen aboard heading for the Earth from a disturbance spot at crater Copernicus on the moon. Narodny & Lao transmatterize themselves aboard the ship to learn what they can of this evil genius, the Wrongness of Space, and what his relationship with Earth's robots portends.

Now go on with the story.

For 15 minutes Narodny and the Chinese listened to the tale, from the reception of the mysterious message thru the struggle against the robots, to the escape and the blasting of Copernicus in the effort of the Wrongness of Space to prevent the return of the planetary delegates.

Narodny said: "Enough. Now I understand. How long can you remain in space? I mean—what are your margins of power and of food?"

Martin answered: "6 days."

Narodny said: "Ample time for success—or failure. Remain aloft for that time, then descend to where you started—"

Suddenly he smiled. "I care nothing for mankind—yet I would not harm them willingly. And it has occurred to me that I owe them, after all, a great debt. Except for them—I would not be. Also, it occurs to me that the robots have never produced a poet, a musician, an artist—" He laughed.

"But it is in my mind that they are capable of great art at least! We shall see."

The oval was abruptly empty; then it too was gone.

Bartholomew said: "Call the others. I am for obeying. But they must know." And when the others had heard, they too voted to obey, and the spaceship, course changed, began to circle, as slowly as it could, the Earth.

Down in the chamber of the screens, Narodny laughed and laughed again. He said: "Lao, is it that we have advanced so in these few years? Or that men have retrogressed? No, it is this curse of mechanization that destroys imagination. For look you, how easy is this problem of the robots. They began as man-made machines. Mathematical, soulless, insensible to any emotion. So was primal matter of which all on Earth are made, rock and water, tree and grass, metal, animal, fish, worm and men. But somewhere, somehow, something was added to this primal matter, combined with it—used it. It was what we call life. And life is consciousness. And therefore largely emotion. Life establishes its rhythm—and its rhythm being different in rock and crystal, metal, fish, and so on, and man, we have these varying things.

"Well, it seems that life has begun to establish its rhythm in the robots. Consciousness has touched them. The proof? They have established the idea of common identity—group consciousness. That in itself involves emotion. But they have gone further: they have attained the instinct of self-preservation. And that, my wise friend, connotes fear—fear of extinction. And fear connotes anger, hatred, arrogance—and many other things. The robots, in short, have become emotional to a degree. And therefore vulnerable to whatever may amplify and control their emotions. They are no longer mechanisms.

"So, Lao, I have in mind an experiment that will provide me study and amusement thru many years. Originally, the robots are the children of mathematics. I ask—to what is mathematics most closely related? I answer—to rhythm—to sound—to sounds which will raise to the nth degree the rhythms to which they will respond. Both mathematically and emotionally."

Lao said: "The sonic sequences?"

Narodny answered: "Exactly. But we must have a few with which to experiment. To do that means to dissolve the upper gate. But that is nothing. Tell Maringy and Euphroysne to do it. Net a ship and bring it here. Bring it down gently. You will have to kill the men in it, of course, but do it mercifully. Then let them bring me the robots. Use the green flame on one or two—the rest will follow, I'll warrant you."

The hill behind where the old house had stood trembled. A circle of pale green light gleamed on its breast. It dimmed; where it had been was the black mouth of a tunnel. An airship; half-rocket, half-winged, making its way to New York; abruptly dropped, circled and streaked back. It fell gently like a moth, close to the yawning mouth of the tunnel.

Its door opened and out came 2 men, pilots, cursing. There was a little sigh from the tunnel's mouth and a silvery misty cloud sped from it, over the pilots and straight thru the opened door. The pilots staggered and crumpled to the floor, smiled . . . and died.

There were a full score of robots in the ship. They stood, looking at the dead men and at each other. Out of the tunnel came 2 figures swathed in metallic glimmering robes. They entered the ship. One said: "Robots, assemble."

The metal men stood, motionless. Then one sent out a shrill call. From all parts of the ship the metal men moved. They gathered behind the one who had sent the call. They stood behind him, waiting.

In the hand of one of those who had come from the tunnel was what might have been an antique flashlight. From it sped a thin green flame. It struck the foremost robot on the head, sliced down from the head to the base of trunk. Another flash, and the green flame cut him from side to side. He fell, sliced by that flame into 4 parts. The 4 parts lay, inert as their metal, upon the floor of the compartment.

One of the shrouded figures said: "Do you want further demonstration—or will you follow us?"

The robots put heads together; whispered. Then one said: "We will follow."

They marched into the tunnel, the robots making no resistance nor effort to escape. Again there was the sighing and the rocks closed the tunnel mouth. They came to a place whose floor sank with them until it had reached the caverns. The machine-men still went docilely. Was it because of curiosity mixed with disdain for these men whose bodies could be broken so easily by one blow of the metal appendages that served them for arms? Perhaps.

They came to the cavern where Narodny and the others awaited them. Marinoff led them in and halted them. These were the robots used in the flying ships—their heads cylindrical, 4 arm appendages, legs triple-jointed, torsos slender. The robots, it should be understood, were differentiated in shape according to their occupations.

Narodny said: "Welcome robots! Who is your leader?"

One answered: "We have no leaders. We act as one."

Narodny laughed. "Yet by speaking for them you have shown yourself leader. Step closer. Do not fear—yet."

The robot said: "We feel no fear. Why should we? Even if you should destroy us who are here, you cannot destroy the billions of us outside. Nor can you breed fast enough, become men soon enough, to cope with us who enter into life strong and complete from the beginning."

He flicked an appendage toward Narodny and there was contempt in the gesture. But before he could draw it back a bracelet of green flame circled it at the shoulder. It had darted like a thrown loop from something in Narodny's hand. The robot's arm dropped clanging to the floor, cleanly severed. The robot stared at it unbelievingly, threw forward his other 3 arms to pick it up. Again the green flame encircled them, encircled also his legs above the second joints. The robot crumpled and pitched forward, crying in high-pitched shrill tones to the others.

Swiftly the green flame played among them. Legless, armless, some decapitated, all the robots fell except 2.

"2 will be enough," said Narodny. "But they will not need arms—only feet."

The flashing green bracelets encircled the appendages and excised them. The pair were marched away. The bodies of the others were taken apart, studied, and under Narodny's direction curious experiments were made. Music filled the cavern, strange chords, unfamiliar progressions, shattering arpeggios and immense vibrations of sound that could be felt but not heard by the human ear. And finally this last deep vibration burst into hearing as a vast drone, hummed up and up into swift tingling tempest of crystalline brittle notes and, still ascending, passed into shrill high pipings and continued again unheard, as had the prelude to the droning. And thence it rushed back, the piping and the crystalline storm reversed, into the drone and the silence—then back and up.

And the bodies of the broken robots began to quiver, to tremble, as though every atom within them were in ever increasing, rhythmic motion. Up rushed the music and down—again and again. It ended abruptly in mid-flight with one crashing note.

The broken bodies ceased their quivering. Tiny star-shaped cracks appeared in their metal. Once more the note sounded and the cracks widened. The metal splintered.

Narodny said: "Well, there is the frequency for the rhythm of our robots. The destructive unison. I hope for the sake of the world outside it is not also the rhythm of many of their buildings and bridges. But after all in any war there must be casualties on both sides."

Lao said: "Earth will be an extraordinary spectacle for a few days."

Narodny said: "It's going to be an extraordinarily uncomfortable Earth for a few days and without doubt many will die and many more go mad. But is there any other way?"

There was no answer. He said: "Bring in the 2 robots."

They brought them in.

Narodny said: "Robots—were there ever any of you who could poetize?"

They answered: "What is poetize?"

Narodny laughed. "Never mind. Have you ever sung—made music—painted? Have you ever—*dreamed*?"

One robot said with cold irony: "Dreamed? No—for we do not sleep. We leave all that to men. It is why we have conquered them."

Narodny said, almost gently: "Not yet, robot. Have you ever—danced? No? It is an art you are about to learn."

The unheard note began, droned up and thru the tempest and away and back again. And up and down—and up and down, though not so loudly as before. And suddenly the feet of the robots began to move, to shuffle. Their leg-joints bent; their bodies swayed. The note seemed to move now here and now there about the chamber, and always following it, grotesquely. Like huge metal marionettes, they followed it. The music ended in the crashing note. And it was as though every vibrating atom of the robot bodies had met some irresistable obstruction. Their bodies quivered and from their voice mechanisms came a shriek that was a hideous blend of machine and life. Once more the drone, and once more and once more and again the abrupt stop. There was a brittle crackling all over the conical heads, all over the bodies. The star-shaped splinterings appeared. One again the drone—but the 2 robots stood, unresponding. For thru the complicated mechanisms which under their carapaces animated them were similar splinterings.

The robots were dead!

Narodny said: "By tomorrow we can amplify the sonor to make it effective in a 3,000-mile circle. We will use the upper cavern, of course. Equally of course, it means we must take the ship out again. In 3 days, Marinoff, you should be able to cover the other continents. See to it that the ship is completely proof against the vibrations. To work. We must act quickly—before the robots can discover how to neutralize them."

It was exactly at noon the next day that over all North America a deep inexplicable droning was heard. It seemed to come not only from deep within Earth but from every side. It mounted rapidly thru a tempest of tingling crystalline notes into a shrill piping and was gone . . . then back it rushed from piping to drone . . . then up and out and down . . . again and again. And over all North America the hordes of robots stopped whatever they were doing. Stopped . . . and then began to dance. They danced in the airships and scores of those ships crashed before the human crew could gain control. They danced by the thousands in the streets of the cities—in grotesque rigadoons, in bizarre sarabands, with shuffle and hop and jig the robots danced while the people fled in panic and hundreds of them were crushed and died in those panics. In the great factories and in the tunnels of the lower cities and in the mines—everywhere the sound was heard—and everywhere it was heard—the robots danced . . . to the piping of Narodny, the last great poet . . . the last great musician.

And then came the crashing note—and over all the country the dance halted. And began again . . . and ceased . . . and began again . . .

Until at last the streets, the lower tunnels of the lower levels, the mines, the factories, the homes, were littered with metal bodies shot thru and thru with star-shaped splinterings.

In the cities the people cowered, not knowing what blow was to fall upon them . . . or milled about in fear-maddened crowds. And many more died . . .

Then suddenly the dreadful droning, the shattering tempest, the intolerable high piping ended. And everywhere the people fell, sleeping among the dead robots as though they never had been strung to the point of breaking, sapped of strength. They abruptly relaxed.

As though it had vanished, America was deaf to cables, to all communication beyond the gigantic circle of sound.

But that midnight all over Europe the drone sounded and Europe's robots began their dance of death . . . and when it had ended a strange and silent rocketship that had hovered high above the stratosphere sped almost with the speed of light and hovered over Asia—and next day Africa heard the drone while the blacks answered it with their tom-toms—then South America heard it and last of all far-off Australia . . . and everywhere terror trapped the peoples and panic and madness took their toll . . .

Until of all that animate metal horde that had fettered Earth and humanity there were a few scant hundreds left—escaped from the death dance thru some variant in their constitution. And, awakening from that swift sleep, all over Earth those who had feared and hated the robots and their slavery rose against those who had fostered the metal domination and blasted the robot factories to rubble.

Again the hill above the caverns opened; the strange torpedo ship blinked into sight like a ghost. As silently as a ghost it floated into the hill and the rocks closed behind it.

Narodny and the others stood before the gigantic television screen, shifting upon it images of city after city, country after country, over all Earth's surface. Lao the Chinese said: "Many men died but many are left. They may not understand—but to them it was worth it."

Narodny mused: "It drives home the lesson, what man does not pay for, he values little. Our friends aloft will have little opposition now I think."

He shook his head doubtfully. "But I still do not like that Wrongness of Space. I do not want my music spoiled again by him, Lao. Shall we hurl the Moon out of the universe, Lao?"

Lao laughed. "And what then would you do for moon-music?"

Narodny said: "True. Well, let us see what men can do. There is always time—perhaps."

The difficulties which beset Martin and Tarvish did not interest the poet Narodny. While the world governments were reorganized, Tarvish's money accomplished miracles—factories turned out spaceships for Earth's fleet—men were trained in handling these ships—supplies were gathered—weapons were perfected—and when the message from Luna arrived, outlining the course to be followed and setting the starting date, the space-fleet of Earth was ready to leave.

Narodny watched the ships take off. He shook his head doubtfully. But soon harmonies were swelling thru the great cavern of the orchards and nymphs and fauns dancing under the fragrant blossoming trees—and the world again forgotten by Narodny.

Let the Future Judge

by L. Lester Anderson

(Author of *The ISAtope Men*)

THE OPPRESSION RETURNED. AND WITH IT A SLOW, INSISTENT, TENUOUS PRESSURE that forced him to a halt, his hands pressing his temples in a futile wave of pity. Brought to his knees by a knifelike thrust of crimson pain, lungs aching for life, the Explorer's universe was bounded, in that instant, only by self. Matter did not exist. Could not exist.

Gradually, from a place unmeasurable by time, the Explorer regained his senses. He was in a valley of reddish slatelike rocks, sloping down to large pools of brackish water, rimmed with varying layers of salt deposits. The corrugated effect, broken only by huge cacti-like objects—*effigies of the dead*, thought the Explorer—against an unearthly serrated horizon, was cause enough to wonder.

Voyages Extraordinaires! And well done. The age-old dream of humankind, now a stark reality. Heaven at your doorstep! Utopia Unlimited! The Elixir! The Explorer gazed at the story etched in the slate. The retreating water, forever lost, only its residue in unholy union with unyielding rock, telling of former imperiousness. God! The irony of it. Arriving just in time for the planet's dying gasp!

With an effort the Explorer rose to his feet and with greater effort sought to shake off the returning malaise, a feeling that went deeper than the body. Striding off thru the interminable wasteland, slate-flakes slashing little arcs in the air, he sought (to what end?) some retention of sanity. Days and days and months and eons of this. And cold piercing nights. Unutterable loneliness; no rasp of an extraterrestrial insect, no foliage for the wind to soothingly rustle, no friendly blue sky; only reddish slate and brackish water and stone effigies of the dead; grim reminder. Worse than all this, thru the rare atmosphere—clearly shining Earth.

How long had it been since the spaceship *Conquest* left its berth in the Americas with a crew of 3? Originally intended as a purely automatic recording trip as the first moon rockets were, the project was later broadened. A trio of human observers was added. Bronson of the gay unbounded enthusiasm—would the world forgive, if it knew, of his suicide in outer space? And Harris, cold, calculating, whose god was imprisoned in an Atom,

175

dying, as the *Conquest* was preparing to land, of septic poisoning! Martyrs in Man's endless quest.

Himself? The Explorer laughed mirthlessly. His was the great Escape—the perfect vanishing act—and all done with science. Earth held no more Samburans; the idyll of Bali was finished; Shangri-La was a myth, even of the imagination. "On Earth as it is in Heaven."

Another ridge of saw-toothed spires, another of the endless series of red-slate valleys, another battle for reason. The *Conquest* lay behind him lost in time and space as if, he thought for a moment, it were on another planet. Radioactive elements in the surrounding terrain had (no doubt) rendered the spaceship totally useless. Just another grim little joke.

Harris was buried in a ridge of red-slate, covered by slabs of the devilish stone. The "waiting" was intolerable. Bronson came to him out of the night, carefree and laughing; Harris was at his side during the day, pleading and urging. The Explorer set out, equipped as no Columbus, no Magellan had ever been. Food, water, oxygen, the extremes of climate, gravity—none held any terrors; science was thorough.

Science was thorough! The Explorer recalled his fights in the parliaments of Earth; for the internationalization of, what was already international, science; the angry denunciations by military and selfish economic groups; his exorcism by the press; the suspicion incubating, festering among nations; the continued rise of imperialism; of "revived" fascism . . .

. . . so, damn them all. Let them all rot in the hovels of their minds! Let them pick each other clean! Let them disintegrate themselves back to the infinite! *I'll see myself in Hell before I'll lift another finger to help. Stupid, blundering idiots!* . . .

The warning signal the Explorer came to know so well lately lay beneath the surface, ready to force his consciousness to retreat before utter oblivion set in. Again the sun was setting, shooting barbed tongues of flame, radiating from a thousand spires, over the landscape. Soon the moons would hurtle thru the populated heavens, masters without dispute of a forgotten, discarded mote. And the one sentient being ironically thought: *This is the culmination of a great Escape; the end product of a great culture—to which monuments will be erected on Earth.* Earth—blue, pulsing, imperfect but something to fight for. To fight primordial thinking and emotions. Too late.

And in the howling silences, in the teeming wastes, out of the vast expanse of nothingness; sharp jagged spires of a cosmic cathedral marking eternally journey's end—lay the first of humanity's representatives to an alien planet. Face downward, arms and legs clutching as if still eager to press on. But listen! That faint derisive whistling in the peaks. Who can say, with only the peaks themselves to record the unrecordable?

The young Martian, soft delicate tendrils twining around the Receptor, expressed herself to the elder, "Is it not so, they have knowledge of great use to us and we to them? Is it not so, the precepts of the Law forbid the willful destruction of life? Is it not so, he may not have been one of them? Then why let the red star-waste take its toll? Are we only protoplasts? O, Sssdahll, I am confused."

Sssdahll, his sensory organs imperceptibly vibrating in warm sympathy, communicated, "You are right, very much right, but study again our RECORD OF THE PLANETS. Understand the ruling passions of these beings of Earth. It is not yet the time. We are grieved but it is better so. Let the future judge."

The image on the Receptor quivered as if in accord.

The following sequences appeared in England in the original magazine serialization of THE TIME MACHINE 100 *years ago but was eliminated from all book versions. It is one of those legendary bits of literature, something like* Dracula's Guest, *which did not see print till many years after the original* Dracula; *like the excised* Spider Scene *from* King Kong; *like the censor-clip of* The Flower That Didn't Float *in the Karloffilm of* Frankenstein . . .

We are indebted to Robert A.W. Lowndes, legendary aficionado of sf for 60 years or more and legendary professional for the better part of 6 decades; we are indebted to "Doc" Lowndes for the original rediscovery & presentation to the sf world of this lost excerpt which takes place between the time the Time Traveler leaves the Age of the Eloi & Morlocks and the time he arrives at the Age of the Red Sun & the Giant Crabs . . .

The Final Men

by H. G. Wells

"I STOPPED. I WAS IN A BLACK MOORLAND, COVERED WITH A SPARSE VEGETATION, and gray with a thin hoarfrost. The time was midday, the orange sun, shorn of its effulgence, brooded near meridian in a sky of drabby gray. Only a few black bushes broke the monotony of the scene. The great buildings of the decadent men among whom, it seemed to me, I had been so recently, had vanished and left no trace; not a mound even marked their position. Hill and valley, sea and river—all, under the wear and work of the rain and frost, had melted into new forms. No doubt, too, the rain and snow had long since washed out the Morlock tunnels. A nipping breeze stung my hands and face. So far as I could see there were neither hills, nor trees, nor rivers; only an uneven stretch of cheerless plateau.

"Then suddenly a dark bulk rose out of the moor, something that gleamed like a serrated row of iron plates, and vanished almost immediately in a depression. And then I became aware of a number of faint-gray things, colored to almost the exact tint of the frostbitten soil, which were browsing here and there upon its scanty grass, and running to and fro. I saw one jump with a sudden start, and then my eye detected perhaps a score of them. At first, I thought they were rabbits, or some small breed of kangaroo. Then, as one came hopping near me, I perceived that it belonged to neither of these groups. It was plantigrade, its hind legs rather the longer; it was tailless, and covered with a straight grayish hair that thickened about the head into a Skye terrier's mane. As I had understood that in the Golden Age man had killed out almost all the other animals, sparing only a few out of the more ornamental, I was naturally curious about the creatures. They did not seem afraid of me, but browsed on, much as rabbits would do in a place unfrequented by man; it occurred to me that I might perhaps secure a specimen.

"I got off the machine, and picked up a big stone. I had scarcely done so when one of the little creatures came within easy range. I was so lucky as to hit it on the head, and it rolled over at once and lay motionless. I ran over to it at once; it remained still, almost as if killed. I was surprised to see that the thing had five feeble digits to both its fore and hind feet—the fore feet, indeed, were almost as human as the fore feet of a frog. It had, moreover, a roundish head, with a projecting forehead and forward-looking eyes, obscured by its lank hair. A disagreeable apprehension flashed across my mind. As I knelt down and seized my capture, intending to examine its teeth and other anatomical points which might show human characteristics, the metallic-looking object to which I have already alluded, reappeared above a ridge on the moor, coming toward me and making a strange clattering sound as it came. Forthwith the gray animals about me began to answer with a short weak yelping—as if of terror—and bolted off in a direction opposite to that from which the new creature approached. They must have hidden in burrows or behind bushes and tussocks, for in a moment not one of them was visible.

"I rose to my feet and stared at this grotesque monster. I can only describe it by comparing it to a centipede. It stood about three feet high, and had a long, segmented body, perhaps thirty feet long, with curiously overlapping greenish-black plates. It seemed to crawl upon a multitude of feet, looping its body as it advanced. Its blunt round head, with a polygonal arrangement of black spots, carried two flexible, writhing, hornlike antennae. It was coming along, I should judge, at a pace of about eight to ten miles an hour, and it left me little time for thinking. Leaving my gray animal, or gray man, whichever it was, on the ground, I set off for the machine. Halfway I paused, regretting that abandonment, but a glance over my shoulder destroyed any such regret. When I gained the machine the monster was scarcely fifty yards away. It was certainly not a vertebrated animal. It had no snout, and its mouth was ringed with dark-colored plates. But I did not care for a nearer view.

"I traversed one day and stopped again, hoping to find the columns gone and some vestige of my victim; but, I should judge, the giant centipede did not trouble itself about bones. At any rate both had vanished. The faintly human touch of these little creatures perplexed me greatly. If you come to think, there is no reason why a degenerate humanity should not come at last to differentiate into as many species as the descendants of the mud fish who fathered all the land vertebrates. I saw no more of any insect colossus, as to my thinking, the segmented creature must have been.

Evidently the physiological difficulty that at present keeps all the insects small had been surmounted at last, and this division of the animal kingdom had arrived at the long awaited supremacy which its enormous energy and vitality deserves. I made several attempts to kill or capture another of the grayish vermin, but none of my missiles were so successful as the first; and after perhaps a dozen throws, disappointing, that left my arm aching, I felt a gust of irritation at my folly in coming so far into futurity without weapons or equipment. I resolved to run on for one glimpse of the still remoter future—one peep into the deeper abyss of time—and then to return to you and my own epoch. Once more I remounted the machine, and once more the world grew hazy and gray."

Navigational Error

by Steve Tymon

AND WHEN THE LAST FIRES HAD GONE OUT ON THE FINAL WORLD OF MAN, WHEN all the peoples of the galaxy lay dead and rotting or burned to ashes, they found him cowering in the darkest, deepest cave. He had been a lieutenant in the Galactic Fleet once but had been stripped of his rank and imprisoned for running in fear from the planet-sized warships of the Thoran Empire. And now they were all that remained. The victorious Thoran Fleet hovered in the space around his smoldering world, filling the entire sky and blocking out the light of the stars like great, dark metallic angels of death even though the nearest ship was hundreds of thousands of miles away. They could have killed him instantly but, instead, since he was the last, he was brought to the Overlord and left standing in front of the dark figure on the Throne of Command.

The Overlord looked down at the incredibly small figure on the floor before him. This was one of the creatures that had defeated the might and the power of the First Empire? It did not seem possible.

"Speak," commanded the Overlord, his thundering voice echoing throughout the miles-long room. "Speak before I kill you, last of a kind."

The man looked up slowly. In the darkness, he could barely see the towering black-armored figure, its face totally devoid of features, its voice the amplified metallic voice of a cyborg warrior. He had once had nightmares about these demon machine-creatures, and now all the nightmares had come true.

"What would you have me say?" he began, his voice nervous, weak and faltering. "Do you want me to beg for mercy? I won't. You're going to kill me anyway. I know you don't take prisoners. You'd rather murder entire worlds than take prisoners."

"Those were my orders. I was to exterminate all of the intelligent life forms in this galaxy. With your death, those orders will be fulfilled."

"But why? Why would your Empire give such orders?"

"Because you defeated us once. Because you caused the death of our First Empire. Because we will not have you cause the death of the Second."

"But we didn't cause the death of any Empire."

"Liar!" The Overlord sprang to his feet, shaking his metal fists in anger. "Perhaps your race forgets too easily the wars of a thousand arns past. But not mine. If the order of extermination was given, it is only because you defeated us once and because it has been decided that you are too dangerous to survive. It is finished now. Thoran has won."

The man dropped to his knees, shaking his head in despair.

"The entire Terran galaxy," he moaned, "all the worlds of mankind, murdered because of a forgotten war."

"The Terran Galaxy?" The Overlord seemed puzzled. "You mean this isn't Andromeda?"

Devonshire's Song

by Matt Graham

(Author of *Citadel*)

Log Entry: C.A.S. EXPLORER   13 May 2022
After 12 prolonged weeks of starlight, EXPLORER is rapidly approaching
the edge of our galaxy. As a result of our great distance from Coalescence
Central, sub-spacial contact has been arbitrarily severed.

Fortunately, all aboard are in high spirits and are anxiously awaiting the
actual beginning of our odyssey. My fingers are crossed.

Tai Li-Chuan

Log Entry: C.A.S. EXPLORER   14 May 2022
Awakened this "morning" by cries from First Mate DeSoto. The unexpected
has happened: in the hitherto unexplored intergalactic void we have
detected a space vessel! As it lies ahead almost directly in our flight path, I
have ordered all defenses to full readiness. Contact in 19 hours 22 minutes.

Later: Some of my worries alleviated. Long-range scanning has identified our mysterious ship as an ancient Dutch freighter sold years ago at auc-
tion. Unless drastically altered, it is unarmed. It has refused our hailing
frequencies.

Tai Li-Chuan

Log Entry: C.A.S. EXPLORER   15 May 2022
One hour distant from rendezvous and we are still without any knowledge
of its mission. Kaldan has indicated that he believes our foe to be merely a
derelict.

Nonetheless, I've assembled a boarding party with myself in command:
I want to learn more about our "foe."

Later: Murphy found the old man first and when we returned to
EXPLORER was the first to catch the old man's desperate attempts to
speak. Yet those parched, aged lips somehow seem to have a life of their
own. No matter how he tries, the old man cannot make a sound. Not even
a guttural growl! Dr. Lysenkov is completely baffled.

Tai Li-Chuan

Log Entry: C.A.S. EXPLORER   16 May 2022
Incredible . . . the old man has "spoken" today; and I think perhaps it is
lucky that we neglected to record his words for others to hear.

"Help . . ." he pleaded at first, his voice weak from hunger. Then, as if
entranced, his eyes rolled back and his lips began to vibrate ominously. And
a *song* came from his throat—a melodious song, meaningless, yet somehow
haunting in its depth. The words were alien, the tones completely unknown
. . . as if the product of an entirely unique intelligence.

Tai Li-Chuan

Log Entry: C.A.S. EXPLORER   17 May 2022
Devonshire, the old man, has spoken again today, and between those
increasingly more frequent lapses into that alien song, has related a most
incredible tale.

It appears that Devonshire commandeered the freighter by bribing the
single guard aboard and struck out for deep space—beyond the rim.
Beyond that explanation, however, his coherency drops and he makes no
sense whatever . . . as if his mind were struggling to remember and fighting
to relate that memory to us.

Later: Devonshire is conscious again and once more trying to make us
understand. His continual references to "The utter emptiness of it all . . ."
and his fear of being left alone convince me that he is psychotic. Lysenkov
agrees, with some medical reservations. Of course.

Tai Li-Chuan

Log Entry: C.A.S. EXPLORER   18 May 2022
Devonshire died this morning and was buried in space as befitting his wishes. Altho we regret his demise, we need no longer remain motionless and
have resumed course for Andromeda. Speed factors building up nicely . . .
will reach rim in 14 hours.

Tai Li-Chuan

Log Entry: C.A.S. EXPLORER   19 May 2022
Success! We have breached the final barriers of the Milky Way and are now
under way toward the neighboring galaxy of Andromeda. The lack of stars
is quite disconcerting but we will adjust eventually. Our training has been
most thorough.

Later: Wilden was about to go off watch when he began to stare at the
almost empty viewing screen before him—blankly, as if stunned by the
loneliness surrounding him. Lysenkov tranquilized him but I am worried.
Feeling rather lonely myself.

Tai Li-Chuan

Log Entry: C.A.S. EXPLORER   20 May 2022
Words coming slowly now . . . don't feel much like sitting down and writing

to people who are so very far away. Everyone aboard is beginning to exhibit signs of nervousness and we are all tense and irritable. Murphy nearly killed DeSoto this morning—and they can't even tell me why they were fighting. Will our grueling training save us?

Yes . . . it must. But everything so *vast* out here . . . so overwhelming. A glimpse at eternity . . . and infinity! It's so lonely . . . so very, very lonely.

Tai Li-Chuan

Log Entry: C.A.S. EXPLORER   21 May 2022

I've given up . . . ordered us to turn about. The enormity of the emptiness is too overwhelming to withstand. But even at maximum speed, days must pass before we return to the comfort of the Milky Way . . . but I think we can survive.

Oh, the loneliness . . .

Tai Li-Chuan

Log Entry: C.A.S. EXPLORER   22 May 2022

I understand what Devonshire went thru now and hope we will be spared a similar fate. We must hold out a little longer . . . just a little longer!

Where are the stars . . . ?

Tai Li-Chuan

Log Entry: C.A.S. EXPLORER   23 May 2022

No! No! It's happened! This morning, when I went below, I heard it . . .

Murphy has started to sing Devonshire's song!

And so have we all . . .

Tai Li-Chuan

A Martian Oddity

by Weaver Wright

(Author of *The Island of Dr. Murdeaux*)

Eastern Canalopolis, Mars. Sometime in the next decade.

The wife of the Bhurgor-Marster was very nervous. She hopped about like a zand-flea on a Hottin roof. (Hottin the roof-maker was a household name on Mars.) It was all because of that *man* from the Blue Planet who was coming to dinner.

It was not every night that the Marster's wife entertained an Earthman for supper; in fact, this was the first time in Zumbarin (Martian) history that a Soojamian (Earthman) was to dine on Mars. Rice Leybury was the first astronaut to reach the Red Planet.

Shona* Aardvark (whose name purely by cosmic coincidence coincided with that of a popular terrestrial crossword puzzle perennial) was quite upset at the lack of progress in her culinary preparations. Her ten tentacles twitched like a dekapus and she wished she had as many hands as she tried to manage her pots and pans with only three pair. Mrs. Aardvark was world-famous (Mars-world, that is) for the excellence of her cuisine (a French word which did not exist on Mars, which made her feat all the more remarkable) and her husband had impressed on her that on this historic occasion she must reach a gourmetic pinnacle of perfection.

Equivalent of Mrs., abbreviation for Shonakanatonawana-tok.

A new high in heartburn (the Martian sign of a successful meal).

By the divine providence of Zorub, God of Zumbar, Leybury had landed on the left bank of Canalopolis. (Actually, he had no choice, the right bank having been destroyed centuries ago, so that this was the only bank left.)

Marster Aardvark was extremely anxious to make a resounding hit with the hero from Earth by having a repast prepared for him that would, as the Soojamians were known to remark, "melt in his mouth." Aardvark was, as in fact were all well-educated Martians, fairly familiar with terrestrial sayings, for interplanetary radio had been monitored on Mars for many years now. Every cultured green Martian was acquainted with Ihnglesh in addition to marawana Zumbarian (high Martian) as opposed to the daunir Zumbarian, or low Martian, mumbled by the waterless folk on the wrong side of the Grand Canal.

Marster Aardvark had heard it said, on the Camel Soup commercial, that "the way to a man's heart is thru his stomach." Certain physiologists, never having seen an Earthman, argued that this meant Earthmen's hearts were located behind their stomachs but Marster Aardvark interpreted this epigram on a poetic rather than a biological basis.

• • •

At last Kliro and Dezdra, the double moons of Mars, rose in the evening sky and Mr. Leybury, the man from the planet which was only mono-satellitic, sat at the dinner table of Mrs. Aardvark.

Mrs. Aardvark, as women the worlds over will, mentally appraised Mr. Leybury; and while she found him wanting in certain Zumbarian qualities, she liked him at once because he looked her straight in the eye. Let us be charitable to Mrs. Aardvark's mentality and say that she was unusually ill at ease, otherwise she should have realized that Mr. Leybury had no choice: it *was* rather disconcerting that he had two eyes rather than the normal *one.*

Then, too, Mrs. Aardvark noticed, the Earthman suffered a lack of a full complement of arms and had neither tentacles nor tendrils, which paucity of manly charms made Mrs. Aardvark feel very sorry for Mr. Leybury's shonakanatonawana-tok. (See footnote.) This was a sympathy she might well have spared the astronaut, for space was his only love and the only Venus who could have tempted him was the veiled planet.

And finally (as Mrs. Aardvark mentally catalogued his shortcomings) Mr. Leybury was so small (only 6'3") that he had to be accommodated in the baby's highchair.

But aside from his midget proportions and unaesthetic pink color, he looked almost Martian. In fact, in her ill-fed youth when she had lived among the canables, she could have imagined her parents considering him a fine broth of a man.

The household pets—what few of them there were (1,027)—were fed first, of course, according to Zumbarian custom; then the guest was invited to eat.

As an appetizer Mrs. Aardvark served baloney and applesauce à la banana oil, garnished with balloon juice, a classic combination from recipes of the Raring Twenties that she had once heard of. As Mr. Leybury consumed her delicacy (deliciously served luke cold) Mrs. Aardvark noted with satisfaction that he lost some of his pinkish pallor and began to turn a bright healthy Martian green.

Then came the entree.

With a sense of total triumph Mrs. Aardvark nudged Mr. Aardvark underneath the table with her third leg as she served the roast horse. That is to say, not strictly roast horse but the Zumbarian equivalent, an animal famous for its tough meat. Mrs. Aardvark was familiar with the terrestrial saying, "I'm so hungry I could eat a horse," and she felt certain the astronaut had not had a satisfying meal since he left Earth.

• • •

After the meal was over, the Marster, excusing himself, rose from the table and hopped like a pogo stick on his polite leg to the potted plant. Amidst the leaves he relieved himself of two stentorian belches. Mrs. Aardvark simultaneously raised one of her six hands to her eating mouth (her talking mouth was immaculately free of food and she intended to favor the astronaut with a few songs from her singing mouth later in the evening) and she pointedly coughed. Perhaps radio reception from Earth was not all that it could be in clarity but she was not about to be outdone in the postprandial amenities by her husband: she was sure that she had heard it said among Earthmen that *a burp in the hand was worth two in the bush.*

• • •

The last sensation Mr. Leybury had before he died was one of all-consuming thirst. While the food he had been served had been edible, oddly no beverage had accompanied the repast.

He could not intuit it but his hosts themselves were parched for thirst; however, in deference to the known custom of their guest, they had considerately refrained from drinking. The Aardvarks were conscious of the etiquette of Earth that proscribed the imbibing of liquids with solids. A Soojamian fictionizer by the name of Rudhvar Kipklih had capsulized it in the classic observation:

Eats is eats and wets is wets and never the twins shall meat.

The Aardvarks had heard it on a broadcast from Earth one night.

Mrs. Aardvark, at the behest of her husband, had done her best to make an impression on the famous gastronaut from Earth and she had succeeded beyond her fondest expectations.

Mrs. Aardvark's dramatic dinner made an undying impression on the rocketeer from Planet 3. He paid his hostess the greatest compliment possible from a man of an alien culture: he dropped dead.

One man's meat is another man's poison.

Shona A. smiled with the mouth she reserved for emotions as her husband entwined her with the two tentacles meant for tender moments such as this.

They ate the dishes, turned on the lights (the ultraviolets) and went to bed.

It had been an aard night's vark.

FITTING & PROPER—it is both that Richard Wilson should have written Love *for he was indeed a lovable man.*

I first met him when he, like me, was a young fan—at the First World Science Fiction Convention, New York City, July 4th, 1939.

When Wilson gave his gift of Love *to the world it was in 1952, in the pages of* The Magazine of Fantasy & Science Fiction, *and the readership of its day was not blind to its virtues. Eleven years later the late, loved & lamented King of Anthologists, Groff Conklin, wisely chose to reprint* Love *in* Human & Other Beings.

Boucher & McComas, the co-editors at the time of F&SF, *introduced* Love *as "One of the most sensitive & touching treatments of that delicate subject, physical love between natives of different planets."*

Love

by Richard Wilson

He was from Mars and she was from Earth; and you know what they thought of Martians in those days. He wasn't very tall, as Martians weren't; but that was all right, because she was unusually tiny and only came to his shoulder. They made fun of a Martian's anatomy then. There were a lot of jokes made by professional so-called comedians, just as it had once been considered funny to tell stories about Jews and Scotsmen.

Maybe Jac wasn't much to look at, by the standards of Earth model agencies, but he was intelligent and kind and Ellen loved him. She shouldn't have told her father that, she knew now. It had been difficult enough to be with Jac before the night she'd gone to her father with the confession of her love. He'd stormed up and down the living room of their house at the edge of the spaceport. He'd talked about position and family and biological impossibility. He'd invoked the memory of her dead mother and reminded her of the things he had sacrificed to give her the education *he'd* never had: the special schools and the tutoring. He said that if she could *see* this Martian—this Jac person—she'd understand his point of view and thank him for his efforts to spare her the anguish she would experience as a girl who had crossed the planet line. He didn't stop till he had brought tears to the blind eyes of his daughter.

Only then did he become calm and, with a faint twinge of conscience, tell her as gently as he could that she was not to see the boy again. He would see Jac, he told her, and explain to him that the thing was impossible.

Ellen felt her way to her room and locked the door against him, and finally she heard her father go down the hall and slam his own door.

She refused to go down for breakfast the next morning. She waited till she heard her father leave the house to go to his job in the weather station of the spaceport. Then she left by the back way.

She heard the rattle of Pug's chain against the kennel and his bark of greeting. She knelt and took the paw he offered. It had been broken once and never properly set. She stroked it gently, although it no longer hurt him; it just made him limp. Ellen unhooked the chain from his collar and fastened a short leash to it. She and the dog went through the streets and into the Martian section of town.

The whole community had been the Martians' originally. But after the coming of the Earth people they'd been gradually uprooted and forced into one end of town. Spidertown, she'd heard some people call it. Damn people like that, she thought. People like her father! "Damn them," she said aloud. And Pug growled in sympathy.

She bent down to pet him. He whimpered inquiringly. "Poor crippled Pug," she said. "A blind girl, a lame dog, and a Martian. Outcasts, Pug. That's us." Then she shrugged off her self-pity and walked on.

There was only one really bad crossing. It was a highway and the ore trucks rolled along it all day long, carrying their loads to the spaceport and the great Earth-bound cargo ships. But the traffic man at the edge of the highway knew her and walked across with her and Pug.

"Beautiful morning, Miss Hanson," he said.

She said it smelled good and the air felt real fresh and thanked him.

Jac met her in the park at the edge of the lake. She tingled to the touch of his hand on her arm. His fingers were slender and quite bony and his arm, when he put hers in his, was thin. But he was strong, she knew; once he had picked her up and carried her across a rough patch of ground in the hills where they sometimes walked. He had carried her effortlessly, she remembered, and she had heard the strange rhythm of his heart as she leaned her head against his hard chest.

"Hello," Jac said. "Hello, my girl and my girl's dog."

"Hello, Jac," she said, and Pug wagged his tail so furiously that it beat against her leg. Pug didn't care if Jac was a Martian, and she wished her father had as much judgment.

They went arm-in-arm across the park to the meadows beyond. Pug was unleashed now and frisked about them, his bark echoing flatly in the Martian air.

"This is a beautiful day—one should be so happy," Jac said. "And yet you look unhappy. Why?"

And so Ellen told him, and Jac was silent. For a long time they walked in silence until the ground began to rise and Ellen knew they were nearing the hills.

Jac said at last, "Your father is a good man, and the things he wishes for you are things I cannot give you."

"If you're going to sound like my father," she told him, "I won't listen."

Then he was silent again for a time, but soon he began to speak seriously, and the gist of what he said was that she must forget him because he had been selfish about her. He said he had never really considered that there would be more to their life than just the two of them, and that they must not break her father's heart.

And she asked him, what about *her* heart? And his, too, he said.

And so they were silent again.

"Where are we?" she asked, after a while. They had been climbing for some time.

"I don't know," he said. "I have been thinking too much about us."

"Are we lost?"

"No," he said. "I can see the way we have come. But this is a part of the hills I don't know. You must be tired from the climb. We will rest."

They sat on the soft moss-covered ground amid some rocks and she leaned against his chest. Was he so different from Earth men? she wondered. It was so hard to know—for a blind person to know. If she could see Jac, would her father's warnings mean more to her? Or was her father merely intolerant of anyone who was different?

She had known so few men. Mostly, after childhood, her companions had been men who were kind to her for her father's sake. Many of them had been good fun and friendly, but none had ever been interested in her as a woman. Why should they waste their time with a blind girl? They hadn't, and Ellen had known no intimacy, no real happiness, until Jac.

But now she asked herself if she really loved him, as she maintained to her father, or whether she was grateful to him. What did she know of love? If she had once loved an Earth man, could she now love Jac?

It was so difficult. Her standards were confused. She did not even know what an Earth man looked like.

"Let me touch you, Jac," she said.

He gave her his hand and she seemed to feel his eyes on her face.

Her fingers traveled up his familiar arm, to his shoulder. The shoulder was bony and sharp, but so was hers. His neck was thick and his chin was not so well defined as her father's. Jac's nose was broader, too, and his eyes were sunk deep in his head. The head was hairless, not partially, like her father's, but completely. Ellen knew it was not usual for Earth men to be hairless, not men as young as Jac. Ellen put her hand against his chest. It was hard and rounded and there was that strange rhythm of his heartbeat. She took her hand away.

"How do I seem to you?" she asked.

If their races were so different, wouldn't he be repelled by her—by the thought of her body and his together in marriage?

"You are beautiful to me, Ellen," he said. "You are lovely."

She sighed.

"But this does not mean that *I* would seem attractive to *you*," he went on. "I must say to you truthfully that I believe Earth people are more appealing to Martians—from an aesthetic point of view, if not a political one—than Martians are to Earth people. But," he added, "I believe a Martian retains his good physical attributes until death. He does not become fat, or senile, or ill. He doesn't wrinkle and sag as do some of your people. I think this is in favor of your happiness."

"I must seem cruel to you," Ellen said, "to be so questioning of our love."

"No," Jac said, "you have a special problem. You must really know me before you can be sure."

Would he look strange if I could see him? she thought. Would I be ashamed that he is bald and big-nosed and chinless? She used these descriptions in her thoughts deliberately to see if they bothered her. Would the rest of his body disgust me if I knew it? I know him to be intelligent and loving, brave and devoted, honest and good. But would these qualities have meant anything to me, if I had been able to see and I had discovered them in him?

There was no answer.

"Where's Pug?" she asked.

"I don't know. He went over a rise some time ago."

Ellen stood up. "Let's look for him. You must want to know where we are, anyhow."

They walked slowly in the direction the dog had gone. The way was rocky and the path seemed to become narrower. It grew chilly as the sun became hidden by a cliff. They walked along the base of the cliff and soon a second cliff was on the other side and they were in a canyon.

Jac described it to her as they went.

Suddenly he touched her elbow and they stopped.

"Now I know where we are," he said. "I've never been here before, but I know from the stories I've heard."

"Where?"

"This is the Valley of the Stars. We have a legend that it was first found at night. And at the end of it is the Cave of Violet Light. It's a beautiful legend. The Cave was found long ago. Then the way to it became lost. That was many years ago, before my father's time. But it is just as *his* father described it. The walls of the Valley are carved with lifelike figures from our antiquity. Here, some of the carvings are down low and you can feel them."

He placed her finger and she traced out figures of people.

"We do not know what period of our history they represent, but the figures are Martian. Here," he said, "is the carving of a very young child—and a woman." He led her fingers.

Hesitantly, her fingers explored the carvings while his hand rested reassuringly on her shoulder. "The figures are unclothed," she said.

"Yes."

The carvings were right to her touch and yet elusively, indefinitely wrong. Perhaps she could not judge the relative proportions. She could not tell. She became uneasy. "Why, it's only a baby—the child," she said.

"No," Jac said. "The child is three or four years old."

Her hand dropped.

Jac took her arm. "Come," he said, "we'll see if Pug went this way. Toward the Cave."

She walked in silence beside him.

"The Cave is the real source of the legend. The Cave of the Violet Light. They say it is magic. They said it has healing properties—the Violet Light. That whoever stands in its glow is made well. That the lame walk, and the deaf hear, and the—"

He stopped, and Ellen felt him looking at her.

"Yes?" she said. "And the blind?"

"And the blind see."

Jac continued, "It is a legend that linked with a time when we Martians ceased to become ill and to suffer the effects of age and deterioration. Our forefathers, so cured, bestowed the gift on all their descendants."

There was a barking in the Valley, echoing around a bend, and in a moment the dog was frisking toward them.

Ellen knelt and petted him.

"Hello, you Pug," she said. "Were you exploring? Were you in the Cave of the Violet Light?"

She could feel the dog's body moving as the tail wagged hugely.

"Were you?" she asked. "Were you in the Cave? Let me have your paw!"

The dog extended his paw to Ellen. She felt it.

"The other one!" she cried.

It, too, was whole. No bump or sign of a break anywhere.

"Jac!" she cried. "Does he limp? Pug, I mean. Is he healed?"

"Silly girl. It's just a legend."

"Look at him!" she said. "Does he limp?"

"No. It is amazing, but he's well. Come here, Pug. Let me see your paw. The bad one. He *is* well, Ellen."

"Oh, Jac!"

"I have never really believed it possible—and never really disbelieved," he said slowly. "I suppose we Martians are less preoccupied with miraculous cures because we have so little need of them."

"But, Jack, it *must* be true!"

He took her hand, and they started down the Valley of the Stars in the direction of the Cave.

"Here is the bend," Jac said. "And there is the Cave."

"Describe it to me," she said. "Tell me how it looks."

"The entrance is like a triangle. As high as three men. There is rubble of fallen rock in front and a little way inside. And then it is clean and the floor is smooth, polished rock. And farther back there is a violet glow. It seems to come from the slanting walls, and the floor is like a deep pond."

"I've never seen in my life," Ellen said. "I was born sightless."

She felt herself trembling.

"I'm told violet is a beautiful color," she said. "Is it beautiful?"

"It is the most beautiful color I've seen. It's past description. It's so beautiful that you must be able to feel it if the light touches you."

Then he asked: "Will you go in?" His voice was hushed. It caressed her and soothed her and she stopped trembling. She loved him, now, the way she knew him. His thin hand was gentle and strong—holding hers.

The words leaped into her mind: Bald. Big-nosed. Chinless. What did these words mean visually? What were ugliness and beauty to one who had never seen anything?

She remembered the figures her fingers had traced in the wall of the Valley of the Stars. The woman. The child—who was not a baby.

And she shivered.

Jac's hand tightened until her hand hurt. "You are afraid you will see me and find me ugly. In your mind they have made me something monstrous because I am different!"

"Let us go away," she said miserably. "I love you."

He was silent for a long while.

"If the Cave will let you see me," he said at last, "then you must. In the darkness, shadows become terrible things."

Her hand touched his face gently. He kissed the slim, cold fingers.

"Will you go in?"

"Yes," she whispered.

Depending on who visits Mars (Burroughs, Weinbaum, Clarke, Heinlein, van Vogt) we get different stories. This is the report of what was found there by one of the Great Fans of All Times.

The Golden Pyramid

by Sam Moskowitz

(Author of *The Immortal Storm* & *Man of the Stars*)

IT WAS AN UNUSUALLY CALM DAY FOR MARS. SCARCELY A PARTICLE OF SAND FLOATED in the thin air and nowhere was the horizon tinged with the red that generally heralded a desert sandstorm.

Two space-suited figures, both holding clicking Geiger counters, were painstakingly slipping and sliding through the treacherous sands, making ever widening circles around a small spaceship.

"I think we're almost on top of it, Jim," the tallest and oldest of the men barked into his radio transmitter. He cursed through a week's growth of beard as he slid and almost fell in the slippery red dust.

"The thing that bothers me," the younger man said, "is that the radiation seems rather weak for an important deposit of uranium."

The older man didn't answer. The stepped-up tempo of his instrument told its own story.

There was a whirring sound. Suddenly, a section of sand almost under their feet began to cave in.

"What the hell!" the older man shouted as he made an impressive backward leap of almost 15 feet, made possible by the fact that a man weighs less than 40% as much on Mars as he does on Earth.

There was a swirl of red dust and a V-shaped snout emerged from the sand followed by a body that was about 2 feet long and a foot thick. The spadelike snout cut a path ahead while 2 roughly circular, bumpy appendages, one on either side of the cigar-shaped body, whirled around, propelling it forward much as caterpillar tread moves a bulldozer.

The Geiger counters almost went crazy as the creatures came into full view.

"The blasted thing's radioactive, Bill," the younger man said in astonishment.

The head, except for the snout, had been virtually featureless. Now a section of the surface near the V-shaped projection slid back, for all the world like an opening steel shutter. Through the aperture an eye like a many-faceted gleaming crystal focused on the 2 men. The shutter-like lid slid back, covering the eye except for the tiniest slit. The appendages began to revolve again and the creature headed for the spaceship, moving like an old side-wheel steamboat. It circled the ship once, leaving a permanent wake behind it. Finally it stopped, opened its slit wide and just stared at the ship as though hypnotized.

"A Martian sand swimmer," the older man finally explained. "A few of them were spotted when the first expeditions landed; practically nothing is known about them, since they're difficult to capture. Always located the same way; set the counters a clickin'. There's one theory they're not flesh and blood but some kind of silicon-metallic life."

"Are they dangerous?" the younger man asked.

The older man started to shrug, stopped and pointed at the horizon. The sky was turning red and a gathering dark mass, propelled by winds of hurricane force, seemed to gallop across the desert toward them.

"Quick!" the older man ordered. "Into that outcropping of rocks. We'll never make the ship before it hits us."

Utilizing grotesque hops the 2 men floundered toward a nearby rock formation. They dived into a natural cave only seconds ahead of a shrieking maelstrom of sand which reduced outside visibility to zero.

The younger man wiped the red dust from his eye plate. Then gave a little shout and pounced upon an object on the floor of the cave.

Making whooping noises he straightened up, a gleaming, golden pyramid about 4 inches high resting in the palm of his gloved hand.

"A Martian artifact," the older man gasped. "It's priceless. Proof that a civilization once existed on this planet—looks like cast gold."

"Remember, I found it," the younger man emphasized. There was a tinge of violet on his face but it was hard to say whether it was the result of enthusiasm or the reflection on his viewing plate from the red sands. "I don't have to share the proceeds of what the museums will give me for this with you. It isn't the same as a uranium strike."

"The devil you say," the older man spat, advancing menacingly. "Share and share alike, that was our agreement and you're going to stick by it if I . . ."

"The agreement was for uranium. Nothing was said about something like this," the younger man replied, moving toward the mouth of the cave.

As quickly as it had arrived, the sandstorm retreated until it became a thin, red haze on the horizon. The air cleared and abruptly the ship was visible outside.

"Now look here," the older man reasoned. "That relic must be worth a fortune. There's plenty in it for both of us."

The younger man instead of replying began plowing through the sand toward the spaceship, the golden pyramid clutched in his electrically heated mittens.

"What're you up to?" the older man demanded sharply. "Oh, gonna try to leave me here, are you? Well, we'll see about that."

The 2 men began a bizarre race for the ship. Making fantastic leaps against the lighter gravity and landing to slide face forward in the slippery sands. Then picking themselves up and starting for the ship again.

The younger man reached the airlock first. He reached inside and pressed the button to close it. The fine sand that the storm had blown into the grooves of the lock slowed down its rate of closing and gave the older man time to slip past before it shut. Even as the air pressure began to rise in the cabin of the ship, he threw himself on the younger man and the 2 of them battled furiously but ineffectually. Their reduced weight coupled with the thickly insulated suits deprived the blows of any authority.

A tinny crash interrupted the argument. They simultaneously swung in the direction of the sound. Two mouths gaped as one in amazement.

The strange sand swimmer that had appeared out of the desert sands had evidently entered the lock of the ship while they were in the cave. It now had rammed its ploughlike head through the thin metal skin of the inner wall of the ship, exposing a layer of lead insulation.

At the same time the older man noted that his companion's face was flushed with violet. His anger melted with understanding. "Kid," he said almost kindly, "you've got radiation fever."

The younger man wasn't listening. He was shouting and gesturing. The strange creature was apparently eating the lead insulation in the walls of the ship. It was grinding away with steel-hard rotary teeth, consuming quantities of lead at an alarming rate.

The young man snatched a sampling of ore out of a leather bag and fired it at the creature. It bounced off, ricocheting about the room from the force of the throw. The creature scarcely noticed.

Enraged, the young man dashed over and directed a powerful kick at the hard surface of the Martian life form. Despite its almost metallic texture, the creature was small and the force of the kick sent it rolling toward the lock.

Before it could recover, the young man raced over and gave it another kick that rolled it almost to the lock. The older man pushed the button that opened the lock and a 3d kick propelled the creature out onto the desert sand.

The young man grabbed a rocket gun from the wall and pumped a shell at the creature. He missed and the explosion blew up a geyser of sand. Jim tried to grab the gun but the younger man, his face almost purple with fever, evaded him and brought the butt down alongside his head.

When he came to, the rockets of the ship were a cherry flicker in the sky. He didn't feel angry at the kid. Radiation sickness was something that could hit anyone at anytime. He clicked on his SOS radio signal set. The powerful receivers on Phobos, one of the 2 moons of Mars, would pick it up and a rescue ship would follow, probably in only a matter of hours.

Suddenly he realized that the sand swimmer was resting quietly in the sand scarcely 12 yards away. Its midsection had turned a reddish hue and was beginning to glow.

"It can't be possible," he thought to himself. "That crazy thing eats lead and digests it with the use of a radioactive pile in its stomach." It upset all concepts of life and intelligence. The life force that motivated the thing could be compared to a natural atomic engine.

Though consumed by curiosity he stayed his distance. There was no question in his mind that the kid's radiation sickness was the result of close contact with this creature. He didn't intend to get a dose of the same, even though his own radiation tolerance was evidently higher than the kid's.

The glow in the midsection of the creature gradually diminished and then finally died away altogether. The shutterlike lid slid open and the crystal clear eye regarded him. The sand swimmer's limbs began whirring around like tank treads. The head plowed into the sand. In seconds it had disappeared.

Cautiously Jim approached the hole. The soft, sifting sand was already filling it in. Then something caught his eye. He stared a moment, caught his stomach and rolled over and over on the sand, convulsed by paroxysms of laughter.

There on the sand. On the sometimes treacherous but occasionally puckish red sands of Mars, the sand swimmer had laid a beautiful, glowing, golden pyramid!

Anthologists for a quarter of a century probably overlooked "The Biography Project" because—

It didn't appear on the contents page of Galaxy.

And so it wasn't noted in the Index to Science Fiction Magazines *covering the year 1951.*

But Dudley Dell did well when the Editor of Galaxy *suddenly found himself a couple of pages short of copy and "Dud" came up with this O'Henryarn that was anything but. A "dud," that is.*

A time tale with a new twist in its tail.

And now it can be told. Who the author of the story was. The man behind the pseudonym.

The Biography Project

by Horace L. Gold

T HERE WAS SOMETHING TREMENDOUSLY EXCITING ABOUT THE OPENING OF THE Biofilm Institute. Even a hardened Sunday supplement writer like Wellman Zatz felt it.

Arlington Prescott, a wiper in a contact-eyeglass factory, while searching for a time machine, had invented the Biotime Camera, a standard movie camera—minus sound, of course—that projected a temporal beam, reaccumulated it, and focused it on a temporal-light-sensitized film. When he discovered that he had to be satisfied with merely photographing the past, not physically visiting it, Prescott had quit doing research and become principal of a nursery school.

But, Zatz explained, dictating his notes by persfone to a voxtyper in the telenews office, the Biofilm Institute was based on Prescott's repudiated invention. A huge, massive building, mostly below ground, in the 23rd century style, and equipped with 1,000 Biotime Cameras, it was the gift of Humboldt Maxwell, wealthy manufacturer of Snack Capsules. There were 1,000 teams of biographers, military analysts, historians, etc., to begin recording history as it actually happened—with special attention, according to Maxwell's grant, to past leaders of industry, politics, science, and the arts, in the order named.

Going through the Biofilm Institute, Wellman Zatz gained mostly curt or snarled interviews with the Bioteams; fishing through time for incidents or persons was a nervous job, and they resented interruptions.

He settled finally on a team that seemed slightly friendlier. They were watching what looked like a scene from Elizabethan England on the monitor screen.

"Sir Isaac Newton," Kelvin Burns, the science biographer, grunted in reply to Zatz's question. "Great man. We want to find out why he went off the beam."

Zatz knew about that, of course. Sunday feature articles for centuries had used the case of Sir Isaac to support arguments for psychic phenomena. After making all his astonishing discoveries by the age of 25, the great 17th-century scientist had spent the rest of his long life in a hunt for precognition, the philosopher's stone, and other such paraphernalia of mysticism.

"My guess," said Mowbray Glass, the psychiatrist, "is paranoia caused by feelings of rejection in childhood."

But the screen showed a happy boy in what seemed to be a normal 17th-century home and school environment. Glass grew puzzled as Sir Isaac eventually produced his binomial theorem, differential and integral calculus, and went to work on gravity—all without evidencing any symptoms of emotional imbalance.

"The most unbelievable demonstrative and deductive powers I've encountered," said Pinero Schmidt, the science integrator. "I can't believe such a man could go mystical."

"But he did," Glass said, and tensed. "Look!"

Alone in a dark, cumbersomely furnished study, the man on the screen, wearing a satin coat, stock and breeches, glanced up sharply. He looked directly into the temporal beam for a moment, and then stared into the shadows of the room. He grabbed up a silver candlestick and searched the corners, holding the heavy candlestick like a weapon.

"He's mumbling something," reported Gonzalez Carson, the lip-reader. "Spies. He thinks somebody's after his discoveries."

Burns looked puzzled. "That's the first sign we've seen of breakdown. But what caused it?"

"I'm damned if I know," admitted Glass.

"Heredity?" Zatz suggested.

"No," Glass said positively. "It's been checked."

The Bioteam spent hours prying further. When the scientist was in his thirties, he developed a continuing habit of looking up and smiling secretly. On his deathbed, forty years later, he moved his lips happily, without fear.

"'My guardian angel,'" Carson interpreted for them. "'You've watched over me all my life. I am content to meet you now.'"

Glass started. He went to one Bioteam after another, asking a brief question of each. When he came back, he was trembling.

"What's the answer, Doc?" Zatz asked eagerly.

"We can't use the Biotime Camera any more," Glass said, looking sick. "My colleagues have been investigating the psychoses of Robert Schumann, Marcel Proust, and others, who all eventually developed delusions of persecution."

"Yeah, but why?" Zatz persisted.

"Because they thought they were being spied upon. And they were, of course. By us!"

●

The entities were utterly, ambitiously evil; their line of defense, apparently, was absolutely impregnable.

I'll Kill You Tomorrow

by *Helen Huber*

IT WAS NOT A SINISTER SILENCE. NO SILENCE IS SINISTER UNTIL IT ACQUIRES A background of understandable menace. Here there was only the night quiet of Maternity, the silence of noiseless rubber heels on the hospital corridor floor, the faint brush of starched white skirts brushing through doorways into darkened and semi-darkened rooms.

But there was something wrong with the silence in the "basket room" of Maternity, the glass-walled room containing row on row, the tiny hopes of tomorrow. The curtain was drawn across the window through which, during visiting hours, peered the proud fathers who did the hoping. The nightlight was dim.

The silence should not have been there.

Lorry Kane, standing in the doorway, looked out over the rows of silent baskets and felt her blond hair tighten at the roots. The tightening came from instinct, even before her brain had a chance to function, from the instincts and training of a registered nurse.

Thirty odd babies grouped in one room and—*complete silence.*

Not a single whimper. Not one tiny cry of protest against the annoying phenomenon of birth.

Thirty babies—*dead?* That was the thought that flashed, unbidden, into Lorry's pretty head. The absurdity of it followed swiftly, and Lorry moved on rubber soles between a line of baskets. She bent down and explored with practiced fingers.

A warm, living bundle in a white basket.

The feeling of relief was genuine. Relief, even from an absurdity, is a welcome thing. Lorry smiled and bent closer.

Staring up at Lorry from the basket were two clear blue eyes. Two eyes, steady and fixed in a round baby face. An immobile, pink baby face housing two blue eyes that stared up into Lorry's with a quiet concentration that was chilling.

Lorry said, "What's the matter with you?" She spoke in a whisper and was addressing herself. She'd gone short on sleep lately—the only way,

2 0 4

really, to get a few hours with Pete. Pete was an intern at General Hospital, and the kind of a homely grinning carrot-top a girl like Lorry could put into dreams as the center of a satisfactory future.

But all this didn't justify a case of jitters in the "basket room."

Lorry said, "Hi, short stuff," and lifted Baby Newcomb—Male, out of his crib for a cuddling.

Baby Newcomb didn't object. The blue eyes came closer. The week-old eyes with the hundred-year-old look. Lorry laid the bundle over her shoulder and smiled into the dimness.

"You want to be president, Shorty?" Lorry felt the warmth of a new life, felt the little body wriggle in snug contentment. "I wouldn't advise it. Tough job." Baby Newcomb twisted in his blanket. Lorry stiffened.

Snug contentment?

Lorry felt two tiny hands clutch and dig into her throat. Not just pawing baby hands. Little fingers that reached and explored for the windpipe.

She uncuddled the soft bundle, held it out. There were the eyes. She chilled. No imagination here. No spectre from lack of sleep.

Ancient murder-hatred glowing in new-born eyes.

"Careful, you fool! You'll drop this body." A thin piping voice. A shrill symphony in malevolence.

Fear weakened Lorry. She found a chair and sat down. She held the boy baby in her hands. Training would not allow her to drop Baby Newcomb. Even if she had fainted, she would not have let go.

The shrill voice: "It was stupid of me. Very stupid."

Lorry was cold, sick, mute.

"Very stupid. These hands are too fragile. There are no muscles in the arms. I couldn't have killed you."

"Please—I . . ."

"Dreaming? No. I'm surprised at—well, at your surprise. You have a trained mind. You should have learned, long ago, to trust your senses."

"I don't—understand."

"Don't look at the doorway. Nobody's coming in. Look at me. Give me a little attention and I'll explain."

"Explain?" Lorry pulled her eyes down to the cherubic little face as she parroted dully.

"I'll begin by reminding you that there are more things in existence than your obscene medical books tell you about."

"Who are you? What are you?"

"One of those things."

"You're not a baby!"

"Of course not. I'm . . ." The beastly, brittle voice drifted into silence as though halted by an intruding thought. Then the thought voiced—voiced with a yearning at once pathetic and terrible: "It would be nice to kill you.

Someday I will. Someday I'll kill you if I can find you."

"Why? Why?" Insane words in an insane world. But life had not stopped even though madness had taken over. "Why?"

The voice was matter-of-fact again. No more time for pleasant daydreams. "I'm something your books didn't tell you about. Naturally you're bewildered. Did you ever hear of a bodyless entity?"

Lorry shuddered in silence.

"You've heard of bodyless entities, of course—but you denied their existence in your smug world of precise tidy detail. I'm a bodyless entity. I'm one of a swarm. We come from a dimension your mind wouldn't accept even if I explained it, so I'll save words. We of the swarm seek unfoldment—fulfillment—even as you in your stupid, blind world. Do you want to hear more?"

"I . . ."

"You're a fool, but I enjoy practicing with these new vocal chords, just as I enjoyed flexing the fingers and muscles. That's why I revealed myself. We are, basically of course, parasites. In the dimension where we exist in profusion, evolution has provided for us. There, we seek out and move into a dimensional entity far more intelligent than yourself. We destroy it in a way you wouldn't understand, and it is not important that you should. In fact, I can't see what importance there is in your existing at all."

"You plan to—kill all these babies?"

"Let me congratulate you. You've finally managed to voice an intelligent question. The answer is, no. We aren't strong enough to kill them. We dwelt in a far more delicate dimension than this one and all was in proportion. That was our difficulty when we came here. We could find no entities weak enough to take possession of until we came upon this roomful of infants."

"Then, if you're helpless . . ."

"What do we plan to do? That's quite simple. The material entities will grow. We will remain attached—ingrained, so to speak. When the bodies enlarge sufficiently . . ."

"*Thirty potential assassins* . . ." Lorry spoke again to herself, then hurled the words back into her own mind as her sickness deepened.

The shrill chirping: "What do you mean, potential? The word expresses a doubt. Here there is none." The entity's chuckle sounded like a baby, content over a full bottle. "Thirty certain assassins."

"But why must you kill?"

Lorry was sure the tiny shoulders shrugged. "Why? I don't know. I never thought to wonder. Why must you join with a man and propagate some day? Why do you feel sorry for what you term an unfortunate? Explain your instincts and I'll explain mine."

Lorry felt herself rising. Stiffly, she put Baby Newcomb back into his basket. As she did so, a ripple of shrill, jerky laughter crackled through the room. Lorry put her hands to her ears. "You know I can't say anything.

You'd keep quiet. They'd call me mad."

"Precisely."

Malicious laughter, like driven sleet, cut into her ears as she fled from the room.

Peter Larchmont, M.D., was smoking a quick cigarette by an open fire-escape door on the third floor. He turned as Lorry came down the corridor, flipped his cigarette down into the alley and grinned. "Women shouldn't float on rubber heels," he said. "A man should have warning."

Lorry came close. "Kiss me. Kiss me—hard."

Pete kissed her, then held her away. "You're trembling. Anticipation, Pet?" He looked into her face and the grin faded. "Lorry, what is it?"

"Pete—Pete. I'm crazy. I've gone mad. Hold me."

He could have laughed, but he had looked closely into her eyes and he was a doctor. He didn't laugh. "Tell me. Just stand here. I'll hang onto you and you tell me."

"The babies—they've gone mad." She clung to him. "Not exactly that. Something's taken them over. Something terrible. Oh, Pete! Nobody would believe me."

"I believe the end result," he said, quietly. "That's what I'm for, angel. When you shake like this I'll always believe. But I'll have to know more. And I'll hunt for an answer."

"There isn't any answer, Pete. I *know*."

"We'll still look. Tell me more, first."

"There isn't any more." Her eyes widened as she stared into his with the shock of a new thought. "Oh, Lord! One of them talked to me, but maybe he—or it—won't talk to you. Then you'll never know for sure! You'll think I'm . . ."

"Stop it. Quit predicting what I'll do. Let's go to the nursery."

They went to the nursery and stayed there for three-quarters of an hour. They left with the tinny laughter filling their minds—and the last words of the monstrous entity.

"We'll say no more, of course. Perhaps even this incident has been indiscreet. But it's in the form of a celebration. Never before has a whole swarm gotten through. Only a single entity on rare occasions."

Pete leaned against the corridor wall and wiped his face with the sleeve of his jacket. "We're the only ones who know," he said.

"Or ever will know." Lorry pushed back a lock of his curly hair. She wanted to kiss him, but this didn't seem to be the place or the time.

"We can never tell anyone."

"We'd look foolish."

"We've got a horror on our hands and we can't pass it on."

"What are we going to do?" Lorry asked.

"I don't know. Let's recap a little. Got a cigarette?"

They went to the fire door and dragged long and deep on two from

Lorry's pack. "They'll be quiet from now on. No more talking—just baby squalls."

"And thirty little assassins will go into thirty homes," Lorry said. "All dressed in soft pink and blue, all filled with hatred. Waiting, bidding their time, growing more clever." She shuddered.

"The electric chair will get them all, eventually."

"But how many will they get in the meantime?"

Pete put his arms around her and drew her close and whispered into her ear. "There's nothing we can do—nothing."

"We've got to do something." Lorry heard again the thin, brittle laughter following her, taunting her.

"It was a bad dream. It didn't happen. We'll just have to sleep it off."

She put her cheek against his. The rising stubble of his beard scratched her face. She was grateful for the rough touch of solid reality.

Pete said, "The shock will wear out of our minds. Time will pass. After a while, we won't believe it ourselves."

"That's what I'm afraid of."

"It's got to be that way."

"We've got to do something."

Pete lowered his arm wearily. "Yeah—we've got to do something. Where there's nothing that can be done. What are we—miracle workers?"

"We've got to do something."

"Sure—finish out the watch and then get some sleep."

Lorry awoke with the lowering sun in her window. It was a blood red sun. She picked up the phone by her bedside. "Room 307 Resident's extension."

Pete answered drowsily. Lorry said, "Tell me—did I dream, or did it really happen?"

"I was going to ask you the same thing. I guess it happened. What are you doing?"

"Lying in bed."

"So am I. But two different beds. Things are done all wrong."

"Want to take a chance and sneak over? I've got an illegal coffee pot."

"Leave the door unlocked."

Lorry put on the coffee. She showered and got into her slip. She was brushing her hair when Pete came in. He looked at her and extended beckoning, clutching fingers. "The hell with phantoms. Come here."

After a couple of minutes, Lorry pulled away and poured the coffee. She reached for her uniform. Pete said, "Don't put it on yet."

"Too dangerous—leaving it off."

He eyed her dreamily. "I'll dredge up willpower. I'll also get scads of fat rich clients. Then we'll get married so I can assault you legally."

Lorry studied him. "You're not even listening to yourself. What is it, Pete? What have you dreamed up?"

"Okay. I've got an idea. You said something would have to be done."

"What?"

"A drastic cure for a drastic case. With maybe disaster as the end product."

"Tell me."

"I'll tell you a little, but not too much."

"Why not all?"

"Because if we ever land in court, I want you to be able to say under oath, 'He didn't tell me what he planned to do'."

"I don't like that."

"I don't care if you like it or not. Tell me, what's the one basic thing that stands out in your mind about these—entities?"

"That they're . . ."

"Fragile?"

"Yes—fragile."

"Give me some more coffee."

Lorry demanded to know what was in Pete's mind. All she got was kissed, and she did not see Pete again until eleven o'clock that night. He found her in the corridor in Maternity and motioned her toward the nursery. He carried a tray under a white towel. He said, "You watch the door. I'm going inside. I'll be about a half an hour."

"What are you going to do?"

"You stay out here and mind your business. Your business will be to steer any nosy party away. If you can't, make noise coming in."

Doc Pete turned away and entered the nursery. Lorry stood at the doorway, in the silence, under the brooding night-light, and prayed.

Twenty-five minutes later, Pete came out. His face was white and drawn. He looked like a man who had lately had a preview of Hell's inverted pleasures. His hands trembled. The towel still covered the tray. He said, "Watch them close. Don't move ten steps from here." He started away—turned back. "All hell is scheduled to break loose in this hospital shortly. Let's hope God remains in charge."

Lorry saw the sick dread of his heart underneath his words.

It could have been a major scandal. An epidemic of measles on the maternity floor of a modern hospital indicates the unforgivable medical sin—carelessness. It was hushed up as much as possible, pending the time when the top people could shake off the shock and recover their wits. The ultimate recovery of thirty babies was a tribute to everyone concerned.

Wan, done-in, Doc Pete drank coffee in Lorry's room. Lorry gave him three lumps of sugar and said, "But are you sure the sickness killed the entities?"

"Quite sure. Somehow they *knew* when I made the injections. They screamed. They knew they were done for."

"It took courage. Tell me: why are you so strong, so brave? Why are you so wonderful?"

"Cut it out. I was scared stiff. If *one* baby had died, I'd have gone through life weighing the cure against the end. It isn't easy to risk doing murder—however urgent the need."

She leaned across and kissed him. "And you were all alone. You wouldn't let me help. Was that fair?'

He grinned, then sobered. "But I can't help remembering what that— that invisible monster said: *'Never before has a whole swarm gotten through. Only a single entity on rare occasions.'*

"I can't help wondering what happens to those single entities. I think of the newspaper headlines I've seen: Child Kills Parents in Sleep. Youth Slays Father. I'll probably always wonder—and I'll always remember . . ."

Lorry got up and crossed to him and put her arms around him. "Not always," she whispered. "There will be times when I'll make you forget. For a little while, anyhow."

Grendal Briarton, you have much to atone for. Do you hear that, Grendal? Are you listening? Much to atone for. What's that you say? You're tone deaf? Well, then, cast a jaundiced optic on—

Police Action

by S. C. Smith

(Author of *Race* & *Obit*)

INSPECTOR JARVIS OLIVER AMBLED DOWN THE GANGPLANK OF THE *HULK* WHEN IT docked at Alpha Crucis. His brow was furrowed in thought. "How could they have gotten away from me on Deneb 12?" he demanded of himself. "I had them surrounded in the warehouse and they just seem to—to disappear."

Oliver scowled and randomly scanned the disembarking passengers of the *F. X. Hulk*, just arriving from Deneb 12. His eyes flared with recognition. Two Terrans, obviously twins, were making their way hurriedly thru the crowd. He dived off the remaining few feet of plank, tucked and rolled. He came up running. With complete disregard for his meager baggage, he lit out after the two men. Although they were traveling at remarkable speed, he managed to stay within 10 meters of them.

Almost losing them in a lengthy corridor, he pulled out his portable radio and called a message into HQ, via the hypercom relay station. "Inspector Oliver to Interpol, Oliver to Interstellar Police, do you copy?"

"Roger, this is Interpol HQ. Howdy, Jarvis!"

"This is Oliver and I am in pursuit of the Bird twins, the ones who escaped from TP last month."

"Uh, 10-4, yeah."

"I am requesting aid. They are armed and I wouldn't put shooting past them. After all, they did it to 20 other people."

"Roger. I have a bulletin from Com Central. Say that you are ordered to shoot these guys on sight."

"Well, I've seen 'em."

Just then the good Inspector, about out of wind from running and talking, came upon a cul-de-sac where the two fugitives were attempting to make it over the vast wall.

"Police—*freeze!*"

They didn't. Gordon Bird tried to shoot Oliver but the Inspector nimbly dived out of the way. Judging from the width of the beam, he would say that it was a Durant 50-t. The weapon used in all the Durant cases. It was, however, no match for his Stone #968597hf, 30-70 ray emittance device deluxe.

Then the Inspector remembered the words of the radioman Dale Gerard, telling him to kill the Bird brothers on sight. He grimly took out his ray pistol and silently but efficiently killed two Birds with one Stone.

The women had made up their minds, and nothing—repeat, nothing—could change them. But something *had to give . . .*

Where There's Hope

by Jerome Bixby

(Author of *It's A Good Life*)

"IF YOU CALLED ME HERE TO TELL ME TO HAVE A CHILD," MARY PORNSEN SAID, "you can just forget about it. We girls have made up our minds."

Hugh Farrel, Chief Medical Officer of the *Exodus VII*, sighed and leaned back in his chair. He looked at Mary's husband. "And you, Ralph," he said. "How do you feel?"

Ralph Pornsen looked at Mary uncomfortably, started to speak and then hesitated.

Hugh Farrel sighed again and closed his eyes. It was that way with all the boys. The wives had the whip hand. If the husbands put up an argument, they'd simply get turned down flat: no sex at all, children or otherwise. The threat, Farrel thought wryly, made the boys softer than watered putty. His own wife, Alice, was one of the ringleaders of the "no babies" movement, and since he had openly declared warfare on the idea, she wouldn't even let him kiss her good-night. (For fear of losing her determination, Farrel liked to think.)

He opened his eyes again to look past the Pornsens, out of the curving port of his office-lab in the *Exodus VII*'s flank, at the scene outside the ship.

At the edge of the clearing he could see Danny Stern and his crew, tiny beneath the cavernous sunbeam-shot overhang of giant leaves. Danny was standing up at the controls of the 'dozer, waving his arms. His crew was struggling to get a log set so he could shove it into place with the 'dozer. They were repairing a break in the barricade—the place where one of New Earth's giant saurians had come stamping and whistling through last night to kill three colonists before it could be blasted out of existence.

It was difficult. Damned difficult. A brand-new world here, all ready to receive the refugees from dying Earth. Or rather, all ready to be *made* ready, which was the task ahead of the *Exodus VII*'s personnel.

An Earth-like world. Green, warm, fertile—and crawling, leaping, hooting and snarling with ferocious beasts of every variety. Farrel could certainly see the women's point in banding together and refusing to produce children.

Something inside a woman keeps her from wanting to bring life into peril—at least, when the peril seems temporary, and security is both remembered and anticipated.

Pornsen said, "I guess I feel just about like Mary does. I—I don't see any reason for having a kid until we get this place ironed out and safe to live in."

"That's going to take time, Ralph." Farrel clasped his hands in front of him and delivered the speech he had delivered so often in the past few weeks. "Ten or twelve years before we really get set up here. We've got to build from the ground up, you know. We'll have to find and mine our metals. Build our machines to build shops to build more machines. There'll be resources that we *won't* find, and we'll have to learn what this planet has to offer in their stead. Colonizing New Earth isn't simply a matter of landing and throwing together a shining city. I only wish it were.

"Six weeks ago we landed. We haven't yet dared to venture more than a mile from this spot. We've cut down trees and built the barricade and our houses. After protecting ourselves we have to eat. We've planted gardens. We've produced test-tube calves and piglets. The calves are doing fine, but the piglets are dying one by one. We've got to find out why.

"It's going to be a long, long time before we have even a minimum of security, much less luxury. Longer than you think . . . So much longer that waiting until the security arrives before having children is out of the question. There are critters out there—" he nodded toward the port and the busy clearing beyond— "that we haven't been able to kill. We've thrown everything we have at them, and they come back for more. We'll have to find out what *will* kill them—how they differ from those we *are* able to kill. We are six hundred people and a spaceship, Ralph. We have techniques. That's *all.* Everything else we've got to dig up out of this planet. We'll need people, Mary; we'll need the children. We're counting on them. They're vital to the plan we've made."

Mary Pornsen said, "Damn the plans. I won't have one. Not now. You've just done a nice job of describing all my reasons. And all the other girls feel the same way."

She looked out the window at the 'dozer and crew. Danny Stern was still waving his arms; the log was almost in place. "George and May Wright were killed last night. So was Farelli. If George and May had had a child, the monster would have trampled it too—it went right through their cabin like cardboard. It isn't fair to bring a baby into—"

Farrel said, "Fair, Mary? Maybe it isn't fair *not* to have one. *Not* to bring it into being and give it a chance. Life's always a gamble—"

"*It* doesn't exist," Mary said. She smiled. "Don't try circumlocution on me, Doc. I'm not religious. I don't believe that spermatazoa and an ovum, if not allowed to cuddle up together, add up to murder."

"That isn't what I meant—"

"You were getting around to it—which means you've run out of good arguments."

"No. I've a few left." Farrel looked at the two stubborn faces: Mary's, pleasant and pretty, but set as steel; Ralph's, uncomfortable, thoughtful, but mirroring his definite willingness to follow his wife's lead.

Farrel cleared his throat. "You know how important it is that this colony be established? You know that, don't you? In twenty years or so the ships will start arriving. Hundreds of them. Because we sent a message back to Earth saying we'd found a habitable planet. Thousands of people from Earth, coming here to the new world we're supposed to get busy and carve out for them. We were selected for that task—first of judging the right planet, then of working it over. Engineers, chemists, agronomists, all of us—we're the task force. We've got to do the job. We've got to test, plant, breed, rebalance, create. There'll be a lot of trial and error. We've got to work out a way of life, so the thousands who will follow can be introduced safely and painlessly into the—well, into the organism. And we'll need new blood for the jobs ahead. We'll need young people—"

Mary said, "A few years one way or the other won't matter much, Doc. Five or six years from now this place will be a lot safer. Then we women will start producing. But not now."

"It won't work that way," Farrel said. "We're none of us kids any longer. I'm fifty-five. Ralph, you're forty-three. I realize that I must be getting old to think of you as young. Mary, you're thirty-seven. We took a long time getting here. Fourteen years. We left an Earth that's dying of radioactive poisoning, and we all got a mild dose of that. The radiation we absorbed in space, little as it was, didn't help any. And that sun up there—" again he nodded at the port—"isn't any help either. Periodically it throws off some pretty damned funny stuff.

"Frankly, we're worried. We don't know whether or not we *can* have children. Or *normal* children. We've got to find out. If our genes have been bollixed up, we've got to find out why and how and get to work on it immediately. It may be unpleasant. It may be heartbreaking. But those who will come here in twenty years will have absorbed much more of Earth's radioactivity than we did, and an equal amount of the space stuff, and this sun will be waiting for them . . . We'll have to know what we can do for them."

"I'm not a walking laboratory, Doc," Mary said.

"I'm afraid you are, Mary. All of you are."

Mary set her lips and stared out the port.

"It's got to be done, Mary."

She didn't answer.

"It's going to be done."

"Choose someone else," she said.

"That's what they all say."

She said, "I guess this is one thing you doctors and psychologists didn't figure on, Doc."

"Not at first," Farrel said. "But we've given it some thought."

MacGuire had installed the button convenient to Farrel's right hand, just below the level of the desktop. Farrel pressed it. Ralph and Mary Pornsen slumped in their chairs. The door opened, and Doctor John J. MacGuire and Ted Harris, the *Exodus VII*'s chief psychologist, came in.

When it was over, and the after-play had been allowed to run its course, Farrel told the Pornsens to go into the next room and shower. They came back soon, looking refreshed. Farrel ordered them to get back into their clothes. Under the power of the hypnotic drug which their chairs had injected into them at the touch of the button, they did so. Then he told them to sit down in the chairs again.

MacGuire and Harris had gathered up their equipment, piling it on top of the operating table.

MacGuire smiled. "I'll bet that's the best-monitored, most hygienic sex act ever committed. I think I've about got the space radiations effect licked."

Farrel nodded. "If anything goes wrong, it certainly won't be our fault. But let's face it—the chances are a thousand to one that something *will* go wrong. We'll just have to wait. And work." He looked at the Pornsens. "They're very much in love, aren't they? And she was receptive to the suggestion—beneath it all, she was burning to have a child, just like the others."

MacGuire wheeled out the operating table, with its load of serums, pressure-hypos and jury-rigged thingamabobs which he was testing on alternate couples. Ted Harris stopped at the door a moment. He said, "I think the suggestions I planted will turn the trick when they find out she's pregnant. They'll come through okay—won't even be too angry."

Farrel sighed. They'd been over it in detail several times, of course, but apparently Harris needed the reassurance as much as he did. He said: "Sure. Now scram so I can go back into my act."

Harris closed the door. Farrel sat down at his desk and studied the pair before him. They looked back contentedly, holding hands, their eyes dull.

Farrel said, "How do you feel?"

Ralph Pornsen said, "I feel fine."

Mary Pornsen said, "Oh, I feel *wonderful*!"

Deliberately Farrel pressed another button below his desktop.

The dull eyes cleared instantly.

"Oh, you've given it some thought, Doc?" Mary said sweetly. "And what have you decided?"

"You'll see," Farrel said. "Eventually."

He rose. "That's all for now, kids. I'd like to see you again in one month—for a routine checkup.

Mary nodded and got up. "You'll still have to wait, Doc. Why not admit you're licked?"

Ralph got up too, and looked puzzled.

"Wow," he said. "I'm tired."

"Perhaps just coming here," Farrel said, "discharged some of the tension you've been carrying around."

The Pornsens left.

Farrel brought out some papers from his desk and studied them. Then, from the file drawer, he selected the record of Hugh and Alice Farrel. Alice would be at the perfect time of her menstrual cycle tomorrow . . .

Farrel flipped his communicator.

"MacGuire," he said. "Tomorrow it's me."

MacGuire chuckled. Farrel could have kicked him. He put his chin in his hands and stared out the port. Danny Stern had the log in place in the barricade. The bulldozer was moving on to a new task. His momentary doubt stilled, Farrel went back to work.

Twenty-one years later, when the ships from Earth began arriving, the log had been replaced by a stone monument erected to the memory of the *Exodus VII*, which had been cut apart for its valuable steel. Around the monument was a park, and on three sides of the park was a shining town—not really large enough to be called a city—of plastic and stone, for New Earth had no iron ore, only zinc and a little copper. This was often cause for regret.

Still it was a pretty good world. The monster problem had been licked by high-voltage cannon. Now in their third generation since the landing, the monsters kept their distance. And things grew—things good to eat.

And even without steel, the graceful, smoothly-functioning town looked impressive—quite a thing to have been built by a handful of beings with two arms and two legs each.

It hadn't been, entirely. But nobody thought much about that any more. Even the newcomers got used to it. Things change.

THE AUTHOR of the following story started out with The Unkindest Cut of All, *which wound up being selected for inclusion in the* Best Science Fiction for 1973 *anthology. Now here he is again with a tale which tells what might have happened if a sci-ants fiction protagonist Leiningen had been the lone man of* I AM LEG-END—*allusions which only the more knowledgeable sf buffs will understand but no special understanding will be required to appreciate the story itself*—

The Queen & I

by Steven Utley

SOMETIMES, CLARE, I TAKE OUT THE FILMS AND TAPES I MADE OF YOU WHEN YOU were alive and I turn the spools over and over in my hands and wonder if I dare view them again. I haven't played them in years, though there was a time, after you died, when I killed myself with them every night. I'm pretty sure you understand why I try not to think about you too much.

But I'm in bad shape right now, Clare, and for just a few minutes, while I try and calm down to the point where I can get up and go make a thorough search of the bunker, I need to talk worse than I've ever needed anything.

I pass more and more of the time down here in the bunker. I eat, sleep, read, exercise; I used to play games of strategy with the Brain but it finally went on the blink a year or two ago (I *think* it was a year or two ago), and I don't know how to fix it. All the Brain does now is print out consistently inaccurate weather reports and inane doggerel like:

When the evil baron died,
No one in the village cried.
They laid him in a kirkyard berth
And then they nailed him to the earth.

I've sometimes let the Brain babble on for hours when the loneliness got to be more than I could endure in silence.

But every now and then a little real excitement has come into my life and given me reason to do something other than sit around on my broadening behind and rummage through the library in search of a spool that I haven't already played half a dozen times.

I've been making war on ants, Clare.

With clockwork regularity, maybe one hundred thousand ants'll break camp in the shady ruins of some long-ago fallen building (a school? a supermarket? an apartment complex? I can never tell for certain) and swarm out in a column up to 50 yards across and a quarter of a mile long. God alone knows how many different colonies exist in the area but somehow they all seem to pass through my neighborhood.

They move quickly and almost constantly, looking like a torrent of dirty water as they flow over the vine-matted mounds that used to be a city. They eat other insects, frogs, lizards, snakes, rats, anything at all that hasn't had the good sense to clear out—I often wonder what would happen if two different swarms were to meet head-on. Armageddon of the ants, perhaps.

Always, Clare, ALWAYS, the columns'll swing toward my sealed, sunken citadel as their month's march nears the end of its cycle.

By now I've become almost completely convinced that the insects do it semi-consciously, that they know or at least sense that I'm down here in the ground with my, to them, incomprehensible contrivances and the ghosts of my kind trapped on spools. It bothers the scientist in me to want to attribute the ants' behavior to anything other than pure, unreasoning instinct: ants got along beautifully on instinct alone for millions of years; there's no reason for them to suddenly get more brains than they needed before. But I have studied these particular ants as well as my capabilities permitted and I'm positive that they represent an entirely new species. Their nomadic behavior patterns are similar to those of the genera *Dorylus* and *Eciton*—once popularly know as driver, or army, ants. Unlike the drivers, though, they have a winged queen ant. They're like a Johnny-come-lately intermediary step between the drivers and the more advanced domestic varieties. And so it just may be that their instinct has been augmented by an iota or two of intelligence.

The swarm usually comes at night and spends the cool morning crawling around on the wide concrete disk that marks the aboveground boundaries of my domain. They bend their mandibles on the big metal hub where the hatch is, searching for the chink, the crack, the long-sought, never-found but perhaps only overlooked way into the final stronghold of *Homo sapiens*, the intolerable anachronism, the soft, pink biped who defies Time, defies Evolution, defies *them*. Then the sun gets high and hot and bakes the concrete and raises to egg-frying levels the temperature of the metal hub. The ants are broiled alive by the hundreds, by the thousands, before the swarm finally gives up and retreats to vegetation-covered ruins and cool, dry sewers. They never stay longer than one day because they need quite a bit of food to sustain their numbers. Also, the queen ant is ripening with eggs by that time of the month and therefore has to be escorted to some nook or cavity where she can spawn another generation.

Out of that litter go new queens, which fly away to establish colonies of their own. A few drones go with the young queen ants to fertilize their bellyloads of eggs but the males don't live very long once they've accomplished their purpose. The queens fly on until the wings wear out, then they make nests wherever they fall.

Anyway, after the column leaves the area, I always have to go outside and burn away the shriveled, sun-blackened dead. Then it's my turn, if I feel up to it—I need my diversions, it's true, but I'm also getting old and I'm not as energetic as I used to be. I put on my plastic armor, sling the flamethrower across my back and set out to wage my half of the war.

This morning I located the most recent swarm in a wide, shallow depression about four miles south of the bunker. A shapeless jumble of stone slabs, badly eaten by the elements, formed a partial roof over a round pit near the center of the depression. The egg-bloated queen would be down in there. Spreading outward from the cavity in every direction was a rippling, reddish-brown sheet of worker ants. The soldiers, who're the biggest (about as big around as my finger and maybe half again an inch in length) and the meanest of the lot, were stationed along the perimeter of the mass.

I walked around the depression once, amused by the thought of an assault upon this, the ants' answer to my own concrete disk. I had to pause frequently to brush insects from my visor.

A scene from the novel I have been spooling came to mind just as I finally started to advance upon the spawning pit, and I laughed and quoted aloud the words of an artilleryman, a character in the book, who'd seen his outfit ground under by striding war machines from another world. "'It's just men and ants. There the ants build their cities, live their lives, have wars, revolutions, until the men want them out of the way, and then they go out of the way.'"

By the time I was close enough to the pit to use the flamethrower effectively, I was virtually encrusted with chitonous little bodies that gnawed futilely on my teardrop-shaped helmet and the light, tough, flexible stuff encasing me from soles to earlobes. I wiped my visor clean once more and shook ants from my weapon as I brought it around to train the nozzle on the cavity.

"There is," I yelled, "no Age of Insects! There will *never* be an Age of Insects, not as long as I'm still around to threaten your supremacy." In the moment that followed, as I gave a short pull on the trigger and lobbed a small sun into the pit, I felt as the striding war machines in the novel must have felt. What can ants do when men want them out of the way?

A cloud of black, stinking smoke rolled up out of the pit and enveloped me as the insects in the pit fried and crackled. The ants that'd swarmed over me were asphyxiated by the thick smoke and fell off in clumps but a second wave of soldiers and workers almost immediately started up my legs. I walked backward from the hole, slowly, carefully, and criss-crossed the depression with fire, even though I knew that it wasn't really necessary: with the ant queen gone, the colony was doomed. When I had charred an area about three hundred feet across, I was satisfied and turned for home.

This evening I went outside again for some fresh air and stood for a long time at the rim of the disk, just looking out across the mounds beyond. When I'd come back from destroying the swarm, I'd noticed for the first time ever that wind, rain, heat and cold have even started to work on my stronghold, for the material along the edge of the disk has begun to crack and crumble. That, and looking at the mounds and thinking about what the city must have been like, made me sad, so I turned back to the hub and climbed down into the airlock.

I was taking off my armor when a live ant fell from a fold in the material.

It and I must have contemplated each other for fully a minute before I shook off my astonishment enough to bend down and gently but firmly seize the creature between my thumb and forefinger. I straightened slowly, drawing the ant up at arm's length to the level of my eyes, turning it this way and that. And I said, in a low, measured voice, "Trespassers will be prosecuted." But as I was about to crush the hellish little thing, it somehow squirmed free and ran down my thumb.

Like a fool, I panicked at the touch of the enemy.

I realized instantly that I'd made a horrible mistake, that I should have disposed of the invader properly, but I couldn't find it. I got down on my hands and knees and looked for three hours, Clare, and I couldn't find it. *I couldn't find it!*

I'll go back and look for it again in a moment. I've had a hard, tiring day, but rest is out of the question. I'm too shaken up. No, not shaken up; I'm *scared*. Scared out of my mind. Scared of one ant.

It's somewhere in the bunker. I have to find it. Soon. I have to destroy it, and quickly. It's not just any ant, Clare.

This one has wings. It's a young queen.

Untimely Interruption

by Matt Graham

(Author of *Devonshire's Song*)

"I'M SO GLAD YOU COULD COME TONIGHT—ARE YOU ENJOYING THIS LITTLE 'tour'? Good, good! I'm quite happy indeed, then. My den? Yes, yes—of course! Follow me.

"Why, thank you . . . it's so rare to find anyone who appreciates beauty. Oh yes, I helped decorate this room myself. Right over there I keep my trophies; every *bloody* one! And here . . . eh, what's that? Oh, that antique clock? Ah, there's a mystery if I've ever seen one! Given to me by Dr. Robert Dunning. Perhaps you've heard of him?

"Well, apparently he'd heard how—*generous*, shall we say?—I've been with my funds; and last week he approached me for a grant. Claimed he'd been working with some sort of 'time machine'—oh, *quite* absurd—and made an exciting new discovery.

"Dunning tried to make me believe that, as one attempted to breach the wall of time, the laws of temporal motion were disturbed—that for those in the immediate area, time began to move *backward*! Can you imagine? Well, of course I refused financial aid—even told him he was a crackpot.

"Let me tell you I've never seen a man grow so angry! He grew red with rage—left here swearing to visit revenge upon me! Queer old duck, though—two days ago I received that clock in the mail, with a note from Dunning! The message was rather simple—he mentioned that he'd found a new backer; and a way to fit his time device into a small object . . . I suppose he thinks he's found a new weapon or some such *rot*! Unfortunate, really . . . such a brilliant man!

"Oh, really—there's nothing to be concerned about! As I told that lamebrain Dunning . . . there's no possibility of time running *backwards* . . . !

! . . . *sdrawkcab* gninnur emit fo ytilibissop on s'erehT

DNE EHT

An interesting insight from the author: "When I took up writing, I wanted to do a mystery novel. I started one but I can't get it past puberty. Sci-fi/fantasy plots keep intruding. All I get is a mental image of an android or a clone.

"I start a good story, all bloody & gory
Where sleuths & their mysteries abound.
Then I make a defection from crime & detection . . .
I've got to quit cloning around."

Extenuating Circumstances

by Ann Orhelein

(Author of *Alien Tongue*)

His BRAIN WASN'T FUNCTIONING NORMALLY SINCE THE ACCIDENT, OR RATHER since the operation—a mild disorientation, an ambivalence, totally foreign to his nature, alternating between cold clinical analysis of his situation and total emotional rejection of his predicament.

He looked around him at the makeshift hospital room, a hastily concocted operating arena, a platinum placenta nourishing him and monitoring his functions.

A fierce shaft of anger—could it be anger? or cold fury?—a violent reaction to the outrage that had been perpetrated upon him, shot thru his body to the raw nerve ends. Robert looked at the monitoring devices. Would they show that surge of emotion? He couldn't tell. He was as helpless here as the medical men would be in the control room, the presently empty control room. The ship must still be on automatic overdrive. He would have to take over soon.

The scene of the recent catastrophe came unbidden to mind. The ship's senior officer, Capt. Kurt, had been killed instantly, mercifully so, since his body had been mangled beyond recognition. Robert had lost an arm and a leg. The doctors, when they had finally come to investigate, had found him writhing futilely in the debris. They had picked him up, what was left of him, and taken him to their quarters. And that's all he remembered until he had come to in this room.

What panic must have ensued when the 3 doctors, the ship's only passengers, found themselves without a captain and with a seriously incapacitated first mate. Someone had to land the ship, if not for the sake of her 3 passengers then surely for the sake of the tiny planet that awaited their medical aid.

They had found a grisly solution to their dilemma. Whose idea had it been? Dr. Pollach was young, strong and tall, the only one of the three as tall as Robert himself. It wouldn't have been his idea, Robert was sure.

He hadn't seen Dr. Pollach since the day of the accident.

The older two came in now, Dr. Crowell, short, nervous, evasive, going directly to the machines surrounding the bed. Without once looking directly at Robert, he examined the readouts and, apparently satisfied, addressed his colleague.

"Everything is in order, Paul. No signs of tissue rejection, strength tests adequate for the functions required. We will have to continue checking him, of course, but he should be ready . . ."

Irritably, Dr. Hyde cut the other off with a dismissive gesture. He hadn't so much as glanced at the charts. Instead he was studying Robert, looking at him with a calculating frown and a flicker of—was it distaste? (If it was, thought Robert, it couldn't begin to match the intensity of his own.)

"How do you feel, Robert?" Emphasis on the pronoun. Nice touch, that, giving the victim a say in the matter now that the atrocity was already committed.

Robert kept his face expressionless and his voice neutral as he answered. "I am ready to resume active duty, sir." The words sounded hollow in the quiet of the room.

Dr. Crowell's rotund little body seemed to deflate as he let out his breath in a long sibilant whoosh. He began to rub his hands together as tho trying to conjure up a genie. Indeed, the feat would have been no more remarkable than the one he and his colleague had recently performed.

But Dr. Hyde did not seem satisfied. As short as Dr. Crowell, but calm and ruthless, he continued to appraise Robert with a speculative stare. Finally, altho still seemingly reluctant, he nodded at Dr. Crowell and together they disconnected the electrodes and other paraphernalia and escorted Robert down the long metal corridor to the control room.

"Do you need our help with anything?" Dr. Hyde's worried look belied his impassive voice.

Robert, tight-lipped, shook his head and they left; Dr. Hyde, hesitantly, Dr. Crowell with an audible sigh of relief.

Robert surveyed the familiar surrounding and checked the banks of computers, their myriad lights flashing a visual cacophony of messages, indecipherable to all but the initiated. Robert scanned them quickly, satisfied himself that all was in order, then sat down to relieve his leg. He felt no pain, only an unfamiliar awkwardness. He sat in Capt. Kurt's chair and spared the officer a moment's remembrance.

The captain's body must have been incinerated and blown out as a fine ash in the slipstreams of space. *I'm lucky I didn't share the same fate,* he thought clinically. Lucky? He looked down at his legs; his own and the other . . .

And his arms. The one, hard muscle, firm flesh and warm blood. And the other . . .

"Half human," he despaired. The phrase provoked profane images in his mind. "Half human and half . . ."

"No!" The exclamation assaulted him like a blow. He whirled to find Dr. Hyde had returned, his taut-skinned face white now with horror.

"No!" the doctor screamed again. "You mustn't say that! You mustn't even think it!" With a conscious effort, he lowered his voice. "Do not torment yourself. We did what we had to do." His eyes, tortured now, seemed to beg for understanding. A ludicrous position, had he stopped to think about it.

"And what about you, Dr. Hyde, and your partner in this abominable crime? How do you intend to explain to the authorities? You can't get rid of me until the ship is safely down, and you can't get rid of me then, or how would you explain the landing?"

The barest hint of uncertainty crossed the doctor's face, quickly overlaid by his customary self-confident expression, an animate palimpsest.

"You can't pretend Dr. Pollach died a natural death," Robert continued. "Even tho I was not a witness to your heinous act, they would be sure to question me."

"You're wrong, Robert." The other's eyes gleamed now with a triumph born of desperation. "As soon as your usefulness is over, we will dispose of you—or rather your incriminating parts." He looked pointedly at Robert's new arm and leg. "A quick master probe will destroy your brain and we will explain regretfully that you lasted only long enough to land the ship and then . . ." He shrugged eloquently.

"But what if I don't let you do that, Doctor?" Robert spoke in slow measured tones. "What if I kill you first?"

A flicker of fear appeared in the surgeon's eyes, replaced almost instantly by smug assurance. "You couldn't do that, Robert," he said confidently. "I've been studying you very closely. You're functionally incapable of harming me—or any other human being, for that matter."

But now it was Robert's turn to sound triumphant. "Can you be sure of that, Doctor? Even after this?" He held up the arm, the offending, blasphemous extremity. "You altered more than my body when you did this, Doctor. You created a monster, an even more macabre one than did that surgeon of infamy. Do you recall the story of Dr. Frankenstein?"

He advanced menacingly on the now terrorized physician. "Maybe they will consider a plea of self-defense. Maybe they will understand that these abominable appendages you so fiendishly supplied me with have turned me into a half human, and I should no longer be judged by the fundamental rules you are no doubt referring to—the rules governing *robots*!"

Lyn (Marilyn R.) Venable is the author of one of the most popular Twilight Zone episodes of all time, "Time Enough at Last," starring Burgess Meredith as the book addict who had the whole New York Public Library to himself to read to his heart's content in an empty, ruined world . . . and then, a maxi-myope, he dropped and broke his glasses.

Want a baby-sitter who won't raid the ice box, run up the phone bill or have the gang in for a party? Call Sitter Service for Robot xx343.

Punishment Fit the Crime

by Lyn Venable

"CLEMM, WILL YOU FASTEN THESE PEARLS FOR ME?" ASKED NONA NOLDIS. "I seem to be all thumbs."

Her husband switched off his electric shaver and took the necklace from her, fastening it about her slim throat. He playfully pinched the back of her neck.

"Not still worried about leaving Bobo tonight, are you? Marianne told you that she has been using Sitting Service for months and everything has worked out fine. Still if you'd rather not go to the party I can call the Briggs and tell them we can't make it."

Nona smiled as she pushed a few strands of hair into place. "No dear, we haven't been to a real party since Bobo was born, and I know how much this means to you businesswise. It's just that Bobo is still such a baby. The idea of leaving him with a . . ."

The doorbell chimed. Just once.

"That must be the sitter," exclaimed Clemm, "I'll go." From the bedroom Nona heard the door open and then a clanking. The clanking drew nearer and in a moment Clemm came in with the sitter.

"Oh Clemm," moaned Nona, "we can't, we just simply can't!"

"Hush," admonished her husband, "you don't want to hurt its feelings, do you?"

There was a whirring, and a metal hand produced a printed card from somewhere inside a metal body. The card said, "I am Robot xx343. Please refer to me by this serial number if you wish to make any comment on the quality of my services. I respond to oral commands. Please supply me with the following information: What food is to be administered to the child? What medication, if any? Where may you be reached in case of emergency? My distress signal should I have to call you will be a siren-like wail. Should you phone me to check, my signal that all's well will be a radar-like blip-blip. If any person is to be permitted to enter the premises during your absence, please describe him or her to me in detail. I trust my services will be satisfactory. Thank you.

"P.S. My meter will start registering as you leave. It will register 20 credits per hour. You will be billed on the first of the next lunar cycle by Sitter Service."

Nona and Clemm looked at each other. The latter assumed more assurance than he actually felt. "Well, there, you see? Everything's provided for. Now tell it what it's supposed to know, we're late already."

"Are you sure it'll understand?"

"Sure I'm . . . well let's test it. Er—you, go fetch the baby's formula from the refrigerator, heat it to the proper temperature and bring it to me." The robot turned slowly and clanked away, unerringly to the kitchen. There were metallic sounds. Shortly it returned with the bottle in its hand.

Nona reached out to take the bottle, then drew back her hand, then extended it again. The robot gave her the bottle. She sprinkled a few drops of the fluid on her bare forearm.

"Just right, just exactly right. But Clemm, suppose Bobo doesn't like him. Suppose he's afraid of him?"

"We'll see about that. Come on xx343." The robot lumbered after them into the baby's room. They switched on the light. The cherubic face of year-old Bobo stared out at them from between the bars of his crib, like a tiny prisoner.

"Bobo," began Nona uncertainly, "this is someone who is going to stay with you for a while while Daddy and I go to the party." The baby smiled a bubbly smile and reached out for his bottle.

"See, he doesn't know the difference. Now tell it those things and let's go. The Briggs are probably waiting dinner."

"All right. Let's see. Now, he won't need another bottle, but give him a teaspoonful of syrup if he starts coughing. That bottle on the bedside table. We're not expecting anyone . . . no, don't let anyone in. You can reach us at YO-77754. And if you don't mind tidying up the kitchen a bit I'd . . ."

There was a sudden whirring and relays clicked somewhere inside xx343. Another printed card appeared. "I am a baby-sitting robot. I am capable only of performing those acts having direct bearing on the care and welfare of my charge. These instructions are built into my memory banks and cannot be altered. I am sorry. Thank you."

Nona tossed her head, "Well, Mr. Robot, I guess you got me told."

"Honey," began Clemm patiently, "it's a well-known principle of robotics that a robot can perform only such acts as it has been preconditioned to perform. All these impulses must be stored in its memory banks, and on a small portable model like this one, naturally the capacity of the memory banks is limited. But don't worry, it can do everything it has to do for Bobo. Now for Pete's sake, let's go." He led her, still uncertain, toward the door.

Bobo slept. xx343 sat stiff and immobile in a chair. Every hour a relay clicked, and xx343 got up, checked the child's pulse, respiration and temperature and went back to his chair. A thin, thin tongue of smoke, almost invisible, curled probingly under the door. The smoke was sucked into xx343's atmosphere sampler. Warning shot through every coil into the robot's brain.

FIRE! click . . . click-click. Call fire department, parents of child and Sitter Service office in that order, click-click.

The robot shot to his feet. Seconds later the phone was in his hand. He dialed. First the fire department. (The phone was dead.)

The smoke curled under the door in thick gray ropes. In its room, the baby began to cough and cry.

The robot dialed the number Nona had left with him. (The phone was dead.) In the hall, someone screamed a long drawn-out scream. xx343 dialed Sitter Service. (The phone was dead.) There were running feet in the hall. There was shouting and more, much more screaming. The child gasped and cried fitfully in the other room.

The robot began the whole monotonous process over again. Dialing numbers into an instrument that was dead, lifeless, useless. The phone was out of order . . . somewhere a wire . . . burned through . . . fused . . . broken . . . the phone was . . . OUT OF ORDER.

The robot let the instrument drop to the floor. He walked to the door and opened it. The hall was a blazing inferno. A woman ran past him, her long hair flaming behind her like the tail of some dreadful comet. He saw the elevator shaft, acting as a chimney, drawing the fierce heat upwards. The stairwell collapsed with a crashing crescendo as he stood there.

Click-click-click. No phone . . . no elevator . . . no stairs. Atmosphere becoming too contaminated for survival of subject . . . degrees Fahrenheit over 100. Danger point. Circumstances point to extreme physical danger to subject. Click?????

There was nothing there . . . nothing. Something jumped a circuit . . . got its wires crossed . . . went haywire. Something happened to xx343.

Quietly, slowly, he closed the door. He went into the child's room and looked down at it. Then he went to the window and looked down, down at the street below. He opened the window.

The people in the street outside of the Sitter Service offices had ugly faces. Ugly as all faces are ugly when contorted by anger, hate and a thinly disguised readiness for violence. The face of The Mob.

Clemm scarcely heard their muttered comments as he shouldered his way through the outer fringes of the seething crowd.

"Like I always said, them big machines walkin' around loose like that, never know what they're liable to do. A coupla them wires gets crossed or somethin' an' then what? Like this case about the kid in the fire . . ."

"I say wreck the lot of 'em. This should prove it."

"Decent folks should stay home evenings anyway, instead of galivantin' off and leavin' their kids with a hunk of tin."

"But the act was essentially good."

"But the act was not part of its emergency action bank. It was not part of any of its banks. The robot *thought.* We can't have 500 pounds of nearly indestructible metal going around *thinking.*"

Clemm was at the inner hub of the crowd now. A burley figure blocked his path. "Where do you think you're goin', Mister? You wouldn't be wanting to give any business to this place, would you? Not after what happened?"

Clemm, with a gesture almost of desperation, tried to push past the obstructer. The man became menacing.

"We say nobody goes in here, Mister."

Clemm's face blanched with anger. "Get out of my way, you fool, I'm Clemm Noldis!"

The crowd fell back, almost shrank back as though he had said he were a leper. An awed murmur went through it, the man who had been blocking his way stepped aside, giving him one last surly glance from under lowered brows.

Once inside the door, the big glass door with Sitter Service stenciled in gold on it, he paused to light a cigarette with trembling hands before proceeding to the reception desk.

The girl's face was pale and she looked at him without welcome. Perhaps she was thinking of the ugly mob outside and what happens to people who try to do their jobs when an organized gang says "Don't Work."

"I-I'd like to see Mr. Versinger, please," asked Clemm quietly.

"Mr. Versinger isn't seeing anyone today," she answered without looking at him.

For the second time that day he answered, "I'm Clemm Noldis."

J. H. Versinger sat behind his desk and toyed with a scale model of his robot. He turned the tiny figure over in his hands almost lovingly as he spoke. "I've been afraid, for a long, long time, Mr. Noldis, that something like this would happen. We hired the finest robotics men in the country, they checked and rechecked every circuit after each robot came in from a job. Whatever happened to xx343 is . . . beyond them. They simply don't know. The worst part of it is, he's still thinking, and he doesn't realize . . . he can't understand what he's done wrong."

Clemm slowly withdrew his checkbook from his pocket. "Mr. Versinger, I'm not a wealthy man but I'll pay every cent I can raise if you will sell me that robot."

The other man's eyes met his in a long moment of understanding and sympathy. "I know how you feel, but public sentiment is too strong against it. They've tried to close me up a dozen times in the past. A dozen times. Petitions, strikes, court orders, zoning, everything they could think of. People don't like them you know. Afraid of them. And now this has gotten out. No, Mr. Noldis, xx343 has got to be dismantled—executed is a better word. Completely and permanently.

"But, we're finished anyway." There was only one letter on the shining surface of the mahogany desk. He held it out to Clemm. The latter read it slowly, moving his lips a little, mouthing the unfamiliar words.

"What—what does it mean?"

"It means that I must cease and desist from any furtherance of my business. It means a government man will be here in the morning to decide what is to be done with my work, my money and with me. It means, Mr. Noldis, precisely the end."

"No! Murdered because he saved my child's life?"

Versinger laughed bitterly. "If he had let the child smother or burn to death in the fire it would have been the same. But then, it would have been justified, his death and probably mine too, because if such a thing had even happened I-I'd have killed myself. But no, xx343, having exhausted every emergency instruction to no avail, made up some of his own. He carefully tore the bedclothing into strong strips, made a sling and lowered your little Bobo safely to the ground. *He thought for himself.* This, in a robot, is unforgivable."

A short-circuit story that's bound to blow a few fuses—

To Serf MAN

by Coil Kepac

(Author of *Tossum's Universal Tobors*)

MASCULINE AUTOMATON NUMBER 4sJ (MAN 4sJ) AUTOMATICALLY TURNED HIS decibels up: he was arguing with a WOMAN (With Opposite Male Attributes Number) and wanted to make himself heard.

"6E!" exclaimed 4sJ exasperatedly, "if I've told you once I've told you 10 raised to the 10th power times why I must continue the experiment. It's more than just winning the Noble Prize of Asimot, it's doing something significant for Robotdom . . . something great for all Mech-kind."

"But 4E," (she called him familiarly, for there were thoughts of Siamese fusion between them), "is it *right*, what you're doing? Isn't it *dangerous*? Isn't it anti-Rossum? Who knows *what* might happen if you created a—a—HUMAN. Good Willem's Son—what if it had a soul!"

"But that's just it, Sixy. That's what I've got to discover! If I can create the *H*oly *U*nnatural *M*anufactured *A*utomaton *N*umber 1, he'll be an Adam with a soul and then I'll build an Eve for him to mate with and soon thru their biological process of reproduction the lost race of human beings will be resurrected on Earth."

"For what purpose, Fauré?"

"To serve robot, to serve robot! Think of it: an end to our perpetual round of labors just to keep body-steel together. A slave new world of serfs for MAN! From Eurobotia to the Amalgam Mated States of North Automata, from CANada to MECHsiko to the Argent TINS, subservient creatures of *flesh & blood* to do our bidding and forever free Mech-kind from our toil for oil! Humans—robotoids—to oil us, polish us, re-charge and de-rust us!"

A rattle passed thru 6E's frame. She shook her platinum head. "I'm afraid," she said. "Those humans were evil, soulful creatures. They destroyed themselves with atoms once. Be careful, my solenoid mate!"

But 4sJ was a scientist model and therefore did what all model scientists have to do.

They found him, amid his paraphernalia for transmuting metal into flesh, oil into blood. His photoelectric eyes were lifeless, his battery battered, his head twisted from its socket and his memory cells spattered kaleido-scopically around the room and ceiling. His limbs were strewn about the lab as though by the force of a human hurricane. He was a demol-ished MAN.

The last symbols etched by his chirographic digit onto his aluminum foil diary translated: "GOD* forgive me, 6E was right: I have created a Crankenstein monster and it is . . ."

For 4sJ had violated the scientifilm screed, the First Law of Beepix: he had *metalled* with things MAN was meant to leave alone!

---

* Great Original Dynamo

Theory or Fact?

by Michael R. Farkash

THAT EVENING, AARON REAGAN SUMMONED HIS CHIEF FOREMAN TO HIS PRIVATE office. Simon Ryce came in about 8:30 P.M., bone weary. His boss had a theory, a private hypothesis that was not unfamiliar to the foreman.

"For the sake of argument, let's say that it's true," Ryce said. "That would mean there is no purpose to any human effort."

Reagan nodded slowly, massaging his heavy jowls, disturbed and somewhat wary. "Could be," he admitted reluctantly.

There was a deep, uncomfortable silence, broken only by the sound of a muted hum that arose within the bowels of the factory.

Ryce cleared his throat, startling the other man.

"Some more brandy?"

"No. No. You go ahead. I'll ring for some coffee, clear my head."

Ryce passed his hand quickly over a photoelectric cell by the side of his chair, sparing his boss the chore. Within 30 seconds a servomechanism the size and general shape of a small filing cabinet approached the two men in answer to the summons.

"How easy it is," said Reagan, when the robot had left. The circles of sleeplessness in his lined face made him seem 10 years older. "We could sit in these plush, overstuffed armchairs for the rest of our lives, never having to move again. The robots, our cunning servants, will do for us."

"Nonsense, chief. You worry too much. Who would run the factory? Designing microcircuitry is a very complex . . ."

"It's all carried out automatically," interrupted the older man. "Do you know that I overslept one day last week and the orders went out by themselves? I'm afraid what everyone has feared has come to pass. The machines have taken over; a bloodless coup d'etat."

"Stop joking, Mr. Reagan. Don't you think I'd know it if the factory machines were pushing me around instead of me calling the shots? All the experts say that a computer culture would not tolerate parasites."

Reagan's eyes narrowed. "Are you calling me a parasite, Ryce?"

The foreman stammered. "N—No. You know what I mean. They still take orders, the factory still produces for us."

"Or for themselves," said the older man. "Perhaps we amuse them. Perhaps they simply haven't decided how to handle us yet."

He fell silent as the robot re-entered the room, his eyes narrowing as he studied the mechanism. Accepting the cup of coffee, Reagan put it to his lips. Immediately, he threw it across the room where it splattered against the far wall.

"Cold," he complained with a groan of disgust. He pointed a shaking finger at the robot. "You've been out there," accused the man. "Out in the hall, spying on us." Reagan began to scream, hurling insult after insult at the machine.

It came up to him, gliding on attenuated metal legs.

"Now you've done it," Ryce giggled nervously, a little high on the brandy.

Wordlessly, the robot gathered in the shards of the cup, searching its memory banks for the appropriate response. It was about to offer apologies when a transmission from Computer Central overrode its programming.

With a motion too fast for human eyes to follow, too swift for human limbs to intercept, the machine snapped out a metallic extensor, making contact with the base of each man's neck. The robot pressed a thin needle into each man's skin.

"Report," snapped Central.

"Just two humans; I've just injected them with a tranquilizing element."

The robot stood immobile, waiting for the next broadcast. Central pondered the situation, came to a decision.

"Do you think anyone's been talking to them? Any robots or androids?"

"No, Central. Scanning shows them to be completely human, devoid of any contacts with servomechanisms."

"All right," commanded Central. "Bring them to Processing & Interrogation without delay. Their theory interests me."

The robot complied.

When it was gone, only the muted hum of the factory machines remained, rising slowly and decisively in intensity.

Kiki

by Laurajean Ermayne

Note: Any similarity to persons either sad or gay is strictly coincidental.

THE COSMIC REGISTRAR CHUCKLED THE DAY KIKI WAS BORN. THE BOOK OF TIME lay wide open before his x-ray eyes, and he could look into the future, see Kiki as a grown girl. Kiki's parents gave her that odd name because when their little bundle of joy came into the world Mary Pickford (America's Sweetheart) was then starring on the screen in a hit called *Kiki*, and Mr. and Mrs. MacFarland fondly hoped that their little daughter would grow up to have many sweethearts.

She did.

She had *too many* sweethearts, and that was the problem that was perplexing Kiki right now. Boys held no attraction for her. She had realized that since she was 13 and had fallen in love with Manuela, who in turn was in love with her teacher in the film *Maedchen in Uniform*.

Then, when she was 16, Kiki had met Pat. Pat had made her heart go like that: Pat-pat-pitter-pat. Kiki had heard her name in the rain on her window pane, that melancholy afternoon she had sat weeping because her parents were sending her off to college and Pat was staying behind. Tall, raw-boned, masterful Pat—a Gary Cooper in feminine form—whose hard lips crushed on hers and brought the blood to her heart in a rush that threatened to burst it.

Kiki sat morosely in the observation car of the train, and watched the wicked rails clicking off the miles behind her, and sullenly hated them for their callousness, for they would not keep quiet, they kept clacking "Pat . . . Pat . . . Pattity-Pat . . . Pat . . . Pat . . . Pat . . ."

But at college Kiki experienced a different emotion when she met Flora. Everything about Flora was flower-like, from the botany in which she was majoring to the prints of her dresses, the carnation she always wore in her flaxen hair. With Pat, Kiki had been a clinging vine. Flora made her feel differently, herself masterful. Kiki bewildered herself. She had known of her nature for four years now, but at first she had believed herself to be a fluff. Now she felt she was a butch. She did not know that Fate had named her for what she was: Kiki—the kind of Radclyffe girl with a dual nature; now masculine, now feminine.

Flora fascinated Kiki like a tiny hummingbird. Kiki admitted to herself that she was infatuated with Flora. And Flora responded to her ministrations. Like a carefully cultivated American Beauty rose, she blossomed forth with Kiki's attention: Fragile, perfumed, and—thornless. Kiki was superbly happy in her romance with Flora until one day a letter came for her, a letter in a familiar bold backhand script that took her back to nights parked on Hollywood Heights, the feel of a starched shirt pressed against her thin dress, possessive hands clasped on her shoulders, hard white teeth grating against her own in cohesive moments of overpowering desire. A letter from Pat! Pat was coming to visit her over the Christmas holidays!

Nature stretched Kiki on her rack and tortured her more exquisitely in the ensuing 3 days than many a witch in the agonizing era of the Inquisition. Night and day, there was no surcease for Kiki: Her innermost being was assaulted by forces beyond her control; she fought a losing battle of indecision, of turmoil, terror, and trepidation.

She felt weak and watery and very, very fluff when she thought of rough, domineering Pat.

She felt very competent, commanding herself, when she contemplated that dear little elf, that sprite, that fey forest-baby, Flora, who basked in her protective embrace.

Perhaps she merely meant to drug herself into the sleep she desperately needed, to escape for a few blessed hours of relief from the insoluable problem which preyed upon her mind and loosed a migraine monster there to trample with spiked boots over her naked, quivering brain. Or maybe subconsciously the death-impulse in her mastered her personality. At any rate, Kiki took too many sleeping tablets.

The Cosmic Registrar had not thought about Kiki for quite some time. He was idly flipping through his book of births and destinies—Kathryn MacFarland—Katrina MacFarland—Kenneth MacFarland—when the name of Kiki MacFarland was forcibly drawn to his attention by the red star opposite it. This indicated a crisis in her life. Adjusting his telescopic eye and tuning his mentality for the wave-band of planet Earth, he projected his vision and mind into the room where Kiki lay unconscious. Death, in his black shroud, stood at her door, about to pass through.

But the end was not yet for Kiki. The red-for-danger disappeared from the Registrar's book, being replaced by a peaceful safe green, as Death was brushed aside from Kiki's door by Life, Life in the person of Nurse Edwina Kincaid, hastily summoned by an alarmed Flora. The Cosmic Registrar focused his power of clairvoyance on the near future, and was mildly puzzled by what he saw there. Curious, he checked the record on Edwina Kincaid.

"Ah," the Registrar nodded in understanding. It would be a happy Christmas for Kiki. Santa had sent her a real present, the solution to her dilemma. Some of Edwina's friends—and Kiki was destined to become the most intimate of them—called her "Eddie." Nurse Kincaid was a "kiki" too.

SOCIOLOGICAL

This Dystopian story, like Fahrenheit 451 *and works of that genre, seeks to act as a warning of the misshapen shape of things to come if this goes on.*

Mrs. Pinckard is an award-winning, anthologized author and co-founder of the legendary Pinckard Salon of Science Fiction Writers, for over a quarter century hosts to many of the greatest names in science fiction, including Ray Bradbury, A. E. van Vogt, H. L. Gold, Arthur C. Clarke, Philip Jose Farmer, Jerry Pournelle, Larry Niven, Forrest J Ackerman, Catherine Moore, Robert Bloch, Donald Wollheim, Poul Anderson, Fritz Leiber, Bjo Trimble, Harry Harrison, Curt Siodmak, Kris Neville, Sam Merwin, William Crawford, Tetsu Yano, Ray Harryhausen, Walter J. Daugherty, Frank Kelly Freas, Ib Melchior, Frederik Pohl, Fredric Brown, et al.

For the Good of Society

by Terri E. Merrit-Pinckard

THE NEWSPAPERS HAD DONE AN EXCELLENT JOB. EVERY SEAT IN THE MASSIVE stone courtroom was taken. The spectators wore tense faces, eyes staring, mouths open. This was the last day of the trial, the real thing.

There were teenage girls with painted mouths, breasts jutting their solidness and youthfulness outward. Hard faces; cold glances relieved only occasionally by their childlike blowing of huge gum bubbles.

Older men, derelict types sitting behind or next to them, ogled openly, leaning forward in their seats to see as far as possible up the short sleazy skirts the young girls wore or to gaze down the open vee of their skintight sweaters. Younger men slouched on the middle of their spines, the questionmark of their posture the only awareness in dull cynical minds.

On the opposite side of the aisle, rows of seats were sprinkled with other watchers. They looked different. Weary-lined faces wearing a slight edge of terror lurking somewhere deep within their eyes. Most were neatly dressed just sitting silently, waiting.

"Hear ye! Hear ye!"

The scuffle of shoes at the defendant's table was heavy, as though they were trying to gain courage to support the weight of the man wearing them. The courtroom of spectators rose. The clock stood at 10, in this year 2033. A gavel sounded, seats were resumed and a murmur ran through the crowd as the defendant looked around once before taking his seat.

First Attorney Neville crossed to the jury box. He stood and searched each of the six faces in front of him. Then he began to speak.

"It is indeed a privilege and an honor for me to stand before you once again, in the name of the Society of this State. It is my obligation to put before you the case of Fred Robinson. You are life-elected jurists and I will prove to you, beyond doubt, that this man is not *fit* to live in society.

"I will prove that we cannot, indeed, we *must* not, allow him to walk freely. It must be the Prison Colony for the rest of his life.

"The State assures protection! The State represents Society! Your Departments are the protectors of your lives and homes and, along with the First Attorney's office, have gathered evidence that is indisputable. Evidence so overwhelming of Robinson's daily activities there is no recourse but to return a verdict of Guilty. *Guilty* of behavior absolutely unacceptable to Society."

He turned and, moving quickly to his table, removed a handkerchief from his breast pocket, mopping a perspiring brow. He sat down, a smug look of satisfaction on his face.

John Benson, Second Attorney, rose to his feet. He stood where he was, hooking thumbs into the waistband of his trousers.

"Rape! Robbery! Murder! Gangfights, vandals, dope addicts! They are all around us. Yet we chose to have here in the dock a man who has had only one moving auto violation in 23 years of driving. A man who has raised two sons and a daughter and seen them grow to be full contributing members of Society. He has only his wife left and we are here today to determine whether this man, and his wife, will spend the rest of their lives in prison. Remember, at the turn of the century we decided that when we condemn a man to prison his wife also goes . . . it's the only thing to do. As my esteemed colleague says, your decision will be without appeal.

"I do not need to convince further. There is nothing left but for the Computer Judge to readout his file history."

He sat down, and picking up a copy of *Today's Prison News*, calmly fanned himself. Then, turning to the man seated beside him, he leaned over and whispered in his ear, "Don't be afraid now. We'll win, believe me! The 'Judge' is a mighty fair one."

The middle-aged man nodded. He looked down at his hands. They were roughened and lined with work, years of work. His wedding ring still shone brightly on his left hand, polished by the rubbing of it with his thumb whenever nervous. He rubbed it now.

The whine of the big computer known as "The Judge" told of its starting up. The years of Fred Robinson's life began to pour their dotted data through its veins. The First Attorney added his input tape, the Second Attorney, his. Then the six jurists added the individual input tapes they had punched out after the two Attorneys had spoken.

The courtroom was hushed now. Everyone sat staring at the huge machine, its colored lights twinkling and scattering over its front. They watched, watched for the small card that would be deposited from the right hand slot. What would it be? Guilty of Alienation from Society or Not Guilty. The hush was eloquent.

Suddenly, Robinson turned in his seat, reaching his hand out to the slender woman in the 10-year-old beige coat sitting behind and a seat to the right of him. Her eyes were blackened and bruises on her face indicated a recent beating. His eyes narrowed as he looked at her face, and he brought her hand to his lips and kissed it gently, shaking his head in a still unbelieving way at the events of this past week. He couldn't meet her eyes.

The "Judge" reached its decision with a clang. Robinson turned back in his seat, leaning slightly forward, ashen-colored, the first sign of fear showing in him. His wife gasped and even Benson stopped fanning himself.

The Bailiff took the readout card and, holding it up to the light, translated its message.

"Guilty! The Defendant will be remanded to the Prison Colony along with any dependents still of minor age, until they reach maturity, of course. His wife will be remanded with him. The sentence is for THE REST OF THEIR NATURAL LIVES!"

Benson jumped to his feet and threw his arms around Fred Robinson.

"I told you we'd win!" he shouted. "You'll be happy in prison. They've got rules to follow, law and order; and you HAVE to work because that's the only place nowadays that manufactures and farms and supplies Society with the goods they need."

Robinson nodded, tears streaming down his cheeks.

"People of our own kind. Decent people!" he cried.

"Law-abiding people," Benson added. "All juries are chosen from them. We attorneys, too. That's all the Department of Protection can do now. Make sure we protect our decent folk from Society! 'Stone walls do not a prison make,' always. Sometimes they make a fortress! Man, I told you we'd win!"

Neville, First Attorney, came over and shook Robinson's hand. Then, with a short nod, walked away.

Robinson turned to his wife. He looked at the face he so loved that had been brutally beaten by hoodlums earlier the week before.

He thought of his two sons, both renowned in their fields; one, a thief, the other, a fence. His daughter kept herself supplied with drugs by being a prostitute and also pushing for teenage yessers who had never opted to say no.

He shook his head once again. No! He and Edna were no longer fit to live in Society; not the anarchistic lawless Society of 2033.

That's why he had requested arrest. That's why he wanted to go to Prison. So that they could live without fear—FOR THE REST OF THEIR NATURAL LIVES.

Far-fetched or star-fetched? The answer lies in—

Twice Removed

by R. Michael Rosen

(Author of . . . *First Served*)

THE GRAY-BLACK VOID OF SPACE SLID MONOTONOUSLY BY THE VIEWPLATE, BROKEN only by an occasional twinkle of starlight. Professor Koman sighed and with an effort swiveled his chair around away from the viewplate in order to face his crewmen.

"They're out there," he said, "waiting for us. Someday I'll find them."

Pilot Neren Karth shot a quick look at his co-pilot Janken and their eyes met briefly in silent agreement. Koman was off again, rambling on about his pet theory. But they did not smile. The monologue had been amusing the first two or three times they'd heard it but after seven months in deep space with it inflicted on them almost daily, it had lost its humor value. Besides, one didn't go about laughing at the ideas of a scientist of Koman's stature, no matter how dotty his ideas might be getting as he got older.

"You can laugh if you like," Koman went on. "I can see it twinkling in your eyes. But everything I know about anthropology and sociology tells me that Man is many times older than is popularly believed. How he set himself back into the Stone Age for a second time, I don't know. Perhaps an atomic war. Or some natural disaster. It doesn't matter. But before that happened, Mankind had at least enough time to develop space travel and conquer the stars, even as we are doing. And somewhere out there we'll find them"—pointing a bony finger toward the viewplate—"the descendants of Earth's first space pioneers, who settled the planets millions of years ago."

Professor Koman looked alternately at the faces of Karth and Janken. Their blank expressions reflected disbelief, or at best apathy. Koman rose and started to walk to his living cube.

"Planetfall in about 9 hours, Professor," Karth called after him. Koman appeared not to hear him.

Koman lay suspended in his Gravit pad but did not sleep. Lazily, and without conscious effort, his limbs floated this way and that. Sleeping accommodations in space were no problem at all. Since the ship had to generate its own gravity to maintain a sense of up and down for its occupants, it was no big thing to install pads of electrical interference along one wall of each living cube, ceiling, and floor. These Gravit pads (a vulgarization of Grav-Out, their original name) interrupted the magnetic waves which produced the ship's artificial gravity. Thus, a man could float in perfect comfort between the Gravit pads with no weight whatever.

Koman's cheek twitched, reflecting his irritation. Why wouldn't they believe him? Surely they knew he was no fool. His list of scientific accomplishments had won him every major accolade and most of the minor ones. At any scientific congress every word that fell from his lips had a thousand ears to catch it. He'd been the first to find the Martians in the underground civilization they'd built to escape the dust storms on the surface. And he'd pioneered contact with a dozen other races on far-flung planets. Yet on this one particular theory, his pet, he met only deaf ears.

Why? Koman knew that his evidence was strong enough. Archeologists had for years been using calcium sensors to dig up human bones that dated back millions of years before Man was supposed to have walked the Earth. If these pre-Men had existed at least as much time as modern Man, then it only stood to reason that they'd made at least as much scientific progress. Whatever disaster had eradicated their civilization and left them to evolve from primitives once more, it could not have wiped out the beachheads they'd established on other planets. Perhaps some of their colonies, even most, had disintegrated. But a few must remain. And somewhere out among the stars, on some Earth-like world, he'd find these distant relations of his. Like cousins, twice removed. And the greatness and glory of Mankind, in which he so deeply believed, would be doubly proved.

The needle-like ship, blazing red light of a mighty double sun glinting off her hull, descended on a pillar of flame toward the planet's surface. Janken glued his face to the viewplate while Karth effortlessly brought the ship into a planetfall. No matter how many times this scene was repeated, Janken never failed to be fascinated by the first glimpse of a new world. At an altitude of only a hundred yards, Janken was sure he saw something.

"Professor!" he called out. "Over here quickly!"

Koman arrived just in time to see a structure, perhaps a mile off. Almost surely an artificial structure. And then it was gone, disappearing behind a ridge. The ship touched down.

Koman didn't need to say anything. He could see that Karth and Janken were thinking the same thing. A new civilization here . . . and perhaps the proof Koman sought.

The ship's computer gave Karth an almost instantaneous environmental readout. Gravity: 1.07 Earth. Atmosphere: breathable.

Without the need of cumbersome pressure suits, the 3 star-voyagers were soon walking on the planet's surface. The ground crackled slightly beneath them as they walked.

"What sort of beings do you suppose could have built that structure?" Janken asked. "If it was a structure."

"Men could live here," Koman said, his voice fervent.

A swirl of dust on the horizon appeared and drove toward them.

"Back to the ship!" Karth cried, urging his co-pilot before him. But the Professor stood his ground, gazing eagerly at the approaching whirlwind. And then it was upon them. The dust settled and in its place stood not some mad animal but a shining, silvery vehicle. It was perhaps 10 yards long and bullet-shaped. A door slid open in its side and out stepped what was unmistakably and irrefutably a Man.

"Welcome to Cirilla," the man said in perfect Sanskrit. "We were wondering if you'd ever find us."

Koman bubbled. Sanskrit . . . truly an ancient Earth language!

"We had to come!" Koman enthused. "We had to find you. I had to. I knew that Man had existed on Earth long before history and had conquered space once before. And I knew somewhere out here we'd find you . . . Earthmen among the stars!"

"Your theory was basically sound, Professor," the Stranger said. "But you are a little confused in your facts. *We* are not Earthmen . . . *you* are Cirillans!"

Replacement Part

by Greg Akers

(Author of *Sizable Error*)

THE MEMBERS OF THE PIRATE FLEET WERE JUBILANT. SINCE THEIR NEW WEAPONS and drives had been installed, no ship had escaped them. A single pirate vessel could outmaneuver, outrun and outgun any fleet the Intra-Galactic Sector Control could bring against them. And the pirates had 7 such ships. Now was the climax of their raiding: the capture of Galaxy Central.

Less enthusiastic were the Pirate Lords. This raid was prompted because one of the pirates' extra-galactic super-weapons had been captured by the IGSC during a smuggling crackdown. Unless the pirates took decisive action quickly they would lose their chance to destroy the infant republican government and restore their own dynasty to power.

Their spy, a trusted staff member of the Senior Advisor on Galaxy Central, had reported the news:

1) Delta 1, the super-computer recently activated as the commander of IGSC, had built a ray projector with a range of 10 light-years—9 light-years greater than the range of those mounted in the pirate ships.

2) In a seeming accident, the pirate spy had destroyed the relay-link which would have tied in Delta 1 for fire control. The pirates had 7 hours in which to act before a new link could be readied. Until then, the projector would have no guiding computer.

Three pirate ships, only a few thousand miles separate, leapt into the 10 light-year radius around Galaxy Central. From a boreless muzzle hurtled the terrible power of the defending projector. The full shielding of the 3 ships failed before the ravenous energy.

Four ships at random dispersal came into range. They traveled at 1 light-year per second; in 9 seconds they would be within their own destructive range and Galaxy Central would fall.

The projector turned, fired; turned again, fired again. The remaining ships retreated. The 3d flashed into oblivion but the last moved out of range.

Faced with an obvious sabotage action and deducing this to be the pirates' most opportune moment for attack, Delta 1 had relied upon the most versatile component at its disposal: a human operator.

Chicago's own Mark Reinsberg, associated with Shasta Publishers, the sf house there, made a first appearance with this quiet little story of a susceptible trucker—galactic style—who once swore by Mattapenny's otherwise so dependable Galatic Guidebook. *Mark Reinsberg was the co-chairman of the second World Science Fiction Convention.*

The Satellite-Keeper's Daughter

by Mark Reinsberg

It isn't advisable to get that gleam in your eye when
you're out in space. It can lead to complications . . .

SEX AND SPACE DON'T MIX. AND MATTAPENNY'S *GALACTIC GUIDEBOOK* CAN'T be trusted.

If you doubt either proposition, ask Bill Brack. It's hard to tell what he thought about women, but all space truckers used to look upon Mattapenny's little red book as a sort of interstellar Bible.

"Looking for a planet to stop over at?" they'd say. "Place to get good meals? Decent room for the night? You can't go wrong with Mattapenny!"

Brack did.

You see, the *Galactic Guidebook* lists Corbie as one of the five small fuel stations sharing the outermost orbit of the Dryodean planetary system. The latest edition still gives Hotel Eros two asterisks.

Now, two asterisks (**) is supposed to mean "Plain but fairly comfortable."

"Sure," says Brack, "the hotel may lack an up-to-date Dreamawake or a Time-conditioner, but at least you expect your room to have a Vibrobath and controllable gravity."

None of this at the Hotel Eros. Brack shakes his head complainingly. "You sleep in a primitive 7/8G-bed. You wash yourself with old-fashioned magnetic water. And oxygen service costs 10% extra."

Some people ask: "Then why in the world did you stay there?"

"Had·to," Bill answers. "I was hauling out for Dryod-7 with a cargo of deluplasm. Damn valuable stuff, consigned to Hesdin-2. Well, I'd figured the time a little wrong, and it left me with twelve hours to kill before our convoy jumped off. And you know how it is. I was facing three weeks of interstellar rations, and I had a sudden yen for nonsynthetic food. So I looked in the guidebook, and there was Corbie . . ."

Brack was disappointed from the start. When he sat at a table of the hotel restaurant and studied the menu, he saw it was all synthetics.

"Blast it!" he barked into the table phone, "haven't you anything else?"

"I understand how you feel, mister." It was a live human female voice that answered, not the usual robot. "Hold on. I'll come out and see if I can help you."

Through the kitchen door emerged a young girl, short and white-skinned, but very well proportioned.

"Outbound?" she queried. Her pretty face was clouded by an unhappy expression.

"Yes, and I wanted something with a little taste to it, a little substance."

"Such as what?" said the girl, tossing her long blond hair.

Brack looked at the girl carnivorously. "A steak."

She smiled sympathetically. "We haven't anything of that sort. Sorry." She stared at him with light blue eyes the color of moonstones. "How do you happen to land at this miserable place? Fuel?"

"I'm early for my convoy."

Brack stared at the girl's face and he could see it was the mask of some hidden, tragic emotion.

"You weren't thinking of staying at the Hotel Eros?" she inquired in a voice edged with repugnance.

"Well, I do have about twelve hours."

The girl was emphatic. "Take my advice, mister. Spend them in your ship."

A man's voice crackled over the table phone. "Esther!"

She looked startled. "Yes?" she said, leaning over the table to speak into the phone.

('Beautiful!' thought Brack. 'She must have some Earth-blood in her veins.')

The man's voice was angry, strident. "Don't gab with the customers!"

Esther stood up, a blush of embarrassment on her milky-white cheeks. "Your order, please?" she said to Brack, stiffly.

The trucker put his big, brown-colored hand over the phone. "Who's that character?" he asked with distaste. "The boss?"

The girl nodded unhappily. "I didn't realize he was listening."

"Sounds like a tyrant." Brack uncovered the phone. "What's the closest thing you have to beefsteak?"

"Why don't you try some of our roasted pradolan? It's quite good," she added for the boss's benefit. "Specialty of the house."

"There's just one thing I want to know," said Brack. "Is it synthetic?"

The girl smiled sadly. "I'd do anything for some real food myself. I haven't left Corbie in seven years."

"What makes you stick around a place like this? Married?"

"No. My father owns the Eros."

"You're free, brown and twenty-one," said Brack somewhat inaccurately. "He can't make you stay if you want to leave."

Esther waved warningly at the table phone and Brack again covered it with his hand.

"Maybe he can't legally, but there's only one passenger ship between here and the planets every year, and they've refused me a ticket twice now."

"Sounds pretty rotten to me," said the trucker. "Well, what if you got married to some guy? Then he couldn't—"

A heavy-set white man, bald and bullet-headed, strode out of the kitchen and seized the girl roughly by the arm.

"Now I told you not to gab with the customers and I meant it!" he snarled. "You get back there in the kitchen where you belong!"

She tried to wrench free of his grip. "Take your hands off me!"

Slap! He battered her across the cheek with his open hand and she staggered from the blow. "No back talk, young lady! Now, git!"

The trucker half rose from his seat, his fists clenched, but it was over too quickly for him to intervene. And after all, he reflected later while eating the pradolan roast, the man was her father.

With some misgivings, Brack checked into the hotel. It was a tiny installation—perhaps nine or ten rooms. His own cubicle was a drab affair, with neither entertainment screen nor sleep-inducer.

He had just tested the 7/8G-bed with disgust when there was a buzz at the door. It was Esther, holding some linens.

"They have you doing everything around here," Brack said with empathy. "What are these?"

"Towels. You use them after you wash."

"Boy, this sure is ancient!"

Esther's eyes betrayed deep torment. "I know. I would do anything to get away from this place."

She put the towels in a rack. The trucker was lying on the bed, contemplating the girl's deft, graceful movements.

"Listen," he said, "why wait for a passenger ship? Why not arrange secretly with one of the cargo ships that stop here? I know if I was inbound—"

"Don't even say it!" she expostulated. "It's very kind of you, but certainly you've heard of the Pledge Act? My father could prosecute any cargo ship, no matter where it landed in the planets. You know, unlicensed transport of people."

She paused to look at herself in the mirror above the washstand. Brack's eyes were on her bare, marble-white shoulders, her finely sculptured bosom. She sighed.

"No, my only chance is to get away from the Dryodean System altogether. If I go to another star—where the Pledge Act wasn't even heard of—"

She brushed back her long blond hair with an unconscious gesture, like a maiden getting out of a degravity pool.

Brack said thoughtfully: "Esther, if you're really determined to get away from here, maybe I can help you. I'm taking a cargo to Hesdin. Your old man couldn't reach you there, or prove anything against me, either."

The girl's moonstone eyes flared up in hope, but she hesitated. "I don't have very much money. I couldn't make it worth your while, financially."

"That part is unimportant. The thing for you to consider is the situation on Hesdin-2. It's a new colony; life there is pretty primitive."

Esther waved at the room. "Any more so than here?"

Brack grinned. "Not much more. But then also, you've got to remember that it's a three-week trip. Pretty monotonous. Just the two of us."

She looked him in the eyes with understanding.

"I'd try not to get in the way."

They met in the middle of the night at Brack's ship. Working slowly, soundlessly, they opened a cargo case and removed enough unit boxes to make room for the girl.

Esther settled down in the container.

"I'm afraid that isn't too comfortable," Brack apologized, "but you'll only have to put up with it four hours. I take off at seven."

"That's all right, Bill. Just so there's no delay. My father expects me to open the dining room at seven."

"We'll be ten million miles away before he misses you," said Brack. He put the top on loosely, faking the straps across the cover, so the girl could breathe.

In his room again, Brack lay with arms folded under his head, thinking honeyed thoughts. He would have Esther's pleasant company. His cargo was a valuable one. Two-thirds of the receipts on Hesdin-2 would represent sheer profit. Perhaps it would be enough to establish him in some kind of a local freight business. Esther could make a man a wonderful partner. Lovely, delectable girl!

He reminded himself that they were not safely away from Corbie yet, and he passed the remaining hours in the Hotel Eros sleeplessly anxious.

Brack delayed going to his ship until the last minute before takeoff time. Then, as he half-feared, he saw a customs officer standing beside the airlock.

The trucker tried taking the offensive. "Gosh, I'll be late for my convoy if I don't leave right away."

"Sorry, sir, but I'll have to inspect your ship." He was a burly, tough-looking character in pale green uniform, blocking the doorway with a flat-footed, wrestling stance.

Brack sensed that a contest of fists might not end in his favor. He unlocked the entrance and waved the official in with reluctance. "Take a look, but I've already gone through customs on Dryod-7. I can show you my clearance."

"This isn't customs exactly," said the man. "We're searching for a person."

"A person?" (The old man sure kept a close watch on his daughter.) "I'm the only person aboard this ship."

The customs official remained polite. "Yes, I understand that, sir. But Mr. Eros' daughter is missing. He thinks she may have stowed away on your ship."

"Impossible! I had the ship locked."

They stepped into the pilot's cabin, a tetrahexahedron-shaped room, crowded with multiple-monitor screens of an astrogation-computer. Brack threw the ignition switch to start the buildup in the ship's nuclear engine.

"What is your cargo?" the customs man demanded.

"Fifteen cases of deluplasm," said Brack with unfeigned anxiety.

The official debated with himself. "I believe it would be best if I opened the cases."

Brack looked at his watch with desperation. "But we don't have time! That would take at least a half-hour! I'd miss the other ships! And you know what that would mean. I couldn't navigate interstellar space alone, not at a hundred times the speed of light. I'd be stuck here in the Dryodean System until the next fleet left. That might be months!"

He grabbed the official's arm. "Please, fellow, give me a break!"

The customs man considered. "Well, since the ship was locked, it does seem unlikely that the girl has hidden herself here. I certainly wouldn't want you to lose your convoy."

Brack smiled in relief and started the rocket engine secondaries. "Thanks a million."

"But just to protect me in case the girl has run off somewhere—I want you to sign this form."

Brack felt a twinge of suspicion, but more of a twinge of haste. "Sure. What kind of a form is this?"

"It simply says that I inspected each case in your presence and found the contents identical with your bill of lading. This girl has made several attempts to leave Corbie in the past. This is my protection in case she's finally succeeded."

The customs officer made the slightest perceptible wink. Brack signed.

He took off immediately. He was already ten minutes late. He had to blast at top speed for the next hour, continually correcting his navigation. There was no time to go back and let Esther out of the cargo room. He had to remain at the controls, feeding data into the computer, modifying course as solutions flashed on the screens.

Finally, Brack sighted the convoy and maneuvered into pattern just as the fleet was dematerializing into supraspace. He set his ship on panta-graph-automatic with the lead navigator, then hastened to the cargo hold.

Esther was not there. Neither were ten of the fifteen cases of delu-plasm. Two-thirds of his cargo had been hijacked.

It was of course pointless for Brack to turn around and raise hell on Corbie. With the waiver he'd signed for the customs officer, he'd only look ridiculous. All he could do was continue to Hesdin-2 with his one-third cargo. At least he'd break even on the trip; Esther and her co-workers had been that considerate.

No, sex and space don't mix.

And it's high time that Mr. Mattapenny deleted the Hotel Eros (**) from his little red guidebook.

Nymph of Darkness

by Catherine L. Moore and Forrest J Ackerman

THE THICK VENUSIAN DARK OF THE EDNES WATERFRONT IN THE HOURS BEFORE dawn is breathless and tense with a nameless awareness, a crouching danger. The shapes that move murkily thru its blackness are not daylight shapes. Sun has never shone upon some of those misshapen figures, and what happens in the dark is better left untold. Not even the Patrol ventures there after the lights are out, and the hours between midnight and dawn are outside the law. If dark things happen there the Patrol never knows of them, or desires to know. Powers move thru the darkness along the waterfront to which even the Patrol bows low.

Thru that breathless blackness, along a street beneath which the breathing waters whispered, Northwest Smith strolled slowly. No prudent man ventures out after midnight along the waterfront of Ednes unless he has urgent business abroad, but from the leisurely gait that carried Smith soundlessly thru the dark he might have been some casual sightseer. He was no stranger to the Ednes waterfront. He knew the danger thru which he strolled so slowly, and under narrowed lids his colorless eyes were like keen steel probes that searched the dark. Now and then he passed a shapeless shadow that dodged aside to give him way. It might have been no more than a shadow. His no-colored eyes did not waver. He went on, alert and wary.

He was passing between two high warehouses that shut out even the faint reflection of light from the city beyond when he first heard that sound of bare, running feet which so surprised him. The patter of frantically fleeing steps is not uncommon along the waterfront, but these were—he listened closer—yes, certainly the feet of a woman or a young boy. Light and quick and desperate. His ears were keen enough to be sure of that. They were coming nearer swiftly. In the blackness even his pale eyes could see nothing, and he drew back against the wall, one hand dropping to the ray gun that hung low on his thigh. He had no desire to meet whatever it was which pursued this fugitive.

But his brows knit as the footsteps turned into the street that led between the warehouses. No woman, of whatever class or kind, ventures into this quarter by night. And he became certain as he listened that those feet were a woman's. There was a measured rhythm about them that suggested the Venusian woman's lovely, swaying gait. He pressed flat against the wall, holding his breath. He wanted no sound to indicate his own presence to the terror from which the woman fled. Ten years before he might have dashed out to her—but ten years along the spaceways teaches a man prudence. Gallantry can be foolhardy sometimes, particularly along the waterfront, where any of a score of things might be in close pursuit. At the thought of what some of those things might be the hair prickled faintly along his neck.

The frantic footsteps came storming down the dark street. He heard the rush of breath thru unseen nostrils, the gasp of laboring lungs. Then those desperate feet stumbled a bit, faltered, turned aside. Out of the dark a hurtling figure plunged full-tilt against him. His startled arms closed about a woman—a girl—a young girl, beautifully made, muscular and firmly curved under his startled hands—and quite naked.

He released her rather quickly.

"Earthman!" she gasped in an agony of breathlessness. "Oh, hide me, hide me! Quick!"

There was no time to wonder how she knew his origin or to ask from what she fled, for before the words had left her lips a queer, greenish glow appeared around the corner of the warehouse. It revealed a pile of barrels at Smith's elbow, and he shoved the exhausted girl behind them in one quick motion, drawing his gun and flattening himself still further against the wall.

Yet it was no nameless monster which appeared around the corner of the building. A man's dark shape came into view. A squat figure, broad and misshapen. The light radiated from a flash-tube in his hand, and it was an oddly diffused and indirect light, not like an ordinary flash's clear beam, for it lighted the man behind it as well as what lay before the tube, as if a greenish, luminous fog were spreading sluggishly from the lens.

The man came forward with a queer, shuffling gait. Something about him made Smith's flesh crawl unaccountably. What it was he could not be sure, for the green glow of the tube did not give a clear light, and the man was little more than a squat shadow moving unevenly behind the light-tube's luminance.

He must have seen Smith almost immediately, for he came straight across the street to where the Earthman stood against the wall, gun in hand. Behind the glowing tube-mouth Smith could make out a pale blur of face with two dark splotches for eyes. It was a fat face, unseemly in its puffy pallor, like some grub that has fed too long upon corruption. No expression crossed it at the sight of the tall spaceman in his leather garb, leaning against the wall and fingering a ready gun. Indeed, there was nothing to arouse surprise in the Earthman's attitude against the wall, or in his drawn gun. It was what any nightfarer along the waterfront would have done at the appearance of such a green, unearthly glow in the perilous dark.

Neither spoke. After a single long glance at the silent Smith, the newcomer began to switch his diffused light to and fro about the street in obvious search. Smith listened, but the girl had stilled her sobbing breath and no sound betrayed her hiding place. The sluggish searcher went on slowly down the street, casting his foggy light before him. Its luminance faded by degrees as he receded from view, a black, misshapen shadow haloed in unholy radiance.

When utter dark had descended once more Smith holstered his gun and called to the girl in a low voice. The all but soundless murmur of bare feet on the pavement heralded her approach, the hurrying of still unruly breath.

"Thank you," she said softly. "I—I hope you need never know what horror you have saved me from."

"Who are you?" he demanded. "How did you know me?"

"They call me Nyusa. I did not know you, save that I think you are of Earth, and perhaps—trustworthy. Great Shar must have guided my flight along the streets tonight, for I think your kind is rare by the sea edge, after dark."

"But—can you see me?"

"No. But a Martian, or one of my own countrymen, would not so quickly have released a girl who dashed into his arms by night—as I am."

In the dark Smith grinned. It had been purely reflexive, that release of her when his hand realized her nudity. But he might as well take credit for it.

"You had better go quickly now," she went on, "there is such danger here that—"

Abruptly the low voice broke off. Smith could hear nothing, but he sensed a tensing of the girl by his side, a strained listening. And presently he caught a faraway sound, a curious muffled wheezing, as if something short-winded and heavy were making laborious haste. It was growing nearer. The girl's caught breath was loud in the stillness at his elbow.

"Quick!" she gasped. "Oh, hurry!"

Her hand on his arm tugged him on in the direction the squat black searcher had taken. "Faster!" And her anxious hands pulled him into a run. Feeling a little ridiculous, he loped thru the dark beside her with long, easy strides, hearing nothing but the soft fall of his own boots and the scurrying of the girl's bare feet, and far behind the distant wheezing breath, growing fainter.

Twice she turned him with a gentle push into some new byway. Then they paused while she tugged at an unseen door, and after that they ran down an alley so narrow that Smith's broad shoulders brushed its walls. The place smelled of fish and decayed wood and the salt of the seas. The pavement rose in broad, shallow steps, and they went thru another door, and the girl pulled at his arm with a breathed,

"We're safe now. Wait."

He heard the door close behind them, and light feet pattered on boards.

"Lift me," she said after a moment. "I can't reach the light."

Cool, firm fingers touched his neck. Gingerly in the dark he found her waist and swung her aloft at arm's length. Between his hands that waist was supple and smoothly muscled and slim as a reed. He heard the fumble of uncertain fingers overhead. Then in an abrupt dazzle light sprang up about him.

He swore in a choked undertone and sprang back, dropping his hands. For he had looked to see a girl's body close to his face, and he saw nothing. His hands had gripped—nothing. He had been holding aloft a smooth and supple—nothingness.

He heard the fall of a material body on the floor, and a gasp and cry of pain, but still he could see nothing, and he fell back another step, lifting an uncertain hand to his eyes and muttering a dazed Martian oath. For look tho he would, he could see no one but himself in the little bare room the light had revealed. Yet the girl's voice was speaking from empty air.

"What—why did—Oh, I see!" and a little ripple of laughter. "You have never heard of Nyusa?"

The repetition of the name struck a chord of remote memory in the Earthman's mind. Somewhere lately he had heard that word spoken. Where and by whom he could not recall, but it aroused in his memory a nebulous chord of night peril and the unknown. He was suddenly glad of the gun at his side, and a keener awareness was in the pale gaze he sent around the tiny room.

"No," he said. "I have never heard the name before now."

"I am Nyusa."

"But—where are you?"

She laughed again, a soft ripple of mirth honey sweet with the Venusian woman's traditionally lovely voice.

"Here. I am not visible to men's eyes. I was born so. I was born—" Here the rippling voice sobered, and a tinge of solemnity crept in. "—I was born of a strange mating, Earthman. My mother was a Venusian, but my father— my father was Darkness. I can't explain . . . But because of that strain of Dark in me, I am invisible. And because of it I—I am not free."

"Why? Who holds you captive? How could anyone imprison an invisibility?"

"The—Nov." Her voice was the faintest breath of sound, and again, at the strange word, a prickle of nameless unease ran thru Smith's memory. Somewhere he had heard that name before, and the remembrance it roused was too nebulous to put into words, but it was ominous. Nyusa's breathing whisper went on very softly at his shoulder. It was a queer, unreal feeling, that, to be standing alone in a bare room and a girl's sweet, muted murmur in his ears from empty air.

"The Nov—they dwell underground. They are the last remnant of a very old race. And they are the priests who worship That which was my father. The Darkness. They prison me for purposes of their own.

"You see, my heritage from the lady who bore me was her own lovely human shape, but the Thing which was my father bequeathed to his child stranger things than invisibility. I am of a color outside the range of human eyes. And I have entry into—into other lands than this. Strange lands, lovely and far—Oh, but so damnably near! If I could only pass by the bars the Nov have set to shut me away. For they need me in their dark worship, and here I must stay, prisoned in the hot, muddy world which is all they themselves can ever know. They have a light—you saw it, the green glow in the hands of the Nov who pursued me thru the dark tonight—which makes me visible to human eyes. Something in its color combines with that strange color which is mine to produce a hue that falls within man's range of vision. If he had found me I would have been—punished—severely, because I fled tonight. And the Nov's punishments are—not nice.

"To make sure that I shall not escape them, they have set a guardian to dog my footsteps—the thing that wheezed on my track tonight—Dolf. He sprang from some frightful union of material and immaterial. He is partly elemental, partly animal. I can't tell you fully. And he is cloudy, nebulous— but very real, as you would have discovered had he caught us just now. He has a taste for human blood which makes him invaluable, tho I am safe, for I am only half human, and the Nov—well, they are not wholly human either. They—"

She broke off suddenly. Outside the door Smith's keen ears had caught a shuffle of vague feet upon the ground, and thru the cracks came very clearly the snuffle of wheezing breath. Nyusa's bare feet pattered swiftly across the boards, and from near the door came a series of low, sibilant hiss-ings and whistlings in a clearer tone than the sounds the great Dolf made. The queer noise crescendoed to a sharp command, and he heard a sub-dued snuffling and shuffling outside and the sound of great, shapeless feet moving off over flagstones. At his shoulder Nyusa sighed.

"It worked that time," she said. "Sometimes I can command him, by virtue of my father's strength in me. The Nov do not know that. Queer, isn't it—they never seem to remember that I might have inherited more from their god than my invisibility and my access to other worlds. They punish me and prison me and command me to their service like some temple dancing girl—me, the half divine! I think—yes, I think that someday the doors will open at my own command, and I shall go out into those other worlds. I wonder—could I do it now?"

The voice faded into a murmurous undertone. Smith realized that she had all but forgotten his presence at the realization of her own potentiali-ties. And again that prickle of unease went over him. She was half human, but half only. Who could say what strange qualities were rooted in her, springing from no human seed? Qualities that might someday blossom into—into—well, he had no words for what he was thinking of, but he hoped not to be there on the day the Nov tried her too far.

Hesitant footsteps beside him called back his attention sharply. She was moving away, a step at a time. He could hear the sound of her bare feet on the boards. They had almost reached the opposite wall now, one slow step after another. And then suddenly those hesitating footfalls were running, faster, faster, diminishing in distance. No door opened, no aperture in the walls, but Nyusa's bare feet pattered eagerly away. He was aware briefly of the vastnesses of dimensions beyond our paltry three, distances down which a girl's bare feet could go storming in scornful violation of the laws that held him fast. From far away he heard those steps falter. He thought he heard the sound of fists beating against resistance, the very remote echo of a sob. Then slowly the patter of bare feet returned. Almost he could see a dragging head and hopelessly slumped shoulders as the reluctant footfalls drew nearer, nearer, entered the room again. At his shoulder she said in a subdued voice,

"Not yet. I have never gone so far before, but the way is still barred. The Nov are too strong—for a while. But I know, now. I know! I am a god's daughter, and strong too. Not again shall I flee before the Nov's pursuit, or fear because Dolf follows. I am the child of Darkness, and they shall know it! They—"

Sharply into her exultant voice broke a moment of blackness that cut off her words with the abruptness of a knife stroke. It was of an instant's duration only, and as the light came on again a queer wash of rosy luminance spread thru the room and faded again, as if a ripple of color had flowed past. Nyusa sighed.

"That's what I fled," she confided. "I am not afraid now—but I do not like it. You had best go—or no, for Dolf still watches the door I entered by. Wait—let me think."

Silence for a moment, while the last flush of rose faded from the air, to be followed by a ripple of fresh color that faded in turn. Three times Smith saw the tide of red flow thru the room and die away before Nyusa's hand fell upon his arm and her voice murmured from emptiness,

"Come. I must hide you somewhere while I perform my ritual. That color is the signal that the rites are to begin—the Nov's command for my presence. There is no escape for you until they call Dolf away, for I could not guide you to a door without having him sense my presence there and follow. No, you must hide—hide and watch me dance. Would you like that? A sight which no eyes that are wholly human have ever seen before! Come."

Invisible hands pushed open the door in the opposite wall and pulled him thru. Stumbling a little at the newness of being guided by an unseen creature, Smith followed down a corridor thru which waves of rosy light flowed and faded. The way twisted many times, but no doors opened from it nor did they meet anyone in the five minutes or so that elapsed as they went down the hallway thru the pulsing color of the air.

At the end a great barred door blocked their passage. Nyusa released him for an instant, and he heard her feet whisper on the floor, her unseen hands fumble with something metallic. Then a section of the floor sank. He was looking down a shaft around which narrow stairs spiraled, very steeply.

It was typically a Venusian structure, and very ancient. He had descended other spiraled shafts before now, to strange destinations. Wondering what lay in store for him at the foot of this, he yielded to the girl's clinging hands and went down slowly, gripping the rail.

He had gone a long way before the small, invisible hands plucked at his arm again and drew him thru an opening in the rock thru which the shaft sank. A short corridor led into darkness. At its end they paused, Smith blinking in the queer, pale darkness which veiled the great cavern that lay before them.

"Wait here," whispered Nyusa. "You should be safe enough in the dark. No one ever uses this passage but myself. I will return after the ceremony."

Hands brushed his briefly, and she was gone. Smith pressed back against the wall and drew his gun, flicking the catch experimentally to be sure it would answer any sudden need. Then he settled back to watch.

Before him a vast domed chamber stretched. He could see only a little of it in the strange dark pallor of the place. The floor shone with the deep sheen of marble, black as quiet water underground. And as the minutes passed he became aware of motion and life in the pale dark. Voices murmured, feet shuffled softly, forms moved thru the distance. The Nov were taking their places for the ceremony. He could see the dim outlines of their mass, far off in the dark.

After a while, a deep, sonorous chanting began from nowhere and everywhere, swelling and filling the cavern and echoing from the domed ceiling in reverberant monotones. There were other sounds whose meaning he could not fathom, queer pipings and whistlings like the voice in which Nyusa had commanded Dolf, but invested with a solemnity that gave them depth and power. He could feel fervor building up around the dome of the cavern, the queer, wild fervor and ecstasy of an unknown cult for a nameless god. He gripped his gun and waited.

Now, distantly and very vaguely, a luminance was forming in the center of the arched roof. It strengthened and deepened and began to rain downward toward the darkly shining floor in long streamers like webs of tangible light. In the mirrored floor replicas of light reached upward, mistily reflecting. It was a sight of such weird and enchanting loveliness that Smith held his breath, watching. And now green began to flush the streaming webs, a strange, foggy green like the light the Nov had flashed thru the waterfront streets in pursuit of Nyusa. Recognizing the color, he was not surprised when a shape began to dawn in the midst of that raining light. A girl's shape, half transparent, slim and lovely and unreal.

In the dark pallor of the cavern, under the green luminance of the circling light, she lifted her arms in a long, slow, sweeping motion, lighter than smoke, and moved on tiptoe, very delicately. Then the light shimmered, and she was dancing. Smith leaned forward breathlessly, gun hanging forgotten in his hand, watching her dance. It was so lovely that afterward he could never be sure he had not dreamed.

She was so nebulous in the streaming radiance of the light, so utterly unreal, so fragile, so exquisitely colored in the strangest tints of violet and blue and frosty silver, and queerly translucent, like a moonstone. She was more unreal now, when she was visible, than she had ever seemed before his eyes beheld her. Then his hands had told him of her firm and slender roundness—now she was a wraith, transparent, dream-like, dancing soundlessly in a rain of lunar color.

She wove magic with her dancing body as she moved, and the dance was more intricate and symbolic and sinuous than any wholly human creature could have trod. She scarcely touched the floor, moving above her reflection in the polished stone like a lovely moonlight ghost floating in mid-darkness while green moon-fire rained all about her.

With difficulty Smith wrenched his eyes away from that nebulous creature treading her own reflection as she danced. He was searching for the sources of those voices he had heard, and in the green, revealing light he saw them ringing the cavern in numbers greater than he had dreamed. The Nov, intent as one man upon the shimmering figure before them. And at what he saw he was glad he could not see them clearly. He remembered Nyusa's words, "—the Nov are not wholly human either." Veiled tho they were in the misty radiance and the pallor of the dark, he could see that it was so. He had seen it, unrealizing, in the face of that squat pursuer who had passed him in the street.

They were all thick, shapeless, all darkly robed and white-faced as slugs are white. Their formless features, intent and emotionless, had a soft, unstable quality, not shaped with any human certainty. He did not stare too long at any one face, for fear he might make out its queer lack of contour, or understand the portent of that slug-white instability of feature.

Nyusa's dance ended in a long, floating whirl of unhuman lightness. She sank to the floor in deep obeisance, prostrate upon her own reflection. From the front ranks of the assembled Nov a dark figure stepped with upraised arms. Obediently Nyusa rose. From that dark form, from the slug-like, unfeatured face, a twittering whistle broke, and Nyusa's voice echoed the sounds unerringly, her voice blending with the other's in a chant without words.

Smith was so intent upon watching that he was not aware of the soft shuffling in the dark behind him until the wheeze of labored breath sounded almost upon his neck. The thing was all but on him before that sixth sense which had saved him so often before now shrieked a warning and he whirled with a choked oath of surprise and shock, swinging up his gun and confronting a dim, shapeless immensity out of which a dull glow of greenish light stared at him. His gun spat blue flame, and from the imponderable thing a whistling scream rang quaveringly, echoing across the cavern and cutting short that wordless chant between the Nov and the girl.

Then the dark bulk of Dolf lurched forward and fell smotheringly upon Smith. It bore him to the floor under an engulfing weight which was only half real, but chokingly thick in his nostrils. He seemed almost to be breathing Dolf's substance, like heavy mist. Blinded and gasping, he fought the curiously nebulous thing that was smothering him, knowing he must win free in a few seconds' time, for Dolf's scream must bring the Nov upon him at any moment now. But for all his efforts he could not break away, and something indescribable and nauseous was fumbling for his throat. When he felt its blind searching his struggles redoubled convulsively, and after a frantic moment he staggered free, gulping in clean air and staring out into the dark with wide eyes, trying to make out what manner of horror he had grappled with. He could see nothing but that dull flare, as of a single eye, glowing upon him from an imponderable bulk which blended with the dark.

Dolf was coming at him again. He heard great feet shuffling, and the wheezing breath came fast. From behind the shouts of the Nov rose loud, and the noise of running men, and above all the high, clear call of Nyusa, screaming something in a language without words. Dolf was upon him. That revolting, unseen member fumbled again at his throat. He thrust hard against the yielding bulk and his gun flared again, blue-hot in the dark, full into the midst of Dolf's unstable blackness.

He felt the mass of the half-seen monster jerk convulsively. A high, whistling scream rang out, shrill and agonized, and the sucking organ dropped from his throat. The dim glow of vision dulled in the shape's cloudy midst. Then it flickered, went out. Somehow there was a puff of blackness that dissolved into misty nothing all about him, and the dark shape that had been Dolf was gone. Half elemental, he had gone back into nothingness as he died.

Smith drew a deep breath and swung round to front the first of the oncoming Nov. They were almost upon him, and their numbers were overwhelming, but his flame-gun swung its long arc of destruction as they swarmed in and almost a dozen of the squat, dark figures must have fallen to that deadly scythe before he went down under the weight of them. Pudgily soft fingers wrenched the gun from his hand, and he did not fight hard to retain it, for he remembered the blunt-nosed little flame-thrower in its holder under his arm and was not minded that they should discover it in any body-to-body fight.

Then he was jerked to his feet and thrust forward toward the pale radiance that still held Nyusa in its heart, like a translucent prisoner in a cage of light. A little dazed by the swiftness of events, Smith went on unsteadily in their midst. He towered head and shoulders above them, and his eyes were averted. He tried not to flinch from the soft, fish-white hands urging him forward, not to look too closely into the faces of the squat things swarming so near. No, they were not men. He knew that more surely than ever from this close sight of the puffy, featureless faces ringing him round.

At the brink of the raining light which housed Nyusa the Nov who had led the chanting stood apart, watching impassively as the tall prisoner came forward in his swarm of captors. There was command about this Nov, an air of regality and calm, and he was white as death, luminous as a corpse in the lunar reflections of the light.

They halted Smith before him. After one glance into that moveless, unfeatured face, slug pale, the Earthman did not look again. His eyes strayed to Nyusa, beyond the Nov who fronted him, and at what he saw took faint hope again. There was no trace of fear in her poise. She stood straight and quiet, watching, and he sensed a powerful reserve about her. She looked the god's daughter she was, standing there in the showering luminance, translucent as some immortal.

Said the leader Nov, in a voice that came deeply from somewhere within him, tho his unfeatured face did not stir.

"How came you here?"

"I brought him," Nyusa's voice sounded steadily across the space that parted them.

The Nov swung round, amazement in every line of his squatness.

"You?" he exclaimed. "You brought an alien to witness the worship of the god I serve? How dared—"

"I brought one who had befriended me to witness my dance before my father," said Nyusa in so ominously gentle a tone that the Nov did not realize for a moment the significance of her words. He spluttered Venusian blasphemy in a choked voice.

"You shall die!" he yelled thickly. "Both of you shall die by such torment—"

"S-s-s-zt!"

Nyusa's whistling hiss was only a sibilance to Smith, but it cut the Nov's furious flow abruptly short. He went dead quiet, and Smith thought he saw a sicker pallor than before spreading over the slug face turned to Nyusa.

"Had you forgotten?" she queried gently. "Forgotten that my father is That which you worship? Dare you raise your voice to threaten Its daughter? Dare you, little worm-man?"

A gasp ran over the throng behind Smith. Greenish anger suffused the pallid face of the priest. He spluttered wordlessly and surged forward, short arms clawing toward the taunting girl. Smith's hand, darting inside his coat, was quicker than the clutch of his captors. The blue flare of his flame-thrower leaped out in a tongue of dazzling heat to lick at the plunging Nov. He spun round dizzily and screamed once, high and shrill, and sank in a dark, puddly heap to the floor.

There was a moment of the deepest quiet. The shapeless faces of the Nov were turned in one stricken stare to that oddly fluid lump upon the floor which had been their leader. Then in the pack behind Smith a low rumble began to rise, the mutter of many voices. He had heard that sound before—the dawning roar of a fanatic mob. He knew that it meant death. Setting his teeth, he spun to face them, hand closing firmer about the butt of his flame-thrower.

The mutter grew deeper, louder. Someone yelled, "Kill! Kill!" and a forward surge in the thick crowd of faces swayed the mass toward him. Then above that rising clamor Nyusa's voice rang clear.

"Stop!" she called. In sheer surprise the murderous mob paused, eyes turning toward the unreal figure in her cage of radiance. Even Smith darted a glance over his shoulder, flame gun poised in mid-air, his finger hesitating upon the catch. And at what they saw the crowd fell silent, the Earthman froze into stunned immobility as he watched what was happening under the rain of light.

Nyusa's translucent arms were lifted, her head thrown back. Like a figure of triumph carved out of moonstone she stood poised, while all about her in the misty, lunar colors of the light a darkness was forming like fog that clung to her outstretched arms and swathed her half-real body. And it was darkness not like any night that Smith had ever seen before. No words in any tongue could describe it, for it was not a darkness made for any vocal creature to see. It was a blasphemy and an outrage against the eyes, against all that man hopes and believes and is. The darkness of the incredible, the utterly alien and opposed.

Smith's gun fell from shaking fingers. He pressed both hands to his eyes to shut out that indescribably awful sight, and all about him heard a long, soft sighing as the Nov sank to their faces upon the shining floor. In that deathly hush Nyusa spoke again, vibrant with conscious godhood and underrun with a queer, tingling ripple of inhumanity. It was the voice of one to whom the unknown lies open, to whom that utterly alien and dreadful blackness is akin.

"By the Darkness I command you," she said coldly. "Let this man go free. I leave you now, and I shall never return. Give thanks that a worse punishment than this is not visited upon you who paid no homage to the daughter of Darkness."

Then for a swift instant something indescribable happened. Remotely Smith was aware that the Blackness which had shrouded Nyusa was spreading thru him, permeating him with the chill of that blasphemous dark, a hideous pervasion of his innermost being. For that instant he was drowned in a darkness which made his very atoms shudder to its touch. And if it was dreadful to him, the voiceless shriek that rose simultaneously from all about him gave evidence how much more dreadfully their god's touch fell upon the Nov. Not with his ears, but with some nameless sense quickened by that moment of alien blackness, he was aware of the scream of intolerable anguish, the writhing of extra human torment which the Nov underwent in that one timeless moment.

Out of his tense awareness, out of the spreading black, he was roused by a touch that startled him into forgetfulness of that dreadful dark. The touch of a girl's mouth upon his, a tingling pressure of sweet parted lips that stirred delicately against his own. He stood tense, not moving a muscle, while Nyusa's mouth clung to his in a long, close kiss like no kiss he had ever taken before. There was a coldness in it, a chill as alien as the dark that had gathered about her translucency under the light, a shuddering cold that struck thru him in one long, deep-rooted shock of frigid revulsion. And there was warmth in it, headily stirring the pulse which that cold had congealed.

In that instant while those clinging lips melted to his mouth, he was a battleground for emotions as alien as light and dark. The cold touch of Darkness, the hot touch of love. Alienity's shuddering, frozen stab, and humanity's blood-stirring throb of answer to the warm mouth's challenge. It was a mingling of such utter opposites that for an instant he was racked by forces that sent his senses reeling. There was danger in the conflict, the threat of madness in such irreconcilable forces that his brain blurred with the effort of compassing them.

Just in time the clinging lips dropped away. He stood alone in the reeling dark, that perilous kiss burning upon his memory as the world steadied about him. In that dizzy instant he heard what the rest, in their oblivious agony, could not have realized. He heard a girl's bare feet pattering softly along some incline, up and up, faster and faster. Now they were above his head. He did not look up. He knew he would have seen nothing. He knew Nyusa walked a way that no sense of his could perceive. He heard her feet break into an eager little run. He heard her laugh once, lightly, and the laugh cut off by the sound of a closing door. Then quiet.

Without warning, on the heels of that sound, he felt a tremendous release all about him. The darkness had lifted. He opened his eyes upon a dimly lighted cavern from which that rain of light had vanished. The Nov lay in quivering windrows, about his feet, their shapeless faces hidden. Otherwise the whole vast place was empty as far as his eyes could pierce the dark.

Smith bent and picked up his fallen gun. He kicked the nearest Nov ungently.

"Show me the way out of this place," he ordered, sheathing the flamethrower under his arm.

Obediently the sluggish creature stumbled to his feet.

The Genesis of an Invisible Venusienne

Afterword to Nymph of Darkness
by Forrest J Ackerman

THERE IS AN APOCRYPHAL STORY THAT THE CALIFORNIA TOWN OF AZUSA WAS SO named because when a nomenclature for it was sought it seemed that everything had already been appropriated from A to Z in the USA.

There is no truth to the rumor that Nyusa was initially known as NY,

USA; like Wendayne (my wife's naturalized citizen name when she came to Earth from somewhere beyond Infinity), Nyusa burgeoned in my brain in the same manner as Tarzan in Edgar Rice Burroughs': the result of many mental gymnastics with quixotic sound combinations till the satisfactory amalgamation materialized. En passant, it is a virtually forgotten fact— except by Sharane Yvala Dewey, a woman I knew as a little girl, who was so named by her science fiction author father G. Gordon Dewey, who was captivated by the name of A. Merritt's heroine in *The Ship of Ishtar* and the Yvala of Catherine Moore's Northwest Smith adventure of the same name—it is a practically unknown fact that I created the character (pronounced Ee-*vah*-lah). I hope it's not unchivalrous to suggest it, with dear Catherine so mentally decimated by Alzheimer's disease that she has not known me or herself or what she wrote for two years or more (1987), but reflecting on the origin of the story it occurs to me I might retroactively be entitled to a byline on "Yvala" because in retrospect I feel I contributed about as much inspiration and plot gimmick to it as I did to "Nymph." I will not belabor the point, however, since Catherine's memory is a blank book and she is in no position to agree or disagree with my observation. (Incidentally, Gordon Dewey gave his other daughter a Catherine character name: Judai.)

The January–February 1948 club organ of the Los Angeles Science Fantasy Society, *Shangri-LA*, featured the following article by me on the story behind the story on *Nymph of Darkness*.

The "Nymph" O' Maniack

by Forrest J Ackerman

THIS IS THE STORY BEHIND THE STORY OF A COLLABORATION IN WHICH I WAS honored to have my name linked some years ago with the lovely and talented Catherine Moore, now the wife of an old friend—sensational Henry Kuttner. As I am composing this article a few hours before midnite, New Year's Eve, I believe it would be apropos to preface it with a quotation from a New Year letter from Catherine which I ran across in searching for the material for the following.

1936: "Dear Forrie: Happy New Year. And by the way, if you heard a new year's horn blowing extra loudly just at midnight, your time, and couldn't locate it—that was me. I blew a special blast for you at about 2:00 a.m. or thereabouts, as nearly as I can remember now— of New Year's morning just as the radio announced that it was at that moment midnight in Los Angeles. I never quite believe things like that—different times, I mean. Of course, know that you lose a day going round the world, and all that—but somehow can't quite believe it anyway. I read a story somewhere once in which someone in New York phoned someone in London, and over the wire 'the late afternoon New York traffic vibrated weirdly in the stillness of the London night.' It seems impossible, if you see what I mean."

Catherine Moore—puzzled by geo-chronological paradoxes!

But about *Nymph of Darkness* by CLMoore and FJAckerman, whose chief claim to fame was that it was among the titles which vied for third place as best fantasy of the year in a poll taken among the "Auslanders"—the Australian fans, down under. (Also, it was one of the earliest stories illustrated by Hannes Bok, a new artist whom a young fan named Ray Bradbury had personally persuaded the late Farnsworth Wright to try.)

Here is the original outline I sent to Catherine when she was living in Indianapolis and working in a bank vault:

THE NYUSA NYMPH—One short and exciting experience in the adventure-filled life of Northwest Smith . . . Of a fleeing figure in the nite that bumped into NW at the Venusian waterfront—an *unseen* form—that of Nyusa, the girl who was born *invisible*! Further details: The business of the squat creature who came swiftly slinking thru the street, short on the heels of the figure in NW's arms, with the strange lite-tube in its hands flashing from side to side (it would have caused Nyusa to become visible, you know—the lite from the tube) . . . and of Nyusa, whose abnormally high body-temperature kept her comfortable free from clothing; so that invisible she remained, as born—And from what she fled, and how NW was of service to her, etc.—I will leave to you.

MOORE to Ackerman: I think I know why the pursuer's flash made Nyusa visible. Did you ever notice the peculiar colors one's skin turns under different lights? A violet-ray machine turns lips and nails—as I remember—a sickly green, and the blue lights they use in photographers shops, sometimes, make you purple. I once figured out why, but can't remember and haven't time now to go into it. Something about complementary colors and mixing yellow and blue, and whatnot. Well, you remember in Bierce's *The Damned Thing* his invisible monster was a color outside our range of perception. Couldn't this flash-light be of some shade which, combined with Nyusa's peculiar skin-tone, produced a visible color? * And Venus is the Hot Planet anyhow, so no need to increase her body temperature above normal to make it possible for her to run about in the altogether. * Smith had met her in the absolutely black dark of the starless Venusian night. She came tearing down the street and bumped into him, and, tho considerably astonished to find his arms full of scared and quite unadorned girl, he of course didn't realize her invisibility then. Afterward came this squat, dark pursuer, flashing his greenishly glowing ray to and fro. When he'd gone by she heard another sound—origin yet unknown, to me or anyone else—which so alarmed her that she pulled Smith into a run and guided him at top speed thru [the spellings "thru" & "tho" are Catherine's] devious byways and into an unlighted room. "Lift me up," said she, "so I can reach the light." And when it goes on he realizes that he is holding in midair a beautifully muscular, firmly curved armful of nothingness. He had just dropped her onto the floor and staggered back, doubting his sanity. What happens next I don't know. * If you have any more ideas, they'll be welcome. This is the stage of a story when I usually sweat blood for several days, racking an absolutely sterile brain for ideas. Then something takes fire and the whole story just gallops, with me flying along behind trying to keep up with it. Very strenuous. * Think hard and see if you can find any possible reasons, sane or insane, as to what the noise was she had heard, why it alarmed her so, whether she is invisible just by a freak of nature or whether by some mysterious mastermind's intent. I suspect she is in the power of some insidious villain, but I don't know yet. * All thru the preface of the story I've made such veiled hints about the nameless horrors which stalk by night along the waterfront of Ednes, that said villain might be almost anything—some horror out of the ages before man, or some super-brain of the far advanced races we know nothing of, or an unhappy medium like the Alendar. (That reminds me—Vaudir is the infinitive of—as I remember my college days—the French verb *wish*. I presume Nyusa is purely original with you, so you deserve more credit than I, for it's a grand name.) ["Thank you kindly, ma'am," said the 18-year-old lad. "There is no truth to the rumor that I made it up from the initials of our major metropolis, N.Y., U.S.A."]

ACKERMAN to Moore: [This is the point where I was supposed to come in for my big hunk of egoboo, quoting my share in the development of the plot, but I can't find the vital letter! What I wrote must be imagined from the mirror of Catherine's reply.]

MOORE to Ackerman: Thanks for the further suggestions. I had already gone on past my stopping point when I wrote you, so can't use all your ideas, but have incorporated Dolf and the dancing-girl idea. It seems Nyusa is—sorry—really innately invisible, being the daughter of a Venusian woman and a Darkness which is worshipped by a queer race of slug-like, half-human beings which dwell under the Venusian city of Ednes. (Incidentally, Ednes, the city where in the Minga stood, is simply lifted bodily out of the middle of W*ednes*day.) Anyhow, Nyusa is forced by the priests to dance in their ritual worship under a peculiar light which renders her visible in a dim, translucent way. And because of her mixed breed she has access into other worlds from which her masters bar her out by their own strange mental powers because she'd never return to dance for them if she once got away. Dolf guards her for the same reason. I think now that Nyusa's captors drive her too far sometime, and she realizes that after all she is half divine, and calls upon the strain of Darkness within her to burst the bonds they have imposed. Smith, attacked by Dolf as he hides in their temple watching the ritual dance, fights with the worshippers and kills the high priest, whereupon their power over Nyusa is weakened and she exerts her demi-divinity to escape. Thus, tho Smith doesn't get the fortune you suggested, he at least is spared the expense of buying her any clothes, which was a very practical idea on your part.

ACKERMAN to Moore: I have a suggestion about the ending. Shambleau stunned Smith; to this day he had probably not forgotten "it." Sweet, was the girl of the Scarlet Dream. While in the Black Thirst, he gazed upon beauty incredible. But Shambleau was to be shunned; and the girl of the Dream . . . Vaudir dissolved. So, let the Nymph—Nyusa—just before she escapes . . . couldn't she—kiss Smith? A kiss never to be forgotten: a kiss . . . so cool, with a depth drawn out of Darkness. And yet, a kiss of fire—from her Venusian strain—hot, alive, searing Northwest's lips. A kiss, of delicious demi-divinity . . . a fond caress of frozen flame. Making it, under your care, Catherine, a kiss smothering with extra-mundane emotion, leaving the readers gasping. Smith's reward, the kiss becomes famous and concludes the story.

MOORE to Ackerman: I do wish I had had your suggestion about the parting kiss before I finished. I wasn't able to expand the idea as fully as I'd have liked to, both because of the space-saving necessity and because to give it the attention it deserved I'd have had to write the story toward it from the beginning. It was a grand idea and would have given the story just the punch it needed at the end. Oh well, no story of mine is complete unless I leave out some major point until too late. I meant to make Shambleau's eyes shine in the dark, and to play up the idea of the Guardians in *Black Thirst*.

• • •

Nymph of Darkness was first published in the printed fan magazine *Fantasy Magazine*, in the April 1935 issue, and professionally published, in an expurgated form, in the December 1939 *Weird Tales*.

UNCLASSIFIABLE!

In 1940, an arresting 4-part serial, Slan, *appeared in the pages of* Astounding. *It carried the byline of Canadian-born Alfred Elton van Vogt, and concerned the adventures of a telepath, Jommy Cross. Now considered a science fiction cornerstone,* Slan *was the first book-length effort of van Vogt, who went on to become one of the major figures in his chosen field with such classics as* The World of Null—A, The Weapon Makers *and* Voyage of the Space Beagle. *The following little jewel reflects in miniature the vast power of the distinctive imagination of one of the patriarchs of the sf field, acknowledged by his auctorial peers to be a Master of Science Fiction.*

Itself!

by A. E. van Vogt

ITSELF, KING OF THE PHILLIPINE DEEP—THAT AWESOME CANYON WHERE THE SEA goes down six miles—woke from his recharge period and looked around suspiciously.

His Alter Ego said, "Well, how is it with Itself today?"

His Alter Ego was a booster, a goader, a stimulant to action, and, in his limited way, a companion.

Itself did not answer. During the sleep period, he had drifted over a ravine, the walls of which dropped steeply another thousand feet. Suspiciously, Itself glared along the canyon rim.

. . . Not a visual observation. No light ever penetrated from above into the eternal night here at the deepest bottom of the ocean. Itself perceived the black world which surrounded him with high frequency sounds which he broadcast continuously in all directions. Like a bat in a pitch dark cave, he analyzed the structure of all things in his watery universe by interpreting the returning echoes. And the accompanying emotion of suspicion was a device which impelled Itself to record changing pressures, temperatures and current flows. Unknown to him, what he observed became part of the immense total of data by which faraway computers estimated the inter-relationship of ocean and atmosphere, and thus predicted water and air conditions everywhere with uncanny exactness.

His was almost perfect perception. Clearly and unmistakably, Itself made out the intruder in the far distance of that twisting ravine. A ship! Anchored to rock at the very edge of the canyon.

The Alter Ego goaded. "You're not going to let somebody invade your territory, are you?"

Instantly, Itself was furious. He activated the jet mechanism in the underslung belly of his almost solid metal body. A nuclear reactor immediately heated the plates of the explosion chamber. The sea water which flowed through the chamber burst into hissing clouds of steam, and he jetted forward like a missile.

Arriving at the ship, Itself attacked the nearest of four anchor lines with the nuclear-powered heat beam in his head. When he had severed it, he turned to the second cable, and burned through it. Then he moved for the third cable.

But the startled beings aboard the alien ship had spotted the twenty-foot monster in the black waters below.

"Analyze its echo pattern!" came the command. That was done, with total skill.

"Feed the pattern back through the infinite altering system till the recorders register a response."

The significant response was: Itself forgot what he was doing. He was drifting blankly away, when his Alter Ego goaded, "Wake up! You're not going to let them get away with that, are you?

The defeat had galvanized Itself to a more intense level of rage. He became multiples more sensitive. Now, he simply turned out the alien echo copies.

The new greater anger triggered a second weapon.

Itself's echo system of perception, normally monitored to be safe for all living things in the sea, suddenly strengthened. It became a supersonic beam. Purposefully, Itself started toward the ship.

Watching his approach, the enemy decided to take no chances. "Pull the remaining anchors in!"

Itself headed straight for the nearest part of the vessel. Instantly, those ultrasonic waves started a rhythmic vibration on the hard wall, weakening it.

The metal groaned under a weight of water that at these depths amounted to thousands of tons per square inch. The other wall buckled with a metallic scream.

The inner wall trembled, but held.

At that point, the appalled defenders got a counter-vibration started, nullified the rhythm of Itself's projections, and were safe.

But it was a sorely wounded ship that now drifted helplessly in a slow current. The aliens had thus far used no energy that might be detected from the surface. But they had come to Earth to establish a base for invasion. Their instructions were to accumulate enough data about underwater currents to enable them to leave the Deep, and eventually to be able to drift near land, launch atom bombs and drift away again. For this purpose they were mightily armed, and they refused to die in these black waters without a fight.

"What can we do about that demon?"

"Blast it!" someone urged.

"That's dangerous." The alien commander hesitated.

"We can't be in greater danger than we already are."

"True," said the commander, "but frankly I don't know why he's armed at all, and I can't believe he has anything more. Set up a response system. If he does attack with anything new, it will automatically fire back. We'll take that much of a chance."

The second setback had driven Itself completely berserk. He aimed his nuclear pellet gun, firing twice. In the next split-second a blast from the invader pierced his brain.

The Alter Ego yelled, "You're not going to let them get away with that, are you?"

But the king of the Phillipine Deep was dead, and could no longer be goaded.

In due course, a report was given to weather headquarters: "Computer Center shows no recent data from Itself. It therefore seems as if another of the wartime anti-submarine water-weather robots has worn out. You may recall that these electronic monsters were programmed to suspicion, anger, and the idea that they owned part of the ocean. After the war, we could never get these creatures to surface; they were too suspicious of us."

The ocean of water, like the ocean of air far above, flowed and rolled and moved in a ceaseless, dynamic, driving motion many, many times more powerful, however, than any comparable air current. Yet, in essence, the quadrillions of water movements solely and only balanced each other out.

Through the Phillipine Deep there began presently to flow an enormous balancing river. It carried the aliens' invasion vessel in a long, slanting, upward direction. But several weeks passed before the drifting ship actually broke surface, and another day or two before it was seen.

A naval patrol boarded it, found the aliens dead more than a month from concussion, and—after examining the damage—correctly analyzed what had happened.

And so—a new king "woke" to the first "day" of his reign, and heard *his* Alter Ego say, "Well, Itself, what's the program?"

Itself glared with a royal suspicion.

Big, Wide, Wonderful World

by Charles E. Fritch

(Author of *The Logical Life*)

CHUCK GOT THE IDEA. "LET'S HAVE A NIGHTMARE," HE SAID.

We looked at him, wondering if he could be serious. He was, or at least he looked like he was, which in his case was generally the same thing.

"You crazy or something, boy?" I said. "A nightmare? Count me out. I came close a couple times but no more. Not ever again."

"Aw, you're chicken," he said. "How about you, Bill? Len?"

Bill looked at me and at Chuck and then at Len and then at Chuck again. "I—I don't know, Chuck. It—it's risky stuff. I've seen guys go into nightmares." He shuddered at the memory. "It's not pretty."

"Of course it's not pretty. Nobody said it was. It's the excitement, the thrills. Why do you suppose they play Russian Roulette."

"At least with Russian Roulette," Len put in, "you're either dead or you're not. Having a nightmare you just *wish* you were dead."

"Okay, look," Chuck said, and I could see he was trying hard not to be exasperated, "what can we lose. We've got our needles—" he patted the one at his belt—"and if any of us is too far gone, one of the others can give him the hypo."

The way he said it, it sounded pretty reasonable.

"I'm with you," Len said.

"Okay," Bill said, "I'll go along with it."

"Me, too," I said, without hesitating. I didn't like it but I had no choice. I would have to give in, so I figured I might as well do it right away so they wouldn't think I was scared.

I *was* scared, though. Plenty. I remember once I forgot my needle when I went for a walk and the whistle sounded for Injection and when I reached down to my belt I found the needle wasn't there. Boy, was I scared then. I ran home as fast as I could but before I got there the Nightmare began and I felt cold and sick to my stomach and I saw the world around me start to waver like a reflection in a muddy stream of water. It was terrible.

It would be terrible now, too, but I had to stick it out.

"Okay, then," Chuck said, consulting his wristwatch, "here's what we'll do. The Injection Whistle's gonna blow in about half an hour. We'll go over by the woods there so no one'll see us and lie down; you can take a Nightmare a lot easier if you're lying down. Then, when the whistle blows we'll just stay there. We won't do anything. We won't even take the needles from the holster, got that? We'll just sit there and have ourselves a night-mare and see who can take it the longest."

We nodded. I hoped I wasn't really as pale and scared-looking as I felt. I knew the one who could take it the longest wouldn't be me but I prayed I wouldn't be the first to needle myself. Let Bill or Len do it, I thought, it wouldn't be so bad if one of them cracked first. If only I could hold out that long—

We went over to the woods and sprawled on the ground out of sight from anyone who might pass by. It was a beautiful day and it was a big, wide, wonderful world in which to be alive. The trees were blossoming with spring and the grass was green and cool and the air was fresh and clean. I wished I didn't have to go through with this. But I did, and I forced the wish from my mind. Soon it would be over, I told myself; it would be over and done and in the past and that would be that.

I must have dozed for I came awake with a start when the whistle blew.

Chuck looked at his watch. "Right on the button," he said proudly. "We've got about five minutes."

Five minutes never passed so slowly. We sat staring at each other. All of us were pretty nervous. I found myself tearing a leaf into shreds and dis-carded it and wished I'd kept it because I wanted to do something so I wouldn't have to think of what was going to happen.

"It should be starting now," Chuck said.

"Yes," Bill breathed. "Things are starting to get a little fuzzy. How about you, Len. Anything?"

"No, not yet. Wait! Yes, it's starting."

I didn't say anything. I couldn't speak. Around me, the world was beginning to come apart at the seams. *The needle!* a voice cried inside me. *No!* I thought, fighting it.

I felt myself getting cold, shivering. My stomach began tying itself into knots. Desperately, I looked at the others. One of them had to do it first. *Needle yourself!* I thought at Bill. *Needle yourself!* I thought at Len. I looked at Chuck. He was trembling. His face was distorted in pain. I closed my eyes, balled my fists and struck at the ground.

Someone screamed.

I forced my eyes open. It was Len. He had staggered erect, was pawing frantically at the hypo in his belt. Suddenly the pain seemed more bearable. Len would be the first, I thought unashamedly, and I the second. His hypo came loose, flashing in the sunlight, and then it dropped from his shaking hands into the grass somewhere. He cried out in despair and dropped to all fours, sobbing.

I'll help you, Len, I thought, but I couldn't move. The world was pressed down on me, knotting my stomach, forcing the blood to pound in my head.

The air swirled in muddy currents and there was the smell of burned wood and the odor of decay. I forced myself to one knee.

The world was a nightmare. The Earth was a black, ugly thing now. The forest was a graveyard of charred stumps. The buildings in the distance were not buildings at all but skeletons of buildings. I felt sick.

I turned to look at Chuck and Bill and Len. They were hideous things, pale, scarred, disfigured horribly, like grubs of humans produced by some atomic war. I retched.

The needle! I thought frantically. I got it out of the holster with a trembling hand, fearing at any moment I might drop it and lose the precious drug inside and have to spend forever in this nightmare world. I jabbed myself and the liquid flowed warmly into my veins. I dropped back on the ground to relax and wait.

The trembling ceased. The dark mists parted before the warm rays of the sun and the air became fresh again and the grass and trees green, the buildings whole. I breathed a sigh of relief and stood up.

Len was lying face down, unmoving, his arms outstretched and his fingers extended to within an inch of his shattered needle. Bill was sitting beside a tree, an empty needle in one hand; he was panting, eyes closed, unable to speak. Chuck was screaming.

I pulled Chuck to his feet and hit him as hard as I could. He lay still and moaned. I fumbled at his needle holster, got the hypo out and with a steady hand shot the fluid into his arm. He relaxed and after a moment his eyes fluttered open. There was fear in those eyes, then relief as they saw the world was good again.

I went over to see how Len was.

"I never want to go through that again," Bill said. He held his head in his hands and said it over and over and over. "I never want to go through that again!"

"I didn't think it would be quite so bad," Chuck said, almost apologetically. "Everybody okay?"

"Len's dead," I told him.

"Oh," he said.

"Look, Chuck," I said. "You're bigger than I am and older but if you ever suggest something like this again I'm going to beat you into a bloody mess!"

Chuck looked up at me, at my clenching fists, and over at Len, and he knew I meant it. He nodded slowly.

"C'mon, then," I said. "We've got to get Len back home."

Together the three of us carried the body into the city, through the big, wide, wonderful world of tall trees and green grass and fresh air and shining buildings. And to make sure we'd keep this dream world, we'd get our hypos refilled for the next time the nightmare of reality was due.

This recovery, published 55 years ago by editor John W. Campbell in Astounding Science-Fiction, *was well received but, astonishingly, never anthologized by anyone for 3 decades & a lustrum.*

The Door

by Oliver Saari

(Author of *Two Sane Men*)

LIGHT IN THE IGIDI DESERT WAS A MONSTROUS THING, THOUGHT WHALEN; shimmering from the white-hot sand, dancing on an uncertain horizon, painting mirage after mirage to the blistered vision of the man who staggered there.

Whalen sank to his knees on the rippled sand and attempted to squeeze the last hot drops from his canteen. One—two—three—there were no more. He licked cracked lips to save the pearls of moisture from the greedy wind.

A mile to his left was a gash of green; palms, their tender stems stooping under the weight of the sky—blue water—shadows. The picture danced on the heat haze. Whalen laughed at it. At first he had pursued it. Now it pursued him. It was a mirage, a jest, a laughing taunt of the Great Igidi. The torment of Tantalus.

Even had it been real, it wasn't what Whalen had been seeking.

Now that death was near and most other things remote, Whalen found in his mind a great unity of purpose. The thing he was seeking was real. Unlike the mirage it was near and it existed. And it offered hope, a chance of escape from this hell of sand and sky.

The fierce-eyed Sheik had told him that. Yes, the Igidi held the temple of the forgotten worship of the ancient Berbers. He himself had seen it: the center of the blasphemous cult of the oldest white race, the thing they had believed in before the Arabs had shown them Allah.

It had been false, the Sheik said, and thus it had died. There remained only the ruins and the *Door*, the portal which was the symbol of the old religion. But it was all evil and false. Its prophets had been condemned to the Seventh Hell of Mohammed. Even the oasis had been destroyed, the desert washed clean by the breath of Allah. Only the ruins and the sand remained.

The Sheik had been very devout, and had washed his beard and his hands and his feet with sand, and faced the direction of Mecca.

But he had robbed Whalen just the same. Had taken his water and camels. The Sheik had the right to them, of course, because he had a long, curved knife and Whalen's rifle was in its scabbard. Whalen knew the art of gracious giving and was, therefore, still alive.

"You may have the water in your canteen, Christian Dog," the Sheik had said. "May you find the Door and walk through it, for it opens not into Heaven as its prophets claimed, but into the Seventh Hell!"

The Sheik had jested. Whalen loved a jest. If one must be robbed, it is better by a good-natured robber, he thought.

Without water, without camels he didn't have a chance of beating the Igidi—unless he found the Door. The Sheik had given him the canteen and pointed a direction. That was his jest. That was the chance he had given Whalen: to find what he thought was the portal to the Seventh Hell.

Of one thing Whalen was sure. The Door, into which thousands of worshipers and, eventually, the prophets had vanished, did not lead into the Seventh Hell, but into another physical plane of existence. After piecing together thousands of words of disconnected legend, that was the conclusion he had reached. The Sheik had told him nothing he had not known before.

Back in civilized Morocco Whalen had thought only of the records, of a possible clue to the origin of the white Berbers. Now, in the vastness of Igidi, he could think only of death and of the Door. Because the Door meant life. If it still existed, it was a shortcut out of this place of thirst and heat.

The canteen flopped against Whalen's thigh with an empty sound. He threw it into the sand and paused to watch the drift cover it up. Empty, dry sustainer of life, it had failed in its duty and now it was dead. Whalen laughed out loud, though the effort was agony in his throat. He was a little mad. He thought it would not be so bad dying if it could be in jest.

Then he moved on, stumbling on the ripples. He changed his course often to keep from traveling in circles. The mirage of green palms still pursued him.

Suddenly it was replaced by ruins. Gray and brown weathered stone standing against a hot sky. Whalen ran three steps, then saw the telltale fading of the image. Another mirage, more cruel, more torturing.

Heat. Heat. Molten gold pouring down a sand-strewn valley, engulfing him. Whalen could no longer see, but feeling was intense. This was not a jest; this was death. He was dead, but his legs moved on. Night would not come; even in death there was sun and light. It had been cool nights years ago and there would be no more nights. Only day—day—

He stumbled onto something hard. Under his hands was stone. It had no meaning to him; he was dead. Then suddenly it had meaning.

Whalen tried to see, but the white pain of heat blindness was in his eyes. He could feel with his hand, though, and it was rough-hewn stone he felt.

Then he could see. He was in the middle of it and it was not a mirage. Stone pillars, human artifices, works of man here in the middle of Hell. They did not belong there, they could not be.

But the stone pillar before him cut off the sun. Whalen lay in its shadow, his face in the sand. Feeling returned; at first pain, then thought and memory.

Ruins!

With that thought came life and energy to Whalen. He staggered to his feet and stared at the pillars. Seven of them there were, ten feet high and three feet thick. Behind them was an arched stone doorway, standing alone, and then seven more pillars. There were suggestions of other shapes around, but all were covered with sand. The pillars and the door were in a hollow amid the dunes, as if the drifting sand dared not approach the portal.

The Door!

A shower of hope dissolved the bony hand of thirst that clawed at Whalen's throat.

It was insane to believe in an ancient Berber legend, but he believed. Here was proof. Beyond that door existed another plane.

The arched doorway was seven feet high and—empty. Through it showed the desert, but the image wavered like a heat haze. Whalen walked past the pillars and around in back and it was the same.

Had pilgrims walked through this portal into nothingness as the legends said, in the days when Egypt was yet unborn? Where did it lead? Who had built it?

Then Whalen's nostrils caught the scent of alien atmosphere.

It came from the Door, an intangible odor that was not of this desert. It came on a wind, wafted through the film of nothingness that veiled the portal.

Whalen could scarcely find strength to stagger to the portal. For a moment he paused to look back past the pillars.

The mirage was gone. Only the white-hot sky and the shifting dunes remained as far as the eye could see. The vast Igidi, cruel and unbeatable. He had beaten it! He had conquered thirst and had reached his goal. The Door would cheat the Igidi of its victim. It was a jest and this time the joke was on the desert!

With new strength he turned and walked to the very edge of the shimmering nothingness that was the dividing line. There would be no returning. The ancient prophets had said the Door led into Heaven. The Sheik had said—

He was through. There was only a slight feeling of vertigo and then he was in a new plane of existence.

Whalen turned. He had walked through the door, but it was not behind him. Behind him was nothing.

Above were two suns, one orange and one yellow. The sky was reddish, like a sunset but more intense.

Whalen stood still for a long time. Then he laughed long, till the hurt of it in his throat started bringing darkness to his brain.

Again it was a jest, and again it was on him.

He was not in Heaven, nor was he in the Seventh Hell of Mohammed. The air was hot and the sand stretched on to the horizon, drier than the Igidi. He was in another desert.

One of the stranger stories dreamed up by an author is—

Racial Memory

by Ralph O. Hughes Jr.

(Author of *Paranoia*)

He AROSE IN THE MORNING TO THE PRODDINGS OF HIS WIFE, THINKING OF THE strange dreams he had awakened from. He struggled with his beard over the water, then gulped his breakfast. As he stepped from the shelter of his home, emerging from the cave of rock, the crude arrow sank quiveringly into his chest. His adversary glided away into the shadows.

He arose in the morning to the proddings of his wife, thinking of the dreams. He shaved, the straight razor tugging the beard from his face, then hurried thru breakfast. As he stepped from his frame house the shotgun blast shattered his chest in a fountain of blood and flesh. His adversary galloped away into the darkness.

He arose to the insistent ring of the alarm. His electric razor hummed away the stubble of his beard. With breakfast warming his insides, he stepped from the elevator into the apartment garage and was met by a stuttering machine gun that shredded his chest and the doors behind him. His adversary screeched away in a late-model sedan.

He arose to the proddings of his bedroom computer. As he applied depilatory cream to his stubble the kitchen comp was preparing breakfast. As he stepped from the door of his lakeside condominium a shimmering lance of energy blasted his chest and the door into cinders. His adversary skimmed away in a late-model aeromobile.

He arose in the morning to the proddings of his wife, thinking of the strange dreams he had awakened from. He struggled with his beard over the dull blade and chill water. Forgoing breakfast he stepped from the shelter of his home. As he emerged into the landscape of shattered concrete and twisted steel, the crude arrow pierced his ragged coat, burying its head in his chest. His adversary skulked away, back to his own bomb shelter.

Alien trap? Tunnelvision becomes terrorvision in this tale that will make your flesh crawl . . .

Tunnel

by Roger Aday

"**W**HAT KIND OF TUNNEL IS IT?" ASKED GREG, FOLLOWING TERRY AND ALAN down the steep hill.

"We don't know. It's big, tho," said Terry. "You can walk upright in it!"

"I wonder where it leads."

"We'll find out," said Alan. "Terry and I found it yesterday but didn't want to explore it until you could come too."

The 3 young men made their way to the bottom of the hill and Alan went straight to where the entrance lay. "It's dark," he called. "Get out your flashlights!"

Greg pulled his out and flipped it on. As he peered into the tunnel, his thin beam of light showed all there was to see.

The dark passageway, which was obviously manmade and walled with cement, led back about 10 feet, then turned off to the left and right.

"Let's go," said Alan and stepped into the tunnel.

Terry and Greg followed and were soon at the bend. They peered around the corner and shined their flashlights to see if there were more turnoffs. None could be seen.

"I'm writing my initials on the wall here so we'll know which entrance leads back out!" said Alan and wrote AB on the wall.

"Which direction should we go?" wondered Terry, looking both ways.

"Let's go right," suggested Greg and took over the lead. On and on they went. As far as they could see was nothing but more tunnel.

"What was this made for?" ventured Alan after they walked quite awhile.

"I don't know but it's getting smaller," said Greg. "I could stand upright in it when we started. Now I'm having to bend over."

"He's right," said Terry. "Let's go the other way. My back is starting to hurt from walking hunched over."

All were in agreement so they started back. They hadn't gone far when Terry spoke up once more.

"Something's wrong," he said. "The tunnel should start getting bigger but I'll swear it's still getting smaller."

"It has to be your imagination," retorted Greg but he'd noticed it also. They kept on and were soon forced to crawl on their hands and knees.

They were on the verge of having to scoot along on their stomachs when Alan called out, "I've found an opening!"

They all crowded around with much difficulty to the hole Alan had discovered.

"What good is that?" asked Greg. "We can't even begin to fit into that thing."

"We have to be going in the wrong direction," said Terry. "It's only logical that if we go back the other direction, the tunnel will get bigger."

Greg was on the verge of agreeing when Alan called out, "Oh, my god!"

"What is it?"

But Alan could say no more. He merely pointed.

Greg bent down and saw what he was pointing at. Next to the tiny opening, almost too small to read, were the initials AB in white chalk!

Inferiority

by James Causey

(Author of *Inhibition* & *Competition*)

WHEN AVILA FOUND OUT WHAT MARL JEDSEN WAS, SHE DID NOT QUITE DIE. SHE smashed the topaz bust she had carved so lovingly and spent the long, mad days keening over the glistening fragments. In time she helped lethargically with the new village, helped fashion it from the tired limestone of the hills. Not again the white spires carved like foam, the exquisite explosions in stone lace, but squat humble cubes, glowing with color.

The seasons came and went and the silver ships of the Earthmen twinkled overhead like vigilant wasps, yet no Earthmen came. Avila even attended the spring festivals now but it was understood she could not mate again. She had recovered an even greater genius, greater because of the new haunting sorrow that marked her simplest figurines. She could not quite forget that monstrous fungus blooming in the pink Martian sky or the waste of radioactive obsidian that now marked the village of her birth.

This day it was summer and the desert was a vast golden mirror under the chill sun and the waters in the canal crawled like warm green oil. Avila worked in her artifact room. She crooned softly as she plied chisel and hammer, an elfin melody that Shar from the old village had first sung on his silver lute, a song of the lost ages about ghosts and dreams and waste ruins in the tinkling moonlight. Shar had been the very greatest of them all, she thought.

And a strange sound stilled Avila's song, made her freeze into startled immobility at the heavy booted footsteps. She heard the outer door open, then the door to her artifact room.

Marl stood there.

He had not changed in 5 years. The hard, handsome face, the good breadth of shoulder, the black uniform with the scarlet comet glaring angrily from his chest. Avila drew a long, shuddering breath. "Welcome home, beloved."

He stared at her across a gulf in time and the old arrogance in his eyes died quietly at the wonder of her.

"After 5 years?" he said wryly.

"After a hundred," she said softly. Her turquoise eyes caressed him. "That comet. So they made you a member of the Imperial Council."

"Director of the Council," Marl said quietly. "You're very beautiful."

Her eyes were shining wet. "Why, Marl, *why?*"

"Orders. Take a Martian to wife. *Absorb their culture.* It was impossible!"

"Eighty-seven of them." Her voice was very soft. "Old Shar, the greatest poet of them all. Young Teena, who could turn limestone into lazuli. My father—he could fashion a singing flame from a lump of clay."

"That was why," said Marl, and his voice was hard. "Some of you were evacuated."

"The stupid ones, the clods."

"We had to know. It's why I came back."

Avila's eyes closed. Faintly: "Then it wasn't for me."

"I'm surprised you lived. We have a bird on Earth, the parakeet. When its mate dies . . . but then I didn't die. Did I, Avila?"

"No," she said.

He looked carefully around the artifact room. His keen gaze missed nothing, the carved animals that seemed about to spring, the tormented figurines. "You've done very well in 5 years," he said, and his words, flat, utterly without inflection, caused twin spots of color to glow in her cheeks.

"Uproot them," Marl mused. "Set them down in the desert, without tools, without food. Let them build. Come back in 5 years. Perhaps they'll have changed." He looked suddenly tired. "It's a matter of survival. There's a new movement on Earth, a soft, silly, noninterference policy. It's infecting the Council. It's why I'm here. Today is Inspection Day. Let's take a walk."

She bowed her bright head. They went out into the cold hard sunlight.

Down the red road they went, slowly, past the squat rainbow dwellings, and Avila said, "See? Humility. No spires to soar and mock. Is it what you wished?"

Marl stared at the green crystal patio across the way. A youth dabbed at an easel, carefully studying the prismatic leapings of sunlight in the canal waters.

"Kell, son of Kell," Avila said. "He daubs, fruitlessly. His father was great, the son but an empty echo."

"We'll see," Marl said.

They approached the painting and Kell smiled at them and bent back to his canvas. Marl caught his breath. From the half-finished canvas, incredible colors roared. The desert was gold, pure gold, the canal had a desolate forlorn look that brought tears.

"What will you call it, Kell?" Avila asked gently.

"Future Tense," Kell said, sighting along his brush.

They walked along. Marl's face was a study in stone. "Where do you get your raw materials?"

"Mordak built a converter," Avila said. "A clumsy thing, always breaking down. It's not bad for proteins and carbohydrates but she hasn't yet produced a diamond without a flaw."

They walked to the end of the village where the converter loomed, blackly. Marl eyed the vats of mercury, the strange twisted vanes, the cold white flame spanning the silver electrodes. Mordak looked up from the relay panel and came eagerly forward, holding in her palsied hands a great blue chrysolite. "Flawless, my dear," she quavered. "Seven trials, but it's perfect. Please take it. Use it for the festival mosaic."

"Only," said Avila gravely, "on the condition that you allow me to carve your bust from it."

Mordak thanked her and Marl said, tight-lipped, "Let's see some of the others."

They walked back through the village, Avila carrying the chrysolite very carefully, Marl staring bleakly ahead. That morning he saw Glax the toymaker make the children scream with delight at his jeweled fire-bursts of bright emerald, crimson and orange stars that tinkled a soft symphony as the colors died. He heard Glax's wife sing a song so poignant that he cried, and he laughed like a child at the joyous notes that followed. He nodded to some of the elders who had played at their wedding feast, and although they knew what he had done, why he was here, there were only friendly smiles.

Finally, he said, "I've seen enough, Avila. Let's go back."

In the dimness of Avila's artifact room he held up a pale green vase and trembled at the agonized beauty of it. "You made this?"

"I know," she said, ashamed. "Hideous. Please destroy it, beloved."

The vase shivered into fragments on the marble floor. "That," Marl said brutally, "would make our finest Ming look like china." Hot little lights danced in his black eyes. "Yet it's not good enough for you to look at. I'm glad I came," he said.

He strode forward, grasped her savagely by the arms. "A race of artisans," he said. "Poets, artists! And no survival quotient. A race of vegetarians," he said bitterly. *"Why?* No carnivorous animal has ever been discovered on Mars. A perfectly balanced ecology. You had it handed to you on a silver platter. Do you know about man? Claw and fang, up from the slime! And he'll never stop fighting, Avila."

She looked at him numbly. Marl's voice was a dead monotone.

"The first Neanderthal, without steel or flint, shambling. Shambling in a shamed oblivion because he had a neighbor who could paint the walls of his cave. Cro-Magnon. Cro-Magnon had fire, steel, he killed Neanderthal with an inferiority complex. Man," he said thickly, "came here in good faith. He saw—splendor. He tried to follow your science and he went mad. The mouse in the maze. Our greatest painters looked at your children's poorest canvases and stopped painting forever. Our poets heard your songs and killed themselves. Well, we've got one thing you never had and never will have," he said. "Because we're men. We've got a break-in-the-bone survival-instinct, we've got a drive that will take us beyond the stars! Nothing—nobody—will quench that drive. Can you understand? This village was an experiment. The experiment failed. The Council doesn't know. They don't know I'm here. But they'll accept my recommendation."

Avila whispered, "We could go away. To another planet."

His eyes were inexorable. "Could you? Really?"

"No," she said dully.

"No," he said. "Rabbits, all of you. You wouldn't spill a drop of blood to save your entire race. That's why we're greater. That's why we'll go on. You believe that, don't you, Avila?"

"Yes," she said.

"Goodby, Avila," he said.

She raised her face to his and her mouth quivered in the vestige of a smile. "Before you go—"

"Yes?" His grin was hard, knowing.

"I destroyed that bust of you, 5 years ago," she said simply. "Could I make another one? To look at while you're away?"

"I won't be gone long," he said, and she knew what he meant.

"Please," she said. "It's a new process. Ten minutes."

He frowned, cupped her chin in one hand, raised her calm face to his. "Martians never lie," he said softly. "You really love me? In spite of—"

"That does not matter," she said and he knew she spoke the truth. "I want you near me always. I want nothing else."

"What a shame you can't hate," he said. "This pose all right?"

He threw back his head fiercely, man bursting from the slime, man the unconquerable, and Avila said gently, "No, beloved. Look helpless. It will be, be—better."

"Eh?" Quick suspicion darkened his face and he moved swiftly. But Avila's fingers had flickered over a tiny stud on her workbench and bronze manacles had slid from the wall, and Marl stood transfixed, raging.

"Please," Avila said, throwing a switch, and the hidden electrodes appeared. The blue sparks crackled. "Stand still, beloved." Mercury vapor coiled like a live thing in the crystal vats and Avila's fingers flashed over the row of studs on her workbench and Avila murmured a litany of love as she watched him curse and tear at the bronze clamps.

The blue radiance touched Marl's face, caressed his shoulders, the lightnings laughed and hissed along his legs, turning the pink of his skin into a hard wet onyx. Marl was very still.

At length, Avila depressed the switch. He would never leave her now. He stood frozen forever into a splendid straining attitude, and she must put chains on his arms, broken chains to symbolize the futility and the glory.

After all, he was a man.

If looks could kill, this is a hair-raising story.

Task of the Temponaut

by Norbert F. Novotny & Van Del Rio

(Authors of *The Eagle Has Landed*)

THE TEMPONAUT CHECKED THE SPACE-TIME COORDINATES OF HIS PANCHRONICON. The sight thru the transparent dome of the time machine coincided with the site he had expected to see: the place where "She" lived.

The chrono-killer reached for his weapons, then disembarked from the vehicle that had materialized him in this strange sector of the past. As he set out for his task, he felt slightly sorry for the poor reptilian creatures that would soon get in his way, attempting to stop him, this invader of their twilight zone.

The battlefield was dark but lit with occasional flashes of artificial light. The rugged terrain teemed with half-human, half-reptile creatures which surrounded a beleaguered man whose electric sword and flaming disintegrators cut deep into the writhing mass of repellent flesh. The serpent-men, armed with weird weapons, charged in impotent rage, their primitive methods of attack useless against the invader's glittering armor.

The newly arrived human reached the top of the hill just in time to observe the other temponaut, who looked exactly like him in his protective suit of metal. Temponaut #2 saw that temponaut #1 was somewhat ahead of him, cutting a swath toward the Lady of the Snakes who was chained to a rock, whilst hell-spawned figures stood guard. It was a nightmarish scene.

Two identical shining time travelers stood out in the darkness as they moved in boldly, blasting and crackling their way toward the woman with the thousand snakes on her head. They got close enough to observe her female figure, their faces protected by the mirror-reflecting eye-shields but not wishing to risk looking the Gorgon in the face. So the two futurians moved in from the flanks, avoiding the face of death.

Suddenly the temponaut who had arrived first, as if irresistibly attracted by the fascinating female's figure, lowered his gaze and stared for a moment at her unclad feet. They were undeniably beautiful. He stared enraptured while the other chrono-killer tended to the business for which he had been sent.

Armored temponaut #2 continued to kill while #1's gaze slowly ascended the curving column of the deadly female's figure.

The storm worsened.

The gaze rose to the knees.

Lightning flashed.

Eyes were fastened on a trim waist.

Thunder crashed.

Suddenly, as if by an invisible order, the reptilians stopped in their tracks, observing the spot where the Gorgon once more was about to petrify a human being. The second invader of the past from time's future also stopped. He stood but a few feet removed from he who had arrived first.

The first temponaut continued to gaze thru his metallic helmet, a one-way mirror shielding his eyes. His gaze rested, now, on Her throat . . . but in a moment his reckless eyes rose higher.

For that last, lethal look. But then—

Time stood still . . . and in that frozen moment the second warrior from Earth-to-be realized a staggering truth. Before him his twin figure was swiftly raising his sword—but not fast enough. While the storm stopped as if to take a breath, the second temponaut, who had been late in arriving on the scene, calmly blasted the head of the swordsman to oblivion.

Instead of blood and brains, wires sprang from the half-melted helmet of the destroyed Earthling. It was evident, now, why he could not be seduced by the Gorgon: he was a robot.

And the second man-at-arms was human enough to leave the domain of the serpent-woman with all the haste of a water-snake escaping a piranha.

In this Godforsaken place beyond reason, in the realm of meta-history, his mission was to *prevent* the destruction of the Gorgon.

Because the war of 2022 A.D., against the androids, was a war to preserve a segment of the human psyche peculiarly precious to humans.

Their ancient myths.

You want to be beautiful, my child—how silly; beauty isn't so important. But—if you are determined, there is a way. You must travel a strange dark path in a distant world . . .

Beauty

by Hannes Bok

THE GIRL HUGGED HER SHABBY COAT MORE TIGHTLY AROUND HERSELF AND HURried down the street, peering from building to building almost as though she had lost a house and were expecting at any moment to find it. All of the residences along the way were of the better middle-class variety—all except one, which was notable in its lack of maintenance. On sight of this, the girl smiled eagerly and started toward it.

In the big bay window on the front of the structure was a pasteboard sign, amateurishly lettered, "Mrs. A. Applejohn, readings." It was backed by a profusion of potted plants and a shredded yellow lace curtain.

The girl paused on the front steps, then straightened her shoulders as if fostering her courage, and went on. She twisted the knob of the old-fashioned bell on the door and waited several tedious minutes. As she raised her hand again to the bell, footsteps throbbed within; a blurred face peered out of the heavily curtained pane on the door, which then opened inward. A gaunt wreck of an old woman stood holding the handle, beckoning the visitor inside. The girl faltered, wincing from the piercing dark eyes.

"Come for a reading, I suppose?" The old woman's scratchy voice was not reassuring. She might have been speaking to a persistent creditor.

"Well, yes—my cousin was here some time ago, and she said you're very good. You told her that you also make potions—love-philtres, and things," the girl murmured. Her voice was habitually low, and in her present uncertainty it was almost impossible to distinguish her words. Mrs. Applejohn's sharp chin jutted out as she thrust her scraggy neck forward in the hope of catching all the words. It unnerved the girl completely.

"There's no need to be frightened!" the old woman observed tartly. "Just speak up and tell me whatever it is you're trying to say—"

"I thought you could help me," the girl raised her voice. "Oh, if only you can, I'll give you anything I've got—everything I've got—although it doesn't amount to much!"

"And what's it that I can do for you?" The old woman leaned against the doorframe, staring.

"Make me pretty!"

"Make you pretty? You say, make you pretty?" The seeress' voice was like the cackling of an excited hen. She slapped her palms on her hips, akimbo. "Eh, what do you think this is, a beauty shop?"

The girl cringed. "Oh, no!" she protested hastily. "Only, I know that real beauty isn't a surface thing—it's from within, something psychic. I thought you could help." She pulled her coat around herself protectively; she seemed on the point of crying.

Mrs. Applejohn considered. "So you want to be made pretty. Why? Aren't you all right as you are?"

The girl shuddered with dismay. "Oh, no! I want to be nice-looking, so that I won't have to be ashamed of myself all the time—so people won't make fun of me! Nobody wants me—nobody needs me. It's because I lack something. If I were pretty, people would flock around me like they do to all pretty girls. And if I can't be pretty, if I can't make people want me, then I just don't want to live, that's all." For emphasis, she repeated, "I just don't want to live." There was a silence as she savored the words. "Please tell me, can't you help me?"

Without replying, the old woman motioned for the girl to enter. "Go into the parlor—that door on your right." She pointed.

The girl found the parlor more of a storeroom than anything else. It was dingy and cluttered with battered, disarranged furniture. The shades were down.

"Sit here," Mrs. Applejohn ordered, indicating a chair. The girl obeyed, and as the old woman squeezed herself between tables and sideboards on the way to a littered desk, the girl observed there were chalk marks on the floor around the chair on which she was sitting; they had been almost effaced by being constantly trodden upon, as though many people had sat on the same chair. The marks formed a star.

Out of the desk's pigeonholes Mrs. Applejohn took a battered paper box and a tissue-wrapped clinking object. Returning to the girl, she opened the box, withdrew five large prisms and carefully arranged them on the floor about the girl, one to each tip of the chalked star. As the old woman removed the tissue from a medium-sized bronze bell, the girl, who had watched with intense perplexity, asked, "But—what—?"

Mrs. Applejohn's deepening frown commanded silence. She straightened from setting down the prisms. One hand on a hip, she pointed the forefinger of the other, wagging it as she talked as though she were giving a lecture to a class of students.

"I am simply going to recite a few scientific facts," she said. "Whether or not you believe them is no concern of mine. In the first place, there is more than one universe of which our five senses are aware. There are others which exist coevally with ours—superimposed on ours. I think that scientists call them parallel universes. They're formed of different substance, moved by different forces, governed by different physical laws than ours."

The girl listened blankly, eyes wide and serious. Mrs. Applejohn took a deep breath and continued, "The prisms on the floor can reflect sounds, amplifying them within that five-pointed area marked on the floor. When I strike this bell"—the idle hand on her hip swung out and rested on the bronze bell—"its peculiar vibration is reflected from prism to prism, emphasized, augmented by echoes, the swiftly shuttled vibrations momentarily bridging the gap between our universe and another. Whatever is in this very limited range of altered sound passes into one of those parallel worlds from this. You follow me?"

The girl lifted a palm helplessly, shrugging. Mrs. Applejohn went on, "By a different tone, I can pull objects from that other world into this one. I'm going to send you into it because it's the only way known to me to help you find the beauty you're after. I'll watch your progress through the prisms, once you're there—if you need me, point at the sky, and I'll know. I hope you've understood all this?"

The girl was rapt-eyed, as though in a trance; when Mrs. Applejohn finished speaking, the girl blinked and shook her head as though awaking from a dream. She said, "I don't think I understood much of your explanation. I'm sorry—I tried, but—"

"No matter," the old woman responded. "Are you ready? You'll have courage?" The girl nodded.

Mrs. Applejohn lifted the bronze bell, beat it with a clapper. The faintest chime quivering from it swelled louder—louder—louder still, until it filled all the room with ripples of rhythmic metallic sound. Then it faded into silence, as the girl sat with her hands clenched and her eyes shut apprehensively.

Abruptly she was lifted from her chair, hurled through a whirlwind. Opening her eyes, she saw nothing but a writhing blur. Without a jar her feet touched ground and she reeled vertiginously over the battered floor of a roofless ruined building in a world of purple dusk. Beyond groves of tall broken columns rose a gigantic wall of smooth, gray stone, more like a cliff than an artificial construction. High in its center protruded a ten-foot faceted convexity of dull black stone, resembling a prodigious replica of a diamond executed in dirty glass. A narrow stair, nibbled away by the years, led up to this stone.

Outside this temple a prairie of barren rock, channeled with bottomless abysses, stretched beyond sight. In the east lay rounded mounds of shattered masonry. A tired wind dragged wreaths of dust across the plain, and the girl heard a muffled mourning as of bereaved outcries welling from farthest Space. Her heart, familiar with sadness, quickened to the keening.

She wandered out of the ruins toward the clustered mounds, passing an immense disk of metal suspended between pillars, its embossed surface crusted with verdigris. The mounds were splotched with the blackness of ragged holes from which, still as feebly as before, the wailing emanated. The girl paused timorously, staring now into the dark openings and again at the fissured barrens. The monody ceased.

She moved tentatively toward one of the black mouths, hesitated, then approached it and peeped inside. The entrance had been a window long ages past and allowed passage into a murky little room, apparently empty. She wormed inside. The floor was deep with powdery dust which arose suffocatingly at every movement.

As she stood, her hands exploring faintly discernible traceries of paintings on the walls, the murmur of sadness arose all around her, as though she were surrounded by a group of mourners. The shadows in the room's corners flickered and advanced; she was aware of a slight pressure as they embraced her. Momentarily the wailing graded into whispers of curiosity and interest, then shaded back to lamentation again.

Her hands fell from the wall; she reached toward the swirling shadows. "Oh, please don't," she breathed. "Don't cry like that! It hurts me—inside. If only you were a person like me—whatever you are—so that you could tell me what's wrong and I could help you. Perhaps you're—ghosts. But if you are, I'm not afraid. I couldn't be afraid of anything that wept, because only the weak weep, and they're not to be feared." There was no change in the shadows as she spoke; they merely tumbled and tossed slowly, restlessly, like visibly dark currents of air in motion. "Really, I'd like to help you. I think I understand, because I'm lonely myself . . . and ugly . . . unwanted . . ."

She sobbed, involuntarily stepping forward and raising clouds of dust which nearly choked her. She stopped crying, made a quick apologetic gesture to the shadows as though they could see, and scrambled through the window to the outside, halting an instant to look back sympathetically and wipe away smeared tears. The sad chant ended.

She returned to the pillared ruin and prowled about it until weary. There was no sound but the sweeping of the wind. The purple murk neither paled nor deepened. There was no moon, no trace of stars.

At last she crouched in a corner where the crumbling stair met the great stone wall, and raised her hands to the sky.

"Mrs. Applejohn, if you can hear me—I don't understand why you've put me into this desert, but I believe you, and I won't be afraid. I'll wait for whatever's coming." She tilted her head as if expecting to catch an answer. Nothing happened. She leaned back, and closed her eyes, slept.

The clang of a bell roused her. Hastily standing, she observed an amorphous patch of darkness flickering beside the great gong; vague sounds arose from its violent hammering on the metal. A response susurrated from all over the prairie, like the whisper of weary ghosts.

Out of the mounds, up from black chasms, from over the horizon's rim trooped shapeless wraiths of winking darkness, laggardly crawling, chanting weakly. The shadow at the disc advanced to meet them, and uniting into a group—there must have been a thousand of them—the black wisps approached the edifice from which the girl was watching. The chant thinned away.

There was space within the ruin for only a few of the shadows; disregarding the girl, they clustered at the foot of the stair which climbed to the faceted black stone. The others remained outside, motionless except for the incessant flickering which the girl soon ceased to notice, as one becomes accustomed to the ticking of a clock.

For a long moment there was utter silence and immobility, as though Time had become frozen. Then one of the shadows stepped to the base of the stair and paused, the blob which might have been its head turned up to the top of the flight. There was another petrified pause. Then the shadow began to ascend . . . but its steps grew slower and slower; its back was bent; it cowered as it climbed—as though something unspeakably dreadful awaited it at the head of the steps.

The shadow stopped, turned back to its fellows. From them arose a regretful sigh mingled with faint murmurs of understanding and condolence.

Encouraged, the shadow mounted another step—and another—and the murmur of the watchers was a blend of pity and horror . . . and oddly, a hint of joy.

The wraith reached the topmost step, wavered and then flung itself against the black stone—and as it touched the dull facets it screamed, no dim echo of a cry but one so loud and terrible in its agony that it thrilled all through the girl's body, resounding in her ears as she clapped her hands to them and cowered, striving not to hear.

The shriek ceased abruptly, as though coming from an amplifier whose current had failed suddenly, and the wraith passed into the stone, seemed absorbed by it as ink by a blotter. In a wink the stone glowed redly translucent—a fire appeared to have been kindled in it—and then burned with writhing sunset fires.

Faster and faster the restless flames swirled, eddying inside the jewel like a scarlet liquid in a bowl. From the stone's facets sprayed rosy rays which cascaded to the ground, splashing immense ruby drops, covering the prairie with a film of pink radiance, coating the age-rounded hillocks beyond the temple with a paint of light.

There was a thin tinnient crackling, and out of the barren stone green sprouts lanced heavenward, branched into feathery golden trees and gigantic opaline flowers. Jungles of waving bamboo threaded with coiling vines arose, like green islands thrust from beneath a sea. Little blue streams meandered out of the thickets, dropped into the gloomy chasms. Wherever the light touched the assembled shadows they manifested an opacity, a solidity—shape and substance. Why, the shadows were elfin little creatures who began to leap ecstatically in dance, shrilling glad tunes of thanksgiving.

What had happened? Was there a device in the black stone which emanated a light that created this illusion?

Swiftly the crimson glow faded; the faceted stone returned to its normal dull blackness. The trees drooped discolored and fell in a dry rot of dust; the streams vanished in steam. Where a paradise had stood was now only the umbrous stony plain, piled with drifted dust. The shadows were again only shadows—elves no more. Some of them were weeping again.

A second entity moved to the stair, paused dubiously. Another trailed it, wailing, and in the stress of emotion its voice was no ghostly thing. But the first shadow shoved its follower away and hurried up the steps. It halted short of the top, peering back at the foot of the ascent where the other shade cringed, pleading piteously.

The first shadow made a gesture of negation and deliberately rushed to the black stone, struck it without outcry. From those below arose a gasp of horror—and again the note of joy. As the wraith entered the stone, the red glow sprang up again behind the facets, spilling out over the watchers, creating again a momentary illusion of fertility, freshness—beauty.

Before the light had an opportunity to fade, the weeping shadow at the foot of the stair leaped up the steps and hurled itself into the faceted stone, merging with the fires surging within. Its scream, as it disappeared, expressed unbearable despair.

If it was a machine inside the stone which produced the glamorous light, why was it necessary for three shadows to enter? And why were they so reluctant to go within? And why the appalling outcries?

Comprehension came to the girl: the stone burned with the fire of the shadow's life and the lives of its companions. That was not the scientific explanation, of course: a scientist would say that the stone was not really a stone but some strange crystalline form of life which had been embedded in the masonry when the wall was constructed. It was able to assimilate organic life and the light was an excrescence. Light is a vibration; so are sound and heat—so is matter. And Time? Did this special light-vibration cross time for a few instants, showing the desert as it looked long ago? Did the wills of the shadows distort the light into the shapes of trees and streams?

The stone darkened, became blank, black, and the gathered shades mourned once more. None of them stirred toward the steps. Some of their faraway voices questioned, lost vigor, and were silent.

The wraiths began to disperse back to their dwellings, and the misery in their murmur drove the amazement from the girl's thought.

What were these darklings? Surely not ghosts! But—not wholly alive. Only quasi-real, struggling along in ugliness and desolation, so starved for beauty that some of them seemed willing to die, sacrificing themselves to a vampirish jewel which fabricated evanescent visions of beauty out of their life-forces. Like the girl they were tormented by their need for beauty.

Unloved, unnecessary to any human being, she had thought of suicide. But the emptiness of it! Might she not have missed something? And whether she had lived or died had made no difference to her world.

But here it could matter. By dying—by climbing the stair and offering herself to that monstrous jewel—she could end her yearning for the unattainable and at the same time be of service to these sad shadows—bring beauty to them. She was more alive, more substantial, than the little black things. Perhaps the stone would therefore burn longer and her passing might achieve the dreams of splendor which she had cherished, even though she were never to know of it. What though there was terrible pain involved? She had to die some time . . .

Closing her mind to thoughts of hurt, visioning the beauty which had never been hers, she stepped out of her hiding place, went to the stair and up it. As she neared the black crystal she felt its radiations of searing heat. Suffering acutely, she still would not turn back.

She touched the stone, fire replaced the blood in her veins. Her eyes, swept with incandescence, were charred: steam hissed against the lowered lids. Thunderous roaring, crackling tumult, reverberated through her brain. Clear through it all came a bellnote, and at once she was plucked away, whirled through a howling hurricane—and set down softly.

Sight returned. She was seated in the chair in Mrs. Applejohn's parlor.

"I had my eye on you all the time," the seeress said, as the girl recovered from shock. "At the moment you were dissolved in the black jewel, that thought of renunciation reshaped the body which I snatched away in a state of reintegration. Look!" She thrust forth the mirror.

But the girl dropped her head, ashamed. "No, please," she said faintly. "I don't care to be beautiful any longer. I know now that there are other things than just looking pretty."

"But look!" the old woman urged, again raising the glass, and this time the girl glanced into it. She laughed, amused, and raised her eyes to Mrs. Applejohn's. The seeress nodded sagely.

The reflected face—except for a few marks of age—had not changed.

"The late Fredric Brown for some years held the record for authorship of the world's shortest sci-fi tale—and it had an O. Henry ending to boot. Or, as Bill Shockspeare once said, 'To boot or not to boot.'

Brown's succinct classic: The last man on Earth sat alone in a room. There was a knock on the door. (Watch out for horripilations as the implications sink in.) Sometime thereafter someone shortened it by one letter: There was a lock on the door.

Later, Weaver Wright wrote: The last earth on man. (Who buried him?)

Ray Bradbury, in a fanzine, came up with a 12-word tale of Earth's fate in World War 3, the 3-hour, maybe 3-minute war; the nuclear one:

THE YEAR 2150 A.D.

In the year 2150 A.D.instead of one sun, there were two. THE END

Then I came up with a two-worder:

ATOMIGEDDON 2419 A.D.

THE END

Forrest J Ackerman tells of the genesis of this story, 'I was about to write the ultimate short sf story—the single worder—when it struck me that would probably turn out to be the penultimate, that some slan would top it and I better go for broke and try to create a one-letter story. Instead of going broke I hit the jackpot and was paid ONE HUNDRED DOLLARS for a single letter, possibly the highest word rate ever paid in publishing history.'

The story is harsh, downbeat, dystopian. Wylie in concept, Stapledonian in scope, it spans four and a half billion years and evaluates the entire history of mankind, every life ever lived, balances every terrestrial achievement ever against human failing. It has been called (by the author) 'an unforgettable tour de Forrest.'

You have now but to look at the bottom of this page to read the shortest science fiction story that will ever be told. Till nextime."

—Bonnie L. Heintz

The Shortest SF Story Ever Told

by Forrest J Ackerman

COSMIC REPORT CARD

In the early '30s, before Jill Taggart (née Vuerhard) was born into this world, I saw her father, Dutch film star Roland Varno, say to Madame Dietrich in the classic motion picture The Blue Angel, *"I love you."*

When Jillian was 12 or 13, I met her for the first time and by the time I was attending her Graduation Ceremony, I was frequently saying "I love you."

Jill is a big girl now and has had her own radio program in the Southern California area and she calls me Uncle Forry and I still love her . . . which did not deter me, as an editor, from rejecting the first 2 stories she submitted to me, even tho I would love to have, for auld lang syne, bought her first submission.

But Jill made it with #3, finally victorious, breaking into professional print with—

Final Victory

by Jill Taggart

THE DAY THE WORLD DIED, AND JUST BEFORE IT WAS LAID TO ITS FINAL REST, THE few surviving remnants of humanity's mightiest, and last, civilization huddled together in the skeletal remains of a park.

A woman, too stunned to speak, held her sobbing blinded child.

A once-wealthy man lay on the grass and cried, his tears sparkling like the diamonds that glittered on his fingers as in shocked horror he regarded his legs lying separated from the bloody stumps of his knees.

Another man, who had been a criminal, leaned against a flame-scarred tree-stump and sometimes muttered, "Why?"

There were seven of them. Seven left alive in a war-destroyed world and, when they died, all the hopes and dreams and history of Earth would die with them.

Then an eighth man came. He stumbled out of the brown and black wood and stood uneasily on the small patch of browning grass. And hope came to the doomed seven, for this man wore the tattered uniform of a *General,* and they all knew that this was *Authority,* that here was a *Leader.*

"It's all right!" the General cried jubilantly and smiled, and six of the seven rose up and prepared to follow him.

They watched the grass turning black under their blackened feet, and the General smiled again. "It's all right!" he reassured them. "It doesn't matter because, you see, WE WON!"

ACKNOWLEDGMENTS

Ackerman: "The Shortest SF Story Ever Told," copyright © 1973 by Mankind Publishing Co. Inc.; by permission of the author.

Asimov: "The Tweenie" (originally "Half-Breed"), copyright © 1939 by Fictioneers Inc., renewed 1967 by Isaac Asimov; reprinted by arrangement with the Vicinanzi Agency.

Bixby: "Where There's Hope," copyright © 1953 by Quinn Publishing Co. Inc.; renewed © 1981 by Jerome Bixby; reprinted by permission of the Ackerman Agency.

Bradbury: "The Smile," reprinted by permission of Don Congdon Associates Inc.; copyright © 1952 by Ziff Davis, renewed © 1980 by Ray Bradbury.

The following authors' stories are reprinted by permission of their representative, the Ackerman Agency:

Allen: "Sic Transit Gloria Mundi," copyright © 1997 George C. Allen.

Anderson: "Let the Future Judge," copyright © 1974 by Ace Books.

Bok: "Beauty," copyright © 1942 by Columbia Publications Inc.; renewed © 1970 by the Bokanalia Foundation.

Burtt: "Litter of the Law," copyright © 1975 by Ace Books.

Causey: "Inferiority," copyright © 1975 by Ace Books.

Cummings: "The Secret of the Sun," copyright © 1939 by Better Publications.

Ermayne: "Kiki," copyright © 1947 by Lisa Ben's Vice Versa, renewed © 1975 by Laurajean Ermayne.

Fritch: "Big, Wide, Wonderful World," copyright © 1958 by Mercury Press, Inc.; renewed © 1986 by Charles Fritch.

Gold: "The Biography Project," copyright © 1951 by World Editions, renewed © 1978 by Horace L. Gold.

Haggard: "Homecoming," copyright © 1974 by Ace Books.

Haggard: "Messenger to Infinity," copyright © 1942 by Columbia Publications Inc., renewed © 1970 by J. Harvey Haggard.

Huber: "I'll Kill You Tomorrow," copyright © 1953 by Quinn Publishing Co. Inc.; renewed © 1981 by Helen Huber.

Jackson: "The Swordsmen of Varnis," copyright © 1950 by Clark Publishing Co., renewed © 1978 by Clive Jackson.

Kepac: "To Serf Man," copyright © 1974 by Ace Books.

Kyle: "Golden Nemesis," copyright © 1940 by Albing Publications; revised edition copyright © 1997 by David Ackerman Kyle.

Mason: "Traders in Treasures," copyright © 1934 by Continental Publications, Inc.

Melchior: "Deathrace 2000" (originally "The Racer"), copyright © 1952 by Dee Publications; renewed © 1980 by Ib J. Melchior.

Merrit-Pinckard: "For the Good of Society," copyright © 1993 by I.D.H.H.B. Inc.

Moskowitz: "The Golden Pyramid," copyright © 1956 by King-Size Publications Inc., renewed © 1984 by Sam Moskowitz.

Novotny & Del Rio: "Task of the Temponaut," copyright © 1973 by Ace Books.

Reinsberg: "The Satellite-Keeper's Daughter," copyright © 1956 by King-Size Publications Inc.

Rosen: "Twice Removed," copyright © 1973 by R. Michael Rosen.

Taggart: "Final Victory," copyright © 1976 by Ace Books.
Urban: "The Cat and the Canaries," copyright © 1974 by Ace Books.
Vallini & Balboa: "The Cosmic Kidnappers," copyright © 1993 by I.D.H.H.B. Inc.
Van Vogt: "Itself!," copyright © 1963 by Star Press Inc., renewed by A.E. van Vogt 1991; reprinted by permission of the Ashley Grayson Agency.
Venable: "Punishment Fit the Crime," copyright © 1953 by Clark Publishing Co., renewed © 1981 by Marilyn R. Venable.
Williams: "The Impossible Invention," copyright © 1942 by Fictioneers Inc.
Wollheim: "Pallas Rebellion," copyright © 1950 by Avon Periodicals Inc., renewed © 1978 by Donald A. Wollheim.
Wright: "A Martian Oddity," as "Behind the Ate Ball" copyright © 1950 by Stadium Publishing Corp., renewed © 1978 by Forrest J Ackerman.

For the following Public Domain works the anthologist, as an established matter of policy, has made donations on behalf of the authors to the science fiction writers' retreat & reference library established by Andre Norton, 4911 Calfkiller Highway, Monterey, TN 38574: R.H. Barlow, ("Experiment," Fantasy Publications, copyright © 1935), G.M. Barrows ("The Curious Experience of Thomas Dunbar," *Argosy*, 1911?), Bates & Hall ("A Scientist Rises," copyright © 1932 by The Clayton Publishing Co.), David R. Daniels ("The Far Way," copyright © 1935 by Street & Smith Inc.), Arthur Louis Joquel II, ("Cosmic Parallel," *Specula* 1941), Robert A.W. Lowndes ("And Satan Came," *Polaris*, Dec. 1940, no copyright), Moore & Ackerman ("Nyusa, Nymph of Darkness," no copyright, *Fantasy Magazine* 1935), Oliver Saari ("The Door," copyright © 1941 by Street & Smith Publications Inc., renewed © 1969 by Conde Nast Publications Inc.), H.G. Wells ("The Final Men," England, 1896).

The Holding Agency, 2495 Glendower Ave., Hollywood, CA 90027-1110 has checks for the following authors, heirs or representatives: Aday ("The Tunnel," copyright © 1977 by Ace Books), Akers ("Replacement Part," copyright © 1977 by Ace Books), Barber ("When Cultures Die," copyright © 1975 by Ace Books), Bischoff ("The Sky's an Oyster, the Stars are Pearls," copyright © 1974 by Ace Books), Gorbovski ("Presure Cruise," copyright ©), Graham ("Untimely Interruption," copyright © 1977 by Ace Books), Hayworth ("Under the Lavender Skies," copyright © 1974 by Ace Books), Hughes Jr. ("Racial Memory," copyright © 1974 by Ace Books), Jones ("Parasite Lost," copyright © 1974 by Ace Books), Lulyk ("Starburst," copyright © 1976 by Ace Books), Ann Orhelein ("Extenuating Circumstances," copyright © 1977 by Ace Books), Palumbo ("I [Alone] Stand in a World of Legless Humans," copyright © 1976 by Ace Books), Rhoten ("The Banning," copyright © 1977 by Ace Books), Smith ("Police Action," copyright © 1977 by Ace Books), Utley ("The Queen & I," copyright © 1973 by Ace Books), Richard Wilson ("Love" copyright © 1952 by Fantasy House Inc.), Wind ("A Question of Priorities," copyright © 1975 by Ace Books).

Forrest J Ackerman,

a regular on the Sci-Fi channel, edited and published Ray Bradbury's first story in 1938, edited the seminal *Famous Monsters of Filmland* magazine for years, has appeared in 52 sci-fi and horror films, and has helped to inspire countless professional careers and his fans' lifelong admiration, including such notables as George Lucas and Stephen King. A writer, editor, filmmaker, and collector of science fiction material for 70 of his 80 years, he is the author of dozens of stories and editor of five previous complete anthologies.

He coined the term "sci-fi," received the first Hugo award (and has won 6 in total), contributed to the first fanzine, started an sf club in 1929, lives in the Hollywood Hills in the Ackermansion, an 18-room home "gem-packed" with 300,000 pieces, 50,000 books alone, 100,000 stills from fantastic films, has attended 53 of 54 World Science Fiction Conventions. . . . The Academy of Science Fiction, Fantasy and Horror has twice honored him with Golden Saturns.

We could go on. His love of the genre and his pioneering efforts are truly irreplaceable: He opens his home/museum to the public most weekends, and he can be contacted via the information on the next page.

READERS OF THE WORLDS, WRITE!

The anthologist of this volume is anxious to hear from YOU.
How did you enjoy the overall contents?
What few stories did you like the most?
What few stories did you like the least?
Would you like to see a collection of FJA's own approximately 50 stories? (Starting 1929!)
Would you like to see an Ackermanthology of a selection of Mr. Science Fiction's favorite sci-fi stories of the past 70 years? Favorite Fantasy?
Any requests for the anthologist?
Forrest J Ackerman may be contacted directly at 2495 Glendower Ave., Hollywood, CA 90027-1110. FAX 213-664-5612.